"Running away . . . *again.*"

The voice was so bitter David understood why he hadn't recognized it at first.

"Thou are most skilled at leaving at the opportune moment. I said stay where thou art." Despite the words, the hands holding the musket trembled, so David obeyed in case it went off accidentally.

"How did you get here?" He nodded his head at his friend, indicating his uniform. "And how did the Ironsides get you?"

Jonathan looked around nervously, as if he was expecting more of his regiment to join him. "I was pressed."

And you hardly know one end of a musket from the other, thought David. "Let me go, Jon," he said softly. "No one will know. If you ever loved me at all..."

Jonathan snarled at him, and David realized he'd hit a nerve; the gray eyes were as angry as the day Elizabeth had brought their world crashing down. He spoke, but he seemed to be having trouble with the words. "Thou willst...*not*...twist me around thy little finger once more. I am free of thee and thy deceptions. I thought...I might never see thy treacherous face again!"

"Then let me go, Jon, before they come. Please!"

He could see Jonathan was wavering. It was clear from the Puritan's visible emotions that he still cared for David, and if they couldn't be together, at least they could both be alive.

TRANSGRESSIONS

An M/M Romance

BY ERASTES

RUNNING PRESS
Philadelphia • London

9   8   7   6   5   4   3   2   1
Digit on the right indicates the number of this printing

Library of Congress Control Number: 2008939354

ISBN 978-0-7624-3573-9

Cover design by Bill Jones
Interior design by Jan Greenberg
Typography: New Caledonia and Amigo

Running Press Book Publishers
2300 Chestnut Street
Philadelphia, PA 19103-4371

Visit us on the web!
www.runningpress.com

Dedication

To the memory of my mother, Joanne,
with grateful thanks.

◖ CHAPTER 1 ◗

Kineton, Warwickshire 1642

David Caverly was not where he should be.

He rarely was. He was supposed to be in the shed, milking the four cows and then cleaning the barn, but he had not even started. The beasts were at the gate lowing insistently, but David was sprawled in the tall grass on the side of the river, ignoring them and the work to be done.

He was comfortable. He had all day, and the warmth of the sun on his body gave him no inclination to move. The day was perfect; the grass gently grazed his sides and his skin tingled deliciously as the water dried upon it.

Jacob, his father, had left early that morning and had given David enough tasks to keep him busy for the remainder of the day. Dutifully, David had completed the morning milking, but after he let the gentle beasts back out into the water meadow, he had sauntered down to the river and had done nothing more since. It was too hot for chopping wood, and he felt his father was being somewhat overzealous by demanding such a stockpile made ready in this heat when September had not yet arrived. He planned to do it later, before his father returned.

His father had informed him that he was going to be away from the forge all day, although he not told his son where he was going, and David had not particularly cared. He liked being alone.

David longed to be free of the forge and the smallholding. He hated the work, the mindless toil of it all, the inevitable sameness of every single day. He felt that life must offer so much more, and so he would find any way of avoiding work he could, unabashed by his father's speeches on the merits of toil. He tried not to spend time worrying about the inevitable—such as his father's censure, which would ensue upon his returning to find that David had not done the work allotted to him—and preferred to remain cheerful and as lazy as he could be, whilst doing the very minimum he could get away with.

The sun was scorching his flesh and getting too hot at last. David rose, stretched and yawned. His body was sun-dried after his bath, but he could feel his hair clinging damply to his skin. He grinned as he imagined his father's reaction to his son walking naked through the field, and could well imagine his admonition if he saw how long David had let his white-blond hair grow. It was a bone of contention between David and his father, and David was careful to keep it tied back and appearing to be shorter than it was when his father was about; for if his father knew that David was prideful over his hair, he would surely insist on having it cut as short as his own chin length bob.

Resentfully, David dressed and let the cows in from the fields for milking. He slapped their silken rumps a little too hard in unjust punishment for the work they were making him do, tugging at their teats and growling in annoyance when he paid the price for it, losing a whole bucket of milk to an angry kick. He knew his father would react more strongly to the loss of the milk than the chores he had not accomplished, for the milk was money. It was not that they were poor, but it was waste, and waste was sin.

David frowned; everything was sin with his father, who reproved David daily for failing to defeat the demons of the seven sins and being unable to master any of the cardinal virtues.

A joy of food was sinful, getting angry with the cows for stepping on his foot was sinful, wasting money was sinful, even taking a pride in his own handsomeness was somehow wrong in the eyes of the Lord. David knew he was beautiful; he did not own a looking glass (another sin), but he had a river in which, secretly, he would gaze at his reflection. He knew that his face was changing as he matured, becoming leaner, accentuating his cheekbones and his straight dark brows. He knew too, that his eyes were unusual, for his friends had remarked on them. Not quite brown and yet not hazel; in some lights like amber honey, and in others lit with a greenish fire. He never let his father see him looking at his reflection because that, of course, was a sin.

Singing—frowned upon, dancing—forbidden. This did not prevent David doing any of these things, but it did mean that most of everything that he enjoyed he was forced to do in secret in his attempt to keep his father from being disappointed.

Such subterfuge meant that when his father did find out, he was even more disappointed by the deception than the act. Trammeled in this way, David felt caged and trapped, and everything he took pleasure in seemed tinged with guilt.

He'd become used to the guilt; his constant rebelliousness inured him to it, and the more he broke his father's rules the less he worried about it. He could not help but resent it, however, even though his father never beat him for his transgressions, never got angry with him. He simply sermonized or prayed to God to ask Him to intercede, and David had long ago learned to look penitent, beg forgiveness, and promise to pray for strength to change his ways; his father accepted it, every time.

He was chopping his fifth log when he heard the return of Jacob's wagon, and he pretended to ignore it, applying himself to the task before him, and not looking forward to the speech he was likely to receive for the endeavors left undone. As the horse rounded the barn he straightened up when he noticed that his father was not alone. Sitting beside him was a young man clad in somber clothes, overshadowed by a large black hat. David's eyes narrowed at the stranger as the young man jumped down from the wagon and took the reins of the horse whilst Jacob descended.

David didn't much like what he saw. The newcomer was a tall youth about his own age or possibly a little older. Brown straight hair, pale, suspicious and unhappy eyes, plain of face with flat cheekbones and a defiant scowl under his wide-brimmed hat. A plain black coat, black breeches and a high collar confirmed David's worst suspicions: Puritan.

Jacob gestured and called out to David. "Come, make your new brother welcome. I would like you to meet Jonathan Graie. Jonathan, this is my son David of whom I have spoken."

"Master Caverly," the newcomer said, his face unhappy and mistrustful, despite his words. "I am pleased to make thy acquaintance." He bowed stiffly, removing his hat awkwardly then ramming it back onto his head. David looked enquiringly at his father, confused. He wanted some indication as to who this young man could be, and why Jacob was calling him his "brother."

Jacob looked at his son for a long moment, and then his gaze moved around the unswept yard, taking in the pile of uncut timber, with the few logs beside it. With a sound like a suppressed sigh and a flash of annoyance in his eyes, he spoke in a voice that barely concealed his irritation. "Jonathan is come as my apprentice, David."

David's eyes flew open with shock, but he managed to curb his tongue. He knew his father well enough not to begin a discussion in front of a stranger.

His father turned towards their cottage. "Come, lad, I will show you your new lodgings. David, you may join us for supper when you have finished."

In a fit of temper, and only when his father was out of sight, David swung the axe high and broke a log with violent ease. His father's words had left no doubt in his mind of their meaning. He expected David to finish all of the tasks he had been allotted before he was permitted into the house to eat. *Apprentice? What need have we for an apprentice?* David felt resentful at the intrusion into their lives, and annoyed that his father had not let him into the plan. Granted, with the talk of war the forge was busier than ever recently and they were slipping behind on their orders, but did they really need another pair of inexperienced hands?

Without his being aware of it, David was chopping the logs more forcefully with each cut, the pieces flying across the yard, making a mess that he would no doubt have to go and pick up afterwards, but his anger surged through him at his father's secrecy and he was too furious to care. He finished with the pile of timber and strode into the barn, leaving the logs scattered around the yard.

Brother. His new brother. Well, whatever his father might say, Master Graie was not his brother. His real brother had died. Stephen Caverly, his twin, had perished together with his mother when David himself had been born. He swept the floor of the barn, working out his temper. That was his brother; Stephen. The midwife had said they had been as alike as two peas. Stephen would have been like him, another blond Caverly, not a sullen, ugly Puritan with clumsy hands and antiquated speech.

It would be a long, hot, and sunny day in December before he welcomed that awkward Puritan boy into the family.

Hanging up the broom at last, he walked back out to the yard, stripping off his sweaty shirt as he went. As the shirt cleared his head he stopped in his tracks. The yard was clear, clean as a whistle, every log, every twig gone, swept up.

He rounded the barn and found the newcomer at the wood pile. He had just finished stacking it and was now filling the log box from the house. He turned as he heard David approach and smiled a hesitant smile, but it faded before the sight of David's unfriendly frown.

"What do you think you are you doing?"

An ugly flush rose in Graie's cheeks. "Thy father was preparing the meal and needed logs, and I thought that two people would finish thy tasks more speedily." Graie trailed off and turned back to the wood pile, angrily throwing logs into the box.

David noted that he was biting his bottom lip as if keeping himself in check. *Interesting*, he thought. *Looks like I'm not the only one with a temper*. The thought restored a little of his hospitality. Perhaps the other boy was no happier with this new situation than David was himself. He took a deep breath and forced himself to speak with a little more civility. "It was…thoughtful." He wanted to say thank you, but he was still smarting from his father's manner of springing this young man on him, so he said nothing further and strode toward the trough, where he plunged his head into the cool water, refreshing himself and cleaning the sweat from his body before supper.

Jonathan Graie stood by the woodpile, ostensibly filling the log box, but in reality he was watching David, one hand frozen on the next log, staring as the young man washed himself. Jonathan had never seen anyone like David before; he watched, fascinated, as David loosed the tie from his hair and poured water over his head.

He stared at the silvery fountain of David's hair with fascination, marveling at its rare color. The last rays of the summer sun hit David's body, transmuting his hair from silver into a golden fire, as the water droplets on his bare torso made rivulets of gold which ran down the honeyed skin and soaked into his breeches.

David was about as alien to Jonathan's experience as anything could possibly be. His own family was uniformly dark in countenance and dark in comportment. They rarely bared any skin to each other no matter how hot or sweaty they became, so the sight of David washing himself with such abandonment took Jonathan by surprise. He had not seen so much of his brothers' skins before, let alone a stranger's.

There came a shout from the cottage and Jonathan came to his senses with a start, guiltily snatching up the log box, casting a swift glance at David who had his back to him, seemingly indifferent to his father's call, and Jonathan's interest, before hurrying into the house.

✺ CHAPTER 2 ✺

David entered the cottage, which was dark after the bright sunset outside.

He was tidy and clean, his hair folded into his collar, and his expression properly blank and dutiful as he helped get the table ready while his father fussed with the stew. He retrieved three trenchers from the dresser and put them on the end of the table, then cut thick slices of black bread and placed them on top of each trencher. He opened a press and lifted out a large earthenware jug, poured three mugs of ale from it, and handed one across to Graie without looking at him, slopping some of the ale on the table. Graie's face colored again as he looked nervously up at Jacob, but his father was concentrating on stirring the pot. David watched in some amusement as he saw the newcomer surreptitiously wipe up the spilled ale with his sleeve.

Jacob took the pot off the fire and, after doling the thick stew onto the slabs of bread on the hollowed trenchers, he passed them across to the two young men, before taking his seat silently at the head of the table. David found he was ravenous, having not eaten since early that morning, but he sat with his head bowed and his hands in his lap and waited for his father to speak.

"Bless us, O Lord, and these your gifts which we are about to receive from your bounty, through Christ our Lord. Amen."

The boys chorused "Amen" after him. As David ate, he cast surreptitious looks at Graie and noticed that the newcomer watched the two of them constantly, not making any movements, not touching anything, not his spoon, or breaking more pieces from the large black loaf in the center of the table until one or the other of them had done so first. At such timidity, David sneered inwardly. *Why, the oaf does not even know how to eat at table!* His father finished his stew, and ladled another portion for himself and David, Graie not having finished his yet.

"So, Master Graie, your indenture was in Nottingham," Jacob said, in his slow and kindly voice.

"Aye, sir."

David watched Graie as he colored at being spoken to, but his interest was pricked by the mention of the city. "Is that where you are from?" he interrupted.

When Graie answered, David could hear a definite shake in his voice, as if he was unused to being the center of attention. "No, I was raised near Coventry, but the Master was an old friend of my father, sir." David hadn't been called "sir" in all his life, and found it off-putting and somehow wrong. "I was there two years in all as thou knowest," he continued, turning to Jacob once more. "But I have learned a lot in that small time. My master, before he died, sir, was a man who expected quick learning."

"And how far did your study progress?" Jacob asked.

Graie answered in the same nervous manner, explaining his progress with his previous master. Gradually David pieced together that Jacob had bought Graie's indenture cheaply as it was interrupted due to the master's death. The apprentice spoke of his knowledge of farriery, forging, sword craft, and armory, and David found himself impressed. Graie's knowledge, if it were to be believed, was far beyond his own. If he could truly do half the things he spoke of, he might well be an asset in the forge after all.

However, David realized with a sinking heart, the apprentice's presence would mean that most of the farm chores would now be his own. He often worked in the forge, but he did not delude himself; he had not the patience or the talent to be anything more than an average smith. David could not contain his impatience any longer and asked the question he had been longing to ask since Jonathan's town of indenture had been mentioned.

"Did you see the King's army before you left Nottingham?" Graie looked at him sharply, and then shot a confused look at Jacob. The man's face did not move a muscle, but his voice cut across their nascent conversation like an axe.

"David, I have told you more times than I can remember, I will not permit discussion on this matter, and especially so with newcomers and at the table."

Jonathan watched David as his glowing tawny eyes, which had just been so eager and full of life, shut down all their expression at his father's rebuke. He felt a pang of sympathy for David; he knew exactly how it felt to be humiliated in front of others. Being the youngest son in a family of six boys, he had brothers who took ritual delight in finding as many ways as possible of making sure he was embarrassed or caught out, blamed for everything. However, with his own family it had only ever been within the household; most of his brothers would never dream of shaming him in front of strangers. He wondered what was going on behind that closed-down face, those masked eyes.

David was seething. His father would *never* discuss the war, or rather the threat of war, which was on everyone's minds, and this infuriated him. To David the thought, however unlikely it seemed, that there might be a war here in England, instead of off somewhere so far away you only found out whom had won it months later, was exciting, and he and his friends spoke of little else. He knew that his father would never willingly allow him to join a regiment, and although he had had thoughts of running away without permission, there were only the two of them on the smallholding, and David knew his father could not cope alone. *But now*, he thought, with a glimmer of hope, *with Graie here, things might change.* He did not betray these thoughts, he was all too practiced in disguising his ambitions. Instead he sat passive and silent—the picture of a perfect son.

His father rose, the signal that the day was over. David cleared the table, waving away Graie's offer of help without a flicker of expression, and took the remains of the stew outside to feed it to the dogs. Then he walked down to the water meadow, stepped through the fence, and made his way noiselessly down to the river. The cows were billowing ghostly shapes in the gathering dark, as they moved restlessly to the water's edge. Crumple looked up as he approached and snorted a welcome at him, her black eyes huge in her wide brown face, her tongue licking her nostrils as she watched him placidly. He ignored them all and when he reached his favorite spot he lay down in the long grass and looked up at the sky.

The sky was his freedom. For all of his rebelliousness, and with all the sinful escapes he was able to allow himself, he still felt trapped in his small world. It was the sky that fascinated him. Huge, endless and infinite. Mysterious. Sometimes cloaked and invisible, sometimes, like tonight, so clear and full of stars that it seemed that it would only take a raised hand to pull one down to earth.

His thoughts drifted from the apprentice's arrival to the King, rallying his troops at Nottingham. His heart surged when he thought that perhaps a sword forged here at Kineton might one day strike a decisive blow for the King's cause, or that perhaps a breastplate that he had beaten and shaped might save the life of an important man, who might reward him thereafter. *Perhaps*, he thought, his imagination taking flight, *I might carry one of my own swords into battle someday and help win over the rebellious Parliament!* He grinned at that, for the few swords he had completed were of little use to anyone, so badly balanced and brittle that one blow from another sword would fracture them.

Reluctantly he rose and made his way back to the house, finished cleaning up in the kitchen, then climbed the narrow stairs to bed. As he paused outside his door, he realized, feeling foolish that he had not considered this before, that Graie would be sharing his room with him, so it looked like the little privacy he had was gone forever. He sighed deeply as he en-

tered, ducking his head to miss the lintel; he was surprised to
find Graie was sitting on the edge of the large wooden bed, his
hat in his hands, his bundle by his feet, and he looked more
unhappy than ever. As David started to undress, Graie stood
and faced the door. David smiled at this sudden bashfulness; he
thought briefly about leaving some clothing on to spare the
newcomer some embarrassment, but decided against it. It was
far too hot and the blanket was too much as it was. The sheet
would have to suffice. He slid beneath the linen and pulled it
up around his waist.

"You are quite safe now, Master Graie," he said, his voice dripping with sarcasm. "I am now covered well enough to save your
maidenly blushes." Graie spun around and David saw anger flash
in the pale eyes. *He's actually quite nice to look at when he allows
his face to come alive,* David thought. *It's just that sullen expression that makes him seem so plain.* He put his hands behind his
head and watched the apprentice start to undo his waistcoat. As
Graie peeled down to his shirt, he glanced across at David and
paused. David knew what he meant, but brazenly continued to
stare at him, one eyebrow raised in a challenging manner. The
two of them glared at each other and David got the chance to
study Graie's eyes. Not blue, he now saw, but the lightest gray he
had ever seen, made livid with a startling charcoal ring around
the outside, giving him a hunted, feral look.

Although David found them fascinating, they were unrelent-
ing, stubborn to the point of impossibility, and to his annoyance
he found himself losing the battle of wills, finally looking away.

"As you wish," he said shortly, and turned to the wall. The
sheet slid away from his waist and David grinned in the candlelight. Although he wasn't watching Graie undress, the apprentice
had to endure his nakedness. Being raised as an only son, David
had never had any feelings of shame about bare skin, as there
was never anyone around to see. He swam naked, and, if his father was not about, would often walk back to the house un-
clothed, in all seasons. But he realized from Jonathan's innate

modesty that the new apprentice had been raised differently, and he was imagining the fun he could have causing more embarrassment to the young man.

He felt Graie slip into the bed next to him but he didn't move; he knew that he was taking up more than his share of the space, his back was bent and his backside was protruding into Graie's half, but for pure mischievousness he stayed still. He felt the heat of an unaccustomed body in the bed, could feel the pull of the feather mattress as it sank beneath the apprentice's weight. He could tell that Graie had left some clothing on; the wool of his under breeches tickled David's backside and it felt strange yet weirdly pleasant. As he lay there dealing with the odd sensation, he was astounded as his member began to harden, for that was unusual. David was used to having sudden hardnesses, but it had not yet happened in response to another person.

The other boys from the town and he had discussed this at times, and the others boasted of how their pricks would shame them at the worst possible moment, usually whenever one of the maidens approached. This had not happened to David, although he pretended that it had, not to be left out. He assumed it was probably because he found the local maids uninteresting and tiresome. The other boys waxed lyrical over one dull girl and then another, describing their figures, their eyes, their hair, but David had not yet found one he found appealing enough to follow around like a love sick puppy as did his friends.

He discovered as he grew older that he woke hard most mornings, and as sinful as he knew the manipulation of his member was, he did it anyway. He discovered very early on just how pleasurable it was. He found that he could let himself go with the moment; he learned to experiment with speed and pressure to build the most indescribable torment inside his body so it felt that his groin and head would explode simultaneously. That sweet agony of release, as spurt after spurt of seed would shoot from him, often made him bite down on his other hand to prevent his cries of bliss. The wasting of a man's seed was inherently sinful—he knew only too well, but it was so deliciously enjoyable.

It had made him curious to know if all forbidden activities relating to the body were as sweet as this one. *Why was it*, he often wondered, *that everything sinful was so pleasing?*

To take his mind off his needy prick, he rolled over and propped himself up on his elbow. He tugged the sheet up around his waist and shielded his hardness with a hand so it did not intrude in the space between them. Graie was lying motionless in the candlelight, staring up at the ceiling.

"So, *did* you see the King's Army?"

Graie turned his face to David and looked at him full in the face. For the first time since his arrival he had lost the look of worried suspicion he had been wearing. When he spoke, the words tumbled from him as if he was relieved to be speaking naturally. David found the timbre of his voice to be deep, with a different accent to his own, but compelling. It made David want to listen and listen: it was a true storyteller's voice.

"I saw some of them as they marched in. Our forge was near one of the gates, and they entered the city over many days, although the numbers soon became too great even for the city and they camped without the walls. I was told that the King was gathering troops to the north of the city, but I never had the time off to travel to see them all. They say that over eleven thousand men have come to support him; it seems... surprising that such a number could rally so quickly. I think it was the extra work in such heat that caused the death of my ma...Master Langland." He turned away from David, and resumed his stare at the ceiling. "Dost thou think that the King will fight against Parliament, sir?"

David frowned, annoyed once more for being called sir, and irritated that the entrancing voice had stopped. He wanted it to carry on, as it stirred him in a way he hadn't felt before. It was as if the voice caused the same sensation in his brain and stomach that his fingers were achieving on his loins. When Graie described the situation in Nottingham, it became real to him. It seemed as if he could see the troops on the hills, the flags, the shining armor, the restless horses, the rows of white tents.

"I am not a 'sir.' You need not call me that. But I think that there can be no fighting. How could anyone fight against their King? Once Parliament sees that the country is really behind their sovereign, they will not dare to raise a sword against him. Who could? He is the King!" Annoyed, he turned away and blew out the candles.

Jonathan was silent but watched David as he blew the candles out, and rolled back over to face the wall. He felt troubled. Since his master's death his life seemed to have been hanging in the balance, and there had been times when he'd thought that all the work he'd done would be wasted, that he'd never find another indenture. Now, in this place he'd never heard of before, he couldn't help but be a little stunned as to how quickly his life had changed. A village forge could hardly compare with the clamor and pace of his work in Nottingham. And now it seemed that his new master's son was unwelcoming and hostile. Not only that, but he supported the King. Overhearing Master Caverly speaking to his own father that morning, it was more than clear that David's feelings were in direct opposition to Master Jacob's. He had a horrible suspicion that David did not know this, or he doubted he would have spoken as he had. He hoped that what David had said was true, but he had heard many things in the city, things that unsettled him. It was not only the King who was raising a sizeable army, and if the King decided to march to London, Jonathan himself could not see anything but bloodshed ahead.

❦ CHAPTER 3 ❧

Jacob called the boys at daybreak. Jonathan was out of bed before the third rap sounded on the door, but David did not even stir. Jonathan looked down at him, slightly more inured to his nakedness than he had been the night before. The young man was laying face down, the sheet no higher than the small of his brown back, but it was his hair that again had Jonathan entranced. Tousled through the hot night—David had kept Jonathan awake with his restlessness—it hid his face completely, a white-blond tangle of shining cobwebs, which tumbled over his shoulders and across the pillow.

Jonathan dressed hurriedly while he had the privacy of David's inattention, but he paused as he pulled open the door and looked back at the young man with his legs tangled in the linen sheets. He swallowed hard as he walked back to the bed, sat down on the edge, and, tentatively grasping a muscled arm, shook it lightly.

"Master Caverly. Thou must arise. Thy father —"

"Is bellowing..." David's voice sounded weary and muffled. "You will get used to it. It happens every morning." As if on cue, Jacob's voice sounded up the stairs telling them that if they did not hurry they would break no fast with him that day. "David," said David, pushing himself up on his elbows and sweeping the curtain of hair from his face. "Try and remember that, Puritan. It's *David*. Not master anything. I, you will discover, am Jack-of-all-trades and master of none." He grinned disarmingly at the apprentice and pulled himself to the edge of the far side of the bed. "And you and I shall soon quarrel if you wake me on father's first shout. He's patient 'til at least the third."

Jonathan scowled, and left without another word.

David sat there smiling; he had been feigning sleep and had watched Graie dress, sly glances hidden by the mass of his hair. Graie's body was something to behold, a powerful torso showing plainly the "quick learning" of his two years of apprenticeship, large muscled arms, and a very broad back. His skin was surprisingly pale, and certainly appeared pallid compared with David's sun-kissed body. Jonathan had a man's physique; one as powerful as Jacob. There was no trace of the youthful softness of David's own form. Jonathan had kept his underclothes on all night, so David had not been able to compare the parts below the waist with his own. To his own bafflement and amusement, he found he was eager to do so; he had never had the opportunity to see another man's member and wondered if his own was normal sized. *Perhaps*, he thought, *Graie would fancy a swim after the hot working day….*

He did not have time to attend to his morning erection, so he ruefully stuffed it into his underclothes, thankful that his breeches were roomy enough to hide it, and ran downstairs. Breakfast was a silent meal; the Caverlys may not have been rich in coin, but the small-holding and income from the forge provided for their needs and they ate well, shoring up their strength for the day ahead. Slices of pork, oatcakes, and porridge with honey were all washed down with watered ale. After eating, his father took the apprentice to the forge to start the furnaces, leaving David to clear up and start on the farm work.

He was milking his second cow when he heard an unwelcome but melodious voice from the door.

"Why, Master Caverly, still milking the cows? My father said you had come so far up in the world that you had engaged a servant. Surely then *he* should be doing the dirty work?"

Knowing well who the intruder was, David did not even bother to take his head away from the cow's flank as he gave a curt greeting. "Good morning, Mistress Woodbine." He did not need to look at the girl to know that her skirts were hitched up too short, her cap would be missing, and she would already have flowers in her hair. He squeezed the last drops into the bucket and spun around on the stool, smiling as he saw his guesses were correct. Fifteen-year-old Elizabeth Woodbine was the daughter of their nearest neighbor, the thorn in Jacob Caverly's side. The Woodbines were a dissolute family, who ran a farm larger than Caverly's smallholding, but did not do as well upon it for all of its size, due to their laziness and drunkenness. They neglected their water meadows and they rarely mended their own fences, which meant that their beasts often strayed onto the Caverly's land. Master Woodbine was not sharp to collect them either, probably thinking that a few days grazing the good meadows the Caverlys tended would save him time and money. Each time Jacob returned the animals there would always be a bitter argument, as Amos Woodbine would accuse Jacob of attempted theft. A sullen truce between the two of them had existed for many uneasy years.

Elizabeth was short and pretty in a pinched, elfin sort of way; sharp featured, with long dark hair which (when her father was not there to see) tumbled in glossy curls over her shoulders, and eyes the color of lavender. She was adored by most of the other youths of the village, but her eyes were only for David. Whether it was because of his looks, or because he was disinterested in her charms, or even that it would be a good match for her, David did not know and cared less. He only wished that she would let him alone.

"So, where is this new servant then?" She swayed into the barn in a practiced, provocative manner, being careful to get out of the way of the cow as David let it back out into the field.

"He is not a servant. He is an apprentice to my father, a smith. A good one too, by all accounts. We are lucky to have him." He surprised himself by defending Graie so staunchly, but it irritated him to hear her describe the apprentice as a servant and not as the craftsman he would undoubtedly become.

"And is he as pretty as you are, Master Caverly?" Elizabeth ran a slim finger down his arm and looked up at him with an expression that would have made David's friends die of jealousy.

"You must decide that for yourself, Mistress," David said, moving the stool to the third heifer. "Your tastes may be different to mine. He's up at the forge if you wish to compare us."

The girl stood there for a while, swaying her hips slightly as she waited for David to pay her some attention but he didn't, pretending to be too involved in his milking. He could guess how annoyed she was by the way she folded her arms and pulled the flowers from her hair. He was perfectly aware that she fully intended to set her cap at him. She might dally with the boys of the village, but David had a suspicion that both the girl and her father would be more than happy if the two families were joined. There were, David knew, more eligible bachelors in the neighborhood in terms of wealth and position, but Woodbine was greedy for the Caverly's better land and David knew the man would not complain if Elizabeth were to choose David over wealthier suitors. It was well known that Woodbine would stop at nothing, including it seemed, selling his daughter, for a chance to take over the smallholding with its rich water meadows, thriving forge, and well-tended market garden.

Despite her best attempts to catch his eye, David had remained completely indifferent to her. His manner was always polite and slightly mocking. He enjoyed the childish pouting his neglect caused. He knew that every other man she had previously set her cap at had swooned at her feet, and he felt somewhat proud to be immune to her charms. He did not dislike her; he admired her stubbornness even if she did irritate him. He had merely attempted, on more than one occasion, to convey that she was wasting her time, but she was, it seemed, more confident in her powers of seduction than he was in his powers of dissuasion.

She wandered outside and David drew a sigh of relief. When he'd finished with the last cow, he shut the gate on the meadow and started the walk up the cinder path to the forge. It was a low,

long building on the road to the village, about a quarter of a mile
from the house. It had been his father's idea to have the forge at
such at such a distance; originally the forge had been housed in
the barn, but it meant that any passing trade on the main road
was missed, and there was a constant danger that if the forge
burned down it might set fire to the cottage. As he stepped onto
the cinder path, Elizabeth appeared from behind the barn.

"You do not mind if I walk with you?" She smiled brightly at
him, her pretty smirk fading a little at his stony face. "I would be
shy introducing myself to your serv...apprentice alone." She twirled
her ringlets in an affected way but David remained unmoved.

"You are free to walk where you wish, Mistress," he said curtly,
but he did not slow his pace to accommodate her and she soon
had to trot to keep up with him, her unsuitable, dainty shoes slipping on the cinders. To her credit, David noted, she did not complain, or attempt to hang on to his arm for support, but he knew
well why she was loathe to go to the forge on her own: it was because of his father's opinion of her and her family. If she had arrived there unescorted she would be made most unwelcome; the
forge was about the only place David ever felt safe from her.

There were two horses being shod at the moment, giant
beasts from a neighboring farm. Kind faces and huge hooves;
usually Jacob would take one and David would take the other,
but Jacob was methodically beating flat a sheet of metal and
watching the apprentice closely. He had given him both horses
to do, so David stopped and watched, knowing he should not interrupt a shoeing. It soon became clear that Jonathan was either
naturally talented, or his last master had taught him more in two
years than David had learned in ten. Not only was he at home
with the fire, the hammer, and the anvil, making them seem like
extensions of his chiseled body as he moved from brazier to anvil
to bucket; but he had a knack with the horses too, holding on
tightly when he thought that the beast was simply trying its
strength, and letting go swiftly when he realized that the animal
was genuinely frightened.

All Jonathan was wearing over his torso was a leather apron, and from where David watched he could see it sticking to the sweat on his hairless chest. His hair was loose and drenched in sweat, hanging in dark ribbons around his face as he bent over the hoof he was working on. Drops of moisture fell from it onto the hot metal, making it sizzle and steam. As he pressed the hot shoe to the hoof, man and beast disappeared momentarily in a cloud of smoke. Taking the shoe from the foot, he turned again to the anvil to reshape it, and pushed his hair back from his face. The sweat ran down his temples and onto his broad shoulders.

David found himself licking his lips, and unbidden, his mouth watered. From somewhere in his mind there came an image of him licking the sweat from that broad chest, laving the man with an eager tongue and tasting the salt and sweat of him. His stomach leapt and he frowned—where had such a thought come from? And now he had thought it and had realized how terrible it sounded, why did it still seem like it would be a wonderful thing to do? He nearly laughed out loud imagining Graie's reaction if he were even to try such a thing; he would be lucky if he did not get a hammer between the eyes if he attempted anything of the sort. But that small voice at the back of his mind told him that whatever the risk, he wanted to try.

Elizabeth was also watching Graie and her face screwed up in an expression of distaste. "You wanted me to compare you to him?" she said scornfully. "Why, he's an oaf! How can you compare you to...*that*? It is like comparing silver to iron!"

David continued to watch Graie shining in the forge's glow, and hardly heard what she had said. When her voice finally intruded on his thoughts, he frowned down at her. She simpered at him like a puppy pleased for the slightest attention. "Don't you like my dress, David? I wore it especially for you..."

To his enormous relief, David was spared from answering that question as his father called him into the forge to begin work.

"Be off," he said gruffly. "You know well my father will not tolerate you here." She began another pout, but before she had finished pursing her lips, David had spun away and was shaking hands with Graie, joining in Jacob's congratulations at the good job he did with the horses.

Jonathan stammered his thanks to David's approval, knowing he was blushing and feeling more pleased at David's congratulations than any praise he'd had before. Just the warmth in David's eyes was enough to make him feel welcome at last. The look that David gave him was so open and friendly, Jonathan couldn't understand what had caused such an abrupt change. He had sensed not only unfriendliness but an actual resentment from David the day before, but now it appeared it had all melted as quickly as hoarfrost in sunshine. Whatever the reason, Jonathan was glad of it; he had missed his family when he was in Nottingham, and had been very happy when Master Caverly had said that his son was of a similar age. He had found himself disappointed when David had shown signs of hostility the evening before.

They did not get time to speak further, as a wagon rolled up to the forge needing repairs, and suddenly the day became too full of hammering and the roar of the furnace for talk. As the day wore on the two young men would glance at each other from time to time, in a shy and almost curious manner. Working together with fire and molten metals needs a degree of trust, and as the day wore on each of them thought that if he could trust each other, perhaps they might be able to become friends.

ⳗ Chapter 4 Ⳙ

By the end of the first month, David could hardly remember a time before Jonathan Graie's arrival. He could not even remember when he had begun started to call him by his Christian name, for he was firmly Jonathan, or Jon, in his mind.

He would watch the apprentice when he was not aware that he was observed. David would pump at the bellows whilst Jonathan heated, cooled, and shaped the metal to his command, and David wondered how this shy, awkward young man had managed to meld himself so completely into the life of the forge and the farm. David realized he had fewer thoughts of the army and of running away to join it, and, happy to have someone near his own age at the forge, he found that he even spent less time with his friends.

"Iron and Silver," Elizabeth had called them, and she continued to use the terms to their faces, thinking that she was making a great joke. Between themselves they discussed the nicknames and found them more amusing and more true to their natures than the girl had realized.

"But you would not rust," laughed David, beating out sheets which Jonathan would work his magic upon.

"No. I don't think I'd keep still enough for that," Jonathan said slowly, glancing at David. He still felt a little shy, and it seemed blasphemous to think it even, but he compared David's beauty to what he imagined angels would look like. It was sometimes hard not to stare. "But thou would'st tarnish."

He gave David a rare smile, which for some unknown reason always made David's insides flip over in sheer happiness. "Undoubtedly," David agreed, stopping his hammering. "If there were no one around to polish me from time to time and keep me bright, I would be as black as hell itself in no time. It is only you that keeps me pure, you know."

"Thou speaks blasphemous nonsense," muttered Jonathan gruffly, but inwardly he was pleased at what David said and was thrilled to be the one that burnished David's indolent soul. He had noticed that David's absences from the farm had gradually become less frequent in the weeks they had been working and living together; even Jacob noticed and had said that Jonathan must be a good influence on the wayward boy.

"He thinks that I do not know that he goes to the village to dance," Jacob once confided to Jonathan early one morning before David joined them at the forge. "Such pursuits are not necessarily sinful, but he takes them to excess and lets them affect his work. He then he compounds his sins by lying of them. He seems to think that I was never young and that I never looked at maids."

Talk of the war was everywhere. Even Jacob could not avoid it. Rumor flew about. The King was marching to Scotland to form a larger army; the King was marching to London; the King was turning Nottingham into a siege town. No one was sure of the truth until half way through October when the Parliamentarian Army descended on Kineton like a plague of locusts and camped in the fields outside the town, causing consternation and curiosity to all the inhabitants. Jacob returned from a provisioning trip pale and shaking, and David was at the horses' bridle before his father had stepped down from the driving seat.

"Father?" He'd rarely seen his father so rattled. "What happened?"

"Trouble," Jacob said. "I drove into town easily enough, but on my way home a trio of Parliament's soldiers stepped out of the copse by the river." Jonathan appeared at the door of the forge to listen. "They searched the cart and questioned me. When I told them who I was, they ordered me to return to the camp on the morrow with as many weapons as I have ready."

"But they can't do that!" David said, his eyes blazing with anger. "They'll never pay us the price of the commissions!"

"They are not intending to pay us any price at all, son," Jacob said evenly, as he unhitched the horses and motioned for Jonathan to lead them away. "They gave me a choice: an empty forge, or no forge at all."

"But why?"

"Their rhetoric was somewhat garbled," Jacob said with distaste. "They made it perfectly clear however, that if I didn't do what they suggested, I'd be as guilty of treason as is the King, apparently." David went to argue further, but Jacob cut across him with a voice that brooked no dissent. "Half of what we have ready, load it up, and that's what I'll take over to the camp. Hide the rest, particularly the Compton order."

With a face full of thunder David helped Jonathan place half of the completed commissions of swords and armor into the back of the wagon, and in spite of the care and artistry they'd used to create them, they were not gentle with it, uncaring now of dents or scratches. The Compton armor, burnished and beautiful with the Compton coat of arms on the breastplate, was buried, with the remainder of their work, deep in the hayrick in the farmyard. Dinner was quiet and tense that night. Even Jonathan was angry at having to let their work go for nothing, and was no doubt wondering how they'd ever replace it.

The next day Jacob set off, leaving the boys to start the weary task of replacing what was lost. They worked as hard as they ever had, even when Jacob had been watching them—both stung with the injustice of giving their labor away to Parliament's army for nothing. As the afternoon wore on, two horses led by troopers appeared on the road to the town. Jonathan reached for a pitchfork and David a hammer as they watched them approach. As they drew nearer, it was plain to see that one of the horses was lame.

The troopers stopped at the sight of the two young men. One of them, a lean man with dark blue eyes and his hair loose around his shoulders, gave the reins of his horse to the other and took two steps forward, his hands raised slightly. "Gently, good sirs. My name is Aston, Tobias Aston, and we are King's men, if that means much to you in these times. Whichever side you favor, I ask only for aid for my poor beast. He has no side, it has to be said, and cannot be blamed for being forced to take mine."

The boys dropped their defensive stance, and stood aside. Jonathan handled the horses while David spoke quietly and urgently to the soldiers. "You can go no further towards the town," he said.

"We know of the army," the second man said. He was red-haired and tanned, with deep brown freckles that made him look younger than he probably was. He sat down on the edge of the horse trough and pulled off his hat. "We were scouting and my horse threw a shoe. A yeoman on the road told us of you. We'll go no further." Jonathan led his horse into the forge, while David got them both a drink. "The King was on his way to London, but the devil Essex has forestalled us and I think the King will have no choice but to fight. We must break through and get to London where the King will be safe and back in charge where he belongs."

David nodded eagerly, and the trooper named Tobias said, "You have never had a hankering for the King's Army then, lad?" He drank deeply from the tankard of ale David had brought him. "All the maids love a pretty uniform."

"My father needs me here," said David, knowing how stupid it sounded, how cowardly. These men were risking their lives, they could be dead in a matter of days, and here he was worried about whether his father could manage without him. He looked toward Jonathan, as if for reassurance, and his friend nodded at him with a small smile.

"I understand," said the dark-haired man, looking between David and Jonathan with a strange look on his face. Then rising, he gave a sharp intake of breath and said briskly, "Well, I must stretch my legs, it has been a long time on a horse today and I fear it may be a long time again tomorrow if we must meet with Essex. Hal?" He nodded toward his friend, who gave him what appeared to be almost an angry glance in return. "I should not be long." With that he wandered off down the path.

The one called Hal watched him walk toward the farm, and then looked sideways at David for a moment, before saying, "Tobias has left his tankard behind, boy. Be so kind as to return it to him? He will be thirsty while walking and will thank you for it."

David wondered at the thoughtful stare the trooper called Hal gave him, but obeyed, taking one of the full jugs and the empty tankard and setting out after the dark-haired man. He caught him up at the entrance to the barn, where the soldier was gazing up at it with a peaceful expression.

"Sir?" David called tentatively. "Master Tobias?" He filled the tankard from the jug and offered it up. Tobias drained the tankard in one swift draught.

"My father had a barn like this," he said, walking into it and standing with his arms outstretched in a dust-filled autumn shaft of light. He took a huge breath as if drinking in the scents and sounds of the barn.

"Had? What happened to it?" David spoke quietly, not willing to break the dream-like spell the stranger was weaving.

Tobias' voice was remote, his eyes staring somewhere above David's head. "Parliament raid, a retaliation. They attempted to take a baggage train bound for the King's Army. Prince Rupert fought them off and the goods reached the King safely. But the Roundheads raided local farms for supplies instead. They stripped our farm of everything we had and my father's barn was burned, along with the farm and my parents in it." Tobias sat down suddenly on a pile of hay and looked at David with that strange, intense gaze he had given him in the forge. "Shut the door lad, and come and sit with me a while." Without knowing why, and feeling excited and nervous, he obeyed the stranger. The hairs on the back of his neck stood up and goose pimples seemed to shudder all over him. He sat next to the trooper who was still staring into nowhere. When the man spoke, it was almost to himself. "Your name..." It was, but it did not sound like, a question.

David answered it anyway. "David."

"...is David," echoed Tobias, in a voice that was almost a sigh. He turned to face David, looking deep into his eyes. The trooper's eyes were the darkest blue David had ever seen. David liked the look of his face; for all its weariness and slight sheen of dirt from the road, he was quite handsome with high cheekbones, an aristocratic straight nose and glossy black hair. He smiled at David and said softly, "It suits you. Did you know it means 'Beloved'? Was not David of 'a beautiful countenance', too?"

David found himself blushing but unable to tear his eyes from this fascinating man. Tobias reached out and pulled David's plait from the collar of his shirt where he kept it hidden from Jacob's sight, gasping as he revealed the full glory of it. David was startled, his heart thudding in his chest at the unexpected intimacy, but he could not move. It was as if the man's hands on his hair kept him fettered to his side. He felt the man's fingers shake but he didn't pull away as the soldier undid the strands of the braid and separated the silver-gold threads.

A terrible excitement flooded him and his skin tingled. He felt that Tobias was reading his soul with eyes that were dark as an evening sky, dark as midnight caves—wonderful, yet unknown and dangerous. Suddenly, and with a thrill that warmed his cheeks, David understood Tobias' intent, but he was not afraid. His stomach turned over in the same way that it did when Jonathan smiled for him, and he reached to his own shoulder, caught Tobias' fingers, and intertwined them in his own.

Tobias gently took David's hand and brought it to his mouth. He had never seen a boy as beautiful as this, and he was everything the man had ever dreamed of. The softness and beauty of a woman, but the long leanness of a man, and large able hands. He was teetering between adolescence and manhood, and Tobias was grateful beyond words to be here before the butterfly emerged.

His eyes closed, and he opened David's palm and mouthed it gently, letting his lips open and his tongue drag around the hollow, nipping the skin between finger and thumb, suckling and biting each slender finger in turn. The boy gave a groan of pleasure at this and his head dropped back. Tobias bent forward, touching David's throat with his lips, then, gaining in confidence as David relaxed in his arms, he teased at his throat with his tongue, nipping gently at the golden skin.

He pulled David closer and savored the taste of skin on his lips, salty with an undercurrent of something like gunpowder and meadowsweet. As he moved to possess the half-open mouth, the boy still pliant in his arms, his passion rose and the embrace was harder and more fervent than he meant to give. He was amazed at his own intensity, swept away by the beauty of the young man, boneless in his innocent acquiescence. He left David's mouth only briefly, to remove the boy's boots and hose, returning with rising pleasure as David opened his arms to gather him back in.

David welcomed the dominant mouth, his stomach twisting deliciously with each new sensation, and his member, hard from the moment of Tobias' first kiss, was now throbbing for release. He reveled in the ardent attentions, the sting of the stubble on his cheeks, the hard, sinuous tongue, and the fevered breath at his ear. He did not find his body's reactions odd; rather, it was as if his mouth up to this point had been ever empty, waiting dormant, not realizing that it waited for a man's invasion. Every touch was a shivery delight, and he craved more of it. Eager to be as close to his first lover as he could, he arched toward Tobias in a wanton reflex. He heard the trooper chuckle, then felt kneading fingers on the small of his back, whilst Tobias' other hand busied itself at the front of his breeches. At this, David froze and drew back slightly, but Tobias soothed him as gently as one would a nervous colt, running his hands down David's back and whispering words of reassurance and encouragement.

"Softly, lad. I will not harm thee," he said, his speech slipping into a more intimate manner. "Just let me do this for thee, and if you like it not, I shall stop. No one has...?" David shook his head. "Then trust me, David, you will enjoy it, I swear to you."

David felt he was being lifted up above himself, floating in the sunlight in the barn, and seeing himself through the eyes of someone else. The lips on his mouth and neck, the ragged breath of Tobias as he spoke with such need; both of them were immersed in a moment that neither could stop nor would wish to. He felt Tobias unbutton his breeches and was now excited, rather than nervous. With a surprising strength, Tobias lifted David easily and slid his breeches from his legs, and laying him down on the soft, sweet hay. Then the trooper unbuckled his own breastplate and put it aside, lay down and pulled open David's jacket, removing it with the shirt.

David's golden body was as near to perfection as Tobias had seen; it took every ounce of willpower he had not to drag the boy beneath him, and thrust himself inside the honeyed cleft, to ride him as he had other farm boys for his own fulfillment. It was only those hypnotic eyes that kept his control, as they locked on his, changing color with the light, and so very trusting. He wanted to gentle this treasure, not to break him.

He stroked David's knee and the boy flinched at the contact, so Tobias took it slowly. He did not move his hand, but coaxed the sensitive flesh, fingers massaging, and nails scraping the inside of David's thigh. He continued to kiss the younger man until David was trembling with excitement, and he did not object or freeze when Tobias slid his fingers down from the sweet arch of his back and along the rise of his buttocks. Tobias took as long as David needed, letting him awaken to his needs slowly. He could see David was hard and loving every second, but he didn't want to rush him or frighten him. Tobias knew he would not force the boy; he truly wanted him to enjoy it as much as he would himself. His patience was rewarded when David's arms wrapped themselves around his neck and he started to kiss Tobias on his own accord, pressing his erection rhythmically against the older man's hip. The joy of his submission was worth every frustrated second.

"There's my clever boy," whispered Tobias, as his hand began a slow, sure journey up the slim brown thighs, feeling them twitch and push toward his palms. David's breathing was slow and deep, with a catch of pleasure at the apex of every intake, a sigh of bliss that ebbed and flowed as he appeared lost in the sea of sensation. His eyes were nearly rolling back into his head as Tobias reached his goal, wrapping rein-callused fingers around the youth's pink and gold member. David's cry of rapture was very nearly a squeal, and Tobias couldn't help but chuckle into his ear.

"There, am I right? Is that not wondrous?" There was no reply from David except soft whimpers and an answering reflex from his hips as he pushed his length back and forth in Tobias' hand. Tobias kept his hand static, riding the movement with his body, and not taking his eyes off the sight of David in ecstasy, letting the youth pleasure himself within his tightened fingers, relishing the skin moving over the proud head under his palm, the vein bulging with its need for release. He pulled David closer and allowed his own clothed erection to rub very softly against the serge of his breeches and David's naked thigh. The torment it caused was sweet relief, and he knew that if he teased himself any longer he would spend before the boy did. He released his grip, letting David's cock slide through loosened fingers. David's eyes opened with a drugged expression, his lips bruised and full.

"Disappointed?" teased Tobias. "Patience. It is about to get so much better."

David reached up and kissed Tobias voraciously. *"More."*

"So needy!" Tobias laughed. He'd never had such a willing pupil. His joy increased as David began to unbutton his breeches for him, releasing his own cock, angry and suppressed, which David took into his hands in a covetous manner, as if happy to repay the pleasure he had been given. Tobias slid around, so they were top to tail and continued to stroke David gently whilst allowing himself the pleasure building in his groin with David's eager if rough ministrations. He admonished him softly and asked him to slow his fisting, which David did with a sigh, falling back onto the hay as Tobias' fingers crawled up his thighs to join the other hand. He licked his fingers until they were as damp as he could make them and in this way introduced a warm wet sensation to David's member. When the boy was thrusting again gently into his rhythmic slick fingers, Tobias' mouth claimed the head, sucking it in, grazing his teeth around the sensitive skin between head and shaft, and flicking his tongue over the slit. The taste was exquisite; clear liquid was pouring from the youth in anticipation and Tobias knew it would not be long. David arched backward on the hay in a spasm of joy, the forward movement of his hips thrusting the cock deep into Tobias' receptive mouth. One, two, three mouthings were as much as David could take and his seed pumped into Tobias' mouth. Tobias swallowed quickly before sliding up to cradle the boy in his arms, knowing he would likely be shocked and dazed.

Tobias stroked the flaxen hair, feeling protective and yet bitterly sad that within days he would in all probability be dead, and now, so late, he had to find such one as this.

"Would that I had found you before," he whispered to the seemingly insensible boy in his arms.

David's eyes fluttered open and he pulled Tobias down to claim his mouth again. "More..."

Tobias laughed. "No more! We have already been in here too long. Haldane has probably bored your brother thrice over."

"But I have not pleased you!" David remonstrated, his hands finding Tobias' cock again.

"You have, believe me, you have and more than you realize." He leant in and drank of David's mouth, running fingers through the tousled hair. "David..." he whispered, the name sounding like a prayer of regret, "you are very beautiful and I hate to leave you."

"Then come back. Tonight," David said eagerly. "Please. I beg you! I want to do to you...what you did to me, with my mouth, I want to taste you...." Tobias groaned and pushed his cock

through David's fingers, violently aroused by the boy's innocent
sensuality, unable to stop himself.

He was gentler the second time, and Tobias had to tell him to
tighten his fingers just a little. He pumped into the willing fingers, his breath fast and frantic as his balls tightened. He imagined that it was the boy himself that he was thrusting into, and he
closed his eyes in torment that it was not. His rhythm changed,
and he paused briefly before spending himself with a groan of
pleasure. He pulled David toward him tenderly in gratitude and
watched, amazed, as David tentatively lifted his damp hand to
his lips and licked his fingers, one at a time; his eyes closing in obvious pleasure as he tasted Tobias' seed. The trooper could not
believe how erotic this young man was, how unknowingly he cast
an air of sex and arousal around him. How lucky Tobias had been
to find him in a backwater place like Kineton.

"I will. I will return, how could I stay away now? Till tonight,
I promise. Look for me at midnight."

David clung to him, Tobias' mouth tasting semen and ale, and
murmured his plan to him. "Come to the forge; you can't come
down the path, you will be heard...the dogs...I'll meet you at the
forge." They dressed as hurriedly as they could, Tobias hindered
by David's eager kisses, calming him finally and tying his hair for
him.

"I'll go back alone, we've been gone too long, it will look
strange. I will say that you gave me some ale and I fell asleep in
here. Hal will never believe it, but your brother should." He
pulled the slender form into his arms and kissed him again. "I
swear to you I will be back."

David leaned against the door and listened to the man
crunching up the path. His head was reeling, but his thoughts
were clear as a spring river. Those feelings he had been having for
Jonathan, the wanting to touch him, to kiss him, this is what it all
meant; now it all made sense. It was the most beautiful experience he had ever had. He wondered what Jonathan had made of
their absence and smiled broadly; in his mind he put Jonathan in

Tobias' place. He imagined Jon leaning over him with same expression of longing and lust that Tobias had. His cock swelled again
at the thought of it, and he knew that this was something he must
share with Jonathan; he *had* to. As much as he had enjoyed the
touch of a stranger, he thought, *how much better would it be with
Jon?* He imagined Jonathan's mouth on his, Jonathan's wonderful,
muscled body naked and sweating, those feral eyes lost in pleasure;
Jonathan's large able hands on his skin, on his cock, Jonathan's prick
hot and hard in his own hands. But how on earth could he ever
convince his handsome Puritan to let him touch him in that way?
It seemed impossible. His member was aching from the thoughts
of what he had shared with the trooper and what he longed to
share with the apprentice; he could not wait for tonight. At least he
knew that Tobias would welcome anything that David could give.

"You were away a long time." Jonathan's voice was tinged with resentment as they clambered into bed that night, discussing the
troopers.

"Yes, well, I didn't like the look of their horses. You know that
some beasts don't like me. I knew that they would be putty in
your hands, so after taking Master Tobias his ale I went and
cleaned out the chicken house. Father's been nagging me to do
that for days." There was a grunt from Jonathan's side of the bed
as he settled down to sleep. David pulled the covers up over himself to get warm, wishing he could roll over and put his arms
round his friend and feel the heat of his broad back on his chest,
and to ease his erection against Jon's hard thighs.

To take his mind from such temptation he spoke again, "I
hope the fighting is near here. Would you come with me and
watch it, if it is? Jon?" There was no reply except gentle breathing. David lay awake, too excited to even consider sleeping. He
dreaded that if he did try and sleep even for an hour he would not
wake and would miss seeing Tobias again.

Finally the village bell rang twelve and David slipped out of
bed into the darkness, picked up his clothes, and tiptoed down

the stairs. He dressed in the kitchen and ran up the side of the cinder path in the bright moonlight, keeping to the grass, sure-footed, knowing every tussock and depression in the ground. He reached the forge and walked inside; it was warmer in than out, and still dimly lit by the furnaces dissipating their daily heat. He looked about but was disappointed to see that the forge seemed empty. Then he noticed a flickering of a candle on the far wall and went to investigate. As he rounded the central island, there, in front of the largest furnace on a layer of blankets spread on the ground was a sight that made him gasp in amazement.

Tobias was lying stretched out on the floor, his head resting on a bundle, and completely naked, his body a medley of light and shade in the shifting candlelight. He looked up at David's approach and raised an arm as if to invite him down. David paused, drinking in the sight of the man. His body was lean, slender, and hardened; his hips were high with pronounced ridges which angled down, drawing the eyes to the man's cock, mature, hard, and thick, jutting out from a black sea of hair.

Loath to miss a second of skin on skin, David tore off the few things he was wearing and lay down. Tobias rolled over him, stroking his cheek and looking down with an expression of tenderness.

"I think I may be a little in love with you, beloved," he said gently as he ran his fingers through David's hair, "and that is not a good thing for a man about to die. Perhaps it is *because* of that," he added, sliding his hand down between David's thighs and smiling. "Perhaps you are an angel who visits men before a battle." One finger slipped between David's rounded buttock cheeks while his thumb massaged the soft sacs.

David hardly managed a whisper as the hand between his legs set him alight with excitement. "Think of me as your guardian angel then, and you will not, you *cannot* die. You must come back to me!" He realized that he was more than a little in love with this stranger himself.

Tobias said nothing more, but lowered his mouth to David's, taking his breath away with his kiss. David felt himself swept up into powerful arms, and knew that whatever Tobias wanted from him tonight, he would give it, and willingly.

◖ CHAPTER 5 ◗

"So where wert thou?" Jonathan asked the next morning as he forked hay for the cows. David had given up helping, and was lying as if exhausted on a pile of hay, his eyes on the roof, but his mind obviously elsewhere.

"Mmm?" David said, distractedly.

"You heard me." Jonathan was gratified to see David's head snap around hearing his Puritan friend use the formal address of "you" that he had not used before.

"Jon? Are you angry with me?"

"No," Jonathan shrugged and tried to look casual, in spite of his misgivings. "But thou hast been ignoring me all this morning, and the work is hard enough. I miss thy nonsense to take my mind from things. Thou vanished in the night. I woke and thou had gone; thou didst not come back until early this morning. I was concerned, only. Where dids't thou go?"

David's voice was pompous as he reclined again upon the hay. "My beloved watch-dog, you do not have to know everything that I do."

Jonathan went silent at David's false and patronizing tone. He gritted his teeth and turned away, going back to his work without another word. The effect on David was almost immediate; he jumped up, wrenched the pitchfork out of his hands, gave his arm a brief squeeze, and flashed him a smile.

"Forgive me. I am tired and irritable, and I should not take my feelings out on my Puritan. The talk of war unsettled me, and I could not sleep. I walked the road a while and then went to the forge to warm up. Then I fell asleep and woke just before dawn."

Jonathan was not placated by this story. Despite David's smiles, Jonathan had seen sadness in his eyes, and despite his assurances, Jonathan was sure that David was not telling the truth. *Surely he did not see a maid at that time of night? What maid from Kineton would do such a thing?* As forward as Mistress Woodbine was, he couldn't imagine that even that girl would risk her less than perfect reputation by meeting a young man in the lane at midnight. In any event, Jonathan realized, with a family the size of hers, it was unlikely she would even be able to get out of bed without being missed. He knew that in larger towns and cities women walked the streets at night, but he was fairly certain there were none of that type in Kineton.

"Jonathan?" He realized David was speaking to him. "Now who is ignoring whom? I am going to find the army camp tomorrow and discover if there is to be a battle. Will you come?"

"No, I will not. Not only is it madness but it is the Sabbath and thy father—"

"Oh, forget Father," David said, spinning around with the pitchfork. "I was thinking of going after church, and it is not as if we are going to be working in the forge, is it? Just two friends out for a walk, and we often walk together on Sunday, don't we? Would I not be safer with my keeper by my side?"

Jonathan scowled at him; the devious boy could twist anything to suit his purposes, but Jonathan knew he would give in. He always did when David asked him for anything, be it help with chores, or covering his absences. He reasoned to himself that if he was with the impetuous youth, it might at least prevent David from doing something drastic, like joining the army.

The thought of joining the army had, since Tobias had laid hands on him and inflamed his mind and body, resurfaced in David's mind and tempted him hourly. Thoughts of duty to his father and the farm had melted away. Even his growing friendship with Jonathan seemed less important than seeing Tobias again. He was quite determined to join up, and if not in Wilmot's Cavalry like Tobias, then alongside him carrying a musket; he would not be left behind while Tobias rode away to glory. The trooper had been unable to promise whether he could return the next night or even ever at all. As he bade David goodbye in the early hours, he had held him so close, while David had rested his head on Tobias' shoulder, happier than he had ever been.

"I do not know where we are going, whether we are to stand and fight or to march on; if we stay I may be able to come to you again, it all depends on Essex. If I can, I will. But if we fight, you must stay away from the battle, David, promise me this. If we fight here Hal says it will be in all probability on the flood plains to the south. You must not come."

Tobias' warning rang through his head, but he knew—had known, even as Tobias said the words—that he would disobey.

Eventually, as he knew he would, Jonathan reluctantly agreed to accompany David to the campsite, knowing with a sinking sensation in his stomach that he was going to have to deceive Jacob. The next morning at breakfast Jonathan felt so ill at ease he could not trust himself to speak. Even though he would not have to voice the words to Jacob, as David had said he would do so, he considered himself as guilty as David by allowing Jacob to think one thing, while they both did another.

David broached the subject in the casual way he had. "We're going to walk along the river this afternoon as usual, Father. You do not mind?" He looked at his father with wide eyes, the very picture of innocence.

Jacob's words made it clear that he knew his son well enough. "You are not planning to go anywhere near the army are you?"

David shook his head and kept his eyes firmly on Jacob's.

"You give me your word?"

"I swear to you, Father. We have no intention of going towards the village. We found a new holt last week."

"Aye, well, take the dogs. Damned otters." Jacob left the table and Jonathan was relieved that David had succeeded in controlling the conversation, as he was sure that if Jacob had but glanced his way, their intended deception would be clear. Jonathan stood up and cleared the table, glad to be out of the sight of his master and sickened by the glib lies falling from David's lips. With a father as good and as God-fearing as Jacob, it seemed incomprehensible to Jonathan that David found it so easy to lie to his sire, with seemingly no guilt after his perjury.

Jacob, however, seemed not to be entirely convinced by his son's guileless face, and called back to David as he went out to the cows. "Make sure then that you clean the chickens first thing tomorrow morning. I would not ask you to do it today, but I have asked you so many times I am weary of saying it. First thing tomorrow, understand me?"

"Certainly, Father, first thing," quipped his son.

Jonathan's hands tightened around the trencher he was wiping, and his knuckles whitened. He was angry and confused as he realized the import of Jacob's words. *If David can lie so easily to the man he should respect above all others—why then should I be surprised when I find he's also lying to me? What was he doing yesterday afternoon if not cleaning the coop?* His mind re-ran the events of the day before. The dark-haired trooper strolling down the path, David following him. The red-haired trooper who had remained behind had kept up an irritating prattle of sorties and training which had continued long after the horses were shod. He suddenly suspected that maybe, maybe the trooper had been keeping him by talking. *Why?* He closed his eyes and let his mind imagine what could have happened: David walking down the path, catching up with the trooper, handing him the ale...*What is it that David is lying about? Has he enlisted? Is that why he's been so dreamy, inattentive, won't talk...* Suddenly the blood ran from his face and his hands gripped the trencher he was holding so hard that it snapped in two. The noise made David, who was wiping the table, look round and laugh, and he threw his cloth at Jonathan's head.

"You *blacksmith*, you! Those great hands are not suited for such maidenly tasks!"

All the rest of the morning, during the walk to church and during the service, Jonathan was silent and tight-lipped. His mind rebelled against the unnatural thoughts he was having. He tried to be rational and put his mind into order, but every time he did, he could only come up with one conclusion: David had done something with that trooper that he needed to lie about, and something that the one called Hal had tried to conceal from him. Jonathan could not believe it, but he suspected that David, of whom he was beginning to be so fond, was unnatural in more than just his looks.

The church that morning was packed with Parliamentarian troops, and the normal hush before the service was disturbed by the rattle of armor and weaponry. Jacob had warned the boys to keep their eyes firmly on the floor as they passed the soldiers, and not to cause any upset, and they were both pleased to obey. Jonathan was awed by the numbers of soldiers in the village. As they knelt in prayer, Jonathan cast sideways glances at David. With his silvery hair, honeyed skin, and eyes closed in pious supplication, he looked like a veritable angel as he prayed. He was so beautiful, and yet so very corrupt, but Jonathan now knew that he loved him. He felt he loved David deeply, like the younger brother he never had; someone to protect, to teach and to care for, but his friend's sins troubled him greatly.

Although he had only half decided now that he would refuse to accompany David, after church he found himself falling into step with him, simply because David took it for granted that he would. They walked along the river back in the direction of the farm, and when they were out of sight of the village, they forded the river and walked southwest in silence.

Even from the village, they could hear drums and as they neared the flood plain, David broke into a run. Jonathan raced after him and pulled him back roughly, forcing him to stop.

"Be careful!" he said, in an angrier tone than he meant to use. "Thou knowest not who may be watching. There are bound to be scouts, and someone running into the site of a pending battle is likely to get his head blown off." David's eyes widened as if in shock at Jonathan's outburst, but he slowed and let Jonathan lead him round to the north. "Our best bet is to head for Kent's Copse," Jonathan said pointing up the hill, "and we may be able to see better." They walked on, across the grassland and up the hill, coming around the back of the stand of trees to the brow of the hill. To their amazement there were several other onlookers in the wood, and as they stepped forward to the viewpoint, one of the men there turned and greeted them.

"Come to see the battle too, have you, boys?" he said. "I can't say I blame you. My sons were eager to come, but I forbade them." He went on to say that he had been provisioning the King's troops for the past few days. "I realized they would have to fight. Essex wasn't going to let them go any further east or south."

They stood and looked across the valley. Their friend pointed out the King's army, all lined up on the hill to the side, and Essex's command arrayed in the flood plain below. To Jonathan's unschooled eye the numbers looked fairly equal. Nothing seemed to be happening. It was a pretty scene—bright flags, shining armor, and glossy horses, but Jonathan gave a shiver. It was too bright, too shining. It gave no presentiment of the bloodshed that would surely follow. In fact, there seemed to be no activity at all other than the occasional horse galloping from one end of the line to the other, each side seemingly waiting for some signal.

"This is madness," said Jonathan at last. He pointed across to the troops nearest them. "Some of those men have only sickles and pitchforks. What use will they be against musket and pike?"

David said nothing, but his eyes were wide and excited.

Their new companion chimed in. "They probably joined the army as it passed them in the fields, some willingly, some maybe not so. No time or opportunity to arm them all while they are on the road."

There was a raised shout from the King's troops, as if in signal. It seemed that the wait was over. From behind the ranks, three horses trotted forward to the front of the line, high stepping and proud. The watching group could not make out the details from their vantage-point, but it seemed like a man and two young men. They rode in front of the massed army, and between the serried ranks of musket pike and artillery. Wherever they rode, a cheer rose up until the entire army was yelling itself hoarse.

"Do you think that's the King?" David asked in a quiet voice.

Jonathan shrugged. "I could not say, but it seems likely; he's raising morale, I suppose." He could say no more, as in response to the Royalist cheer there came a sound like hell rising, the air and earth were torn apart, and both Jonathan and David threw themselves flat onto the ground at the deafening volley.

Their companion was bellowing, but it took him several attempts to make himself heard. "It's Parliament's guns, they are responding to the King's appearance! It has begun!" Jonathan looked on in pure horror as the first shells landed, initially too short as they tested their range, causing the earth and grass to rend itself out of the ground with clouds of smoke and dust. Screams sounded from the field, the terrible sound of horses crying out in terror. The cheering stopped as abruptly as if every man there had been killed with the first volley. The guns continued to fire, and then the King's artillery replied until the battlefield was filled with acrid black smoke. As the Parliamentary guns found their range, shells landed past the lines and more horrifically into the center of them, causing carnage and screams as men were blown apart.

David clung to Jonathan's arm as the pretty scene they had been observing turned into a bloodbath. Jonathan was shaking as hard as David, but neither boy seemed to be able to look away from the slaughter.

"Why do they not *move*? Why do they not move back?" David shouted, his face ashen. Jonathan did not respond. He felt cold, as if he would never smile again.

"Because that is what they do," yelled their companion. "They must bombard each other, weaken the line, and then advance." The terrible onslaught continued on both sides for an hour at least. The field was covered with a thick black pall and it was becoming difficult to see anything from their vantage-point. Jonathan was thankful for that. He was longing to escape, but now their route back to the river was blocked by Parliament; they would either have to walk a long way around the armies, or wait till it was all over. He wished that he had not come, had not allowed himself to be persuaded.

There was a sudden racketing of drums from the King's side and a valiant shout of many men. The rows of horses on the right flank of the Royalist side started trotting forward into the face of the opposing army. Jonathan glanced at his friend. David was staring intently at the advancing cavalry and Jonathan knew what he was looking for. He followed David's gaze but it was impossible to tell in the smoke and melee which two men were the troopers they had met the day before. Master Tobias could be any one of the men on chestnut horses. They were not in the line of the cannon, but as they closed on the Parliamentarian side, pikes were lowered, musket fire rang out, and horses and men began to fall. The remaining horses broke into a gallop, and their riders bared their swords as they raced toward the opposing cavalry troops on the plain.

Jonathan could hardly bear to look, but he couldn't drag his eyes away. He couldn't believe that anyone could be as brave as to face such certain death. To his amazement, the Parliamentarian cavalry, instead of riding out to meet them, turned and fled the thundering killing wave of horseflesh and steel.

"It's a rout!" shouted David, amazed. The thousands of Royalist foot soldiers started to move toward the Parliamentarian line and the carnage continued. The group of townsfolk were exclaiming in horror as they watched men cutting other men to pieces.

"It may be," said Jonathan, "but it has left the King with no cavalry—look!" He pointed down to the plain. The horses had all galloped towards Kineton and showed no sign of returning. Without the back-up of the cavalry, the foot soldiers were finding it difficult to repel the Parliamentarian's right flank of horse, and it was only the pikemen who were keeping them off with any success, moving inexorably forward, musketeers seeing the advantage and running to be inside the spiky cage they formed. As the sun slid toward the horizon, and despite the murk, it was clear that the King's line had been breached. Parliament's dragoons galloped up the slope toward the King's cannons.

"The line has broken!" groaned David. Mercilessly the gunners were cut down. Around them, Jonathan saw the other watchers close their eyes in fear, as if imagining how it must feel to be sliced through by a cavalry sword, or trampled by iron clad hooves. The remaining gunners and the soldiers nearest to them, turned to attack the invading horses, but one by one they were torn down or chased back across the field. Soon it was too dark to see anything, and all they could hear was the report of cannon and see the flashes of fire as they exploded their payload of death toward the other side.

From the look of revulsion on David's pale face, it was clear to Jonathan that it had not been the glorious battle that he had expected. It was butchery, blood, and horror. There was nothing noble about seeing a man blown to pieces by cannon shot, or seeing gallant men and horses sliced to ribbons by guns loaded with lethal metal fragments.

In the cold dusk the two boys clung together, David shivering in shock, and Jonathan speechless with the carnage. They lay there for a long time as the darkness deepened around them, and it was a while before Jonathan realized that he was holding David tightly in his arms and that he was still shaking. He leaned down and muttered in his ear. "We must *go*. Thy father will be worried out of his wits, and I hardly dare face him; it will be obvious that we both defied him." David seemed almost paralyzed, so Jonathan had to pull him to his feet, and started to lead the way back through the trees. He turned to see that David was not following him, but instead was moving toward the flood plain and in a moment he was racing down the hill. Jonathan stood there in terror for what seemed like hours, and when he started to follow David his legs felt that they would never speed up, that he would never reach the same pace as the figure in front of him. He blessed David's hair at that moment, for in the half dark it was the just about the only thing Jonathan could see, the braid trailing behind him, shining like a beacon in the murk of the battlefield.

He caught up with David at the foot of the hill where his friend was kneeling in the mud and crying by a pile of bodies. Dead men, left where they had fallen; some horribly disfigured, their faces blown away, their legs gone, and some seemingly uninjured, but dead, all dead and not yet even cold. Jonathan walked up behind David and gently touched his arm.

"This is not for us, David. Let us get away while we can." He looked around nervously; there were soldiers milling about in the dark and he did not want to be questioned, or worse, conscripted.

David would not move but simply said, "I must find him. I *must*. You don't understand Jon...He could be...like them...."
Jonathan caught his meaning as he tried again to pull David away, but David ripped himself from his grip and was gone, leaping over the corpses and straight through the battleground, heading to where he had seen the other line of cavalry.

With an angry growl, Jonathan charged after him, his feet slipping from under him on the wet ground, pitching him forward on his hands and knees. He righted himself, wiping his muddy hands on his tunic, and raced on. As he neared David again, he saw his friend was now searching the bodies, examining each trooper's face, or at least those who had one. Jonathan had nearly caught up to him when there was a strident shout and a lone horse galloped toward the pair of them. The dragoon had come from the direction of the King's guns and had his sword bared.

Without a second's thought Jonathan roared at David. *"Get down!"* He raced forward and grabbed David around the waist, pulling him to the ground. As they hit the muddied grass they rolled, over and over to avoid the sword and hooves. The dragoon thundered past, but Jonathan heard David scream out in pain as the blade swept down. All Jonathan could do was to cover his friend's body as the horse galloped by, soon lost in the darkness.

⊂⊙ Chapter 6 ⊙⊃

For the rest of his life, Jonathan could never remember how he had got David home that night. He recalled lying in the mud with David beneath him, remembered how he had wept in sheer relief when he realized David was still alive; but between that and arriving back in the yard well after dark, his memory had wiped itself clean. He knew that unless he had been spirited back or someone had taken them by wagon, he must have carried David home across fields and over the river, but of this there was nothing left in his mind. Nothing except the memory of the fear that the bleeding body in his arms would not live until he managed to get David back to his father.

There was light shining through the windows of the cottage. The door flew open as Jacob was alerted by the dogs barking a welcome, but the anger on his face died when he saw the apprentice holding David, whose arms dangled as if he were dead. Jonathan was weeping, and could hardly speak. In the light of the cottage he was suddenly aware that both he and David were covered in blood and filth. Jacob shoved everything from the kitchen table and Jonathan put David's inert form on it, fussing over it tenderly, re-arranging his clothing, and attempting to clean the grime from his face while Jacob gathered supplies. There was a knife-sharp pain behind Jonathan's eyes when he thought that David's eyes might not open and look him in the face again, that he may never see that mischievous smile or hear anything—even lies—from those lips, now heartbreakingly bloodless. He was vaguely aware of Jacob asking questions but he couldn't understand anything his master said, unable to tear his eyes from his unconscious friend.

He watched, helplessly, as Jacob investigated his son's body with an eye practiced in caring for his stock. Slowly, as Jacob unbuttoned and untied his son's clothes, Jonathan realized that all the blood on David's clothing could not possibly be his, or he would already be dead. Jacob removed David's jacket as gently as he could, then stripped him of his hose, shoes, breeches and underthings. The damage became clear; there was a laceration across the thigh and buttock. It looked deep and Jonathan gasped.

"It looks worse than it is." Jacob said, with a sigh of relief. "Self-heal. *Now*."

Jonathan stared at David, still hardly able to take in what Jacob was saying. He finally came to his senses as Jacob cuffed him hard across one ear.

"You will not help him by staring at him, lad, and there will be no point going for the surgeon; he will be at the battlefield I'll warrant. You and I must do the best for him we can. Cool that water and get the self-heal."

Numbly, Jonathan did as he was ordered, tearing a sheet into strips, and fetching water and the salve Jacob wanted. He helped Jacob roll David onto his side and held him while Jacob washed the mud from the wound until it ran clear. The two of them together bound the top of David's leg, thigh and waist in bandages to help the wound knit. He was almost asleep on his feet when Jacob lifted David from the table.

"Go and clean yourself, Jonathan. I will speak to you of this later." It was with a heavy heart and a mind full of fear for David's safety that Jonathan did as he was bade, before coming back and sitting at the kitchen table to wait for Jacob to return.

Jacob cradled his son to him as he carried him to his room. He put him into the bed as gently has he could, and watched him for a long while, making sure that his breathing was steady and watching a very little color return to his cheeks. Then, suppressing the fear and anger he felt he walked downstairs to speak to his apprentice. He gave Jonathan some ale and listened to him as the boy told him of the battle and bloodshed, and how he blamed himself entirely for what had happened to David.

"If I had not agreed to go with him, he would not have gone, sir. I beg of thee, do not blame him for this. Blame me and I will return home tomorrow if thou wishest it."

Jacob watched the penitent youth and his heart softened. "You are properly repentant, lad, and that shows me that you had no real sin in this; you were persuaded into it. I know my son. If you had not gone with him, he would have gone alone. *Yes*, he would." Jacob said sharply, as Jonathan opened his mouth to contradict him. "He would have told you falsehoods, as he did to me, and then neither of us would have known where he was when he did not return. But if you had not gone, what would have happened? My son would have bled to death on a battlefield on which he had no place to be. It may have begun as a sin, my boy, but you have redeemed that sin three times over. I have you to thank for my son's life, and tonight I truly feel that I have two sons."

Jacob folded the apprentice into his arms and let him weep afresh on his shoulder. "Now, get to bed. You sleep in my room tonight; I will sit and watch him."

"Let me, sir. Please."

Jacob shook his head. "You are exhausted, carrying him home all that way, you need sleep. I will wake you if there is any change, and I will wake you later, for I will need rest myself by then."

Eventually Jonathan allowed himself to be persuaded. His limbs were like lead, and the sense of relief that he was not being sent home in disgrace was palpable, but he did not feel that he could sleep until he had at least seen David again. He stepped quietly into their room and stood watching David's face. The youth was still pale, paler than Jonathan had ever seen him, but he was breathing steadily. Jonathan nodded at Jacob dumbly, went to Jacob's room and fell into the unfamiliar bed, asleep before he had time to think about it.

It seemed only seconds later that there was someone shaking his arm and he woke instantly. It was still dark.

"What? It is not...?"

"Nay, lad" came Jacob's voice, as the man stood over him, ghostly in the candle's glow. "It is nearly morning and he is peaceful. Will you go and watch him for a while? Let me sleep for four hours and that will be enough."

Jonathan slid out of the bed. "Dost thou wish me to milk this morning?" There was a long silence at this, until Jonathan said, "Master Jacob, did'st thou hear?"

Jacob didn't look at him as he undressed and pulled a nightshirt over his head. "Aye, I heard you. There are no cows, son. No cows, no chickens, and precious little of anything left. After the battle, the village and all neighboring farms were raided, but by which army I could not tell you, some of each I would imagine. We have done better than some, for I have money saved, and we have a source of income other than the farm, but it will be a hard winter for most I'll warrant. This is a bad day for Warwickshire...." Without another word he got into bed and closed his eyes.

Jonathan took the candle and went to his room where David was still asleep, his face pale and waxy in the dim light. He sat on the stool next to the bed and held David's hand. It was cool to the touch so he rubbed it to attempt to warm it. Then, because he could not think of anything else to do, he slid onto his knees, and although he knew it was wrong to barter with the Lord, he began to pray.

"Lord, I beg of thee, save him. He is a sinner but he can do better than he does. If thou willst grant me this, I will serve thee however thou guides me to do so, just save him, and I am thine." There was a gentle touch on his hair and Jonathan started, looking up to find David smiling, but clearly dreadfully tired.

"No, my brave Puritan," David said hoarsely, "you cannot go promising yourself to others. You are mine."

Jonathan thought his heart would break. He wanted to say that it was true, that he was David's, completely. But he couldn't find the words to tell him. Instead, his fingers sought David's hand, and tightened around it. "David. Thank the Lord. Let me go and tell thy father —"

"No, not yet." David clutched Jonathan's hand in both of his. "Is he very angry? I'll wager he is. I will be mucking out cows for months after this...." He frowned. "We should not have gone, you were right. You risked your life and saved mine, because I was too stupid to listen to you. I—only I wanted to see... I only hope he...."

Jonathan hated to do it, but he had to, for his own peace of mind if nothing else—he had to know one way or the other. He squeezed David's hand. "It's Master Tobias isn't it? Thou art worried about Master Tobias?"

David turned his head and looked Jonathan straight in the face, his eyes frightened. "Jonathan?"

"It is all right," Jonathan hastened to reassure him, "all *right* I tell thee. Dost thou not understand? Nothing matters to me except that thou art *alive*. If thou ever wishes to tell me about what happened between thee and the trooper, then thou canst, and if thou wishes it, I will go back there and find out if he lives, if I can."

David was crying. It tore Jonathan's heart to ribbons to see the real sorrow and huge tears in his eyes. "I can't bear to think of him lying there cold and...like the others." David gulped. "You would do that? For me? Knowing what you do?"

Jonathan had not known, for certain, but David's words confirmed his suspicions. He found that he did not care; it did not change David in his eyes. He was still his own David, whomsoever he loved. "Let us not talk about it now," he said bringing his friend's hand to his lips and kissing it, comforting him like he would a child. "Thou needest rest, but please David, never lie to me again? Promise me?"

David squeezed his hands. "Never again, I swear..." His voice was soft and affectionate. "Get into bed, Jonathan, I'm so cold."

Jonathan looked doubtful. "I do not think I should, thy injury—"

"Is behind me..."

"Art thou in much pain?"

David nodded with a small weak smile which warmed Jonathan from the inside out. "I think I would be more comfortable on my left side, and not to roll back, I can bolster myself with pillows on one side, but if I had you to support me on the other I would not roll." Jonathan gave up and slid gently in. When David instructed him, he turned his back to his friend, feeling David wrap himself around him. "That's better, Jon, and it doesn't hurt half as much like this."

Jonathan lay as still as he was able, shocked but inexplicably happy by the feel of David pressed against him, the touch of David's head on the back of his neck. He couldn't help but think that David was already lying, that it was unlikely the pain had lessened just by his own presence, but he forgave David for such a sweet calumny. Although David's body still felt chilled where their skin met, from his shoulders to his hips, a warmth spread between them. David's legs tangled themselves around his, his feet icy, yet the warmth traveled through Jonathan like a trail of gunpowder ignited, down his spine, suffusing his hips and thighs until he felt himself harden as the heat moved forward and inward. Thankful he was facing away from his friend, he bit his lip hard in an attempt to wish away the embarrassment.

His wish was granted as after a few minutes, he felt David shaking with silent sobs and his unwanted ardor cooled instantly. He longed to turn and comfort David, but could offer him no words of solace. Although he had promised that he would try and find out what had happened to David's trooper, he could not tell David in all honesty that he felt the man was alive, because he did not. All he could do was hold David's hands in his own and wait in the dark until his friend stilled, his breath slow and regular, showing he was asleep again at last.

The next few days were uncomfortable for everyone, and most especially for Jonathan who found himself in the middle of an unpleasant atmosphere. Jacob rejoiced that his son has recovered, but treated him with no little disdain in an attempt to show his disapprobation of his actions, waiting for David to show the penitence that Jonathan had done. David in turn, because of his guilt and pride, pretended that nothing was amiss, played on his injury, and refused to meet his father's eyes. Jonathan attempted to make a bridge between the two of them, for he knew that Jacob loved his son no matter what, but the gap between them widened daily despite his best efforts, and he wondered if the breach would ever be healed.

Jonathan was unable to keep his promise to return to the site of the battle until four days later, as he was kept so busy with the farm and the forge he could do no more than fall into bed at night. David had not mentioned it again, but Jonathan could feel the unfulfilled promise eating at his conscience. One morning before it was light he retraced their steps to Edgehill, but found he was come too late. The armies had gone, the plain littered with the aftermath of war. Dead horses lay here and there, attracting the attention of carrion feeders. Fabric fragments, many dull with dried blood, were scattered around the ruined grassland, and pieces of shot lay everywhere underfoot. It was sickening. *What*, Jonathan thought, as he looked around him, *did this achieve except for the death of mothers' sons?* Why had men come to this field, fought in this patch of Warwickshire, and then ridden away? *It makes no sense.* Everything else had been taken, even the broken guns. There was no way to find out what he'd come for. If Tobias had died, likely he was in one of the two burial mounds at either side of the field, and it was not as if Jonathan could follow the army and ask them. He dreaded having to give David such inconclusive news.

David, however, took it better than Jonathan had expected, his eyes clear and unusually bright, spots of pink in the pale cheeks.

"Master Butler in the town," Jonathan reported hesitantly, "he told me the King has gone to Oxford, and Essex to Warwick Castle. If Master Tobias lives, perhaps he will..."

"He's dead. I know it. If he were not dead, he would have come back." David's voice was spiked with pain, despite his brave aspect.

"Thou does not know that. Thou didst not see the place today, there is *nothing* left. They would have all been working hard; so perhaps he could not come. Is he not a scout? Would he not have been the first to be sent onwards towards Oxford?"

"*Don't*, Jon," David said sharply. "I know you did your best, but please let us never talk of it...of him, ever again."

Although he was worried about David's sadness that lingered long after he was out of bed and walking about with the aid of a crutch, Jonathan was pleased to obey the embargo on Tobias' name. To allow himself to think of Tobias and David together in that sinful way was torment to his heart. He knew how wrong it was, both lawfully and in the eyes of the Lord, but it was not that that disturbed him. It was his own feelings that frightened him more; feelings that had been surfacing so slowly he did not notice them. Now he suspected himself of this same abomination that David was seemingly infected with. He shut his feelings away, hid them, even from himself. That he loved David, this was a fact. At first he had done so as his Christian duty to his master's son, despite David's early hostility. Later he had come to love him for himself, as a brother; for his wit, his humor, his loyalty and friendship. But he knew there were darker and deeper feelings than any of these which he thrust away from himself, hurling them into the darkest corners of his mind, and refusing to face the truth.

Jacob had predicted the situation rightly. It was a hard winter for Kineton. Many families both in the town and the outlying farms had lost everything in the sacking that had followed the battle of Edgehill. The community rallied round the best it could, and those that had shared with those that had not. The notable exception to this was the Woodbines. They had been spared the cavalry's attentions, possibly because their farm was so dirty and the yard so filled with rubbish that the troopers simply thought it had already been raided, or that they had nothing of value. What little the family had, they had kept, and what they had kept they refused to share freely with anyone.

The pastor had been to the farm, but Amos Woodbine had all but set the dogs on him after he had told him it was Amos' Christian duty to help the less fortunate. The pastor came to the Caverly's immediately afterwards and had related the tale.

"I had to leave rather...peremptorily," the clergyman said, with a wry smile at Jacob and Jonathan. "He was possessed of a most unnatural temper. *'And did the more fortunate ever lift one hand to help me?'* he bellowed at me. His face was as red as his neckerchief. *'When my entire herd died ten years ago, the village turned its back on me and would not even buy the carcasses. No one worried if me and mine starved back then, and by God I will repay the compliment!'"*

Jacob had had to endure the humiliation of going to his hated neighbor to ask to buy some of his cattle; Jonathan had seen the hopeless look in his master's face as he had set off that day, and saw him returning later with two poor rakes trailing behind him, more skin and bone than anything else. When Jonathan opened the shed for the neglected beasts Jacob spat on the ground beside him.

"The thief charged me four times what they were worth. They are too thin to give any milk worth having anyway; we would be doing them a favor to butcher them now." He sighed. "At least we have hay, perhaps in the spring they will be of some use."

David was uncharacteristically quiet all that winter. He recovered his strength quickly, but his accustomed sunny nature seemed to Jonathan to be lying dormant, like yellow crocuses under snow. Jonathan could only hope that the pall of sadness would lift—he had seen his own older brothers suffer in love, and recover. He could only stand by and watch, and hope that David would do the same.

Eventually David was well enough to help in the forge once more and would stand beside Jonathan as before, operating the bellows, beating the iron for him, holding the horses, but something was missing. It seemed to Jonathan that they no longer worked as one unit, and Jonathan missed that. Instead of spending their Sundays together, David would stay indoors lying on their bed, leaving Jonathan to his own devices. No matter how often Jonathan begged him to come for their usual walks, he refused.

Jonathan missed their closeness more than he could bear to admit. He had received bad news from his home which he had not shared with the Caverlys, not wanting to add to their problems. Two of his older brothers had joined Parliament's side in the conflict, and Samuel, the oldest, had lost an arm at Turnham Green. His parents' sorrow for his brother's injury lay heavy upon him, more so compounded by the fact that Samuel was due to be married and had broken his engagement as he vowed that he could not support a wife now.

Thrown upon his own company, Jonathan resorted to an amusement he had laid aside since beginning his apprenticeship; begging parchment from the minister in town, and making his own charcoal using embers from the forge, he began to sketch again. It was a talent he had discovered early on in his life, but it had been disapproved of by his family as being a useless occupation. Once he began to work as an apprentice in Nottingham, he found that he had neither the time nor the inspiration to draw.

Now, with the Sabbath as his day of rest, other than the necessary animal care, he reacquainted himself with his pastime, only indulging in it in secret for fear of Jacob's stricture, or worse, David's ridicule at such an unsuitable occupation for an apprentice smith. He would go and sit by the river out of sight of the farm, wrapped up well against the cold. On his third such expedition the river was frozen over in parts, and the hoarfrost clung to each reed and bullrush in jagged white spikes, the sky a leaden gray portending days more of snow. He put his milking stool on the crunchy grass by the bank, and started to sketch the opposite side of the river, the overhanging willow and the way that the frozen water reflected the trees like a crystal mirror.

"Jon?"

Jonathan spun around on the little stool at David's voice; his friend was standing behind him in the ice-covered meadow. Jonathan stood up sharply, letting the papers scatter around his feet. He bent to pick them up, but David reached them first.

Backing away from Jonathan, who was attempting to retrieve his work, David's eyes narrowed when he reached portraits of his own face. "You did these? Secretive Puritan!" he teased. He stopped at a particularly well-defined one. It was a study of David asleep, his hair tumbled across the pillow and his arm thrown out to the side of him. He looked up at Jonathan with an amazed expression on his face. "These are *good*, even the ones of my odd face! Why have you hidden this from me, Jon?"

Jonathan snatched the parchments from his hands, picked up the stool, and started back to the house. David ran alongside him. "Jon? *Jonathan!* What is it?" They reached the barn where Jonathan returned the stool and went to leave, but David stood between him and the exit. "What is it? What?"

Jonathan exploded with pent up anger. "Thou asks me that? I thought that we were friends, thee and I, but since...since...the battle thou hast shut me from thy life. Now I have something that I share not with thee and *I* am abraded. Thou hast not shared one thought with me for three months! Thou art truly selfish, Master Caverly," he spat, seeing David blink under the formality. "Thou art not the only one to have lost something in this war, and not the only one to have been injured by it!" With words made bitter by concealment, he told David of his brother Samuel's injury.

David's eyes filled with tears and he moved closer, holding Jonathan by the arms. "I do not deserve you," he muttered. "You make me ashamed. What can I do to make it up to you? Command me and I will do it." Jonathan shook him off, but David's eyes roamed the barn, as if looking for something. He flew to the workbench and came back with a corn knife in his hands. "I have it," he said grimly, looking into Jonathan's frowning face. "You have many brothers and you miss them. You do not know, but I had a brother too, my twin who didn't live." Jonathan started at this confession and stared at David. Guilt and contrition flooded through him as David stumbled over his next words. It tore at his heart to see the pain in David's eyes. "I never knew him, but I miss him too. All my life I have felt empty and incomplete, as if a part of me was missing, and I never thought the emptiness could be filled. But then you came along. You are the brother I didn't want, but would now not ever be without. You have slipped into my life and have made me whole. My missing half, the better part of me, my iron conscience." He sliced the heel of his palm with the knife before Jonathan could stop him, and handed the kn   ife over. "Be my blood brother, Jon."

Jonathan stepped forward sharply and grasped David's bleeding hand. "Art thou mad? Hast thou not lost enough blood?" He tore the collar from his neck and went to wrap it around David's wound.

David pulled his arm away with a smile. "Please, Jon? Do you not want to be my brother? Not by birth, but by blood."

Jonathan's stomach flipped over as his anger receded. Once again he found could deny David nothing. "You are already more to me than a brother," he muttered. He gathered David into an embrace. The warmth and shape of David in his arms felt right, as if David belonged as close as this. Always. Reluctantly and blushing, he let David go, then cut himself with more care than David had and watched as David used the fabric strip to bind their hands together. As their blood mingled, Jonathan knew that their lives were now so intertwined they would indivisible from each other. It felt sacred, and yet dreadful and sacrilegious.

David gave him the sweetest smile imaginable and embraced him again firmly, his lips teasing at Jonathan's ear, causing shivers of delight to travel down his spine. "I'll never shut you out again, Jon, I swear. We are one."

CHAPTER 7

In 1643 King Charles planned a strike against London, to take the city back for himself in order to make a swift end to the war. It would be a three-pronged attack, with Sir Ralph Hopton coming from the west, the Marquess of Newcastle driving down from the north and the King's own army completing the pincer movement out of Oxford. But with a campaign that relied on so many commanders, so many regiments, the plan foundered. Hopton's men were reluctant to move too far east, and instead of striking south, Newcastle set siege to Hull, leaving Charles alone and with not enough force to fight by himself. Unable to take the city alone, Charles' war continued.

Seven months had passed since David and Jonathan had become blood brothers and no two brothers could have been closer. Jonathan was more fiercely loyal to David than before. He had managed to convince himself that the hidden feelings he had for David were passionate friendship, and despite Jacob's trust in him, he still covered for David when his friend disappeared on one of his mysterious absences to the village, or when he had not done a chore he was supposed to have done.

David in his turn treated Jonathan like a favorite pet, affectionate and kind but slightly patronizing. Jonathan weathered this, but he hated lying for his friend, and being lied to. Despite David's avowal to Jonathan after Edgehill, David had become no more open or truthful. David seemed to lie as easily as breathing and this talent for deception weighed heavy on Jonathan's conscience. He offered up a small prayer for David's soul every time it happened, attempting—although he was sure to do so was futile—to intercede with the Lord. One day, he was sure, they would both have to be judged for their falsehoods. In the meantime, all he could do was pray, knowing that by abetting David's many falsehoods to his father he was as sinful as David himself. He reasoned with himself so many times, but he always managed to convince himself that David meant no real harm by it, and was careless rather than intending to hurt. When David was close to him, his conscience bothered him less. To be close to his friend was enough for him, to be mentioned in the same sentence, their names to be linked together like their namesakes in the bible story made him proud. They were brothers—blood brothers; they were cleaved together.

One Sunday afternoon, Jonathan was sketching David as he stood throwing pebbles in the river. They had been swimming and David's hair was damp and plastered to his back, reaching almost to his rounded buttocks, their perfection now marred by the long white scar which curved around the right cheek and over his hip. As usual he was naked, worshipping the sun, whereas Jonathan, still more modest, was wearing breeches loosed at the knee.

"What shall we do?" David asked.

"We could wrestle." Jonathan said, putting his paper down and casting a glance at David who had stopped his game and was squinting into the sun.

"It is too hot."

"Is that why thou dost not wish to? Or is it that thou art afraid I will best thee again?" Jonathan laughed and reached out for one of David's ankles, tipping him off balance and pitching him into the river.

Furious, David emerged dripping-wet and launched himself

onto the laughing Jonathan, rolling him over in the long grass as he attempted to get them both back into the water. "Best me, you say?" he growled, laughing. "It was an error in judgment only; I should not have turned my back on you...as you should not have done today!" David held Jonathan down by pressing his whole weight against him and holding his arms behind his back, making it impossible for him to push himself back up. "Let us see how you can best me if I surprise you as you surprised me last time."

Jonathan was suddenly terribly aware of the feel of a naked David lying on his back and was pleased to be lying face down. David's wet hair was falling around both their faces, and to his horror his prick was hardening as David breathed in his ear. This could not be happening to him—not now!

"But as I say, it is too hot to wrestle." David said. He rolled over, pulling Jonathan around with him, and Jonathan found himself on top with a laughing, taunting David beneath him. He scowled. At Jonathan's serious face the smile gradually faded from David's mouth, but his eyes were bright, the generous mouth parted slightly, his breath fast. Jonathan sucked in his stomach and raised his hips in an attempt to disguise his hardness. It was impossible not to notice that David, passive and naked beneath him, was as hard as he, and unencumbered by any clothing his friend's cock tickled the hairs beneath Jonathan's navel, trailing wetness where it touched. He tried to remain calm, to pretend that this was their normal horseplay, but he knew that something was wonderfully, woefully wrong.

David was strangely quiet. His eyes were warm and compelling, his face calm and oddly expressionless. It seemed to Jonathan that endless hours passed, but he couldn't break his gaze. He felt David's hand on the back of his neck and the gentle pressure of his friend's fingers brought their faces close together. Their noses bumped, he felt David surge upwards, and their lips met and opened; natural as a flower unfurling, natural as breathing. David's tongue was a lightning strike, a shocking bolt from out of the clear blue sky, which touched the base of

Jonathan's spine and set his senses on fire. He felt like he must be shining like a summer beacon in the meadow. David's other hand was around his waist, fluttering over his back and without knowing why he did it, Jonathan pushed his hips hard against David's, and their cocks touched. The spell of the kiss broke as Jonathan gasped at the blissful, and yet terrible sensation this had caused. He pulled away, rolling sideways in horror and disgust at his body's reaction.

"Stop!" he ordered, his breathing heavy. He glared at David. "Thou must *not*." His voice was hoarse and he pushed David's teasing fingers away. As if by witchcraft, the hand was back, this time on his thigh and slipping around behind it.

"Why not, Jonathan?" David's eyes were locked on Jonathan's, his fingers rubbing urgently at the hard muscles.

"You *know* why. I find thee...the thought of thee...of us...an abomination."

"That is harsh. Even from you," murmured David, letting go and slumping back onto the bank, wiggling his toes in the soft mud at the edge of the river, watching his own erection as it continued to wave skywards. "What is it that makes me an abomination?" He rolled onto his side and watched Jonathan with teasing eyes,

"Because," Jonathan said, trying to shore up his faith with his words, "Leviticus tells clearly, as thou well knowest. Chapter eighteen verse twenty-two *'Thou shalt not lie with mankind as with womankind: it is abomination.'*" The words came out of Jonathan's mouth like the hammering of steel on anvil.

"Ambiguous," said David tersely in the voice Jonathan recognized as the one Jacob called his most blasphemous. He rolled forward and rested his chin on Jonathan's hip. His right hand snaked forward and gently tickled the muscles between Jonathan's chest and navel, looking hurt when Jonathan pushed his hand away. "'*As with womankind*'? Surely that means that both acts are as bad as each other, and both then can only be permitted or forbidden. In any event," he leant forward and planted a soft lingering kiss where his hand had been, his eyes shining with amusement as Jonathan scuttled backwards in shock at the feeling of wet lips on hot skin, "who is laying with whom? Have we not been 'laying together' since you first came to this house? It is only a kiss, Jonathan. Surely I can kiss my brother without sin?" He paused and looked across the river bank into the distance, saying softly as if to himself, "Our namesakes did..."

Jonathan could not speak for a moment, and tore his eyes away from the brown body and the teasing eyes like crystallized honey that dragged him towards transgression like a siren. He took a deep breath, fighting for control. "I am not Tobias," he said hoarsely, regretting it as soon as he spoke, seeing David's face blanch and the light fade from his eyes. He stood and strode away, leaving David sitting on the grass.

He walked along the riverbank and attempted to marshal his mind into some semblance of order. Twelve months of being so close to David, every day working together, every night sleeping in the same bed. Why was the Devil entering his soul now? Why was this temptation sent to beset him? *For what purpose could God be testing me?* As he thought back over the past year, he realized that this was not a sudden temptation, that he had begun thinking of David all of the time for longer than he could remember.

The opportunity to address the Devil had been a long time back. Perhaps it began in the forge, when he thought Jacob would not notice. He had long been in the habit of watching David as he worked alongside him. Admiring his friend's tanned torso, and the beautiful curve of his back, gleaming red hot in the forge's glow. Jonathan would smile at the boredom in David's eyes. He knew David could never wait to be released from the forge, even if it meant that there was farm work to do. Jonathan was the one impatient to be free of the work he enjoyed, so he could be alone with David and see him smile again.

Or perhaps it started in our bed. Since Edgehill it had become habit for them to sleep close together, the invisible barrier gone forever. David often curled up to him for warmth, and for more nights than he could count, he had lain awake long after David was asleep and reveled in whatever part of his skin was touching David's. Sometimes David would wrap around him like a vine, at other times Jonathan would wake and find David's head resting on his shoulder, a warm brown arm across his chest. Jonathan had never dared reciprocate and embrace him, but his member always responded in a shameful manner every time their flesh met.

Or perhaps, he thought, *it had been after Tobias,* when he'd started to torment himself with the visions of a naked David pressed skin to skin with the dark stranger. Jonathan could not clearly remember when it had all begun, but he knew that he didn't want to feel any differently, however wrong it was.

The night following their encounter at the riverbank, Jonathan made himself scarce after supper waiting an hour for David to retire, hoping he would be asleep before he joined him. He had been unable to meet David's eyes since the afternoon, ashamed—not only of his own feelings, but also that he had deliberately used Tobias' name like a weapon. The memory of the soldier seemed always to float between them, unspoken of since Edgehill but still painful to them both.

Jonathan sat on the edge of the bed, leaving on his underbreeches for the first time since their first night together, despite the heat in the room. David was face down, uncovered by the sheet, which he'd kicked off in the hot moonlit night and seemingly asleep. Jonathan slipped onto the pallet with him, and tried in vain to ignore David's rounded buttocks and the way his hair tumbled across the bed. Gently he lifted a lock of David's hair, and did what he'd longed to do, but had never dared: he caressed the silver strands, savoring their feel under his fingers. As he moved the hair over, his knuckles grazed David's back and the youth stirred and rolled over, his eyes opening slowly.

He did not make any comment on Jonathan's touch, but lay there looking up at him, his eyes full of softness, unfathomable and mysterious. His naked body was patterned with the shadows of uncertainty and discovery thrown by the flickering candle. *Here be dragons*, warned the map of Jonathan's mind, but his roughened fingers moved instinctively to the pointed chin and stroked the beloved face as gently as he ever touched anything in his life. David's eyes closed as he pressed his cheek against the hand like a cat accepting homage. Jonathan's thumb brushed over David's lips and they opened, accepting the tip of the thumb inside. Jonathan felt the lips, teeth, and tongue exploring every callus and line, and saw David's tongue dip out to lap at the cleft between thumb and forefinger. He watched David's beautiful face relax as he took pleasure from Jonathan's hand, and his cock surged, a sinful and delicious arousal that made him glad that David's eyes were closed in pleasure so he couldn't see him blush.

His suppressed emotions tore to the surface like bubbles trapped underwater, the love he felt emerging, suffusing his soul, and joining him to David as surely as if they were manacled together. He would do anything David asked, anything. *But how can this be love? Yet how could this be anything else?* How could he be so sure of one thing, but be so very confused at the same time?

David's eyes opened once more and one arm reached up, as he pulled Jonathan's head down to meet his in the same way as he had done that afternoon.

"It is not Tobias that I want, Jon..." came David's voice, heady and languorous, and without further thought Jonathan fell into the vortex of David's eyes, his mouth seeking David's like a ship seeking safe harbor.

The dawn brought guilt and incrimination against himself; and himself only. He had embraced his master's son. He had *kissed* his master's son. He had allowed his master's son to do the same to him.

"I am lost," he groaned quietly. There was a soft chuckle. The lithe warm body, which Jonathan had woken beside every morning, was clinging to him, his legs entangled in Jonathan's, their skins damp with sweat where they met. David's face was hidden beneath a tangled mass of hair, but Jonathan could feel a tongue gently circling around on his skin and he was unable to do more than protest weakly when a hot mouth enveloped an aching nipple.

"David," he whispered, unable to move to push him away. "We must not. Thou must *not*." There was a low growl from David, which reverberated around parts of Jonathan he had not accepted as belonging to him, and certainly not being under his control.

"Stop talking like the Puritan you are," whispered David. "*Thou must not. Thou shalt not. Thou wilt not. Thou shouldst not.*' All my life I have heard this and nothing else. And I say: Should I not?" He pulled himself up and kissed Jonathan under the ear. "Shall I not?" The voice was irresistible. David possessed Jonathan's mouth briefly. "Can I not?" A palm was on his chest, and he felt it slide down his sweating flesh, lower and lower, almost painful in its slow descent. He was paralyzed; he could not move a muscle as he felt fingers unbuttoning his breeches and opening them, releasing him. His mouth was dry, but he gulped in shock as what he dreaded, what he longed for, what he had dreamed of for so many months finally happened and David's hand was upon his cock. As the sinful pleasure coursed through him, he knew he was damned then, damned for all eternity and no amount of castigation or prayers or repentance would save him now. "I think thou willst find I canst..." said David. After that there was silence except for small whimpers of joy from Jonathan in glorious rhythm to David's sliding hand.

Jonathan felt his head was coming loose and his hips arched upward in a final agony of bliss; his seed shot from him and splattered over his stomach. He could not speak—could not think—his heart was pounding so hard. He pulled David towards him and kissed him, unable to explain his feelings even to himself. David rolled over him and sat across his hips, his own prick teasingly waving.

"Can I?" Jonathan echoed in a hallowed whisper and tentatively reached out and touched David's member with the tips of his fingers, recoiling as it reacted to his touch by twitching to one side. David took his hand and placed it more firmly.

"Please…" David sounded excited, his breath coming in great gasps. "I need you to know me…" The cock was hot under Jonathan's hand, hotter than any flesh he had felt before, familiar to see—for had he not seen it almost every day of their lives together? But oh, *so* unknown, and how wonderful it was to learn its shape and to feel, oh to feel the source of life in his hand, softer yet harder than he could believe. Longer and slimmer than his own, it curved up and back towards David's stomach.

"It bends," Jonathan said in amazement. There was no reply from David, who had leaned back on the cot presenting with his eyes tightly closed. Jonathan felt his groin pool with warmth and his prick began to rise once again in response David's abandon. Emboldened, he reached out with his other hand and cupped David's balls. David gasped and Jonathan felt the balls contract as he continued to stroke David with increasing enthusiasm. The hot hard shaft seemed to burn his fingers, and he worried that the soft groans of pleasure David was making would be noticed.

"David," he whispered. "Thou willst be heard…hush, *please.*"

David's eyes opened, his face soft and dreamy, and a smile like the day beginning spread across his face. He rolled completely off Jonathan's body and lay on his side so they were face to face. "I do not think you realize how difficult you make it to be silent when you do what you do there, and I have waited so very long for you to do it." He put Jonathan's hands back onto his hardness and thrust towards him. "Do it again, Jon. Please." David nestled his mouth into Jonathan's neck and moaned quietly as Jonathan wrapped his eager fingers back around David's prick, and with his other arm pulled David close to him, running his hands down the firm back, slick with sweat. He felt David tensing against him, and within a minute David was clinging to him, crying out into his neck to muffle the shouts of joy as he spent into Jonathan's hand.

There were tears in Jonathan's eyes, as David clutched him like a grateful child. His mind reeled as David, in the dawning light, confessed that he had loved him since the day Tobias had died, the day Jonathan had saved his life.

As his words came to a close and Jonathan had not replied, David propped himself up and asked, "Do you hate me, Jonathan? I have wanted this for us both for so long. Is this not what you wanted after all?"

Jonathan's heart leapt. He took the bright face in both hands and said firmly, "'*And it came to pass that the soul of Jonathan was knit with the soul of David, and Jonathan loved him as his own soul. Then Jonathan and David made a covenant, because he loved him as his own soul,*'" He kissed David again, deeper and longer than before, relishing the feel of the soft mouth, the rasp of the stubble on the pointed chin, the unique quicksilver taste of David, sweat and tears.

"That's all right then..." murmured David sleepily, teasing with voice and fingers as he slipped down beside Jonathan and wrapped around him once more. "I knew you'd find something in your Bible. I love you too, my beloved Puritan."

✿ CHAPTER 8 ✿

What Jonathan found difficult to decide was, what was worse: the guilt at the feelings he had had before, or the guilt that he carried now that David and he were sinning in the worst possible way, abominations both in the eyes of the Lord and the world. Typically, David seemed unaffected by any such feeling and was happy again. It made Jonathan's heart soar to hear David singing as he worked. His attitude to Jonathan had changed immeasurably for the better. He was less teasing, no longer patronizing, and so very affectionate that Jonathan would blush twenty times a day when David would take every available opportunity to kiss or caress him whenever Jacob was out of sight. It was a wonderful torment; David would either launch himself at him, kissing him gleefully, or would stand beside or behind him, muttering terrible things whilst stroking him sinuously, making him harder with every touch of his teasing hands. Just having David stand next to him and whispering wanton words of need and lust into his ear, was enough to drive Jonathan insane, and he knew that David was doing it partly for his own pleasure and partly to torture him with the fear of discovery.

Having unleashed his desire, Jonathan found himself taking the lead in their relationship, particularly in bed. He found that he was not satisfied with simple caresses and a mutual release; his physical expressions of love were demonstrated with an unexpected and torrential passion. Jonathan felt he was possessed of a demon; a desperate, plundering creature of lust and haste. As summer crept inexorably into autumn, Jonathan was ravaging David's body nightly; his mouth and hands laying claim to every inch of the brown skin, almost rending the flesh, as if trying to tear him open and encompass his very essence; his kisses so violent that David's lips were often bruised and swollen, his neck and chest so bitten and marked that he was forced to wear a shirt in the forge to hide the brands of love that Jonathan claimed him with.

There came a time, however, when Jonathan could no longer hold himself back; he needed more than just hands and lips, and when his lusts could not be calmed by their play, he instinctively moved between David's legs, hardly knowing what he was doing, driven by his own desire and instinct.

David gazed up at him, his smile concupiscent, his hips arching up, as he wrapped his legs around Jonathan's waist. "Jon," he gasped, "don't wait for me to beg you."

Jonathan hesitated, his hands hard on David's writhing hips, which were slick beneath his palms with prurient and sweaty need. His member was weeping and he wanted David so much...but he was thoroughly confused and alarmed at what he was about to do.

"*David*," he groaned. "I cannot."

"You must!" David was grasping the sheets as if in agony.

"But I will hurt thee, and I wouldst not hurt thee for any price —"

"It will all be worth it, I promise you, now do it...*please.*"

Hands shaking with impatience, he lifted David's legs and positioned his cock between David's warm cleft. With his eyes firmly fixed on David's he pushed once, stalling as David gasped. It seemed that David was a vice, crushing his cock with delicious pain and setting off sparks through his mind. David took a deep breath and pushed himself closer, causing Jonathan to sheath himself almost fully inside. They were panting in unison; both motionless, both adjusting to the feel of each other.

Jonathan was dazed; he had not thought that they could have been any closer to each other than they were, but now they were truly one. One mind. One beating heart. One body. Joined and conjoined.

As if to encourage him, David slid back and then forward again. He smiled, his breath now fast and shallow. "That's right. And so beautiful."

"It hurts thee…"

"A little, only. It will stop when you warm to your work. You swell within me, Jon."

At the sensual words Jonathan's cock throbbed, making the connection between them ever more wonderful. Slowly he inched back and pushed forward again. Hardly able to breathe, and completely unable to concentrate with the distraction of David in sweaty abandon beneath him, he closed his eyes and was immediately hurled into a dark and horrifying vision. *He saw a silver path in a dark landscape, lit with red and yellow fires, which seemed to pour from the earth itself, and at the end stood a blond angel with a fiery sword held high above his head…*

Terrified at the conflagrant illusion, his eyes flew open. David was still there, smiling, and seemed not to have noticed the sudden terror that Jonathan had experienced. David reached up to pull Jonathan's mouth down to his, and Jonathan kissed him gladly, too frightened to shut his eyes again. As their mouths met he felt shocks batter through him as his seed tore its way from him and into his lover. He fell forward, and his cock slid from David's body. He wrapped his hand around David's cock, and David came, his hips pushing off the bed as hot semen poured over Jonathan's fingers.

Jonathan lay beside David, clasping him close, but his thoughts were dark, the sweetness of the last few moments already stained with guilt and sin. He had no doubt what the terrifying vision had been. It was hellfire—lighting the path to hell, and he knew that he was destined for it. With a lazy smile, David pushed himself up and kissed Jonathan deep and slow, then tucked himself into Jonathan's arms without even seeming to notice the worried look on his lover's face.

As their relationship grew, Jonathan became possessive of David, suspicious and jealous of his movements. David had not altered his habits so very much in his new found relationship, and would still disappear at odd times to the village to meet with his friends, returning home the worse for drink, but so penitent and lovingly affectionate that Jonathan always found it difficult to sustain the anger engendered by David's abandonments. If Jonathan berated him, David would turn hurt eyes on him or occupy his mouth with lingering kisses to silence his accusations, or would slip down to seek the steel of Jonathan's needful hardness. Jonathan was always placated, silenced, and becalmed as David assured him time and time again that his heart belonged only to him.

"So why dost thou go? What dost thou do? Art thou so discontent with my company that thou wouldst seek out other men? Or perhaps it is the maids that draw thee?"

David looked at him with a hurt expression. "Jon? You don't think...*can't* think that I would be untrue to you?"

"No...Yes...No..." he groaned. He grabbed David by the arms and pulled him up to his face, feeling hunted and agonized. "I do not know what to think, thou makest me so confused! I see thee flirt with the Woodbine lass right here in front of me and it kills me to see it, so what must I think that thou dost when I am not around to see?"

"Nothing. There is *nothing* to think, for there is nothing to see. I go to escape here, Jon, not you. Never you. I was unhappy here for years before you came and I have never been happier in it since we... But I still feel trapped here. If you had not come, I surely would have left a long while since."

"Thou wouldst not leave me?" Jonathan felt his heart contract with panic. He had no idea how they would manage their lives, but he knew that it had to be him and David, *together*.

"Fret not, beloved Puritan," David said. "I promise that I shall never leave you. Not until you have finished your indenture, at least." He grinned impishly and bit Jonathan on one muscled breast, seeing the concern stay in his love's face. "And then," he continued, licking his way back up the hard body, "you can come with me."

Jonathan was not convinced by anything David said. The words "promise" and "swear" came far too easily to lips that had years of practiced deception.

The village was recovering its strength after the sacking of the last autumn, thanks in the main part to the efforts of the local minister. Families who might have starved to death in the long cold winter of '43 were spared the worst effects of the weather, and the death toll was significantly lower than any other year. What broke the heart of the recovering village was its missing sons. So many of them had left the area to join the armies; the Fieldings, the Verneys, and the Shuckburghs had all lost family members to the respective causes. The tragedy was compounded by the fact that some families had been cruelly ripped apart as sons chose opposite sides to their fathers, or brother sided against brother. Jacob was pleased that Jonathan showed no inclination to join the fighting, and he gave daily thanks to God that his son, who had at one point seemed captivated by the thought of war and likely to bolt at any time, appeared to have changed his mind after the butchery at Edgehill.

The Caverley's farm recovered quicker than most, having an income from the forge, together with the fact that it had always been fairly self-sufficient. Despite the army taking most of their work, the war rumbled on and there was no lack of orders, and gradually stock was replaced. New chickens were bought from a travelling man, and later a deal was made with Mistress Verney who sold them a replacement horse. Woodbine's poor cows were now as fat as butter, had calved, and were milking well and the forge was operating from early morning till late in the night, not only with new orders but also with free work helping replace much that had been lost or stolen from people in the town. The long, hard work made the boys so exhausted at night it was as much as they could do to roll into each other's arms before sleep claimed them.

Gossip about the progress of the war reached the family regularly from strangers who stopped at the smithy. It seemed the war was going well for the King—he had gained victories at Adwalton Moor and Dartmouth. David would not talk about the war, and although he listened attentively to the stories that were told to them, he made no comment, not even when he heard that Wilmot's Horse had been the victors at Roundway Down.

When news of war came to the forge, Jonathan watched his lover anxiously. He attempted to gauge David's feelings, but David's face gave nothing away. It was as if he had heard nothing of import, that the news did not touch him, and Jonathan relaxed. *Perhaps*, he hoped, *David is truly over the loss of Tobias*.

So the year rolled by; a perfect summer, and a bounteous harvest with no presentiment of the events to come.

Towards Christmas David convinced Jonathan to sneak off to the village with him for the Christmas market. Jacob had given them the Tuesday as a half-day, warning them both that they must work all the harder the day after.

"You must come," David wheedled, persuading Jonathan as easily as he ever did, "for I want to buy you something." Jacob made them attend church at noon, but afterwards they slipped away, hiding in the churchyard, pressed up against the honey-colored brick. They peered around the corner and waited, until finally Jacob urged the horse away from the church, with a shake of his grizzled head. Jonathan's guilt was smothered by David's hot mouth, but he pushed him away, disgusted that David would kiss him here, in daylight, and worse still, against the very walls of the church.

"Hast thou no shame?" he muttered angrily, more with himself for an unbidden hardness in his breeches.

"Seemingly not," said David with a grin as he towed Jonathan north towards the market square. Apart from church, Jonathan had not been to the village much, and had not seen such a bustle of people since he'd left Nottingham behind him. It was bitingly cold: the wind blew the snow around in tiny whirlwinds and the crystals crunched underfoot as they approached the market. The colors and the activities of the square brought warmth and light to the gloomy morning. David moved among the crowd, obviously a favorite, smiling and greeting all he encountered, touching the brim of his hat to the older ladies and bowing deeply in mock respect for younger maids. His contemporaries swarmed around him, complaining of how little they saw of him. Jonathan trailed behind—enjoying the scents and sounds of the market, but burning with jealousy seeing David perform for the village, being in such demand.

They sat at a provender's stall to watch some guisers perform the old favorite of St. George. David laughed uproariously at the Turkish Knight and the Doctor's comic antics. He turned to share a joke with Jonathan and the mirth on his face dropped away at Jonathan's serious expression. "Jon? What's wrong?"

Jonathan was so touched by David's worried face that he hid his unease at what he considered to be blasphemous entertainment, and his jealousy of David's popularity, and smiled, deflecting the question with one of his own. "Where's this thing thou wast to buy me?" He was rewarded by the sun rising in David's face before his friend leapt to his feet and tugged him back into the throng of the stalls. They moved together as one through the market. David's arm brushing against his, his hand grazing Jonathan's fingers almost imperceptibly. Jonathan's attention was caught by a woodturner's stall and, appreciative of another's craft, he stood and watched the man work for a while, admiring the beauty he wrought from seemingly rough pieces of wood. He lost track of time and when he turned back to the crowd David had vanished.

He strode on into the market seeking David's distinctive brown hat and shining hair to no avail, and after ten minutes of being jostled by people he did not know, he decided he'd had enough and to give it up and go home. As he turned to retrace his steps, an unmistakable voice sounded somewhere not too far off.

It was David and his voice was raised. Jonathan could not hear the words spoken, but it seemed he was arguing with someone. Following the sound, Jonathan pushed back into the throng, hoping that David was not in some sort of trouble. He pushed past three gentlemen having their knives sharpened, and spotted David sitting on a small trestle behind the stalls. He stopped dead and the blood drained from his face; Elizabeth Woodbine was sitting on David's lap. The maid was clutched to David's chest and he was stroking her hair and kissing the top of her head. He was able to see that David was speaking softly to her, but Jonathan could not catch his words. Bile rose in his mouth as his suspicions crystallized into truth. What could be more obvious than for David to marry his neighbor's daughter?

Their fathers will surely welcome it, he thought hopelessly. Whatever Jacob thought of the Woodbine family, the land would become one and be a sizeable farm. It was a good match, for the girl at least. Hot, bitter tears came to his eyes, and he dashed them away as he retreated back into the market square, hardly seeing where he was going. How could he stand it? For all his strength he felt his legs weaken, and he leant a while against a stall, dizzied, until a goodwife asked him if she could offer him assistance, worried that he was unwell. He came to himself, thanking her for her attentions and straightened up, glancing back through the throng. Suddenly David appeared, his face angry and set. He hardly seemed to know where he was going and collided into Jonathan without seeming to know who he was.

"Forgive…" He began to apologize, but at the sight of Jonathan the dark expression vanished like a burst bubble and was replaced instantly with a truly happy smile. He was alone, and there was no sign of the Woodbine maid.

"Jon! I thought I had lost you." He grabbed his lover's arm firmly and tugged him toward a tanner's stall. Jonathan was numb, and hardly could trust himself to speak, allowing David to investigate the leatherwork utterly oblivious of the maelstrom of emotion tearing through the apprentice.

Finally Jonathan controlled his temper and spoke quietly and evenly. "Who wast thou talking to? I heard thee shouting and..."

"Me? No one." David was distracted by the leatherwork, but Jonathan was not to be put off, hating himself for wanting to hear the truth, yet longing for David for once in his life to be honest with him. He leant nearer to David, knowing he would not be heard in the noise of the crowd.

"David, tell me the truth. Thou wast shouting, thou canst not deny it."

"Oh, it was nothing. My friends, you know, they wanted me to spend the day with them." He turned and in his hands was a beautiful, engraved leather sword belt. "Here, this is what I wanted to give you." Jonathan blushed as David fastened it around his waist, fiddling unnecessarily with the settlement of it on Jonathan's hips until he was totally satisfied.

Jonathan hardly noticed the gift, his temper and jealousy raged within him. David was lying to him again, and yet he could not argue with him over it in such a public place. He muttered a thanks and David raised an eyebrow as if surprised at the lack of gratitude. Without another word Jonathan led the way out of the market and towards home, and David trailed after him, both of them lost in darkening thoughts that slid between them like a curtain.

ᚳᚲ CHAPTER 9 ᚲᚲ

From Christmas to Valentine's there seemed to be far too much of Elizabeth Woodbine's presence in their lives for either of their liking. It seemed every time that they opened the cottage door she simply happened to be out in the yard, getting in the way as David worked, accompanying him up the path to the forge. The forge was the only place he felt safe for she would not approach it, having encountered Jacob's anger one time too many.

David knew that Jonathan watched him like a hawk and was jealous of Elizabeth's continued advances. Although David was certain that he gave her no more encouragement than he ever did, Jonathan never seemed to be placated, and David was ever having to reassure his Puritan that the girl meant nothing to him.

On the fourteenth of February Jonathan had gone to the forge early. David had just finished the milking and was loading the cart when Elizabeth appeared as was her wont, as if from nowhere, causing David to jump sideways, almost knocking over one of the milk containers.

"For pity's sake, Mistress!" he shouted at the girl. "Why do you come up upon me like that? If I had spilled that milk, my father would do more than shout at you!" He swung himself up onto the cart and picked up the reins, frowning as Elizabeth clambered up on the other side. "Get down, Elizabeth," he snapped, his temper frayed with her presumption.

Instead of climbing down, she shunted along the driver's

bench, giggling. "Let me come with you David, please?" He could tell she was attempting to get him to look at her, but he ignored her, looking straight ahead. "You always used to let me come with you, remember?"

"We were children. It did not matter then. You know what people would think if we were seen travelling to town alone together now. I was given to believe that Somerton and you had an understanding. That is to say," his eyes slid to hers, "your father has been boasting of it all over town. Do you say it is not true?"

She looked away with a sly expression, as if ashamed to meet his gaze. "I may have been made an offer," she said, with quiet rebellion in her tone, "but that does not mean I've answered him, or that I have to, no matter what Father thinks." She put one small hand on his arm. "David. You know that I...care for you. I know that you feel the same."

"Then you err, Mistress. Greatly."

"But at Christmas?" Her voice rose slightly. "You protected me. The soldiers! You have not forgotten how you comforted me? It has always been you, David. I have always known it. Ever since we played together as children, I never really cared for anyone but you. Ever."

David shook her hand from his arm, his face hardening. "Say nothing else, Mistress. You shame us both. I did what any man would have done, even if the maid brought the trouble on herself by encouraging the soldiers. It is not only them I blame." He glared at her, feeling cold and angry. It pleased him to see the look of shock on her face. "Get down, and for the love of God never speak to me in this fashion again." He jumped from the cart and dragged her down from the seat, his voice harsh. "Somerton is a good man, and a good friend. He deserves better than you, and if you ever speak to me of this again, I will tell him of this day, aye, and of the soldiers too, then see what man will have you." He swung up onto the cart again and drove off.

As the cart rattled away, he heard her voice, shrill and angry as she ran beside the lumbering cart. "It's not just Somerton who wants me, Master Caverly, whatever you may think! You should be grateful! I don't see a line of maids chasing the blacksmith's son!" She took a small parcel out of her apron pocket and threw it at him. It bounced off his arm and landed under the cart. David didn't stop to see what it was or what had become of the girl, but hurried the horse forward, his thoughts dark.

Jonathan trotted down the cinder path toward the barn on a quest for more nails. He spotted something lying in the cart track and picked it up, puzzled. It was a small muddy parcel with a card attached by a string. The writing was smeared but readable. It was done with an educated hand, perhaps one of the local scribes, he guessed. The card was inscribed with a small poem, but there was no name on the parcel. He opened it, absolving himself of guilt with the excuse that it was not addressed to anyone and there might be a clue to the owner within. The parcel contained a pair of soft kid gloves, supple enough to be worn whilst riding and were probably quite expensive. The cuffs were of fine linen and had been embroidered painstakingly with leaves and flowers, and Jonathan had a sinking feeling that he knew which small pale fingers had done that needlework.

Jealousy rolled around in his heart as he stood there, stroking the silky leather. With bitterness in his mouth and eyes he read the card again:

"Two gloves lie side by side, and so should we
without a 'y'—together should we bide."

He knew then who they were from and who they were for. A rage swept through him and he tore the card into tiny fragments. As soon as he had done it, he regretted it, but there was nothing he could do to mend his actions. He ran around the back of the barn to the compost heap and, using a pitchfork, he thrust the beautiful gloves into the middle of the steaming mess, his heart secretly jubilant under the guilt for thwarting the insidious girl. He took the pieces of card back to the forge, and when Jacob was busy, threw the fragments into the furnace.

Elizabeth stopped coming to the forge after that. Jonathan thought it was because she had not had an answer to her poem, but David alone knew the true reason. Sometimes she could be seen taking the short cut from the back of the fields through the woods to the village, but she did not bother them, and they were both grateful for different reasons. Apart from the nagging insecurity of loving David and a recurring vision of hell and a blond, avenging angel with a sword, Jonathan could not have been happier.

A few days later, Jonathan missed David at about midday, and if he had allowed himself to curse he would have done so, knowing that there was no excuse he could give Jacob to explain where his son had gone. The last he had seen of David was when he had left the forge on an errand to fill the water buckets; three hours later and he had not reappeared.

He finished the horse he was shoeing and then ran down to the house and searched around, half hoping that David was either in the cottage, or lazing by the river in his favorite spot. There was no sign of him anywhere, and dreading Jacob's return, Jonathan walked back to the forge, his thoughts anxious and angry, and his heart like lead in his chest. He didn't know whether he would prefer David to lie to him as to his whereabouts, or whether he preferred him just to vanish like this, and lie afterwards, which he knew David always did.

The afternoon was spent taking his temper out on the metalwork, envisioning David getting drunk with the young men in the village, or worse....

David's afternoon had been spent in more pleasant environs than the dark and smoke of the forge. He had, as Jonathan feared, spent most of the time with friends, up on the hills near the old battleground. Simon Butler had brought some cider, and while David was not drunk, as he walked home in the warm spring sunshine, he was more than a little inebriated. Any guilt he may have felt had melted with the alcohol, and it was keeping away the

concern he might feel at the threat of his father's censure or
Jonathan's jealous reprisal for his disappearance. He passed
through the woods on the way home. The ground was nearly entirely carpeted with primroses. David was so impressed with the
beauty of the scene around him, he flopped down in the valley
and looked across the yellow carpet to the river. The delicate
scent of the flowers washed over him as his thoughts, as they always did day or night, ran to Jonathan. *Oh*, he thought, *he's going
to be so angry with me again.*

As much as he loved his precious Puritan, he was finding that
his lover was just as controlling as his father. Jonathan was always
quizzing him as to where he had been, who he had been seeing;
always so jealous of every other person David ever spoke to.

Why can't he trust me? He never believed that David could
be faithful, and David found this inconceivable. *How can he think
that I'd ever want anyone else but him?* He couldn't understand
how Jonathan could not see how very beautiful he was in David's
eyes, how his escapes to the village had nothing to do with wanting to escape from Jonathan, but simply a release from the con-
striction of his everyday life.

As he looked around at the beauty on the riverbank an idea
formulated in his mind. He would bring Jonathan here, make
love to him in this place, and try to instill in his starched, staunch
Puritan soul how beautiful David found him and how no one
could replace him. The vision of Jonathan's naked masculinity
amongst such splendor made him smile, and the imagining of
Jonathan's untrammeled lusts in such an otherworldly place made
his member throb pleasantly. He stood up, unwilling to waste a
second more; he would bring Jon here today. Jonathan needed to
know how very much he loved him.

There was a small shriek from somewhere above him.

"Master Caverly!" came a voice, "you frightened me, starting up out of the flowers like that." Elizabeth was sitting at the
top of the glade on a fallen log, shredding primroses with her
fingers. He had not seen her since their argument at Valentine's.

David bowed stiffly and made as to walk past her. "Don't run away... David..." she said, softly. She caught him by the sleeve and held him immobile, and he was unable to pull away without seeming rude. He glanced down at her, impatient to be away, to get home and find Jonathan, and saw her eyes were red. It was clear she had been crying for a long time before David had made an appearance. His heart softened. As much as he found her attentions galling, he had grown up knowing this maid, and he did not like to see anyone cry.

"Mistress?" He sat down beside her and her head dropped into her hands. Her shoulders shook as she burst into fresh cries of grief, her shoulders shaking. He was unwilling to leave her in such distress, no matter what his feelings about her were, or his father's.

He realized his mistake almost immediately as the girl threw herself into his lap, weeping copiously and making it sound like she could hardly talk in her distress. She gulped and sounded so frightened that anyone would have attempted to protect and console her.

"You are too kind," she sobbed. "You have always been so. Not like...You cannot understand. He will not...He refuses— he is a good man...and my father will..." Her words made no sense to David, who was now seriously concerned that the girl was becoming hysterical. He wanted to escape but was unable to, with the girl in his lap, her arms around his neck, and her head on his shoulder. He knew that he at least would have to walk her home, and that would delay him even longer, and his desired union with Jonathan was making him impatient. Elizabeth's sobs continued as David put a gentle hand on her back, suggesting softly that they should start out for home and that he would accompany her.

Somehow he found that she was suddenly far too close to him, her face wet and supplicant. She leant up and her eyes were half opened, as were her lips. She said nothing, but her mouth moved slowly toward his. David's mind was numbed by cider and confused by a gray fog of conflicting emotions he could not name. He struggled for control, but her eyes seemed to draw him in; he was unable to pull back against them. The scent of flowers exuded from her like she was a living woodland as her lips moved closer to his, but as her mouth touched his the spell was broken and he leant backwards sharply. He had only wanted to help and suddenly he was being clung to; her hands were on his breeches, rubbing his prick through the cloth. David was shocked at her wantonness as she kissed him again. He pulled himself to his feet, leaving her kneeling on the woodland floor, pawing at his breeches with greedy hands.

"Please, David! You know I love you," she said "Take me? You can have me. Please?" She was unbuttoning him and this was the last straw.

"What are you doing?" Her face had lost its pleading and seductive look, and had become avaricious and eager. She was breathing heavily as she rose to her feet and attempted to kiss him yet again. In disgust he pushed her off with a little more force than he meant, and she fell backwards on to a log behind her. Her face turned into one of rage as she pulled herself up.

"You don't want me?" she looked absolutely furious. "Every boy in the village wants me! Why not you?" She rubbed her arm which was bleeding from a graze sustained hitting the tree trunk. David looked down at her, his heart racing and fear in his heart.

"I did not mean to hurt you, Elizabeth, but you are not seemly. You are engaged to Somerton! I would not, could never..." He was unable to continue the sentence, so he stepped forward and held out his hand. "Let me attend to your arm."

The girl was not now to be approached; after throwing a look of pure venom at David, she swept away down the hill without a backwards glance. David stood watching her move out of sight, sickened by the girl's lewd behavior. A shudder ran through him when he thought of what she wanted him to do. This beautiful place, which he had such plans for, had now been spoiled by Elizabeth. He couldn't bring Jonathan here now.

He turned for home.

Jonathan was letting the cows back out into the meadow when he saw Elizabeth emerge from the wood. She looked angry about something, and she didn't even glance over to the farm as she stormed up the track towards the stile between the fields. As he shut the watermeadow gate, Jonathan saw David run out of the wood from the same place, with a similar serious expression. Jonathan's heart sank as he turned to walk back to the barn.

David arrived a minute later, out of breath. He closed the doors, pulling the wooden slat over and strode to Jonathan's side. He had a primrose in his hand, and a familiar sweet, intoxicating smile on his face.

"You are going to scold me. So why don't we..." David took the broom from Jonathan and put his arms around his waist, "...just pretend that I have already been scolded, and that I have already apologized and you have apologized to me for scolding me, and we are making friends again..." He kissed Jonathan's neck gently, and tongued his earlobe. "Making friends again is the best part as you well know."

Jonathan succumbed to his seducer, and let himself be dragged him down into the hay as David chuckled softly. "God, I've missed you. I swear I won't leave you again." Jonathan took no notice of the protestations, knowing David better than that.

As David kissed his chest and torso, Jonathan asked the question that was burning his lips. He'd been wanting to get the question spoken before he lost his mind to David's lips and tongue. "Didst thou see the Woodbine lass in the wood?"

David did not falter in his explorations. "No. I was drinking over at Edgehill. I came through the wood, but didn't see anyone."

"Art thou sure? Truth..." He became slightly incoherent as David grazed his teeth on his hipbone, his tongue teasing the hollow beside it.

"Truth, my Jon. I did not see her, nor speak to her. I promised I would not after Valentine's, did I not?" He pulled himself up next to Jonathan's face and put a slim finger on his lips, smiling as Jonathan instinctively kissed the tip. "No scolding and no more questions. We have about half an hour before supper I think, and I want you to know how much I love you."

Outside, Elizabeth walked back into the Caverley's yard, surprised not to see anyone bustling about. She was calmer now, and had formulated a plan. Her moon's cycle had not come, and she knew enough of Nature to know the reason for it. In desperation she had attempted to seduce Somerton, her affianced, but he was a man staunch in his decision that he would not take her maidenhead until after they were wed. And while her maidenhead no longer deserved the name, as made clear by her current plight, she knew that an early child—whilst not unusual in the parish—would not fool Somerton. He would cast her off.

So she had returned, penitent. She wanted to speak once more to David, to try and ask him to tell no one of their meeting today, and how she had acted. She had decided to try the same trick with her second choice, Nathaniel Moulton, and did not want him to learn of her antics of today. She knocked at the cottage. When there was no reply she walked across to the barn, only to find it locked. She was turning to walk up to the forge when she heard David's voice cry out Jonathan's name. She frowned. He sounded...surprised? *Are they arguing? Good!* Moving around the barn she found a bare knothole and peered through, squinting slightly to focus her eyes to the gloomy interior. After a few seconds she gasped aloud, her hand flying to her mouth, as her eyes widened in shock. She staggered back from the peephole, looking around wildly; hardly believing what she had just seen. Then her sharp little mind started to work in its usual manner. Here then was the reason for David's continued disinterest in her...indeed in all women. And here, she realized, was an opportunity she could use to her distinct advantage.

She smiled, moving back to the wall, and re-applied her eye to the hole.

◖◖ CHAPTER 10 ◗◗

Two days after the incident in the woods, David was walking back from the forge. It had been his turn to close up for the day and Jonathan had gone on ahead.

As he neared the farmyard there was an unaccustomed babble of voices; it was clear an argument was taking place. Frowning and frightened for his father and Jonathan, he broke into a run, rounded the bend, and came to a halt only by hitting the gate hard, knocking the wind from his body.

There were a lot of people milling about in the yard and most of them were shouting. David knew each man; there seemed to be all of Mistress Elizabeth's family there, or at least the entire male line, her father, her four brothers, and her uncle. No one spotted David at first, no one except Jonathan, who was staring at him with a look on his face that David had never seen before. He was pale and white-lipped, his eyes wide and looking more frantic and feral than ever, like a cornered wild thing. David's heart leapt: *Jonathan is scared?* That fact alone was enough to put the fear of God into him, as David thought that his Puritan was frightened of nothing.

Then Jacob noticed Jonathan's stare and followed it. He frowned and waved his arms for silence. "Here's my son now. We will see what he has to say about the matter." The crowd surged towards the gate, but David kept on the other side of it, unwilling to enter the yard, baffled as to what this could mean, and wary of the angry faces. Jacob called for silence and the shouting ceased. "David, these men are here, our neighbors, to make charges against you. Serious accusations." He turned to Elizabeth's father. "Let the girl come forward and tell us again, with the boy here."

"He's no boy!" shouted Woodbine. "He's obviously man enough, my lass attests as such!"

Jacob waved his hand again to interrupt him. "Let the girl speak!" he said, his voice as harsh as David had ever heard it. His father's face softened as he looked at Elizabeth, who David noticed for the first time, had been hidden by the morass of her family. "Come, lass. Tell us again what you said, in front of my son, so that he may hear the charge and can answer thee." David's eyes widened as he had a terrible presentiment. He knew with full certainty what the girl was going to say a moment before she spoke.

"Master David has known me," she said softly, staring David full in the face. "Two days ago in the woods, he waylaid me and forced himself upon me as if I were his wife."

David felt himself go cold; time seemed to freeze around him. He glared at Elizabeth in dismay, willing her to read his thoughts. *Elizabeth? What are you doing?* Her eyes met his, unwavering. She looked both triumphant and mocking. Then she bared her damaged arm, showing a half-healed graze and purple bruises. "He took my honor, and then left me there bleeding and violated. Long has he been wooing me, but I have rejected him always. You all know that I am engaged to marry Edward Somerton, or I was…" Her voice shrank away to nothing, her eyes dropped and she threw herself onto her father's breast, weeping uncontrollably.

"Somerton has cast her off!" roared Woodbine. "What do you say, Master David? Answer the charge!"

David dragged his eyes from the girl, and searched the crowd frantically, finally finding Jonathan, but his love would not look at him. He was staring instead at the hysterical girl. David nearly laughed out loud at the situation. *How could anyone believe the lying jade?* he thought. *What a performance she is giving!*

He tried to remain calm. "This is a nonsense, sirs, and those of you who know me well surely cannot believe that I would do something so dishonorable? I do not deny that I met Mistress Woodbine in the woods yonder two days ago, but it was not as she said. She was..." He hesitated, still a little unwilling to let her family know how desperately she had flirted with him. "...*pleased* to see me, and we talked for a while, but I left her there by the river and came home."

He glanced at Jonathan again, and this time his lover looked at him, but his expression was clouded, angry and mistrustful. *I should never have lied to him about Elizabeth. But how could I not? He'd not have understood, he never does.*

David felt a rising of panic within him. This would be so easy to deny if only he could admit to his true nature, but he knew that if he did, this situation would become even uglier. The mob would turn on him and even on Jonathan in a violent manner, or worse, turn them over to the authorities, and that was not to be borne. Suddenly protecting Jonathan was more important than protecting himself. He could see no way out of this, so he held his head high and looked steadily at the crowd. He could not impugn the girl's reputation without looking as base himself so he kept quiet.

His father broke the accusative silence. His voice was hoarse, and David could hear that he was furious. "You deny this?"

"I do," said David resolutely. "What proof has the girl that this was done, if indeed t'was done at all?"

Woodbine pulled Elizabeth from his chest and looked at his daughter straight in the face. "Repeat for Master David what you have told us already." The girl blanched and shook her head, but her father commanded her to speak, and so she began in a small voice, her eyes upon the ground in a fair imitation of modesty.

"He has...he has...a round red birthmark on his..." She would not continue, but trailed a finger from her own knee up the outside of her thigh. "And a scar, like a crescent...on his..." She lent up and whispered to her father.

"On your *arse*, Master David!" Woodbine shouted at the top of his voice. "She saw it when you stood up to dress yourself, leaving her there in the woods!" There were dangerous mutterings from the family, and one brother had to be forcibly restrained by three others. "Well?" Woodbine demanded of Jacob, turning away from David. "Hast thy son such markings?"

David could not believe what he was hearing—*Has the girl been spying on me as I swam? Why is she doing this? Surely she can't be so desperate to marry a man who doesn't care an inch for her?*

Jacob's eyes moved to his son, full of hurt and disappointment. "I cannot lie to you, Woodbine," he said heavily, still staring at David. "He has both those marks the girl describes. You must take my word for it, for it will not do more to ask my son to display himself to all in such a manner."

"Well," Woodbine declared, "I for one, am not prepared to wait for a child to be born with thy son's unnatural hair. They must wed."

"No!" David shouted.

Woodbine continued his tirade. "Aye. *Wed!* And swiftly as the banns allow." He turned to David's father. "For he has ruined her for any other man and he must pay the price for it. I will call on thee on the morrow. I trust I can leave thee to *deal* with thy son." Pulling the girl with him he clambered onto his wagon, and the group followed on after him, silent as they passed, but one by one they cast angry glances at David.

The yard cleared. David realized that Jonathan had gone, and he had not seen him depart, and now he didn't know how long he had been gone. *How much did he hear? What does he believe? Surely he could not believe this tale after everything we have together?*

Jacob was the only one left and, sighing heavily, he spoke to his son, his voice bitter and hollow. "I have tried all my life to raise thee well, and all of my life you have gone against my wishes, my faith, and my expectations. Never have I been more ashamed of my son as I am at this moment."

"Father, it is a *lie*! I know not why she says the things she does. She has been pursuing me all the spring. You know this!"

"You would blacken her name still further?" Jacob was openly angry at his son now for the first time in his life. "Have you not done enough? Wilt thou add calumny to your list of sins?"

David's voice was more desperate as he pleaded for the belief he knew he didn't deserve. "I did not do this, Father, you must believe me—"

"What have you *ever* done that I should believe you now? Jacob's voice sliced across his words. "All your life you have deceived me, evaded work, lied to me, been wherever you should not be. You are untrustworthy, and you have never been anything else. You *know* my opinion of Woodbine and his family—if your lust had to be slaked, you could have made no worse choice than my enemy's only daughter. The very thought of that wench taking your mother's place in this house makes the bile rise in my stomach, but what sickens me even more than that is you. Sinful, disrespectful, dishonest, deceitful. What have I done to deserve such a son?

"Out of my sight, boy. I should strap you this day for the shame you have brought here, but it is too late for that. I should have strapped you from your first transgression, instead of trying to raise you with Godly values. I have failed as a father. Get out of my sight." His voice, at first so angry, had slipped into an expression of sadness and hurt as he turned away to the house.

David did not need telling twice. He pushed his father's disappointment to the back of his mind—it was nothing he didn't already know. Jonathan was the one he knew he had to find, and fast. He flew into the house and raced up the stairs, but Jonathan was not in their room. He charged back downstairs, past his father who was slumped down at the kitchen table, his head in his hands, and out into the yard again, running as fast as his legs would carry him down to the river. No Jonathan. He stopped dead.

Think, he thought, *think... Where would he go? Nowhere with happy memories*, David realized sadly. *Not to where we ever kissed, or were together in that way...The forge!* Back he tore towards the farm and then up the cinder path to the road. He threw open the forge door and was rewarded by being right, but the face that Jonathan turned to him, made him almost wish he had not found him.

"Get out," Jonathan said. There was nothing in his voice. No expression, no hate, not even a request, nothing. Just a hollow statement with all the hope torn from it. David stood in the open doorway for what seemed like hours watching his love's blank face. It had taken a whole year to put life and animation into Jonathan's face and ten small minutes of lies to wipe it clear. David took a step into the shed and Jonathan stood up, making David suddenly aware of the power of the man, the height and strength of him, and for the first time in Jonathan's presence he felt a small shiver of fear. "I said get out, David. I can not look at thee."

"Jon..." David breathed softly, tears rising to his eyes in response to the bitter wall of injustice. "Listen to me; my father does not believe me, but you must. You *must!* This is not true, none of it. She has tricked you all."

Jonathan's eyes flickered; but the blank canvas was replaced by a look of utter disbelief, and David's heart seemed to crack. "Even if thy history of honest dealings is so scarred as to be unrecognizable, and if I were mad enough to listen to thee one more time, why in the name of our Lord should I believe thee now? Why didst thou conceal that thou met her there in that place? When I asked thee, asked thee over and over, and thou denied it! At Christmas, thou swore that thou wast talking to friends and I saw thee—*I saw thee!* With the wench squirming and vile in thy lap. Thou swearest falsehood easier than most men breathe. What power on earth is there to make me trust thee?"

"Because it's not true!" David realized how feeble the whole thing sounded coming from his mouth. "Because I *love* you! Because I never want you to look at me again with the face you have now. I would tear my soul out and ask you to kill me where I stand, if I could avoid the pain I see in your eyes."

"Which thou hast put there." Jonathan made as to walk past, and David put a hand on Jonathan's arm. Jonathan did not react, but stood staring past David. "Wouldst that thou had never ensnared my heart. If only I still thought of thee as my master's son and no more to me than that, it would not bleed the way it does." With an unexpected strike, he grabbed hold of David in his strong hands, his powerful fingers digging into the flesh above his elbows, bruising him. "Why dids't thou not let me alone? Why didst thou make me love thy beautiful lying face and thy corrupt soul? Tell me once again it is not true, just *tell* me." Jonathan's mouth was inches from David's, his voice dark and hypnotic, hiding a simmering violence like sharp rocks beneath smooth water.

"It is not," David managed through the pain of Jonathan's hands, tears pouring down his face. "I *swear* to you it is not, bring me a Bible—"

At the word, Jonathan shoved him away and he fell backwards against the workbench. "Thou swearest truth, but thy lips are poison. If thou thinketh that I willst believe thee more readily because thou art able to lie on the Book with ease, then thou art mistaken. I will not allow thee to pollute the Bible with thy filth and I will not listen more. I cannot stand thee in my sight. If thou willst not go, then I shall. Tonight I will sleep in the barn, the air there is cleaner." Without a second glance at the weeping David he was gone.

David fell to the floor, his hair loose around his face, his body aching from Jonathan's strength, his heart broken and harboring an active fear of what would happen in the morning.

Marry Mistress Woodbine? Let the farm go to that family? Never. That was something he knew he could not allow to happen, not even if he had been guilty of what he was accused of. It would break his father's heart.

He closed his eyes, remembering Jacob's bitter tirade. It would seem that he had already achieved that. And now he had driven Jonathan away from his arms, and thus his only reason for staying in Kineton was gone. If Jonathan had not come to the house, David knew he would have left long since, probably after the battle at Edgehill. Pulling himself to his feet he came to a terrible decision: he would leave tonight.

Supper was an ordeal. No one spoke and no one looked at David or even acknowledged his existence. His pride kept him there until both of the other men had left the room, then he tidied up the cottage as usual and went up to his room, taking a supply of oatcakes and meat with him. He swiftly packed clothes, food, and what little money he possessed into a bundle, and sat on the edge of the bed until he heard his father retire, Jacob's footsteps sounding heavy and slower than usual. Then he waited another hour, waiting to hear the town clock chiming in the darkness, before he let himself out of the room and out of the house. There were tears on his cheeks as he passed the barn, knowing that Jonathan lay within, probably wide awake and so miserable it broke his own heart to think of him there in the darkness. If he could but go in, throw himself on Jonathan's mercy, admit the lie as truth? *Would Jonathan forgive me then?* No, he knew it was folly. His beloved Puritan had no middle way. Everything with him was black or white. Because he had no guile in him, Jonathan could not understand the rest of world when it slithered around in its human deceptions.

David touched the barn door lightly; then with a loss of control he wept silently and leant full length against the rough wood, his palms caressing it, his cheek pressed up tight, braving splinters, the tears on his face sinking straight into the ancient timbers. He willed Jonathan to feel his presence there, to come to the door, to open it, but there was no sound from within. Finally, his control reasserting itself, he gave a lingering kiss to the door then turned to walk down to the river path, the tears drying on his cheeks.

Half way down the dark field, strong arms grabbed him and pulled him close—a familiar scent of leather, fire, and steel, a vice-like grip, and a tortured voice in his ear. *"Thou art running away?* Thou art leaving me? Thou dishonor thyself and thy father more by this cowardice..." Jonathan kissed him violently and hungrily. "Forgive me my words. Thou makest me a madman and I am not myself, I mean everything and nothing of what I say,"

Jonathan's voice sounded ghastly to David's ears; a tragic betrayal of his lover's values, and David knew how Jonathan must be struggling with himself. David surrendered himself to the crushing embrace, giddy and overwhelmed by the force of Jonathan's passion, never before encountered in such violent measure.

"I care not what thou hast done, whatever thou are guilty of," Jonathan continued. "I know well it is me that thou loves, as I worship thee with every fiber of my soul. Thou art my brother and my blood; thy blood runs in mine and I feel thee within me with every heartbeat, with every hardness I have. Thou livest deep in my veins, poison or no. Thou cannot leave me, we are one. Thou willst kill us both..."

David returned his kisses as eagerly as he could, but they rained on his face so fast he was unable to keep up. He managed to tear his face from Jonathan's and gasped, short of breath. "I-I have no choice, Jon...no choice. You had gone when...they discussed it, but they will make me marry the girl. Believe her lies if you must, but I cannot let...the Woodbines to become heir to the farm. I could not—will not—wish that on my father."

Jonathan pulled David down to the grassy meadow, pinned him beneath him, and undressed him as fast as his shaking fingers would allow. In the moonlight his eyes shone with a frantic, mad look. David had the fleeting thought that it seemed that Jonathan was thinking that if he were to couple with David, it would somehow make the nightmare pass, and they would wake up again in their room and none of this would have happened.

His callused hands grazed David's skin, and David looked up, his eyes full of a sudden hope. He felt Jonathan prepare him roughly and hurriedly, and he appeared to take no note of the small grunt of pain that David could not hold in. David arched backwards, and pushed his hips up and wrapped his long legs around Jonathan's waist, moving his body in time with Jonathan's thrusting. Jonathan ploughed into him blindly, as if he could raze the memory of the afternoon with dumb lust. David gradually relaxed and his breath curled up into the cooling air in curls of passionate vapor. There was pain, still, but he couldn't stop Jonathan, didn't want to, and probably would not be able to. Jonathan was there, but David felt more alone than he'd ever been. It was a love he had to give, and punishment he had to endure.

"Stay then," Jonathan gasped finally, his words in rhythm as he thrust. "Remove thy dishonor, face thy sin for once and marry the wench. I will never leave thee, never. All I wish is that thee *stay*." He thrust violently into David as he spent. He fell forward and his member slid from David's body. David rolled away and sat clasping his knees watching Jonathan recover in the moonlit grass.

"You still think that I am guilty?" David was shaking with the violence of Jonathan's lust, but he kept his voice as calm and even as he could. He dreaded the answer that Jonathan would give him. Jonathan went to pull him close to him again but David stood up and over him. "Answer me, Jon. Do you truly believe that I have done this thing?"

Jonathan groaned and knelt before him, clasping his knees and rubbing his head against David's thighs as if begging for a forgiveness he didn't need. "It matters not to me," he groaned.

"Answer me, Jonathan." David's voice was teasing and kind, shielding the hammer blow behind it.

"Aye. I do. Forgive me for it, but how can I think otherwise? She knows thy imperfections! She described thee before you arrived in more detail than she gave to you. She spoke of this, in all its perfection." He nuzzled David's member in a tender manner, his lips trailed along its length. "She spoke of you in such detail that she wept as she shamed herself, but left no doubt to me that she had seen all of you, aye, and up close too. Thou must stay. What if there is a child?"

David stepped backward, pulling away from Jonathan. He felt sickened and bitter. *They should know me better—they should both know me better.* He turned away and dressed, leaving Jonathan kneeling in the grass, and when he spoke he put as much of his pain into his voice as he could, wanting to hurt Jonathan as hard as he'd hurt him. "So is my fate decided. There will be no child, or if there is it will not be mine, and in nine months or more like less—when you find that it looks like Edward Somerton or Richard Oakley or…any other man in the town and not I—you may remember this night. I can not stay for Father's sake, but notwithstanding that, I will not stay where the person I love beyond all measure can not believe me when I tell him the truth.

"With your own mouth you condemn me. With your words you banish me. We are sundered and our covenant is broken." He turned and walked towards the path, and in ten steps he was lost to the night.

⁣ᗙ Chapter 11 ᗡ⁣

Jonathan survived the next few days, but when he looked back at them all he could remember was feeling dark and cold in spite of the heat of the season. It was as if a candle had been snuffed out somewhere deep inside him, and the warmth which had started as a small spark, infusing his very being whenever David was around, had been extinguished and his marrow had frozen.

He had stayed in the water meadow all night after David had left him, certain that David would recant, that this was just another deception. He couldn't allow himself to believe that David would not turn back once he had thought clearly about what he was doing, what he was giving up. Finally, he didn't know when, Jonathan had fallen asleep only to wake shivering and damp with dew in the dawn light. He dragged himself to his feet, and that was when the cold had begun; it felt as if his very soul had turned to ice. He remembered the feeling of heat, the sensation of David's hot flesh beneath his, could recall the roaring passion of yesterday, but it had all died. It seemed to have happened to someone else.

He despised David for what he had done; for his lies, for his inconstancy, for making him love him so fiercely that for one terrible moment of the night before he would have crawled after him on his hands and knees, and said anything, *anything* to make him stay. And he despised himself more than he could have ever imagined for those self-same feelings. Loathed *himself* that he had become so corrupt that he would have considered begging David to stay, even to have him marry the wench, just for the one selfish motive—that they were not parted. The thought of how low he had sunk sickened him.

Somehow he summoned the courage to make his way back to the cottage and he sat bleakly in the half-light waiting for Jacob to appear. After what seemed like forever, his master entered. Jonathan looked up at him and saw his own sorrow reflected in the older man's face. Jacob's eyes closed for a long moment; he looked older than Jonathan had ever seen him, and when he re-opened his eyes Jonathan could see they were red-rimmed and empty of any hope.

"He's gone?"

Jonathan couldn't speak, could only nod. Jacob did not speak again for a long time, and to Jonathan's amazement simply began to do the things he did every single day, preparing the breakfast; cutting bread, and slices of cold rabbit pie, and pouring ale. Several times Jonathan went to speak, but simply could not think of anything to say, and he could not face eating, so he sat there numbly staring at the table.

"You must not fret on this, Jonathan," Jacob said kindly. "It is not your fault. You have been more of a friend to my son than he deserves; do you think I have not seen how staunch you have been? Nay, he has been wanting to leave for many years and I have been expecting it, but am ashamed that he leaves this dis-honor behind him for others to face." He stood up and cleared his trencher and mug away. "Try and eat something, the work will not be easier today with just the two of us."

Jonathan managed a slice of bread dipped in his ale, but could face nothing more. It was not until he went to deal with the live-stock that he broke down completely.

He vaguely remembered Woodbine coming to the farm that morning and a violent argument ensuing with Jacob, but he was working in the forge and didn't leave it all that day. The familiar materials of iron, fire, and water cocooned him and allowed his mind to concentrate on work, work and nothing but work. His eyes focused on the fire, the metal, the hot sparks. Not the last sight of David, his eyes accusing, his words devious and false, his beautiful face... The forge helped him to forget, at least temporarily; his anger tempered by the blows, hard and fast on hot iron.

That evening Jacob questioned him more closely. "Did you quarrel with him?"

Jonathan nodded, his limbs feeling heavy and his mind stupid. "I tried to get him to stay." *That at least is the truth*, he thought bitterly. "We argued. He denied the accusation and said he couldst not stay and marry the girl, and would not stay if I...we...couldst not believe him."

Jacob nodded. "And why would we? The boy does not—has never known—the meaning of the word truth, and for that I blame myself. He did not tell you where he was going?" Jacob's gray face was heartbreaking; Jonathan blamed David afresh to see how very much his treachery had hurt his father. All he could do was shake his head. They both had a fair idea of where David would go. Jacob said nothing more, and after that day they did not speak of him again.

David was indeed intending to join up. He knew from tales in the town that part of the King's army was besieged in York, so it was pointless to try and reach there. Instead he headed for Oxford, where the King's garrison was quartered.

It took him three days to walk there, and he was filthy, tired, and hungry when he arrived. He had been here once before with his father five years previously, but now the streets seemed to be crammed with more soldiers than citizenry. No one paid him much attention, at least not the soldiers at first, although there were several women who attempted to attract his notice, but he walked past them, blushing furiously at the things they called out after him. He had no idea of where he should go. Soldiers were everywhere; outside inns, marching in and out of large buildings, camped in lines around the town, trotting their horses hard through the streets. He approached a group of soldiers who were sitting outside an inn, their muskets leaning against the wall, their blue jackets and bandoliers laying piled up in a heap beside them. They looked up as he stood before them. He could see the amused interest in their faces.

"Forgive me, sirs," David began, removing his hat, "but would you tell me where may I find the recruiting officer?"

There were instant guffaws from the men. "Sorry, *Mistress*," one of them sneered, his eyes raking over David's hair, coming loose from its bounds after his journey. "You are not the first wench to dress up in her brother's clothes and try and follow her sweetheart. Best ye go on home. Your mother will be worried!" All four of the men laughed heartily at this, thinking it a fine joke, getting more uproarious as the speaker stood, a trifle unsteadily. He put his arm around David's waist and attempted to pull him down to the trestle with him. David pulled away in anger, putting his hand on his sword. There were more laughs from the men, obviously the worse for drink. "Look! The wench has a sword! Well, pretty one," he continued, "if you are convinced that you can deceive the officer, then the best of luck to you." He gave instructions to Christ Church College and sat down again, still roaring with laughter, his ale spilling on his shirt as he did so.

David realized it was pointless seeking anything further from the drunken men, so he turned away, ignoring the jeers and shouts from the soldiers, hoping only that whatever regiment he was placed into that it was not with them. One thing he had learned however, was that his hair was going to be a problem, so ruefully he ducked into an alleyway and with his dagger set about cutting his locks from his head, not without a twinge of sadness. After just a few minutes he had reduced the length to chin level and had created a fringe, albeit a horribly uneven one. He held the butchered mane of silver and gold in his hands, and his chest hurt when he recalled how Jonathan had taken such joy in it, tying his fingers in it during his frantic lusts or stroking it smooth after tangling it so in his passion. Since leaving home David had pushed the thought of Jonathan from his mind in his anger and now, looking at the skeins in his hands, he slid down the wall of the alleyway he lost control, sobbing out his grief over everything he'd lost through his own stupidity.

Part of his mind was furious with Jonathan for allowing him to leave; he felt that if Jon had truly loved him, he would have come with him. Another part of him was bitter at himself for breaking his Puritan's heart with a web of lies. *Then again,* he thought in anger, *if he truly had loved me, he should have believed me when it really mattered...*The thoughts went round and round in circles, blaming himself, then Jonathan, over and over until his chin dropped onto his knees and his mind could not cope with his thoughts any longer. He lost track of time as he sat staring blankly at his hands which held the chopped hair, soft and supple in his fingers. Finally he dragged himself up, and without looking at the hair again, he dropped it in the alleyway, letting it fall through his fingers like the dreams one loses in the morning light.

Finally, after having to ask for directions another three times, he arrived at the barracked college. The large square in the center of the building was filled with fenced and restless cattle, and troops lounged everywhere around the quadrangle. He was directed to and found the recruitment officer. He didn't have to wait long, and was ushered into a small room, bare except for a table, the Royal Standard on the wall, and papers scattered on the floor. Looking at the stark surroundings and the grim-faced, recruiting officer seated behind the table, David felt a shudder of fear. Right up until this very moment he had not thought seriously about what he meant to do, and what it might lead to. The blood drained from his face when he realized how serious it was.

The recruiting officer looked up and David felt that he could see himself through the man's eyes, young, inexperienced and not really knowing what was to come. He wondered for a moment why on earth they *would* take him, and wasn't sure whether he wanted them to, or not. The man seemed bored more than anything. He lifted his quill and spoke in a heavy voice.

"What is thy name lad?"

David hesitated for a second, then said, "Graie, David Graie." He noted with some satisfaction that the recruitment officer spelled it Gray on the order book.

"Can you ride, boy?" the man added without looking up.

"Yes, sir. I am...I was...a blacksmith, so I am used to handling horses."

"Not run away from your master, have you?" the officer inquired sharply. "If your master comes after you, there will be trouble."

"No, sir! My father is a blacksmith, and I learned under him. I am under no indenture, I swear to you."

The officer looked unconvinced but not overly concerned. Pushing a paper over toward David, he said. "Make your mark." Then he signaled to the soldier standing behind him,

"Sergeant Winter, take Gray to Pembroke, get him kitted out and settled in." He turned back to David. "Welcome to the King's Life Guard of Foot." The other soldier, who had been leaning against the wall, sighed loudly and led the way outside, not even waiting for David to finish signing the paper he was given. David trotted after the man who made his way back across the quadrangle and entered a long passageway, shadowed and cool, with arched openings on one side. The man did not speak, even when David attempted to get the details of the regiment he had been assigned to, his face was completely impassive, almost bored. He ignored too the other troopers as they called out to him.

"Who's the maid, Winter?" called one man, sitting on a trestle with a wench on his lap, her skirt pulled up around her thighs.

"How is it that ye get such good assignments?" called another, polishing his breastplate. "I only get sent with messages, not fine pieces like that." The man known as Winter didn't even look at his fellow soldiers.

They exited into the street, and David had to concentrate to avoid the teeming townspeople, keep his feet, and follow the silent sergeant, who he was beginning to heartily dislike. Finally they reached another ancient building, another college, impressive and solid, its honey-colored stone stretching a long way down the street. Winter ducked through a large archway half way down the block, but David had to fling himself against the wall as four horsemen came through at a fast trot with no thought for the care of pedestrians. Winter looked at David and for the first time an expression crossed his face: he was smirking. David was so angry he could have happily punched him; he felt he would have done too if the man had not been armed to the teeth.

Winter led David through the archway into an enclosed courtyard and then through a dark oak door. He gestured at a bench and spoke for the first time.

"Wait there." And then he was gone.

David sat down, clutching his hat in his hands. The dark paneled corridor where he had been left seemed utterly deserted. He could hear the muffled sounds of the street, and the noises of people moving about somewhere in the building, but no one entered the area where he sat. The long day crept by, punctuated only by a clock sounding the hour somewhere not too close. He wondered briefly whether he should go and find someone, but he was too warm, tired, and comfortable to care much. His eyelids drooped as the fatigue of the past few days overtook him, the hat slipped from his hands, and eventually he was asleep.

He was woken by a hand on his shoulder, shaking him, not roughly but with some insistence. His eyes slowly opened, his limbs still feeling leaden and his mind drowsy. He focused on the man in front of him. The man who had wakened him was slim and auburn-haired, his uniform dusty. David shook his head and looked up at his smiling face, only to realize that he was looking in the green eyes and the tanned, freckled face of Tobias' friend.

"Master Haldane?"

ᚲᚲ CHAPTER 12 ᚲᚲ

The trooper had stood and watched young David Caverly sleep for a few minutes before he shook him awake, astounded to have come across the boy here so unexpectedly. *What on earth is he doing here?* Remembering the youth's coltish grace at his father's farm, he would not have imagined for one second that he would have given up what appeared to be an idyllic rural life to risk his life in this madness. He frowned. *A boy like this will not even be safe alone here in Oxford,* he thought, *let alone on campaign.* His hands went to shake the broad shoulders and paused. *Tobias!* he thought with a stab of panic, *what the hell do I tell the lad about Tobias?* He frowned. *I will have to think about that later. If he asks me, that is...let's pray he does not.* He shook the lad awake.

"Master Haldane?" David was clearly delighted to see a face he recognized and Haldane felt a thrill of pleasure shoot through him at the boy's warm smile. *No wonder Tobias had been bewitched by this one.* David shot to his feet and pulled off his hat, and Haldane noticed that he was no longer a boy by any means. The boy had grown tall, as high as himself now, and as broad. Haldane laughed, the first laugh he had given in a while, as he noticed David's disastrous haircut. He reached over and pulled a wisp of it from his fringe which came away in his fingers.

David looked rueful. "It was a little long for the army," he said, not noticing when Haldane slipped the lock of hair into his pocket.

Haldane laughed again, a musical sound which echoed through the long hall. He clapped David on the back. "How marvelous that you should be here and that we should meet! Come, come and have a drink and tell me how it came about."

"Should I not report to someone? A sergeant left me here and told me to wait."

Haldane frowned. "Dark hair? Surly features? Large blue-handled sword?" David nodded. "Sergeant Winter. Mmm, thought so. One of his favorite occupations is to dump new recruits in here. He would have left you here all night and then punished you in the morning for not having reported to the Major. Come. I'll take you, then we can go for that drink."

Haldane led David along the corridor and up some stairs where he was presented to the Major who, as usual, seemed less than interested in new canon fodder, then he led the way down to the quartermaster, who gave David his instructions for the next day, who to report to, and when.

David was silent as Haldane led the way out of the dark corridors and into the afternoon light, and Haldane attempted to rally him a little. "Don't worry, lad," he said, as he led him back through the quadrangle into the main street. "There's not much to learn, and once you've learned it, all you need to do is to keep doing more of the same." He saw that the lad had lost a little color in the last half hour and he felt bad for him, wondered what had led to his joining up. He would have liked to have imagined that this one would have stayed safe at home. Haldane bought them beer at the tavern closest to the college, placing David in a dark corner and ignored the inquiring looks he got from the other men in the dark bar.

David looked introspectively into his mug before tasting it, and without looking up asked his companion, asked, "Will I be off to fight?"

Haldane laughed out loud and bade David drink up. "Nay, lad, you came at a fortuitous time it seems. A month since you would have been marched off to shore up Hopton's ranks. Now there are so few of us here, we will need to wait for them to come back. You and I can't win any battles on our own." He sobered briefly and said, "Some advice for you. You note I have not asked you why you are here?" David nodded. "Well, it is not the custom here to ask why a man volunteers, so you would be well to remember that, as each will give you the same courtesy. However," and here he touched David's arm gently, "if you feel the need to tell me why this big adventure makes thee look like your world has ended, then you'll find I listen as well as I speak."

"I don't even know your name," said David, smiling a little as if grateful for a friend. "Haldane, what part of your name is that?"

"It's a terrible name," laughed the trooper, avoiding the question. "Please call me Hal. Even...only my mother only calls me Haldane when she's angry with me."

"Hal then," yawned David, and to Hal's eyes he looked terribly young. "Hal...I am sorry, about Master Tobias. I know you were his friend, his death must have been hard for you."

Hal was shocked at David's words. *Hell. Now what do I say to him?* Tobias was the last person he wanted to discuss with David, so he simply nodded, feeling that it was the easiest way out. *Damn you, Tobias,* he thought savagely. *Damn you and your obsession with pretty virgins.* He changed the subject abruptly, informing the lad what he should know about the new world he had come to and all its myriad rules and regulations.

As Haldane talked, David saw the confusion and anger in his eyes and felt sorry for him. *Perhaps they were like me and Jon,* he thought in a fuddled daze. His head slipped onto his arms and his mind clouded. He was somewhat aware of being helped up and walking through cool streets, but it was all a dim recollection before sleep claimed him at last.

He was shaken awake to find it was morning, and once again it was Hal who woke him. He felt rested and alert although uncomfortable for having slept in his clothes. He looked around to see he was in a long hall with bedrolls laying everywhere in neat rows. He got up and Hal led him out to a yard where he was at least able to refresh his head, if not able to wash to the best of his liking. Then he was taken to the stores where he was presented with his uniform, a musket, a bandolier, and boots. All of the items looked decidedly shabby and second-hand, and David decided he was not going to ask about the mended tear in the chest of the jacket. His uniform was of a dirty burgundy cloth, and as Hal helped him on with his bandolier, it was as if he could sense David's disappointment.

"Cheer up lad," he smiled, shifting the bandolier to the left, showing him the most comfortable way to sling it. "We get fresh supplies from time to time, you may yet get that pretty uniform, although it must be said that the brighter you are, the more you show up." He gave David a wicked grin, then sat him down and attempted to tidy the terrible haircut. By the time he had finished, the hair was a lot shorter, almost round his ears, but at least it was even. "You'll need to make sure you keep a helmet on once you march," he said, ruffling David's hair as he finished. "'Tis too bright, and you will be a beacon for a marksman." He waited for David to gather up his equipment then he led him on through the college to the quadrangle, where there were other obviously new recruits milling about. "Don't worry," he said, pointing the way out to the green. "Just stay out of trouble, don't antagonize the Sergeant, and you'll be fine. Just do as you are told, as soon as are told to do it, all right?"

"Will you be in Oxford for a while?"

"Should be," Hal said, with a warm smile. "When I'm not scouting, I'm a messenger; so sometimes I go, but I generally come back. Or I have, so far anyway. See you tonight." And he was gone, leaving David feeling as if he was ten-years-old and lost in a crowd.

The next week passed slowly for David, who found one thing about the army—that it was exceedingly dull. No doubt that things were likely to get more "interesting" eventually, but he found the training to be mind-numbingly boring. They marched and marched and marched again. They were taught how to han-

dle their muskets, a laborious process which, in able to produce
a volley of a crushingly slow two shots a minute, required at least
forty different actions. At first they were unable to even produce
one shot a minute, and so they practiced. Over and over again
until David was going to sleep with "Prepare, Aim, Fire," in his
head.

Then they marched again. They formed squares, they formed
lines, they practiced formation whilst shooting in lines, one line
firing, one line loading again and again until David though he
would scream with tedium. Someone had said that it took two
months to train a soldier. David felt that another two *weeks* of
this and he would run mad with boredom.

When they were not being drilled, they were expected to
clean their equipment, report for inspection, carry messages, or
wait on the officers in barracks. These tasks at least kept his mind
more occupied. However, the one consolation which became
more important to him as they became friends, was Hal. If it had
not have been for him, David may seriously have considered that
he had made a mistake, as army life was not what he thought it
was going to be. Hal was a fine man, funny and knowledgeable.
He had been in Oxford since before the beginning of the war,
had in fact been at college at their very barracks, and seemingly
knew everyone and everything about the city. David learned a lot
of military gossip from his lips, and a lot more about different
ales than he ever thought possible.

The two men were popular characters in the garrisoned
town, for Hal was handsome in a leonine way with his long
auburn locks and pale freckled face, and David naturally attracted attention wherever he went, even with his shorn hair.
The new style aged him, Hal had said, matured his face, and
had changed him subtly from a pretty boy to a stunningly handsome young man. Hal was a natural pivot to whatever entertainment was on hand; knew all the soldiers' songs and was
always there in the center of the room, beating time with his
tankard with a wicked smile on his face as he lead the inns in

song, each verse bawdier than the next. David noticed that although women greeted Hal, they did not hang on his arm, or flirt with him, or sit on his lap as they did the other soldiers. After a few attempts with David, they left him alone too, the word getting around that David was Hal's friend. David was not so ignorant as to not know what these rumors meant, but he let them slip; at least it meant that he was not put in embarrassing positions with the tavern wenches.

So apart from the tedium of his days, he enjoyed Oxford. The only fly in David's ointment was Sergeant Winter. Haldane's warning had been pointless, as by simply avoiding the sereant's "trick" of his first day, David had already antagonized him. From his first parade on the quadrangle where they learned how to assemble, disassemble, and clean their muskets, Sergeant Winter found fault with him. David was quite at ease with this, never having been able to please his father in any way, so Winter's disapprobation slid from him like water from a duck's back. All this did was to incense the Sergeant further, as he was a man who was used to making new recruits shake in their third-hand boots.

Thus David was seemingly constantly on punishment detail; standing double watches, having his rations cut, or confined to barracks. By the end of the first two weeks he had merited ten lashes, and Hal was furious, both with Winter and David.

"The man is abusing his authority, and you are not helping matters by acting as if you could not care less about what punishments he heaps upon you! I have a good mind to report him to the Major."

"Don't be ridiculous, Hal," laughed David, who was scrubbing all of the new recruits' leatherwork as his evening's punishment. "Hard work may bore me, but it does not bother me, and it saves me spending my money. Or," he added, as he gave Hal a sly glance, "your money. And I cannot afford it, even if you can. And anyway, you are no relation of mine, will the officers not find it odd that you rush to defend a mere musketeer?"

Hal appeared to think on this, calmed down, then went and bought a flagon of ale and kept David company as he did his chores, as he did most evenings.

The routine of his days, and loneliness of his nights allowed his mind to wander frequently, and many times in those first few weeks he found his thoughts drifting back to the forge, the farm—to his father, and to Jonathan. He wondered what they thought, whether they missed him in any measure as much as he missed them. *Will Jon stay with Father? Do they talk of me at night? Would they forgive me, if I were to run from this place and beg them to take me back?* Such thoughts were pointless, and more than painful. He could not go back—not while there was any chance he'd be forced to marry Elizabeth. He had made his bed, and, uncomfortable as it was, it was a bed he had to lie in.

On the third week the drills moved on to wheeling and counter-marching. Apart from being massively boring, it was also complicated and difficult for the Sergeant to explain a move that enabled the swift relocation of some three hundred men, when he only had between twenty to thirty to demonstrate with. The Sergeant was not a patient man, and he did not explain maneuvers well, and the more the recruits got it wrong the more incoherent he became.

The theory was simple. For wheeling on an angle, the men had to form a straight line, move close up to the men on either side, then—looking to the direction the wheel was supposed to move, (either right or left) the line would shuffle around in that direction until all the men were pointing in the appropriate direction. This did not take long with the small number of soldiers David practiced with, but David could only imagine how long a full line would take, all the time having their muskets out of action and vulnerable to the enemy as they shuffled helplessly in a semicircle, with nothing but pikemen to keep the enemy at bay.

At first they were hopeless at it, and Sergeant's Winter's screams of "Watch your dressings!" were all that was heard as the line buckled and bent, lost shape and direction, or forgot to look the opposite way to which they were pressing, but after days of dizzying and tiny steps they accomplished it well enough to stop their Sergeant from dishing out punishments.

Then they had to master center-wheeling, which was worse, as the pivotal point became the soldier in the very middle of the line, and the column spun around him. The significant difference was that whilst one half of the unit was marching forwards, the other half was moving backwards and the first time they tried it, it was utter chaos. It was after a day of constant angle wheeling, which they just about mastered, and Winter had explained the new maneuver so badly no one understood it and no one dared to ask him to repeat himself. Consequently everyone went in opposite directions; half the troop tripped over the other half and most ended up on the ground, helpless with laughter. Needless to say, most men were on punishment detail that night, including David, which surprised no one.

Hal was away; he had been unable to tell David where he was going, so David guessed that he was off with orders or dispatches to one or other of the Generals, and was sworn to secrecy.

As time went on, David found that he was becoming increasingly pleased to see the young officer each time he reappeared, often dusty and always tired. He found that he could not help but worry when Hal was out of Oxford; crossing the country in uniform, could only be dangerous when he might be found by Parliament scouts at anytime. When Hal was absent, David found himself lonely, his thoughts straying back to home, his father and Jonathan.

Jonathan. The loss of his lover was still raw and so painful he continued to put it away from him until he was left alone in bed with nothing else to occupy his mind. Time and again he thought he would get someone to write a letter care of the church at Kineton, to let his father know he was well, and more importantly to let Jonathan know—but he did not do it. Kineton was too close. He was afraid that his father would come and make a scene about Elizabeth. As busy as his time was in his new life, as busy as Sergeant

Winter kept him with his petty vendetta, as happy as Hal made him with his new friendship, David *ached* for Jonathan. At night, lying in a long, draughty hall with all of the other recruits and soldiers, it was as much as he could do not to weep for his empty arms, and a body that needed Jon's touch. A hardness had to stay a hardness in barracks, although there were men who would disappear at night in pairs, and some who were clearly pleasuring themselves in their bedrolls, David could not bring himself to do it. He longed only for the feeling of Jonathan's hands, his lips, his probing tongue. All those nights they had spent together after Edgehill but before their mating, he had taken for granted the strong warm body that he had curled against. Now he would trade every one of those nights just to wake up in the dark and feel Jonathan's breath on his hair and his hands on his cock where they belonged. To have Jonathan wake him once more in the dead of the night for pure lust, to feel him wrap those vice-like arms around him and pull him physically off the mattress and into his lap, sliding into his fundament so sweetly, that just the look on Jonathan's face as he took possession of David was sometimes enough to trigger his own seed to spatter between them.

Many times when he had been roused from deep slumber, he had almost wished for more sleep when Jonathan began his aggressive night time assaults. To punish him, David sometimes took pleasure in pretending to have to be cajoled, persuaded, licked, and sucked until he was a mere piece of clay for Jonathan to mould how he would. When David thought now of that pretence, he wished for just one more opportunity in those arms, between those iron thighs, so that he could not only show, but tell his Puritan how much he loved being loved by him, and that the show of reluctance had just been happy play. He had never really told Jonathan how much he cared for him, not when it mattered, and it seemed the only time he ever told Jonathan that he loved him had been after a quarrel. And now it was too late. It was not something he could ever put into a letter, and now he knew that he would never see his Puritan again.

CHAPTER 13

Hal had been gone a fortnight and David was worried. Of course he had no idea where the man had gone, it could be anywhere in the country, so, looked at from that perspective, two weeks was not that long a time. He had made a couple of drinking acquaintances among the other recruits: Robert Godwin, tall and slim, a natural pikeman, according to the reluctant praise of their Sergeant; and Allan Blake, who, despite being drunk nearly every hour God gave, somehow managed to fire a musket without blowing himself to kingdom come or getting flogged for his inebriation. These two young men had approached David one evening while he was sitting cleaning his musket and asked if he was going to the town. He had thanked them but refused politely, then found himself lifted off his bedroll and lugged like a sack of provisions down the stairs, where they dropped him on the cobbles of the yard.

"You can walk from here, Master Gray," said Blake, removing his hat to give a mock bow. "We are not your packhorses, although my learned friend here may resemble one more than most." At that, Godwin head-butted Blake in the stomach, who fell backwards over the still-seated David and the men had been friends ever since. David was glad of it; being an only child for years, and then becoming so close to Jonathan, now he sorely missed a friend and companion.

Sixteen days after Hal's disappearance all three of them were outside an inn, shaded by leaves in a tree-lined courtyard.

"Still no word of your dashing corporal, David?" Blake teased, pulling the wench he had in his lap closer to him so he could look down her ample bosom.

David shook his head and tried to look as if it did not bother him; it was vitally important that his proclivities did not become common knowledge, as he knew men had been executed for such "unnaturalness." He made a mental note to try and bring the subject up with Hal—as to how he and Tobias managed it in secret—if he could, without upsetting his friend over the memory of the dead trooper. The sorrow of Hal's losing Tobias weighed almost as heavy on David's heart as his own loss of Jonathan. At least after the war he could, if he wanted to, swallow his pride and go home, hope his father had forgiven him, and go on his knees to Jonathan and beg for forgiveness. Hal's love was gone forever.

David's unusual moroseness caused Blake to tear his montero from his head and throw it at David. "Cheer up, for God's sake, David. Anne, my dear," he waved airily at a buxom blonde watching them, "please do me the great favor of attempting to make my poor friend smile. You would think by the way he misses our handsome corporal, that he had no other friends, which offends us." David looked up at the approaching strumpet and laughed out loud as she stalked him, her hips swinging, calling out to the other women about her challenge.

There were a few ribald comments and one wag from Pennyman's regiment shouted, "Ye won't be allowed as far as his lap me girl, you've not got the right artillery!"

David found himself blushing, and in a desperate attempt to take the suddenly riotous attention away from himself, he pulled the girl into his lap and with an elegant wave to Pennyman's men and a dazzling smile, he kissed her hard.

There was an enormous cheer from the entire inn, everyone laughed, and to David's enormous thankfulness they continued with their own affairs. He let the girl sit up straight and muttered his thanks.

"S'all right love," she said quietly in his ear, making it look for all the soldier's benefits that she was whispering lewd suggestions, "We all know that you be under young Haldane's protection. Pretend to say something to me, and then follow my lead." He did as she said, putting his mouth to her ear and she roared in laughter for all to hear.

"Why, you young scamp!" she shouted as she got off his lap in mock affront. "I don't do that for less than a Colonel! Come back when you've been promoted!" This caused another general laugh, but afterwards David was left in peace to drink and sing with the rest. As they swayed and sang their way back to the barracks, Godwin linked his arm through David's as they watched Blake skipping on ahead doing a passable impression of a jackass.

"Did you hear the rumors about the regiment?" Godwin said quietly and more soberly than he appeared to be.

David looked at his friend's thin face in inquiry. "Rumors? No. I've hardly been off the training ground these last few days." The Sergeant had had him working with his musket for hours after the other men had been dismissed.

"I've heard we will be moving, and pretty soon, too."

David felt the color drain from his face. "Do you know where?"

Godwin shook his head. "Not really. Could be west, could be north. Things are muddled; where we are needed I suppose. Doesn't really matter though, does it? *Action!* At last! This is the year that Essex gets what he deserves!" And with a laugh, Godwin pulled a thoughtful David into their barrack. David walked down to the end where his place was, and his heart leapt to find Hal sitting on his bedroll. Hal jumped up and grabbed David by the arms.

"David! God, I've missed you." His handsome face was pale but wreathed in a smile. "I surmised you would be out drinking, you rascal. I have been waiting for hours. I was not going to scour Oxford searching the taverns for you." He ruffled David's still ragged hair. "Come out, walk with me for a while." He ignored

David's concerns about curfews and Sergeants as he led the way out and down the stairs into the moonlit courtyard. As Hal went to step out into the quadrangle which was almost as bright as day, David grabbed him by the arm, still worried about being caught.

Hal winced and David was immediately solicitous. "Hal? You're hurt!" He sat him down on the grass and peeled off his jacket. Hal's shirt was badly bloodstained and cut off at the shoulder; his upper arm was bandaged. Hal smiled ruefully at David's concerned face.

"Looks far worse than it is, believe me. The man who fired at me was not trained by a Sergeant Winter, or I would be dead. I didn't even see him—the horse did, shied, and between the shooter's stupidity and my horse's brains, together they probably saved my life." He pulled his jacket back around his shoulders. "Don't look so tragic. I'll live. The shot grazed my arm, nothing more, and I've had worse. Master Thornell has patched me up." He reached over, took off David's hat, and tipped his chin up so he could see his face. David's heart contracted at the story and he felt his eyes fill with unbidden tears.

Hal was smiling, but his brow was furrowed with concern. "Crying? Nay, not over me?"

"Not really," whispered David quietly, "but so much loss. I can't explain, I'm sorry." He stood up, embarrassed by his lack of control partly due to the ale and partly in concern for Hal's welfare.

Hal caught up with him at the quadrangle door and pulled him round. "Are you ever going to tell me what makes your face twist in agony when you think I do not see? Am I not enough of a friend that you can share your sorrow as well as your drink? If not, then tell me and we will be no more to each other than your new drinking companions, but tell me one way or the other for I deserve at least that courtesy. Don't let me hope..." His voice faltered.

David leant against the warm, shadowed wall and slid down it into a crouching position. He kept his face turned from Hal as he

said, "Don't, Hal, I can't bear for you to berate me. I left behind...someone. At home. Someone I loved."

"A lass?"

David gave a snarl, startling Hal with his sudden unexpected
anger. "Don't play games with me Hal! You know what happened
'twixt me and Tobias. You helped *arrange* it. I was younger then,
but not addled. You met him."

"Your brother?" Hal seemed to struggle to remember that
day.

"No, not my sibling, but my blood brother, my friend, my conscience, my soul. Everything that was good about me, I left behind. With him."

Hal's voice was strangely quiet. "But *you* left *him*. Why?"

"We quarreled. Don't ask me any more for pity's sake."
David's voice broke. "Don't you see, Hal? That's what destroys
me. We *quarreled*. I was stupid, but I had no choice. I left him,
the best person I have ever known. But he goes on, he lives. I
could go back, he might even forgive me. But you... *you*. You lost
your love, and you can never go back. I blame myself for both of
us." His voice came in huge sobs for his own sorrow as much as
Hal's; allowing all the loss of the last year, from Edgehill to this
moment, to wash over him. "Perhaps if Tobias and I...had not...he
would be...would be..."

Hal moved swiftly to David, knelt in front of the youth and
pulled him forward onto his knees and into his arms. "Don't ever
say that. Do you hear me? Not ever! It is not your fault. Tobias
and I... I do not expect you to understand our friendship, but we
had known each other for many, many years. I knew him so well
that I knew that I was not enough for him, he needed more than
I could give him, and I loved him enough to let him go because
he always came back to me."

"But not..."

"No. Not after Edgehill." The bitterness and sadness in Hal's
words tore through David. "Somehow I knew he wouldn't. After
he came back from you that night he was so quiet, somehow I

knew, and I think he did too." He kissed David's hair softly. "It's not your fault, David, I promise. It's just war." Hal pulled David into an alcove between the buildings and bent towards David, grazed his face with the softest of kisses, drew the tears from his eyes, and followed the trail of salt to his mouth.

David returned the kiss, as gently as it was given. Hal's tongue was tender, almost hesitant as he explored David's mouth, their lips barely connecting. Hal brought long fingers up to David's face and outlined the shape of his lips, as if attempting to memorize their shape and feel. As the kiss broke, David whispered, "He said as much to me. He knew he was not coming back. And then he never did...."

"Can we not comfort each other then, you and I?" Hal whispered into David's ear, his arms slipping around his waist. "Is your loss too recent? For mine is not...I have been lonely for too long a time."

David tipped his head back and opened his eyes. His gaze met Hal's, and he saw something he recognized. They were both lonely, but wanting. He gave the smallest of smiles, then leant forward and kissed Hal deeply, his hands fisted in the thick hair, as his hesitation vanished and his teeth clashed with Hal's in his haste. Finally, when David was quite breathless. Hal stopped, and without a sound led David by the hand and out of the courtyard.

Hal's callused hands trawled over David's hips, and he smiled as the young man stirred in sleep. Hal's mouth investigated the skin beneath his ear, and pulled David's pliant body into his arms. The youth slid effortlessly into the holow of Hal's body, fitting neatly, his convex to Hal's concave, his legs hooked around the other man's calves.

"I must go," David mumbled, his voice thick with sleep.

"Not yet." Hal pulled him closer and leant down for a deep kiss, his left hand teasing the sweet skin where buttock met the back of David's thigh. "Reveille is not for at least two hours. God,

David, do you know how perfect you are? How can a man such as myself see you and *not* want you?"

David didn't reply, and Hal made sure he could not, taking claim of his mouth again, each kiss more hungry than the last. He felt he could never have enough of David—in his mouth, under his hands, in his hands. He shifted around, bringing their cocks together then wrapped one large hand around them both. David gasped as Hal used his thumb to tease the head of David's prick, then arched, pushing his cock further into Hal's hand. Encouraged, Hal stroked up and down. David lay with his eyes closed, his mouth open, his hair damp around his temples. He clung to Hal, and Hal was sure, sure as his own seed was rising within him, that the boy was feeling the same.

Hal let the lust wash through him as he continued to rock gently against David and stroke them both with a steady cadence. He reveled in the slim, muscled body tensing against his in such need, and took delight in relentlessly torturing the youth with a firm grip until David began to whimper and beg, thrusting his hips harder with every movement.

"*Hal...*" David cried, his voice staccato; Hal watched him as David flailed helplessly on the cot beside him. He felt triumphant. He had dreamt of David for a year and a half, longed that *he* had been the one to have won the toss that day in Kineton, that *he* had been the one to seduce the blacksmith's son. As he leant over to kiss David, he felt David's cock pulse in his hand and his seed spilled, gentle and hot, causing his own happy release within seconds.

Although they'd been lovers for days, Hal had not taken David yet. Their play had been with mouths and hands only, and he was almost regretting it, for the youth had made it very clear that he would welcome Hal's prick in his body. Hal had hesitated, hardly knowing why, recompensing himself with the task of taking David, time and again, to such a precipice of desire that David was begging Hal give him any release he would. Eventually, when he had been unable to hold back himself, Hal had allowed it.

Watching David in the throes of passion was a sight of such beauty it was almost worth all of the self-control he had to employ to stop himself from opening that tempting cleft and sliding within it. It was a pleasure he was finding more delicious from its anticipation, and the longer he held out, the more he craved it.

David's eyes fluttered open again; he looked dazed and exhausted in the candlelight. He threw a leg over Hal's hips and leaned in, dipping deep into Hal's eager mouth before escaping from arms that were once again attempting to ensnare him.

"No," he said, firmly but not unkindly. He threw on breeches and jacket, and picked up the rest of his discarded clothes. "We've had little enough sleep. I'll have to tiptoe back through the college as it is. I'll be more than lucky if I'm not caught." He looked around the small room. "Who lives here? It's not you."

"One of the ensigns and his wife," Hal said, grinning. "Went west with the rest of the lads."

Abruptly, David sat down on the edge of the bed. Hal slid towards him and kissed his neck, as if attempting to keep him a while longer.

David turned to him, his expression suddenly thoughtful. "When do we march out? You know, don't you? That's what last night was about. It's what Tobias did. A last minute tumble before we die."

Hal's stomach churned. He wanted to lie. It hurt him to see David look at him with such accusation in his eyes. The only expression he wanted to see was passion and need. "But we didn't...I didn't..." Hal was stung by the unfair accusation. He could have fucked the boy for hours, and did not. "I have known that I wanted you since I first saw you, love you, but haven't had the nerve to say it. I didn't believe I really ever stood a chance with you. I still don't, I know you only turned to me because you were lonely, but I didn't take you. That's exactly what I didn't want you think—that I was just repeating what Tobias did." He gave a rueful smile. "Seems I failed."

"No chance, Hal. I'm here, aren't I? It wasn't *just* loneliness you know. I have...wanted you too." David felt suddenly ashamed at his outburst and undressing again swiftly he climbed back into the bed and straddled Hal by the knees, watching Hal's prick stir and then pulse with life. "I'm here, Hal, and I want you. If you had no chance with me, I would not have let things get this far. If we are to fight soon, if anything happens to one of us, the last thing I want either of us to do is regret we didn't do this."

Hal groaned as David suckled his growing cock into his mouth. All Hal was able to do was to fall back onto the bed with happiness, realizing only much later, as he lay spent and finally sated, his softening member still buried deep in David's tight hole, that the youth had not commented on the fact that Hal had admitted he loved him.

◖◖ CHAPTER 14 ◗◗

Another heat wave. Early June and already it was as warm as August. Jonathan was learning to hate the summer. Everything about it reminded him of the fact it was David's favorite time of the year. All the things David loved to do were made easier in the hot weather: sleeping naked, swimming in the river, making love in the long grass by the river.

Even working in the forge, the one place where the heat of the day did not affect the searing furnace already in the place, there were forcible reminders of David. Every drop of sweat that fell from Jonathan's forehead reminded him of David's naked torso gleaming in the forge's glow, soaked and glistening.

It was torment, but a torment he felt he deserved. He did his work mechanically, taking his usual care, but he felt none of the joy or the pride that he had known prior to David's departure. He used to be able to share his skill with the younger man—having an opportunity for the first time in his life to show off his talent to someone who did not simply consider his skill to be a trade, but was impressed with what magic he could bring forth with water, fire, and iron. He also missed teaching; David's skills were limited because of the years he had disliked the work, but he had improved quite substantially in the two years of their working together. Jonathan had loved those times in the forge, working close together, using the excuse of having to supervise David's technique to teach him exactly the best way to fold each bolt of metal, leaning in close to his lover, clutching David's leg between his own two, squeezing tight with his strong thighs. Pushing his member against David's to watch his eyes flutter in pleasure. David's mouth opening involuntarily as Jonathan teased him with secret fingers when no one was looking. Without David, the forge was just a hot, dull hell.

He punished himself by working harder and putting in longer hours than Jacob asked of him. He punished himself for all of the pride he had harbored before, punished himself for loving David, for committing those unforgivable sins with David. For believing his lies, for *not* believing his lies, for begging him to stay, for driving him away. It was a circle of self-condemnation and loneliness, and his bitterness knew no bounds. He started to have difficulty sleeping, his mind unable to slow down after a long day of pounding steel, so he sat up in the candlelight reading the Bible as voraciously as he had neglected it in the past year, attempting to find some solace, forgiveness, *peace*. He found none; he found nothing but accusation and castigation. After weeks of begging God for help, and receiving none, even though he searched every word for absolution, he finally gave up, thrust his belief aside in his anger, and vowed he would never ask for God's help again.

Night after night he lay awake, his eyes shut tight, imagining he could feel David's weight pulling the mattress down on his side. All he had to do was reach out and surely David would roll into his arms, so he did not reach, unable to bear the disappointment of being alone in the darkness.

He knew he made himself pale and weak from loneliness, lack of sleep, worry, and mental flagellation. His appetite had gone, and when he sat by the river, the reflection he saw of himself in the water was not of the man he had been. His hair was unkempt, his face seemed almost skull-like with weight loss, his cheekbones had become prominent, and his eyes dull and uncaring.

Jacob had watched his apprentice's gradual deterioration with some alarm and was truly concerned for his health, worried that the youth was slipping into a decline from which he would never recover. When questioned, Jonathan answered his queries with monosyllables, spoke only when spoken to, and ate even less than he talked. The day finally came when Jonathan, hefting the trencher-sized hooves of a mighty cart horse onto a hoof stand for rasping, gave a groan and keeled over like a mighty pine tree felled.

The horse, with the gentleness such beasts have, removed its hoof from the stand and placed it onto the stone floor, carefully avoiding Jonathan's unconscious body. Jacob was around his bench like a shot, splashing water onto the apprentice's face and reassuring the owner of the horse that no, Jonathan was not ill, but he had been overworking. The man did not look convinced and speedily led his horse out of the forge without payment and only half shod, as if he feared typhus or plague. Jacob watched the apprentice revive, gave him a drink of small ale, and helped him up to sit on one of the benches.

"Forgive me, Jacob," Jonathan said as he revived. "I have not been sleeping well." It was the longest sentence Jacob had had from him since the day after David's departure.

"Or eating well. Or taking enough rest. Or looking after yourself, lad. You must think I am blind not to see the reason you make yourself weaker every day." Jonathan looked up with a guilty start, fearing Jacob's next words. "You still blame yourself for my son's stupidity, even after I told you not to. Do you not?" Jonathan sighed in relief and nodded, grateful to be able to tell Jacob a partial truth. "Look at you," said Jacob, and he gripped Jonathan's arm with one large hand. "You have lost a quarter of your strength in two months. Do you not feel guilty?" Jonathan looked up at Jacob in question. "I bought a fit and healthy apprentice, fed him, treated him like my own, and he repays me by becoming no good for the work I bought him for. I know the cure for that, and one that is long overdue."

He stood up and for one horrible moment Jonathan really thought that Jacob was going to beat him, or worse, sever his apprenticeship. "I should have insisted on this a long while since. In fact I suggested it last summer and you refused it, but this time

I insist. You will go home and see your family. *Yes.*" Jacob's voice was firm as Jonathan felt a grip of fear of being cast out. "I can manage. I can find someone to help around the farm. And in any case, you being here in such a weakened state is of little help to me. If you become truly ill, how will I manage the work on my own then, if I have you to tend to? Your indentures are suspended. Go home and do not come back until you are once again the man I bought." He took the apprentice into his strong arms and held him close, slapping his back, his voice husky with emotion, "Don't be too long though, son, for I shall miss thee."

Jonathan's eyes filled with tears for the true affection in Jacob's voice, which betrayed his own loneliness. For a brief moment he considered refusing Jacob's kindness, the thought of leaving Jacob truly alone, with the forge and his own bitter memories of his son was heartbreaking, but the sudden longing to see his mother, his father, and such brothers as were at home was overwhelming. He nodded in gratitude, swallowing to keep his tears from spilling, and he clutched the blacksmith to him as if he were indeed his own father.

Too few days later and Jonathan was on his way home. He felt strange, adrift and unanchored. Although he had only been in Warwickshire for so short a time, he had slotted into the Caverley's life like he had always belonged. *David and I*...He shook his head. *No. I have spent enough time worrying about David. Enough sleepless nights missing his skin, enough days in torment worrying about where he is, is he well, is he missing me? Is he even alive?* His mind was tired with thinking about him, the constant ache was still there, but he could suppress it now at least. *Now I have something to look forward to.*

After two days travelling, one with Jacob and one with a carter who was going to Coventry himself, he was within two miles of his house. He felt weary and chilled to the bone, in spite of the heat. The road he was walking was so familiar to him, and yet he felt that he was seeing it for the first time. It seemed smaller somehow. He tried to hurry the pace but the potholes and rubble on the roads prevented much of a speed.

Suddenly, there was a clatter of hooves and four riders emerged from the farm on his right, turning into the lane at a swift trot, making straight for him. He stepped out of the road and slid down into a small ditch and waited, head bowed, for them to pass him. To his concern he heard a shouted command for halt and the horses came to a restless standstill, kicking the dusty ground and throwing their heads about as if resentful of being stopped. They were so close that Jonathan could smell the sweat of the animals, could hear the jingle of spurs and bits, but after a brief glance he looked away and kept his head down.

"You, there," said an imperious voice. "You, man. Look up and come here." Jonathan realized there was no chance of escape. He did as he was ordered and climbed out of the ditch. The lead rider spoke again. "Why did you hide in the ditch when you saw us approach? What have you to hide? Speak up!"

"Forgive me, sirs," said Jonathan, attempting to remain subservient. He had heard too many tales of men pressed into the army due to their insolence, and he schooled his speech accordingly. "I was not attempting any concealment, simply to remove myself from thy road so that thou might pass without inconvenience."

There was a brief silence, then another trooper spoke. "He is a most polite Puritan at least, Norton."

"Silence, Willis," snapped the first man. "Can you ride, brother?"

Jonathan swallowed in fear as he realized that there were four horses but only three men. He was relieved that he was able to tell the truth. "No, good masters. I am an apprentice blacksmith, sure, indentured at Kineton. But I have never sat astride a horse in my life. I am just returning home, to my family—"

"I expected you would say no less." The one called Norton looked skeptical. "However I am in need and we ride fast to Oxford tonight. Let me see you prove your claim. Willis…" He barked at the man who had spoke earlier, who now slid from his horse, handed the reins to the third rider, and led the spare beast out into the road. He stood there while he gestured for Jonathan to draw near. Jonathan knew he had no choice, so he put his bundle down and approached the horse; he knew the basics at least; *approach from the near side, put my left foot into the stirrup.*

This he achieved, with the horse held secure by Willis, but he felt unfamiliar muscles complain the huge stretch he had to make. He pulled himself up onto the saddle, hearing the un-named trooper choke with laughter as he landed heavily, over-balancing onto the horse's neck. Willis patiently helped him gather the reins, which had fallen to the ground.

"He could be faking, captain," Willis said, a laugh behind his words.

"That he could, although his performance so far deserves a place on the stage," the man said dryly. He pointed up the road, the way Jonathan had come. "Take her down the road a way and back." Jonathan looked across at him in concern and was about to speak when the third trooper raised a leather glove and slapped the mare on the rump. She bunched her hindquarters behind her and Jonathan was thrown backwards, only his hold on the reins saving him from an undignified exit over her tail. The mare broke into an uneven shambling trot, unwilling to leave her stablemates, whilst Jonathan clung for dear life to the mane and reins, his feet falling out of the stirrups within seconds. It was lucky the horse had not been more fresh, Jonathan thought, for to go faster would be terrifying.

As the mare realized that the passenger she carried had no control, she swerved to a halt, dropping her head to the ground and began to crop the grass. Jonathan's body continued in the same direction and he fell off head first over her shoulder, rolling as he hit the grass on the side of the road. The one called Willis retrieved the mare with a broad smirk on his face, leaving Jonathan sitting there nursing a bruised shoulder and a simmer-ing temper. The troopers did not even stop to inquire if he was hurt, and all four horses trotted past him within seconds, in a clamor of metal and leather.

As they disappeared into the distance, leaving nothing behind but Jonathan's wounded pride and a cloud of dust, he realized that they said they were going to Oxford. Perhaps if he had been able to ride, he might have been seeing David the next day. He pushed the thought aside. He was sick and tired of obsessing over his lost love and each reminder of him was making him less maudlin and more angry. *This was what I was sent away for, to forget it.*

Picking himself up and brushing the dust from his clothes, he gathered up his bundle and started on the last few miles to his home.

⧼ CHAPTER 15 ⧽

Halfway across the bridge, Jonathan stopped. The scene below him caused him to smile, the first genuine smile in weeks. There, beside the water, was his childhood home; a small timber-framed cottage, the last in a row of three. He knew that his family were not expecting him, so he savored the moment to take in the scene below him. His grandfather was sitting outside on his bench, the bench they had made together, with his old clay pipe—which never drew properly and the smell of which drove his mother mad—between his lips. The old man's eyes were closed as he dozed peaceably in the warm early evening sun. Chickens and ducks perched, like his grandfather, all along the bank, enjoying the heat of the day. Jonathan had forgotten just how much he had missed his family, and felt a dull, aching guilt rise up in him when he remembered that he'd had the opportunity to come back here the previous year, but had been so caught up in his love for David he had neglected the people who loved him most.

He wondered where everyone else was. When he had left here—*was it really so long ago?*—the place had been frantic with activity, not at all like the peaceful scene below him. All of his brothers had been here to see him off, some with their sweethearts. His mother had been crying, while his father stood bluff and proud.

His grandfather, Jonathan smiled at the memory, had been attempting to take him off to one side and give him some advice about women. "Never do anything with a maid that thou wouldst be ashamed to tell thy mother about, Johnny," he'd said. *Well Grandfather*, he thought, *I heeded that advice at least.*

Shaking away the torpor he had gathered from the warmth of the sun on his back and on the golden stone of the bridge, he pulled himself upright, made his way across the bridge and down the steps, keeping as quiet as he could. His grandfather's eyes were closed. He leant down to the old man and blew softly in his ear.

"You want to be on your guard, Mister Graie," he said in an attempt at the cultured accents of the riders on the road. "The King might make off with your chickens while you sit there dozing." He laughed to see the old man surface from his somnambulist state choking and spluttering as he inhaled the smoke from his pipe too quickly. His grandfather's face split into an expression of utter glee when he focused on the tall young man casting a shadow over him.

"Johnny!" With his hands clasped tight to Jonathan's forearms he pulled himself up and embraced his youngest grandson. "By Heaven—look at the size of thee, thou art grown a foot and a half!" The old man only came up to Jonathan's chin. "Alice? *Alice!* Come quick!" He looked up to Jonathan again and tears were pouring down his face. "Why didst thou not let someone know thou wast coming, lad?"

Jonathan's mother came out of the front door, blinking in the sunshine, wiping her hands on her apron in such a familiar way that Jonathan could hardly bear it.

"What's the matter, Fa—" Seeing Jonathan she dropped her cloth onto the ground and launched herself into his arms; then they were all crying, his mother was dragging them into the tiny cottage, sitting him down, bombarding him with questions that he was incapable of answering as she did not let him speak. Finally his grandfather told his daughter to let the boy be, to let him eat his food in peace and she quieted, sat by him and watched his face while he ate, her face flickering from love and happiness to what he was sure was concern at his pale appearance.

"Thou art thinner than thou should be, for all thy manly height, my son," she said, with worry in her voice. "Hast thou been ill?"

"Hast thy master severed your apprenticeship?" His grandfather was bristling in anticipated annoyance, as if ready to go and defend Jonathan from imaginary accusations.

Jonathan slid round on the wooden trestle, and put his arms around his mother. She seemed so tiny to him now, but once she had filled his entire world. She smelled of flour and milk, scents from his childhood that made him yearn for a past that could no longer be found. He could not think of what to tell her. He had never lied to his mother. Not even when his brothers had implicated him in their misdeeds. He had never thought that a lie would have saved him from further torments at his brothers' hands. The risk of damnation or the look of disappointment from his mother's eyes was worse than anything the boys could do to him, and so to his brothers' disgust he would tell her the truth. *"Samuel broke it, and put the pieces in my bed."* Or *"Adam pushed me in the river."*

"Not ill. Mother, not really. Just lonely." *That at least is partially true,* he justified. She squeezed his arm, clearly believing him. She had no reason not to and he hated himself. "And no, Grandfather, my master has given me leave to come home and regain some strength." They let him eat then, although Jonathan could see that his mother's eyes were still full of worry. He let their talk wash over him; the general gossip of the village and of the news that the river folk brought. He finished the last piece of cheese and sat back, refusing a spare pipe his grandfather offered him. He'd eaten more in a sitting than he had for many a day and he felt so tired he thought he could sleep for a week. "Where is everyone?"

"Thy father's haymaking. He won't be back till after dark," his mother said.

"I meant my brothers," he said, knowing that his father had

always worked far too hard, doing his best to raise five sons, feed eight mouths. He'd worked at the manor house all his life, a laborer in the service of Lord Marphon.

"Luke and Matthew were last in Cornwall, as far as we know," his grandfather said, "but they could be anywhere now; we haven't heard any news of them for six months." He saw the tense and drawn expression on his mother's face and wished he hadn't asked about his brothers, still out fighting somewhere in this war he couldn't understand.

"And Sam?" Jonathan's voice was tinged with concern knowing how terrible it must have been for his favorite brother to cope with life with one arm. But his grandfather beamed at this.

"Samuel was lucky. They took him back on at the big house. Not his old job of course, but in the grounds. He seems happy enough. His lass would have him back, but the stupid boy is too proud. However, my money's on her." There was a sudden lacuna of sound, a forced awkwardness that Jonathan could not help but feel. He realized they were avoiding the name of the one other brother for some reason. His mother got up and started clearing the table, and his grandfather started packing his pipe with a concentrated expression.

"Take that outside, Father. Thou'rt not stinking the kitchen up," his mother snapped. "I can do without the pair of thee cluttering up the place. I've got to find Jonathan some better clothes, he's as tall as his father, but he looks like a scarecrow. Only Matthew was as tall and broad, I'll find some of his things." Happy to be busy for her youngest, she disappeared into the back bedroom he had shared with his brothers. Jonathan watched her go, his heart warm again at long last.

His grandfather stood up and placed a hand on Jonathan's shoulder. "Fancy a walk before bed, lad?" Jonathan got the hint, following his grandfather out into the early evening. They strolled along the river and Jonathan waited for his grandfather to speak, knowing that this walk wasn't simply to stretch anyone's legs. The ground rose as the river dropped away from them. His grandfather gently lowered himself to the grassy slope of the riverbank, grumbling softly at his old bones. They sat as they had countless nights before watching the swallows gorging themselves on midges, their wingtips grazing the surface of the turgid water, when finally his grandfather broke the silence.

"I'm glad thou art come when thou hast, lad. Strange how the youngest should be the most sensible." Jonathan blushed to hear himself called sensible, remembering with an arousing jolt, skin like musky torment, hands fisting in his hair, and the desperate cries of "*Yes, oh God, Jon, yes...*" The man who had elicited that response from David could never be called sensible.

His grandfather went on. "When the three eldest all joined up, I thought thy mother would never stop crying. When Samuel came home without an arm she wouldn't talk to anyone for weeks." He paused and puffed on his pipe, filling the silence with smoke.

"Is there something I should know?" asked Jonathan, suddenly feeling selfish for still thinking about his problems when there was clearly something troubling his family. He wondered why Adam had not been mentioned. "Where's Adam?"

"Right now? I couldn't tell thee. Oh, he's still living here, lad, if that's what you mean, but he's late to rise and even later to return home. He's made bad connections in the town, people richer than us, thou know well how he always made friends easily."

Jonathan did. His closest sibling was the charismatic one, with dark brown hair in soft curls like his mother's, blue-gray eyes and a beguiling smile that made you think that you were the most important person in the world, just while he allowed you to be in his presence. He was careless though, thoughtless and transitory, not realizing that when he moved from one set of friends to another he broke hearts and displaced trust.

He had done as much to Jonathan, allowed his younger brother to trail along in his wake, making him feel special and honored to hang around with his handsome brother and his older friends. Jonathan didn't realize that they thought he was amusing with his quaint way of speaking, speech patterns he copied from the grandfather who had been everything to him, who had taught him to read and write because his father was always working and his mother was always busy with so many sons. So when one day he heard them laughing about him and telling his brother that they were fed up with him always rag-tagging along he was hurt to hear Adam agree.

"I know, he's just a brat. I'll put him off, he won't bother us again." Then someone said he was a funny-looking brat at that, and they all laughed including his brother, so they didn't hear Jonathan burst into tears and run away.

Adam, in his careless way, didn't even notice that Jonathan was hurt, and that his younger brother didn't speak to him for weeks after the incident. He never seemed to notice Jonathan's feelings. In time Jonathan managed to forgive his brother, re-alizing that it was nothing more than thoughtlessness, but he'd never forgotten it, and he'd never allowed himself to get so close again.

"Does he not work?" Jonathan asked his grandfather, sur-prised that no one knew where Adam was during the day. "He was working with Father when I left home."

"Aye, he was there a good while, but one day he had a row with the foreman and he left without so much as a by-your-leave. It made life very awkward for thy father, I can tell you. Then he took over from Samuel and worked at the house for a while after that, and it seemed that he was going to make a go of it, but he then got into a fight with one of the footmen over some lass or other, bloodied his nose and he was dismissed on the spot. After that he was caught on the grounds of the house and although he didn't have anything on him, it was assumed he was poaching, and he was very lucky that they didn't arrest him." His grandfa-ther spat into the river and paused a while before continuing. "He's done a few days here and there with the harvest, but his reputation here is ruined. Lord Marphon won't have anyone em-ploy him round here."

"He's never thought of following the others?"

"The Army?" his grandfather gave a hollow laugh and stood up. "Thy mother would never hear of it. Oh, he threatens it from time to time whenever thy father tries to get him to see sense, move somewhere else to find work, but thy mother starts to get upset, and then...well, thy father cannot bear that." He patted Jonathan on the shoulder. "It's not good for a mother to have favorites, but she spoiled him, you know that. Always did."

They walked back in the gathering night, and Jonathan was quiet with his own thoughts, darker than the night itself. His father was eating his supper in the candlelit cottage when they got back and although he didn't say much, it was clear by his shining eyes and the strength of his hand-shake that he was pleased to see Jonathan, and proud of the way he had grown up. His mother gave him a pile of clothes, and finally he went to bed, almost too tired to undress. He tried to stay awake so he could speak to Adam when he came home, but within minutes he was so comfortable and safe, being home, he simply drifted away.

When Jonathan awoke, he had imagined it must be dawn, but realized he was wrong for it was still pitch-dark. Something had woken him and for a while he lay there, every muscle tensed. Then came a curse in the darkness and the sound of a footstool knocked over; Jonathan realized it must be his brother, come home at last. He fumbled for the nightstand, struggling with tinder and taper until he finally lit the candles, revealing Adam sprawled on the floor. His brother's eyes were shut, his mouth open, and the smell of alcohol came off him in thick waves. On his forehead there was a dark scar, and blood and dirt stained his shirt. With a sigh, Jonathan grabbed the unconscious man, dragging him onto the bed to get a better look at him.

Adam hadn't changed much in the years since Jonathan had seen him last. He was still handsome, but his face had put on flesh and his cheeks were florid and ruddy. Not, Jonathan guessed, from a healthy outdoors existence, but from too much drink. Rolling him over to the side of the double bed that at one point in their lives had contained all five boys, he crawled over the comatose man and lay down next to the wall, cursing himself as he had to lean back over Adam to blow out the candles.

When he woke in the morning, Adam was already gone. During breakfast Jonathan questioned his family about his brother's whereabouts, but they either did not know, or pretended not to. Jonathan tried not to let it worry him, but he couldn't help being concerned—it was clear that Adam's escalating bad behavior was causing much upset amongst his family. His mother did her best to make his days pleasurable, and they were. He rested, he ate a lot, and he slept longer than he had for years, but the atmosphere was too edgy to completely forget his errant brother. The worry over Adam was almost enough to push his thoughts and concern over David's whereabouts and well-being from his mind, but not completely.

Adam finally appeared after four days, reeking of alcohol and sporting a black eye. After bursting through the cottage door after breakfast, he threw himself onto the bench next to where Jonathan was cleaning his father's duck gun. Jonathan watched as his mother fussed over Adam, bringing out food she had saved for him, pouring him some watered ale, and even wiping traces of blood and dirt from his forehead. It sickened Jonathan. He attempted to catch his grandfather's eye, but the old man was staring at the wall, a blank expression on his face.

"Well, baby brother," Adam said, with that easy nonchalance he had, as if Jonathan had simply been out for a stroll for the past four years, "you are all grown up at last."

Jonathan's expression darkened as he heard his brother's speech, obviously aped from his wealthier friends.

"You haven't grown out of that ugly, sulky face, I see," Adam said, spearing some pork with his knife. Jonathan flushed in response; he had never considered himself handsome, it had only been David's sweet lies that had let him believe it for a little while.

"And thou hath grown no more charming," Jonathan surprised himself by retorting. "Perhaps if I were a maid—or a Lady—thou wouldst be more sweet to me."

"Perhaps I would at that," Adam said. He grinned at Jonathan and bit into his bread, then chewed it with his mouth open, with the manners of a pig. His hands and nails were filthy.

"I am surprised thou art still here," Jonathan said quietly as his mother took some scraps out for the chickens. "When the rest of us are—"

Adam interrupted him, his eyes glinting dangerously. "Samuel tried that tack on me when he was here last, and I bloodied his nose for him, though he's bigger than me. I advise that you keep your sermonizing to yourself."

"Brave man to fight someone with one arm."

Adam stopped chewing. "Mind your mouth, *little* brother. I'm happy enough here, and don't need your sanctimonious, holier-than-thou preaching."

Jonathan found that he was no longer cowed by Adam; handling tons of horseflesh gave him confidence in his strength, and he would no longer be bullied. "I'm sure thou art comfortable to stay here and let others fight thy battles."

"What do you mean by that?" Adam put his bread back down on the trencher.

Jonathan narrowed his eyes and put the gun down beside him. Anger surged through him, wanting someone to lash out at and finding just the subject. "That thou wallows here in safety waiting for thy mother and father to put food in thy fat mouth."

"Now, Johnny..." His grandfather attempted to keep the peace, but Jonathan wasn't ready to back down.

"And you are risking your life, are you?" Adam jeered. "In your nice warm forge, becoming a master smith? Getting your feet nicely under the table, I'll warrant?"

"Thou was offered the opportunity!" Jonathan bridled. "It was *thy* apprenticeship! I took thy place!"

"And so I have taken yours," sneered Adam. He didn't seem

to want to rise to Jonathan's anger and continued to eat. All Jonathan could do was glare across the table at his brother. Adam ignored him until he had finished eating, then, as he walked past to leave the cottage, he cuffed Jonathan around the head with his elbow. Jonathan was on his feet in an instant, but his grandfather was obviously anticipating trouble, his stick crashing down between the two of them.

"I may be half thy size Jonathan Graie, but I will fight thee myself if thou continues this with thy brother—with thy mother sick to worry every day of her life, never knowing how many sons she hast each morn."

Jonathan felt like he was a child again, being blamed for what was not his fault.

"I...I..." He found himself flushing with anger. Pushing Adam out of his way, he left the cottage and stalked toward the river. He didn't stop walking for a long while. He followed the riverbank, and after a mile or so the river dwindled to a stream and threaded its way through woodland.

As always, after he lost his temper, he felt stupid and embarrassed. Although the argument had not come to blows—no matter how much he had wanted it to—it reminded him once more of how bad he had felt the morning after David had left. How he had wished that David would have come back and given him an opportunity to try and take back every violent act, every word that had driven him away.

It was not how he wanted this visit to go. He should not have allowed Adam to make him feel how he used to feel: resentful for being the one who got "the opportunity" to be a smith because Adam had blown his chance with the master.

He sat by the river, throwing pebbles into the water and trying not to think about anything, but his stomach reminded him when lunch and then supper-time slipped by, and eventually he made his way back along the bank, knowing he'd have to apologize to his family.

The cottage came in sight, and, to his surprise, in front of it was his father, his grandfather and Adam. The cottage door was closed; from their faces it was clear that they were waiting for him to return. They stood as he approached.

"Father, I—

"Don't speak," his father said. His face was hard, but somehow he seemed older and more frail than the father Jonathan remembered as a child—no longer the great solid force he had always been. Jonathan felt a pang of compassion; it was hard enough to have brothers one worried about, but he had no conception of what it must be like to worry about children. "I have spoken to your brother, and he will speak to you." He looked sharply at Adam, with an unspoken command.

Jonathan looked at his brother, and for a moment he wanted to touch him, to shout at him. He wanted to explain to him how fragile life was—how everything could be swept away in a moment, but he knew Adam would never understand. He'd never lost anything or anyone he'd cared about.

Adam spoke with a hesitant voice, but there was no conviction in his words. "I apologize for my behavior earlier. Our father has said that you are right, and that I should go from here and seek my fortune."

"This is sudden," Jonathan said, looking suspiciously between his father and grandfather, fearing that he already knew what had been cooked up in his absence.

"It is only a matter of time before the young fool gets himself arrested," his grandfather said.

"Now, Paul," his father admonished.

"It's true and you know it. Johnny knows it. This place is too small for Adam already. Marphon has made it impossible for him to stay here and work. If he goes with Johnny—"

"We were planning to *ask* Jon if he would be willing to take him."

"Tell him. Don't ask him."

"The smith may not have work for him."

Jonathan looked from one to another, resentment welling up

in him. *They've sat down and planned all this behind my back! At least they could have asked me for my opinion—but no, Adam's needs came first, they'd always come first.* Swallowing his anger, he kept quiet and let his father continue talking.

"We've been through this. If not at the smith's, then in the town. There's men gone from everywhere in the country. He'll get work."

His father sighed. "Then it only leaves your decision, Jon. Will you take him?"

"I'm not—" Adam started.

"You'll do as you are told!" Jonathan's father rounded on Adam. "I will not have your mother upset for one day more. Better you were not here, and then she only worries about what you *might* be doing, not knowing what you really are. Jon?"

Jonathan looked from face to face and then at the closed door of the cottage. There was no choice, and perhaps away from here, Adam might calm down. If he said no it would only make more problems for all of them, and it was true—it wasn't as if Adam wouldn't be welcome. "I'll take him. Master Caverly will be pleased of the help. David—his son—has just left the farm." Saying David's name to his father felt like a sin all of its own.

"Then it is meant to be," his father said, patting Jonathan heavily on his shoulder. "Now go and eat, son. Thy mother wants to fill thy belly. Let her spoil you while she can."

The two young men were awkward with each other the next morning. Jonathan had a feeling that the journey back to Kineton wasn't going to be easy, and wondered in fact if Adam would even make it as far as the forge. He wouldn't be surprised if, once out of sight of the cottage, Adam would disappear on paths of his own. As they gathered their belongings together and said their goodbyes, his mother was crying and his father, unusually affectionate, put his arm around his wife's shoulders.

"Now, lass," he said. "They aren't going to war, after all. Jonathan will look after him, won't you, Jon?"

"Promise us, Jon?" His mother caught his hand and pressed it hard. "No harm?"

Jonathan knew exactly what she meant and he sighed inwardly, wondering how he would keep Adam out of trouble even in a small town like Kineton when he was incapable of staying out of trouble in his own village. "I promise," Jonathan said, his heart feeling heavy with the responsibility. "I'll look after him with my life."

He pushed Adam towards the bridge, and with a final kiss from his mother, he walked after his brother into the dawn.

"Up! Get *up*, you filthy footlickers!" Sergeant Winter was moving up the line kicking the men awake. It was not yet dawn. As David surfaced from sleep, hardly having closed his eyes not half an hour since, he realized muzzily what was going on. From the pale faces of the new recruits and the grim lines on the experienced men, he knew. This was it. He felt suddenly sick as he scrambled to his feet and began collecting his gear, lack of sleep and too much alcohol taking its toll. The only cheerful face was that of Blake, surreptitiously taking his normal breakfast drink from his flask that he hid beneath his bedroll. Godwin was ashen, unable to reply to his friend's cheerful banter of victory and glory.

As they went down the stairs David asked Blake, "Have you ever seen a battle?"

The man's eyes were clear and bright, in spite of his inebriation, giving David his answer before he replied, "No. Have you?"

David lied and shook his head, not wanting to speak of Edgehill. Just the thought of battle brought memories of Tobias, and that terrible, frantic race down the hill to find his body. They lined up in the courtyard, David's suspicions were confirmed as the musketeers were led to a powder barrel and told to fill the twelve 'apostles' that hung from their bandoliers: this had not happened before; normally they were only given their powder at the training grounds. In the gathering light noises were encroaching from without the college walls, the sound of wheels and many horses. He realized then that they were about to march right out of the city; but to where? *And what about Hal?* His nausea returned when he thought that he might not see his friend's smiling face ever again.

The sergeant started shouting and they turned sharply to the right, then one by one, they marched out of the gates of the college, joined the column of regiments, and marched out of Oxford to an indeterminate future.

◖◗ CHAPTER 16 ◗◗

June 1645—Naseby

The sparks flew from the sword as David sat in the gray morning, sharpening the gleaming blade on the whetstone held between his knees. The sun had just risen, but it was swathed in fog, not strong enough yet to burn off the miasma that hung over the encampment. David hadn't slept well.

They had marched all the previous day and David was sick at heart. After the successful assault upon the city of Leicester, it seemed for a while they might rest in the city, but word soon came that they could not stay. Cromwell, intent on besieging Oxford, had turned his troops northward, and was coming to pay them back for the sack of Leicester. So, after provisioning at Market Harborough—which meant little more than organized looting—the army, trying to reach Oxford, found themselves cut off by Cromwell's Roundheads. They'd encamped on a ridge between the villages of Little Oxenden and East Farndon. It was almost too dark to see when they stopped, and it was pitch dark when David finally got his tent up on his own.

By the time rations were served he was too tired to eat more than a little dried meat and fruit, and then once in bed he had fallen asleep immediately. He was awoken in the dark by insistent and familiar kissing, hands roaming over his reluctant flesh as Hal teased his body into hard compliance. David had wanted to refuse his lover, but the whispered discussion that would ensue would take longer than the act itself. He feigned acceptance, but hurried more than usual, encouraging Hal lover to take him straight away with little preparation. Within a few heated minutes Hal had satisfied himself and rolled off, snoring long before David had managed to get himself back to sleep.

Since their time together on the road, they had established a routine when it came to the night before a battle. Usually—and silently, always fearful of being discovered—they would make love for a long time. It was as if, in their bitter defiance to death itself, they sought to wring every moment of sweetness from life that they could. But now, David's affection for Hal was waning. As he sat outside his tent in the chill of the June morning, he found that he could not regret being more accepting of Hal's attentions the night before. *God alone knows*, he thought, *if it is destined that I would die today, it might have been better to have one last night of love.* But Hal had come in from wherever he had been, reeking of brandy and with the unmistakable stink of sex upon him, and it was one time too many, and not worth arguing about, not on a night before a battle. They had learned to keep any arguments hidden on mornings like these, until they knew they had another morning in which to disagree, and it seemed to David that with Hal that there were too many arguments.

There was a soft groan from behind him, and he turned to see Hal crawl out of the tent, his auburn hair in disarray, his eyes bleary with too much drink and not enough sleep. David noticed with some disgust that he had only undone his breeches in order to take his pleasure last night.

"Button yourself up," David muttered quietly, as Hal came near, "unless you're touting for yet another man to share your rod." His words were more bitter than he meant them to be, but once said they could not be retracted, and David let them lie between them. Hal crouched down on the grass next to David, clearly trying to get his attention, wantonly rubbing his crotch, but David became rigidly correct, muttering, "Not in the open for God's sake—how many more times must I tell you?"

"Jealous?" Hal said, his breath foul with drink and his words slurring a little. "You have no need, sweet David. For my heart belongs to you, and you know it." Hal tried to cajole the younger man, the way he always used to be able to, but David's mouth was set in a grim line and he refused to look at him. Hal wondered at the change that a year in the army has wrought in David. He was no longer a boy. That leggy eagerness had gone, replaced by a tough, more masculine leanness, and a slow, measured calm, no unnecessary movement, a soldier's trait: stillness.

Since marching out of Oxford the previous spring, David had become a soldier with surprising speed. Not just a man who could fire a musket and be relatively certain he might hit what he was aiming at, but a man who could make a camp anywhere; find a rabbit; make food from nothing; sleep standing up; live in mud and rain and frost and snow without getting ill; and tear the clothes from the bodies of fallen comrades to make rags for wrapping against the cold. All these things and more David had learned, and it had made a man of him.

And while David was learning all that, in the hardest way imaginable—learning not to vomit at the sight of blood and of maggots on putrefying flesh; watching his comrades fall in skirmish after skirmish—Hal had proven not to be any kind of replacement for the faithful Jonathan. David soon discovered that Hal had a short attention span when it came to pleasures of the flesh. Within a very few weeks of seeming to be totally enamored of everything that he declaimed lovely about David's form and face, he had started to disappear at night. One minute he would be around their constantly moving campsites, and then he would vanish without trace. The first time this had happened, David had been frantic with worry, and had made a show of himself by trying to find the man, unable to avoid seeing the ridicule in most of the soldier's eyes, and pity in some. Hal had returned several hours later, and had made an excuse about meeting friends from

a regiment he had not seen for months. David had been so relieved to see him that he had not even questioned it, and the
force of David's lovemaking that night had kept Hal close to his
side for a week or so, but then there was another aberration, and
then another, and David realized slowly that the excuses were
wearing thin, and the scents that Hal brought back on his clothes
were not simply those of drink and platonic male company.

So the arguments had begun; Hal was always so contrite that
David had been forgiving at first, and believed Hal's tales of being
led astray, of drunken fumblings and of not being able to remember what had happened to him. But eventually he became sickened with Hal's licentiousness and simply started to turn over in
their shared tent, to avoid Hal's touch and pretended to be un-
wakable when Hal's insistent fingers crept between his legs. Hal
seemingly was never more ready for sex than when he had just
left the arms of another, and this fact in itself revolted David most.

The souring of their relationship coincided with the decline in
the fortunes of the King's Army. After their success at the battle
of Cropredy Bridge, where David learned that success in battle
meant death on an almost incomprehensible scale, things had
gone sour when Cromwell's butchers, the New Model Army—
or "Roundheads" as they were derogatorily named by the King's
side—had stepped out in force in April '44.

From what David had picked up by listening to older, more
experienced soldiers, this new army was a new breed never before encountered by the haphazard regiments raised by aristo-
crats. A deliberate and organized force, all trained with same
methods, all thinking the same way, and all in red, they cut a
swathe across the country, conscripting, fighting, skirmishing.
Gradually pushing the King further and further into desperation,
so that it all stood here, on a knife-edge, at Naseby.

To David, though, it was just another battle. Just another day
to try and stay alive. To stand and fire into the face of the enemy,
and then to kill them any way you could, before they could kill
you. Each battle and skirmish was different in lots of ways, but

the same in that.

Hal stood up, spoke about going to check his horse, and touched David's head, but David shook him off, not willing to be appeased and wanting to hurt Hal, though knowing in his heart that he had no effect on the man's feelings, if indeed he ever had. He suddenly realized that this was the first time he had allowed an argument to fester into the morning of possible death, but frankly he didn't care. He was tired of Hal and his wanton lusts, and with a bitter taste in his mouth for the memory of his sweet blacksmith, it hurt his heart to think that, with his carelessness, he had made Jonathan feel the same way as he himself was feeling now.

As the sun crept up, burning off the last of the haze, he stood, seeing his sergeant at the end of the line, waking men who were not yet already out and preparing. As he turned to fetch his gear, two strong arms encircled him.

"I *told* you to get off, Hal." David's voice was almost a growl, his temper close to the surface. "If Winter sees us he'll have us both flogged, or worse."

"What? Hal and you? I can hardly believe it!"

David spun round, the blood in his face draining away at the familiar voice. *"Tobias?"* Lack of sleep, too little food, and shock caused his knees almost to buckle from under him.

Tobias caught his arm. "Aye, in the flesh."

The trooper was just as handsome as David remembered, maybe slightly leaner and with a new scar fresh across one cheek; his hair in soft waves around his shoulders.

"And look at you! What happened to my little farm boy?" He pulled David around and between the rows of tents, and had him in an embrace before David could muster his thoughts.

David pushed him away firmly, his mind was churning in confusion. "I...I thought you were *dead*. Hal—he told me you were dead!"

Tobias' face went suddenly and completely blank. "Where is Haldane?"

"He…he went to see to his horse. Tobias, if I'm not dreaming, and I think I must be—how is this *possible?* I thought you were killed at Edgehill!" David could hardly think. His head was pounding.

"Oh, he knows I'm alive all right." There was an edge to the trooper's voice. "Not only were we together for six months after Edgehill, but I bumped into him in Oxford last winter. He never spoke about his current activities, or he was very evasive about them, at least. I thought that was odd at the time, and now I see the reason for it. He told you I was dead?"

David's mind replayed every conversation with Haldane over the last year. *No, he'd never actually said that, did he? But he'd known I'd have thought it, and he'd let me go on thinking it. How could anyone* do *that?* He echoed the thought to Tobias. "How could he let me think you were dead?"

Tobias touched David's chin-length hair with a look of sorrow, as if mourning the death of a cherished pet. "Hal…is… a little strange. He wants everything, and ends up keeping nothing. I may be to blame I fear, for I was never constant to him. I was his first, and possibly he thought that was the way one behaved. I left him alone too often…" His finger slipped into David's mouth and his pupils darkened, making David's heart ache in remembrance of Tobias' gentle seduction. It was so long ago, it seemed to have happened to someone else.

"Gray!" A shadow fell across the men, and they flew apart as Sergeant Winter came on them with only a split second's warning. "Why aren't you…who the devil are *you?*" Winter's eyes narrowed at the sight of the stranger, and his glance flickered suspiciously between the two of them.

Tobias turned and removed his hat with the minimum courtesy owed to someone of lesser rank. "Captain Aston, Sergeant. Of Howard's horse." His words were smooth and convincing, but spoken with the undeniable arrogance of his superiority over a mere sergeant. "Forgive me for withholding your man. He is a cousin of mine and I had a message from his mother." He turned back to David. "Mind her words, sweet cuz; do not get that pretty head shot off. God willing, we will meet hereafter." And with another nod he was gone, striding down the lines, leaving David feeling cold and empty. He dared not follow Tobias' departure with his eyes, not with Winter around.

Winter scowled at David, and David knew that the man was probably chafing at being thwarted. He was hoping to find David in some wrongdoing and he had failed. He was also obviously stung by being patronized by a senior officer in front of David.

"Gray, take Blake with you and join the guard on the baggage train." The man's voice was crowing with the insult implied in the task. David knew that Winter was just longing for him to complain at the detail, but David was carefully guarded around the sergeant. He was sure that the man suspected his sexual preferences, and would be more than happy to hang him if he caught him in any kind of inappropriate behavior. Answering back, as David had discovered on more than one occasion, simply led to pain. So he nodded, his thoughts confused with the sudden reappearance of Tobias. This compliance wasn't enough for the bullying Winter and he stepped up close to David, who was correctly at attention, his eyes fixed on some middle distance. Suddenly he grabbed David's crotch with violent fingers, holding his balls tight in his hand. David could smell the rank breath stinking of sewerage and tobacco. He kept as still as he could under the pain; to show any weakness or sign of fight now could be fatal.

"You have got balls then, Cray?" Winter whispered foully in David's ear. "You do surprise me, after your pathetic, mutinous behavior at Leicester." His hand, to David's disgust, began to knead his balls whilst his eyes remained firmly on David's face, waiting for some reaction. "Next time I tell you to burn a house, you'll bloody well burn it, or by Christ I'll throw you into it before I set light to it myself." The fingers became rougher as the sergeant sought some kind of response. "Don't you like that, girlie? It's not what I hear. I heard you only like a man's rough hand on your equipment, s'that right? Bloody, filthy *scum*." The hand tightened viciously with each word, causing David to wince at last, and Winter stepped away, triumphantly.

"Get out of my sight. I don't want filth like you fighting next to me." He spat on David's boots and marched off. David stood there recovering his breath, his groin feeling like it was burning, every nerve on fire.

"Bastard." Blake staggered up the line and gave David a half-drunken grin. "I saw what he did. You should report him."

"And get worse the next time? No thanks. Did he tell you what we—"

"Yes. Baggage train. Could be worse places. Come with me; I want to show you something." Blake's usual smile had slipped an inch or two. Grabbing his kit, David followed him along the lines and up the brow of the hill, past the gun emplacements, and along to the end of the line. "Look." Blake pointed across the marshy plain. David's heart sunk. Arrayed on the opposite side, in row after row after unbelievable row were the ranks of Fairfax and Cromwell. Blake and he exchanged glances. The King was vastly outnumbered.

They turned as one and made their way back down the hill to find the baggage train, took their orders, and joined the circle. Neither men said much, too stunned by what they'd seen.

At first the battle was like any other David had experienced; cannons sounded, the sound of men shouting as they advanced, the scream of frightened horses. David stood listening, steadfast at his post, knowing that only a victory for the King would keep Blake and himself out of the action. The baggage train was usually the first target once the line had broken—containing as it did, provisions and arms, and in this case, much of the King's personal possessions. If Parliament's forces did break through and reach the carts of the baggage train, it could only mean defeat for the King, his army, and David's fellow soldiers. After that…David didn't like to speculate what might happen *after* a defeat.

The day rumbled on. Blake complained that he had run out

of rum, and David began to think that it might end in a another stalemate after all. No word came from the battlefield, but in mid afternoon there came the unmistakable sound of hooves, many hooves on the compacted grass. All hope of a stalemate melted as they spotted the flags and realized that it was Parliament's cavalry galloping towards them, and not their own side bringing the news of a happy victory.

David paled; the baggage guard was but one line of men, bare muskets with no wall of pike to protect them. One shot was all they would have time to fire, and desperately the men stood to face into the oncoming wall of horseflesh.

Someone in the line shouted, "Aim for their legs!" The muskets sounded; to David it seemed like he was alone in some huge field with the whole of Parliament's horse coming to cut him down. Some horses fell, but far too few of them, and death swept towards them like a thundering nemesis. The circle of guards scattered, knowing the day was lost. David grabbed Blake's arm and ran towards the trees, drawing his sword as shots rang out and the grass around their feet was chewed up by bullets.

As they reached the relative shelter of the trees, Blake stopped and spun round to see what was happening. "It's all right, they're not following—" and then the world blew apart.

A bullet hit Blake square on his bandolier and the apostles on the strap exploded. The force threw David to the ground. Deafened and temporarily blinded, David could only lay and wait for death, but none came. When he was revived enough to be able to move, he crawled to where Blake lay, his blood streaming in tiny rivulets down the grassy slope.

"*Oh God*... Blake..." Hopelessly he tried to stop the bleeding, but the damage to the man's chest and stomach was almost too horrible to look at. Blake's ribs were visible and his stomach was spilling out.

"Get back to your post, Gray!" Winter appeared out of the smoke, his sword drawn, his face muddy and menacing.

"But I've got to get him out of here!"

"I said, *get back to your post!*" He grabbed David by his buff coat and dragged him to his feet.

David's anger rose to the surface, months of bullying and deprivation by this man, compared with the friendship that he had had from Blake with his constant drunken humor, tipped David over the edge. He violently pushed the sergeant away from him, and the man slipped in the blood soaked grass.

"Don't you touch me, you hear? Don't you *ever* touch me again! You bloody bastard!"

Winter scrabbled backwards, cowed by David's sudden show of strength of violence, he sneered as he turned away. "He's as good as dead anyway, and so are you. Make it through today and I'll see you hang you for this! If you stay here, the butchers will have you, and good riddance." He ran back into the enveloping smoke, leaving David sobbing, the blood soaking his knees.

"Blake…" David cut the sleeve from Blake's tunic and held it over the damage, but the blood welled through it, drenching it almost instantly. Blake was coughing, blood coming out in spurts from his mouth. Although the cannon still sounded and screams and shouts were heard from all direction, in the smoke it was as if he and Blake were on an island alone. Everything seemed muffled, and time was horribly slow, as he watched the blood seep through his fingers, and his friend's face become paler and paler, his eyes losing their focus.

"Blake." He tried to modulate his voice so it didn't sound like it was edged with panic. The body beneath his bloody hands, the body that used to be his drinking companion managed a wordless gurgle. "Blake, hang on! I'll get you to the camp…." But he knew it was hopeless, could see the light going out of Blake's face—the face he would never see laugh again—the eyes glazing over. It may not have been the first man he had knelt with as he had died, but this was his friend's blood on his hands, on his tunic, and he would never see him drink, laugh at his songs, or watch him kiss a wench ever again.

"I'll sweep under the wagons, you check near the wood." A

disembodied voice came through the murk, and David realized that Parliament's men were much closer than he had thought. He went to pick Blake up, but the familiar stench of death was already upon him as the body relaxed and all his bodily functions released themselves. The man was dead, and there was no point carrying him anywhere. David staggered to his feet and made for the cover of the trees, choking in the smoke and sobbing as he ran. He had no thought of trying to find the regiment, or even any concern for Hal's welfare; with the baggage train lost, the battle, and probably the war, was over. David tore his jacket off. *The war is over, for me. Now if only I can get away without either side stopping me....*

There seemed to be voices coming from everywhere. He paused, panting with panic, and leant against a tree, straining his ears. Noises came from his right and behind. He was fairly sure that straight on, the path was likely to be swarming with troops, so he ducked left. There had to be a village beyond the woods, and if he could find one, it was just possible he could find someone to shelter him, find some civilian clothes, and blend in. *After that...* he didn't know.

He moved as quietly as he could, creeping diagonally through the trees, using his sword to cut away dense tangles of brambles. His heart was pounding. If he'd been captured on the field, or had surrendered by the train, it was just possible he might have been spared. If he were found fleeing the scene, he'd be shot as a deserter. It didn't stop him. All he wanted to do was get away from the bloodshed. He'd wanted to desert after the sacking of Leicester. Many troops had, carrying with them as much loot as they could carry, but David had stayed, even after Winter had ordered the burning of several houses—and even now he couldn't remember why he'd stayed. *No longer.*

After an hour and half of stealth moving he was exhausted, the strain of the day taking its toll. He could see a village through the trees. He knew there was a chance troops might be headed now, but it was safer than back there. One small dash across the clearing, that was all it would take. He pressed his back against the tree and got ready to run.

"Don't move!" A hoarse voice, tinged with fear, shouted at him. "Thou...You...You have nowhere to go. Drop thy musket!"

David didn't move, only risking a swift glance down at the burning cord used to fire the powder in his musket. It was still smoldering , and he blew on it frantically, trying to stir the embers as quietly as he could, ready to set it to the firing pan of his gun. He knew he would get one shot, and only one. He stepped forward and ducked down as the expected shot went wide and clipped the tree by his head, then he spun round to face the unknown assailant. He grabbed the match and went to hammer it down onto the firing pan...and stopped dead.

It was Jonathan. Frantically fiddling with his musket with obviously novice fingers, unlike David who could perform the moves in his sleep, but still Jonathan. As the shock of seeing him in this place at this unlikeliest of times filtered into David's brain, he realized that the dear, stupid man hadn't even bothered to try and get under cover, and that if David had been anyone else, Jonathan would be a dead man. He called softly, not wanting anyone in the vicinity to hear.

"Jon."

Jonathan's head snapped up and his face paled. David went to step forward but Jonathan warded him back, waving the musket.

"I said, *don't move*." Jonathan said.

"Jon. It's *me*. For God's sake, you've got to let me go. If they catch me, they'll hang me." He wanted to rush at the man, to cover his face with kisses, as incongruous as that was in this desperate moment, but the year apart seemed like seconds. All he wanted was Jon's arms around him, and it would all be all right between them.

"Running away. *Again*." The voice was so bitter David could hardly believe it was the same voice and understood why he hadn't recognized it at first. "Thou are most skilled at leaving at the opportune moment. I *said* stay where thou art." Despite the words, the hands holding the musket trembled, so David obeyed in case it went off accidentally.

"How did you get here?" He nodded his head at his friend, indicating his uniform. "And how did the Ironsides get you?"

Jonathan looked around nervously, as if he was expecting more of his regiment to join him. "I was pressed."

And you hardly know one end of a musket from the other, thought David. "Let me go, Jon," he said softly. "No one will know. If you ever loved me at all..."

Jonathan snarled at him, and David realized he'd hit a nerve; the gray eyes were as angry as the day Elizabeth had brought their world crashing down. He spoke, but he seemed to be having trouble with the words. "Thou willst...*not*...twist me around thy little finger once more. I am free of thee and thy deceptions. I thought...I might never see thy treacherous face again."

"Then let me *go*, Jon, before they come. Please." He could see Jonathan was wavering, knew that if he kept begging then Jonathan would never hand him over. It was clear from the Puritan's visible emotions that he still cared for him, and if they couldn't be together, at least they could both be alive.

Voices sounded from behind Jonathan. David started to panic but dared not move. Several things happened at once, but the soldier in David reacted so fast he didn't assess his actions until afterwards. He saw a madder-red uniform in the undergrowth, and Jonathan's eye flickering away from him. The soldier, whom Jonathan could not yet see, raised his musket and aimed it square at Jonathan; it was a member of David's own company, thinking that David was in dire straits.

No! With lightning reflexes, utilizing Jonathan's inattention, David fired his own musket, a fraction of a second before the Lifeguard fired his. David aimed true, and blew away part of the Lifeguard's face. The other man's shot went off target, but Jonathan fell to the ground at the same time as did the Lifeguard, blood seeping into his coat.

David leapt forward, and once again knelt by the side of a

fallen friend for the second time in hours. He felt sick and near panic. *No, not my Jon. Not him! He doesn't deserve it, none of it!* With a knife, he cut away Jonathan's tunic to find a clean wound, the bullet had gone straight through his shoulder.

Suddenly there was someone beside him—Tobias. "I've been following you, you idiot. Do you realize how *lucky* you are to be alive? What the Devil are you doing? Looting him?"

The accusation made David's stomach heave and he looked up at Tobias with an anguished face. "It's Jonathan." David could say no more, could not trust his voice to speak and could not explain, but the look Tobias gave him let him know that he understood, and together they tore David's shirt to ribbons and swiftly padded the wound as well as they could.

"It's all you can do for him. We *have* to go!" Tobias repeated the urgent statement but David hesitated. He ran his fingers over Jonathan's cheek, drinking in the face he thought he would never see again. Tobias grabbed Jonathan's jacket and forced David's arms into it, then pulled him up roughly and pointed into the copse where shadowy shapes, soldiers that were certainly not likely to be Royalists, were moving stealthily. "Come *on*, David. They'll find him. He'll be fine, but we have to *go!*" With one last anguished look at Jon's pale face, David allowed himself to be led off, leapt up onto Tobias' horse behind the trooper, and they galloped towards the town as bullets whistled past them.

◖◗ CHAPTER 17 ◖◗

"This is your house?" David felt a little awed as he looked up at the building. It looked larger than the cottage in Kineton, probably because of the claustrophobic feel of the overhanging gable of this and of all the other houses in the dark, dirty street.

Tobias glared at the door as if it had affronted him. "Nay, not mine, but an uncle. Not a close uncle either." Tobias knocked on the door for the fourth time. "It's obvious he's not in, and by the look of the grime on the windows, he hasn't been around for a goodly while. Wait here." He walked a little further along the street and then disappeared into an alleyway.

David stood outside the door attempting to look inconspicuous as people bustled past. He knew that his loitering was causing a few curious glances. A few minutes passed before David heard the bar being lifted. Then the door opened and Tobias reappeared, forcing the door open. The door was thick, but it had warped in the damp through disuse. It took several shoves to drag it screeching across the stone floor, and when it was wide enough for David to slip in to the dark hallway, it had left deep scratch marks in the dark gray flagstones.

"At least," puffed Tobias, forcing it closed again, "if someone tries to get in, we'll hear them." He turned around, leaning against the door, exhausted. David launched himself into Tobias' arms, wrapping around Tobias like a young vine around an oak. He tucked a leg behind Tobias' knee and leaned backward, pulling Tobias down with him onto the unforgiving floor.

Tobias landed ungracefully on David who laughed. They wrestled, as best they could in the small space they had, until David surfaced triumphantly, straddled over Tobias' waist.

"At last," David muttered, kissing Tobias again and again. He began to undress, his eyes locked with Tobias', as his lover left him in no doubt of his desire. Not only was his face filled with lust, but the reassuring hardness under David's buttocks told him all he wanted to know. Tobias still wanted him as badly as he had the first day they had met. Once he was naked to the waist, David was suddenly aware of how grimy he was, and he looked down with some distaste at his torso which was covered in a mixture of bruises, dirt, and a soldier's tan. White scars stood livid against his skin, telling tales of sudden skirmishes, and although he knew that his body was far more mature than it had been the last time they had met, the ribs showing beneath the muscles spoke of hard soldiery and no excess of rations. David's fingers tore at the laces of Tobias' shirt, but Tobias stopped him, his hands masterful but gentle.

"Wait, David." David felt a pang of disappointment until Tobias grasped his forearm in reassurance. "Don't worry," Tobias said, "don't doubt that I still want you, oh *God* I want you—can't you feel it? But you are on a comfortable perch, whereas my old bones will feel it afterwards, if we stay on these cold flags, and anyway, you are filthy." He licked a finger, then ran it over David's grimy skin, leaving a cleaner trail. "And I dare say I look no better." He pulled David down and kissed him urgently and deeply, running his hands down his back, and David warmed again, shuddering with want, but Tobias pushed him away again, just as David was getting hopeful. "Patience. First we get clean, then we eat."

"But..." David said. He didn't know if he could wait.

Confronted by David's disappointed expression, all Tobias did was laugh. "Again, I say, patience! We have time now. Time and safety, which is something neither of us have seen for too long."

He got to his feet, but taking David in his arms again, he held him close, whispering into David's ear. "Is it not worth waiting for, David?"

All the dark thoughts returned; all that terrible time when he'd waited for Tobias in Kineton, only to have to admit that he was dead. He felt impatient and violent, wanted to be the aggressor for once, to adulterate Tobias, to claim a place for himself. To take and to never give back, to be for once the person who took; he felt he had wasted so much time in Hal's thrall, giving, always giving.

But he had been forestalled; frustrated by Tobias' sudden practicality, he was halted and dazed with want. He found himself seated at the kitchen table where Tobias had placed him. He watched Tobias as he moved about the small kitchen, finding kindling and logs, and lighting the huge fire, crouching before it as it caught.

Then Tobias turned to him, maddeningly calm. "This will take a while. Go back to the livery stable, and sell the horse. I'll be sad to see him go, but we need the money more. Give a false name and address, and answer no questions, we need to have no one know where we are. The ostler looked like a right bastard, but I don't think he'll give you any trouble—except I'm sure he will haggle over the price."

David left irritated, desire still flowing through him. After a bitter discussion with the ostler—who was, as Tobias had surmised, little more than a crook and a very hard bargainer— David lugged the saddlebags back to the house and let himself in. At least they had a little money now—the tack had gone with the horse, and in fact had fetched almost as much as the horse itself, but David could not deny that they had no choice but to take the best deal he could. The ostler was no innocent; it was clear that the horse was battle fit, and the harness and tack obviously military equipment. They were lucky to have sold them at all with no more than a hard bargain and a low price.

He hid the money in a pot in the press, while calling out for Tobias. There was no sign of the trooper in the small rooms downstairs, although the fire in the kitchen was burning well and a pan of warmed water was sitting on one side. David pulled his boots off, suddenly exhausted as the terror of the last week drained from him. Six days of riding hard, hiding in barns, in forests, dodging patrols…

Jonathan. In the days of their escape he'd kept the thoughts of Jonathan hidden in his heart, unable to speak of them, even to Tobias. What quirk of fate had made their paths cross in that place, at that time? If it wasn't for the memory of the blood seeping through Jonathan's shirt, and the sight of his sweet, pale face David would almost say that he'd dreamed it. *Was he alive? His face…his eyes…* It hurt him almost more than he could bear to think that Jonathan still hated him, blamed him. David still felt the same in his heart; if Tobias had not been there to drag him away, to begin their desperate flight for freedom, he'd have stayed with Jonathan. And no doubt been captured, or worse. *Oh, my Jon!*

People they'd met in their flight had been kind, some spectacularly so, had hidden the horse, hidden the two men—some in outhouses or haystacks, some in their own houses. They'd been invaluable for leads to other Royalist sympathizers, and in this manner David and Tobias traversed the seventy or so miles to London. There had only been one day, when they were skirting around Bedford, when they hadn't had to go to ground to avoid troopers. The patrols were seemingly everywhere

As they had neared the capital there were more soldiers still, and once they had even been stopped. They managed, thanks to David's purloined jacket and Tobias' knowledge and quick thinking, to convince the soldiers that they were returning to London ahead of the main force. But it had been a heart-stopping moment, both of them knew that if they were even suspected to have come from anywhere near Oxford, they would instantly be arrested as spies. Afterwards, as they slipped past the guards and into the city, David's hands were shaking so hard that he had to have some of Tobias' precious store of brandy to calm his nerves.

War, he had become used to; he had faced the enemy to kill or be killed, but the almost fanatical retribution that the Cromwell's troops were displaying in order to mop up all the Royalist troops deserting after Naseby was nothing short of terrifying. *"Better,"* Tobias had said, *"to have died on the battlefield than to suffer as a prisoner."* The thought of being caught chilled David's blood. Tales of atrocities had reached them in their flight. The Parliamentarians had slaughtered many of their prisoners, even killing and maiming the women who had followed the King's army at Naseby, slitting their noses to mark them as whores. Each new story sickened the two men further, and neither of them wanted anything more to do with the whole bloody mess.

Tobias was sure that they could fade away in London, hide any signs of either of them having been in the military, get employment, stay out of trouble. *Be safe. Be together…*Two men living in London would not raise the attention that the same would do in Kineton.

"David?" Tobias' voice rung from upstairs. "Come. I've got some food up here." David stood, his limbs leaden, feeling he needed to sleep, to crawl into Tobias' arms and not wake for months; the desire he had felt earlier had drained from him. He scaled the narrow stairs almost on his hands and knees, and stopped dead when he saw Tobias waiting for him. The trooper was a picture of temptation as he stood in the hallway, his jacket off, his shirt unlaced at the neck, his hair loose on his shoulders. He held a dusty bottle of something in one hand and a platter in the other, loaded with the last of their travelling supplies.

David groaned, thoughts of sleep sliding from his mind. "What a choice. Alcohol, food, or…" He stepped forward and put one hand behind Tobias' head. "I've made my choice."

Tobias chuckled and led him into the musty bedroom, putting the provisions down on the floorboards. The bedroom smelt damp, but to David it was private—and therefore paradise. Gently

Tobias pulled him down onto the bed, and slowly, deliberately, began to undress him. His eyes gleamed, and all the tiredness was pushed from David's thoughts as his excitement rose again. It was as if Tobias was unwrapping him, as if he were the most anticipated present Tobias had ever wanted. Gentle fingers ran up his thigh, and David's whole body shuddered in need and anticipation. "At last," he murmured.

"As you say," answered Tobias, "at last." He ran both hands into David's hair and looked deep in David's eyes. "I have few regrets in my life, but the day I was ordered to ride away from Kineton without seeing you again? That was one of my greatest. Just knowing you were back there, in the forge. Waiting..." His mouth closed to David's and delved deep, roaming at will, taking David's breath away as he remembered the sweet, warm glow Tobias gave him, so unlike the fiery violence of Jonathan. Tobias' hands slid between David's legs, kneading the firm thigh muscles, and David attempted to wriggle downwards, wanting those hands on his groin. He longed to be touched and each time his cock touched Tobias he almost cried out with need.

"*Patience*," Tobias murmured again. "Close your eyes, keep them closed." David did as he was told, and he was rewarded with a brief caress feathering over his scrotum. Tobias' weight lifted, then a delicious feeling of warm wetness swept up each leg and ended with a soft massage of the skin between his thighs. He squirmed in abandoned pleasure, spreading his legs wider and wider to allow Tobias more access, with what he now realized was a sponge.

"Don't stop..." David arched from the bed, hoping the sponge would be moving up further still.

"I have no intention of it. You appear to have mud *everywhere*." Tobias' voice was wryly amused. "Your face, Master David, is filthy." The sponge was rinsed again and David felt his face being wiped gently, and wherever the sponge touched, so did Tobias' lips. As the lips passed David's mouth, David attempted to capture the teasing tongue, but Tobias was moving onwards and would not be stopped. As sponge, fingers and hands explored his chest, swept over aching erect nipples and dragged slowly and blissfully southwards, David stopped thinking completely. With his eyes closed tight, all he could concentrate on was where that tongue would go next. It slid into a newly washed navel, then tickled its way down the trail of every flaxen hair from that point onwards and further down, till he felt the sponge rest lightly on the base of his cock.

"How you got mud here, I can't imagine."

David gasped as the sponge slid across the head, then arched as gentle fingers pulled back the foreskin and once again the cool sponge slid across the tip, which felt like it was on fire, and ten times bigger than usual. He gasped again as water ran in rivulets down the shaft and pooled around his balls before sliding deliciously between his arse cheeks. With his sight removed, every touch was a delight; his skin felt on fire with sensation and the anticipation of where the next touch would come from. It was hard not to pull Tobias down and to forget his orders, but he did it; for love of the man and for love of the sensations he was causing him.

When he felt his cock pulled into the sweet warmth of Tobias' mouth, he had to bite his lip to stop himself from spending immediately. He pushed his hips up, just a little, to stop that wicked tongue from wasting time around the crown. Tobias allowed it, taking David's cock deeper. Tobias kept his head still, and, encouraged, David began a series of slow and wonderful thrusts into his friend's welcoming mouth. It was like nothing he'd experienced before, and although he'd never taken a man in passion, he wondered if it could possibly be as beautiful as this. Was this the pleasure that Tobias took from him? That Hal had—that *Jon* had? Gradually he had to increase his speed, as he wanted release. His thrusts became faster and deeper. When he felt Tobias' hand between his legs, he spread his knees as wide as he could, thinking the man would stop sucking to enter him, but Tobias kept his head in place and slid a wet finger into David's entrance, sending David spiraling out of control as he felt his climax ripping through him.

He shouted Tobias' name, pushing the man's head down even further onto his cock, and emptying himself into Tobias' mouth.

The world went dim and heavy for a long while, filled with whispered endearments and a wonderful lethargy of limbs.

When he woke, the room was gathering darkness and Tobias was dead to the world—fast asleep, but holding David tightly to him with a fierce protective expression on his face. He looked so pale, despite his weathered tan. *Stern as a doomed prince from an older, more fabled time,* David thought. The lines of age and care were lessened but still visible. David knew then, with his strong arms clamped around him, keeping him safe, that he loved Tobias. It was a different love to how he'd felt—still felt—about Jon, but that love was all fire and violence and heat, like the furnaces in the forge, steel and hammering brute force. This was as different as it could be, gentle and patient. David felt that there was nothing more he needed right now than both of those virtues. He softly touched Tobias on the lips and the man's eyes flickered open. Tobias smiled, some of the care vanishing from his face.

"Are you ready to eat something now?" teased Tobias, but thought of food was abandoned once more as David slid down between his legs to repay him in kind.

Darkness, warmth, and a floor beneath his feet, but he dared not move in the darkness. Then the familiar fires, as fierce and as hot as a forge, but subtly and horribly different. Before they had been in front of him, but now they were to either side of him. He felt the heat, heard the roar of the flume of the inferno, but when he spun around to face it, it had gone, and the heat was on his back again— and every single time it was getting closer and he could never see it. He was being driven, herded by the flames, forward and forward into a blackness, into a future that was not of his choosing. There was no path—the fires gave out no light. His head rang with a persistent clanging of bells, and there was blood in his mouth, bitter, thick, coppery. He forced himself to concentrate— this couldn't be real; all he needed to do was to try and open his eyes, so with a huge effort he tried it and gradually light filtered into his nightmare. The fires receded and there was the familiar blond figure in white.

"David?" he called, but the man's face was hidden in his hands. He went to run forward, and lost his footing, fell...

And woke to horrible clarity, finding himself kneeling on the floor.

The clanging was still sounding somewhere far off; it sounded like the bells of Kineton church. *If I'm late, why hasn't Jacob called me?* He tried to stand, but nothing worked; his legs felt like he'd never used them before.

Strong hands lifted him, placing him back on whatever it was he had been lying on. Confused, and a little frightened, he risked opening his eyes. A man stood beside him, his shirt and face covered in blood, a terrifying vision. For one horrible moment, Jonathan imagined that his nightmare of blood and fire was coming true, until the face smiled at him.

"About time you woke up, soldier. You're not as bad as most here. How are you feeling?"

"Sick," said Jonathan, with some effort, "and weak."

"You'll be fine, but I don't know how much use your arm will be for a while. You'll certainly be no good to your regiment, but the way the day went, I doubt that will be a problem."

"We won?" Jonathan tried to sit up, but his shoulder screamed at him, with a fire that ripped down his spine. The surgeon helped him to sit upright, and by the time he was propped up, he was shaking, his forehead clammy and the blood pounding deep in his temples, like Ireton's drums.

"Aye, and roundly too. The King has lost a thousand men, and more than four thousand captured, together with the entire munitions. 'Twas a good day, with a tally of no more than three hundred dead on the side of the Lord." Jonathan went cold. All those dead. He had nearly died, and... *David!* His head swum and he fell back onto the pillow.

Then there was Adam. He'd promised his family he'd look after his brother with his life, and he'd failed even at that. For here he was, wounded but alive, and Adam was dead, two weeks since. One second he had been fighting by Jonathan's side, the next, blown to smithereens on a nameless field, leaving nothing of him to take home, nothing for their parents to bury.

How can I go home? he thought, blankly. *I can't face my parents—or Jacob*...Perhaps Jacob had got wind of the fact that he and Adam had been taken by force and pressed into service. Perhaps he might have guessed why the two of them never returned from the errand Jacob had sent them on into Kineton, but it was of no use. He couldn't go back, look Jacob in the eyes and tell him what David had done. How he'd behaved.

"Let me go Jon, for God's sake, let me go."

He remembered fumbling. Fumbling with his musket. Why had David waited so long, why had he waited for Jonathan to reload?

"No one will know; I could get away." Was he waiting to see if he would let David go? Was he so desperate to run away?

"Please John. If you ever loved me. Put down the musket."

He shot me! The bitter realization sunk in. *He shot me! Would I really have shot him?* He knew the answer without asking himself. Of course he could not, could never. Just the sight of his face again was the sun rising after months in the dark. Just the sound of his voice woke him from the sleep of the last year. *But he tricked me. He kept me talking and then pretended there were others coming, and then he shot me just so he could run away again...*

He tried to kill *me, to save his own skin.* Sweat broke out on his forehead, and the bed seemed to whirl in circles. The next thing he knew the surgeon's assistant was pressing watered wine to his lips.

"Easy, soldier. You're not ready to get out of bed for a while yet." Jonathan let the assistant check his wound, and clearing his mind of thoughts too complicated to deal with, he slipped back into unconsciousness.

◖◗ CHAPTER 18 ◖◗

The defeat at Naseby was devastating for the King. With the loss of the baggage train David had been guarding, all the King's arms and provisions had been taken. Even the King's private papers—sensitive material telling of his plans to bring over Irish Catholics to fight on his side—had been captured, and Parliament lost no time in publishing this information. In an England still very much against the Catholics, this news only helped to worsen the King's position when it came to finding new allies.

Happy, halcyon days stretched into a week and then into another before Tobias woke one morning and announced, "This must stop."

David lifted his head sleepily from Tobias' shoulder, pushed his hair out of his eyes, and squinted up at his frowning friend. "What?"

"This…this avoidance of life. We've been hiding, and that's more suspicious for anyone that was looking for the King's men than if we were out there in the open. All anyone needs to report is that there are two men in here that no one ever sees except to buy provisions, and someone will think we are hiding."

"Well, we are," David said.

"And we shouldn't. Not if we don't want the Roundheads knocking the door down before we can dress." David frowned, and that made the older man laugh. "All right, it's not that serious, or at least it isn't yet, but the money you got for the horse won't last forever. We need to start making acquaintances and finding employment, making new backgrounds for ourselves. We must not give any hints that we were ever in the army, on either side."

David sat up. "I could ask at the stables. They might need a blacksmith, or know of someone who does."

Tobias pulled him back down, kissing him briefly. "That's my boy. And I'll ask in the taverns; someone might know of something. We will have to husband the money we have."

David caught the note of concern in Tobias' voice and nodded, his head still on his lover's chest. He had a cold, sick feeling in his stomach. He had known that this idyll couldn't last forever, but he had been putting it out of his mind, pretending that this dark little house was their whole world, trying to ignore the big city out there, and the dangers it undoubtedly held.

"You're a blacksmith, David," said Tobias gently, "a craftsman—you shouldn't have any problems at all." David nodded again, glumly, without looking up. He hadn't the heart to tell Tobias that the difference between a trained apprentice, one who has completed his indenture, and someone who was simply trained in the trade because he expected to take over his father's business was enormous. "I'm the one who has no trade, after all. But there must be work somewhere. Men have been killed, there must be jobs—even if it is in a tavern."

"You'd work in the taverns?" David said, his father's upbringing showing just a little. David had frequented them, but wouldn't consider working in one.

"I'm a soldier," Tobias said shortly, swinging his legs off the bed. "I've done nothing else, save working on a farm. Nothing more useless than an ex-soldier in peacetime. Not that this is any kind of peace. We need to mingle, *carefully*, find out what is happening out there, whether the war goes on." He paused and looked blankly at David. "Only how it could go on after Naseby, I can't imagine."

David was quiet as he watched Tobias dress in clothes that they had found in the house. He wondered, not for the first time, what had happened to Tobias's uncle, why the house was deserted, but every time he tried to talk to Tobias about his family, the man changed the subject or instigated sex, which was a sure way of making sure the conversation ended fairly abruptly.

After a meager breakfast they set off, both men dressed in the only clothes they could find that did not make them look ridiculous—as Tobias' uncle was taller than David, shorter than Tobias, and stouter than the both of them. Dark jackets, small white collars, black hats they sufficed enough so they were not wearing obvious uniforms at least. What remained of their uniforms they'd burned.

The streets were busy, the streets damp after the night rain. The gutters ran yellow with urine thrown from windows. David thought he would never get used to the smell. As he crinkled his nose, Tobias smiled.

"Fairly strong, isn't it? Believe you me, in a month you'll be saying 'what smell?' to any newcomers."

David raised an eyebrow in frank disbelief but said nothing. He decided he'd try to develop the art of breathing through his mouth. At the livery stable, they parted company; Tobias wished him luck, and told him to make his way back to the house when he'd finished his search for work. David watched him walk away, a tall figure who, for all his height, was soon swallowed up in the throng. With a worried frown, David looked around him. The streets branched away from him in all directions, and he felt small and lost in a city where, apart from Tobias, he had no connections. Oxford had seemed big, but London was endless. If he had to start searching the streets, he knew he'd soon be unable to find his way back. With a resigned sigh, he pushed open the small door inset into the large coach-house gates and made his way between the lines of horses to an old shed at the back. He knocked, pulling his hat from his head as the door swung open. A large and swarthy man glared out at him. Thankfully it was not the ostler that he'd met when selling the horse.

The man still looked him up and down, suspiciously. "Who are you? What do you want?" It was obvious, David realized, that he didn't look like he had the price of a day's rental on him.

He took a deep breath and stepped into the shed; he had been a soldier after all, he knew a lot about standing up to people, although he was well aware that it was a lot easier with a loaded musket in your hand, or with a line of pike before you.

"Good morning, sir," he said. "I was wondering whether you would know if there was any work for a skilled blacksmith in these stables or any parts that you knew of." He felt like turning away and just getting out of there—the man was large, unfriendly and his odor overpowered even the stench of the stables.

"You know a skilled blacksmith then?" the man said with a crooked smile. "You still haven't said who you are. Can't blame me for being suspicious in these times, can you? Lot of the King's Army boys still on the loose, and we've been warned enough to look out for strangers."

David wanted to ask who had been doing the telling, but he could guess. "I never enlisted," he lied, knowing that was the safest option, rather than having to lie about which Parliamentary regiment he'd been in, as this man had the look of a soldier about him. "I'm a blacksmith, myself. My father needed me at the forge, although I would have fought of course, had I been able."

"Of course," the man said with obvious disbelief. "Pretty boy like you would have been first to join up, I'm sure." He moved around to a shelf of tools, effectively blocking David from the door. "Now I've been polite, and I've been patient. But if you don't give me your name soon, I'm going to have to ask some soldiers to ask you for it, instead."

"Forgive me," said David as earnestly as he could manage, feeling trapped and panicky. He used the name he and Tobias had agreed upon. "My name is David Gray. Our forge was burned by Royalists and my father was killed. I came to London, as I could not think of anywhere else to go. I had no money to rebuild my home. I've been working with my father all of my life."

"Please to make your acquaintance, Master Gray," said the man, shaking his hand with a crushing grip. "Ashwell, that's me. My father's father started a stable right on this spot." He stood back and looked David over once more. "Well you have the look of a man who's been in a forge, right enough," he said. "Broad shoulders, scarred hands. Them palms seem less callused than they should be, however," he said, obviously still wary.

"I've been travelling a long while," David said glibly.

"That may be," Ashwell said. "Well, there are few enough craftsmen coming back from the war. Get the bay from the third stall near the gates. He needs new shoes today. Show me what you're made of and I might give you a trial."

David swallowed; he had been about to point out that he was not merely a farrier, but a smith, able to forge more than bent pieces of metal, but he kept quiet. Admitting one could make swords and breastplates might raise questions as to whom you sold them to. He ducked under the man's arm, and found the required horse. He had his suspicions about his instructions, and these were confirmed when he took the halter from a peg and the horse attempted to bite him hard on the arm. Teeth snapped an inch away from his sleeve, but with a little struggle, David won the fight. He pushed the halter over the beast's ears and backed the horse out of the stall. As he turned round to lead him down to the back yard, the horse snaked his neck out and managed to bite David viciously on the buttock.

In a flash David spun around, grabbed the horse by the ear and bit down as hard as he dared without breaking the skin; for a moment horse and man were fighting each other, as the animal shook its head, attempting to dislodge the pain. Then David let go. The horse shook its head again and looked at David with white-rimmed eyes. David stroked the satin neck, hissing gently in ancient tradition until the horse calmed.

"Now you know that's it feels like," he said softly, "you won't do it again." He couldn't help but remember the first time his father had shown his this trick. *"No point hitting him, son," his father had said. "If a horse wants to punish another one, they bite or kick. That's what they understand. But do it fast."* He stood a moment in silence, remembering his father and wishing he could let him know he was alive. But Tobias had said how dangerous that might be, for David and Jacob both.

"You should have bashed him one," said Ashwell, who had come out to watch. "It's the only thing he understands."

"He wouldn't have understood that it was punishment," David explained, tying the horse up, and deliberately turning his back on him. "He knew what I did, and why I did it. He won't bite anyone again, I can guarantee it."

Without further comment, Ashwell stoked the furnace into life whilst David put on an apron and set about inspecting the horse's hooves. True to his word, the horse didn't attempt to bite him again, but it did try and kick him once or twice. Kicks were easy to dodge for a blacksmith, and the horse soon got tired of it. An hour later David straightened up, and a stable boy led the horse back to his stall.

"You'll do," Ashwell grunted, without any sense of whether he was actually pleased or not. "Start tomorrow. Wages are two shillings a week. with Sunday afternoons off and you'll live in the loft."

David paled at the paltry sum; he knew that if he had bothered becoming an apprentice, had papers to his name, he'd be worth five times that, but without those papers he was worth less than the hire of these horses. He had no choice. "I don't need to live here, I have a place."

"You'll live here or you'll not work here," the man said, walking up the aisle without looking back. "See you tomorrow at dawn. Or not. Suit yourself."

Jonathan stopped at a milestone, sat down on it, and stared into nothingness. Mechanically, he ate a little meat and bread from the small pouch at his side. He took scant pleasure from it. Once he would have given thanks to the Lord for the gift of the food; once he would have chewed, relished, enjoyed every morsel. But now he merely subsisted. He walked, he ate, he found a place to sleep. The next day, come rain, shine, snow, or hail, he would repeat it, walking ever onwards, not even aware of the direction his feet took him, or knowing where he was, not even caring.

He had shut himself down in a way he had learned as a child. When his brothers' teasing got too violent, when the horseplay got too much, when he wanted to be alone in a room full of the chatter of his brothers, he had taught himself to retreat completely into his mind. Since leaving home, he had found this the safest place to be in times of stress. His body took over, managing the tasks of the day-to-day, while his hurts were hidden behind what he knew to be a forbidding scowl which put off even the most genial of strangers.

Not that there were too many friendly faces in the country in the days and weeks after the battle at Naseby. Suspicion and fear reigned everywhere as Cromwell's troops rode out in ever increasing patrols, searching for the soldiers of the King who had fled for their lives. Many times Jon was detained, arrested, questioned, and each time he told them which regiment he had been in, and how he had been invalided out. They examined his shoulder, and so far they'd believed his story. But when questioned where he was going, Jon couldn't reply. He didn't even know where he was, and by the end of each session the soldiers were fed up and aggravated. Some became angry, denied their sport, and Jon often found himself on the wrong end of a Roundhead's boot, but they always let him on his way, wherever that was.

He had stopped thinking about David. He had stopped thinking about anything at all. Finishing the little food he had, he stood, and began the laborious process of living. *One step at a time...*

Some indeterminate time later—for he had long since lost count of the number of sleeps he had had—he found himself with company, among people dressed somberly, walking the same road. A few attempted to make conversation with him, but gave

up when he not only didn't reply, but didn't even seem to hear or
see them. He knew from prior experience that some would think
he might be a deaf-mute, others that he was backward or just unmannerly.

The chatter of the fellow travelers roused him somewhat, and
the fog of repression lifted as he took some stock of his surroundings. He was not in a town; indeed, he had avoided anything larger than a village for a long while, not out of fear of the
patrols—for word must have spread about him eventually and
even the more brutish patrols left him alone now—but due to an
unnamed need to stay away from human contact. At the brow of
a hill he stopped; below him and spread across the plain was a
sizeable town.

He looked at the surrounding countryside, searching for a way
to skirt around the town, when a rotund man who had been walking beside him in silence for some way, stopped with him, wiped
his brow with a grubby cloth, and leant against the fence where
Jonathan was surveying his options.

"If you've walked as far as me this morning, you'll be right to
rest." The man sat down on the grassy side of the track with a
grunt. Chatting volubly about the time he had left home and the
state of the roads, he produced a small stone jug from his pack.
He drank deeply from it and then offered it to Jonathan, who
frowned at the man in concentration, almost as if the man was
speaking a foreign language. In fact his accent was strange to
Jonathan's ears, and it was that which finally pulled him from out
of his mental hideaway.

He shook his head at the offer of the drink and spoke the first
civil words he had for weeks. "What town is that?" Deep and
husky with dust and disuse, his voice sounded like a croak even
to his own ears.

"Chelmsford. And not a better town this side of the country
if I say so myself. Some people leave to go to London looking for
their fortune, but most of them come back to Chelmsford in the
end. Mark my words, there's no place better. A God-fearing town,

never was there a more law-abiding town."

"Such a wonderful town, but thou dost not live here?" Jonathan asked, intrigued, in spite of himself. He could not help but feel drawn to the stranger's friendliness.

"You are perceptive, friend," said the stranger. "I would move to the town tomorrow, but my wife will not hear of it. She was raised in the town, me in the country. I had planned to give up my little farm and move to Chelmsford, but she has put down roots in my farm like a veritable oak. There will be no shifting her without an axe." The little man laughed again and held out a hand, "I'm Ben Fuller, at your service, sir. Have you come to see Hopkins at work?"

Jonathant introduced himself. He could hardly believe how far he'd come without even knowing it. Although he didn't know the distance he'd traveled, he knew that Chelmsford was as near to the coast as he had ever been in his life before. He resigned himself to the conversation, for to walk away from the affable little man would be rude, much as he hated to be ensnared in small talk.

"Hopkins?" he asked, in spite of himself, not really being able to think of anything else to say. "All these people are going to see this Hopkins... *work?* What work does he do that draws such a crowd?" No one had ever sat and watched him work, except the occasional curious boy or... He was grateful when Fuller interrupted his thoughts.

"Matthew Hopkins, lad! Surely you must have heard of him?" Jonathan shook his head.

"He's a witchfinder. *The* witchfinder. Has a gift. He can walk into a village and he knows where the evil is." The little man looked nervous, and he glanced about him at the dwindling numbers of people walking past. "It's uncanny, some say, unnatural." He lowered his voice "Perhaps as unnatural as the witches he seeks out. He's found more witches—"

"There was a witch in our village, or so they said," Jonathan murmured, remembering what his mother had told him. "Before

I was born. She drowned."

"Did they test her? Trial by ducking?"

"No," he said, frowning. "She just was found drowned in the duck pond one morning, but my mother said that afterwards they had the best harvest in living memory."

"She was a witch then," said Fuller, obviously impressed with this tale, but seeming slightly put out as well, that his own stories had been interrupted. "God struck her down, and lucky for your village, too."

Jonathan stood, and put a hand out for Fuller to help him up, and the two men walked over the brow of the hill, then down toward the town. As he entered the first built-up area he had been in since his barrack days, he was apprehensive, a little intimidated by the crowds, and nervous of the presence of so many Roundhead soldiers. There were still many troops dotted about, but now they seemed more interested in the main event, which was where the crowds were gathering around what Fuller explained was the Assizes building. Jonathan found himself carried along with the crowds, and when Fuller indicated they should enter the courthouse, Jonathan's curiosity made him follow his new acquaintance.

Fuller found a space by a large pillar, and they leaned against that. Jonathan's eyes drifted around, trying to make sense of the Assizes. He'd never been in a court of law before, had no idea of the process, the personalities, the procedure.

"That's Hopkins," said Fuller, pointing to a bench where several men and one woman were sitting, "in the tall hat."

Jonathan looked, interested in what they'd all come to see. He saw a physically slight man who seemed pent up in some hidden way. The man's fingers played with a sheaf of paper in his hands. As he talked to his companions, his mouth and face were mobile and expressive, and his other hand punctuated his speech, which Jonathan couldn't hear. Whatever he was saying, his companions appeared to be fascinated by it.

"Who are the people with him?"

"John Stearne is the man next to him. They are partners, although it is Hopkins who has the gift. Stearne is the one brings the miscreants in to justice, to be tried, and he keeps the account of their confessions. The woman's name is Goody Phillips. A saint amongst women, she only has to touch a witch for the truth to out. I don't know the other man, he's a new face to me."

Stearne seemed bookish, his long brown hair falling around his face as he bent over a parchment, writing with care and precision. The woman was haughty, or so it seemed to Jonathan. She dressed simply, but she held herself like he imagined a princess would: upright, regal and proud. Jonathan pulled his gaze from the woman and let his eyes rest on the other man, the man that Fuller didn't know. The crowd's chatter seemed to drift away, and the more Jonathan looked at the man on the end of the bench the rest of the scene faded away like hills covered with mist.

The sun was streaming through the side window and striking the group on the bench, as if they were touched with God's blessing. However, the man on the end hardly needed such gilding, for the golden curls of his hair were like the brilliance of wheat in late August. Backlit as he was, the brilliance of the aura around his face hid his features from Jonathan, but he continued to stare at the blond man, hardly aware of the Assizes bustling into life. Jonathan was fascinated by the play of light on his hair, the way the sun seemed to shine on him alone, creating what was almost a halo around his head.

Fuller kept up a running commentary throughout the morning, telling Jonathan where each witch lived, what the village or town had been plagued with, what horrors they had perpetrated, what familiars they were known to have. Jonathan had to concentrate to take it all in. Gradually, as the man poked his arm and pointed out more people he recognized, telling him all he knew about previous trials, Jonathan's gaze was torn from the man with the blond hair, and he had to focus to keep up with the constant stream of facts.

"A little girl died in this witch's village," the man said, as a woman, terrifying in her disarray, with wild eyes and sandy gray hair, was dragged into the center of the room. "After the child had made fun of the crone, she was found stone cold dead in her bed, and..." he lowered his voice, "there was a raven on the doorstep that morning, and 'tis well known that the hag feeds the ravens."

Jonathan nodded; the raven was the bird of the Devil, no one dared to feed them. Hopkins stood up, putting down his papers. Slowly and deliberately he turned to the crowd to give his report of the witch's confession.

Jonathan found Hopkins to be compelling. Unprepossessing and short when he was seated and silent, he was easily over-looked. But when the man stood to present his evidence, he clearly convinced all who heard him. He was eloquent, fiery, and full of a terrible conviction. He spoke to the crowd, telling them of the woman's crimes, her familiars—agents for the Devil—and in no time the court was muttering angrily of the wickedness of the woman on trial.

"We have tested this woman, and that is why she is here be-fore you today!" he thundered. "For she fooled us too when first we came upon her! Innocent she seemed to us, just because she lived alone, *just* because she grew plants poisonous and dubious, *just* because the villagers said that she was an evil influence, *just* because she had animals which seemed...particularly...close to her..." He paused to let the audience take this in and the crowd reacted angrily, shouting and denouncing the woman. Hopkins waited until the noise died down a little before continuing. "All this does not matter! For we do not try a witch on *hearsay!* I went to her cottage and the stench of the evil within it made me nearly insensible.

"Only by holding this handkerchief to my mouth," Hopkins continued, producing an embroidered scrap of material, "this sa-cred cloth, which has been washed in holy water and blessed by the Bishop himself, could I bear to breathe in the putrid air in that evil place.

"She fooled us further, for she was not frightened by us. Why should she be? The Devil looks after his own, she had nothing to fear from *me*—or so she thought! But she was wrong—for God is by my side and we are His instruments. Witches curse, witches commune with the Devil, witches are a direct conduit to hell and all its horror. But what else? *What else?*" he said, menacingly, stalking towards the woman, dramatically holding a long knife in his hand.

Women shrieked as he produced the knife. Hopkins stood before the accused, who seemed to have given up; slumped in her chair as if insensible. Jonathan felt the short hairs on the back of his neck rise. He straightened, suddenly aware that the court had gone silent, and that every eye was on the man with the tall black hat. Jonathan glanced again at the blond man at the end of the bench and saw that he too was watching Hopkins. Jonathan still couldn't see young man's face, as the blond waves of his hair hid his features in profile, but he was suddenly filled with a longing to see the face of the blond man, to erase the forlorn and futile hope that it might be at least close to the face he still wanted, beyond all reason, to see. He began moving, pushing people out of the way with hardly a word of courtesy.

Hopkins was continuing his impassioned evidence. "We all know that marks on the body are a sign of impurity—a way for the Devil to enter our souls and to take us over. Birthmarks, moles, stains on the faces and in places on the skin where we may not easily see. All these can announce the Devil's presence as he marks his victims." Hopkins tore the sleeve away from the woman's arm, and drew a knife from his beltwith a flourish, making her shrink with fear for the first time. "Here is the Devil's mark!" The assembled crowd gasped on cue as Hopkins pointed out a round, red birthmark. Jonathan passed the final bench, just as Hopkins stuck his knife into the woman's arm and the crowd exploded into pandemonium.

"*No blood!*" Hopkins roared. "There is no more proof required!"

The crowds bayed for the woman's death, and guards had to

restrain them from rushing forward and tearing her to pieces. Jonathan was caught in the crush, and fighting to get away without hurting a member of the public or striking a guard, when a hand pulled him out of the mêlée. He turned to his rescuer and met a pair of eyes, blue like periwinkles in the snow, a soft full mouth, and hair like spun gold.

"I'm Michael," the vision said simply. "Let's get out of here."

The man led him back behind the benches where the others sat, and out a side door. Distantly surprised that he was following a stranger so easily, Jonathan found himself being led along a short corridor and into a room in which there was a round wooden table, and a servant girl who bobbed nervously when she saw Michael.

"Food, good lady," he said courteously, and the girl dashed off, while Michael sat. The girl returned almost immediately with platters of meat, cheese and bread, and a flagon of ale.

Jonathan felt unsettled from the emotional scene they'd just left, and also he felt out of place—the paneled room, the gleaming table, it was more than he was used to. In his eyes, it was as if a nobleman had asked him to dine. He was not used to such luxury, however simple. The man smiled; in the dim room it was like a shaft of sunlight shone directly from his eyes, warming wherever it rested. "Please, do me the great favor of eating with me. And a further boon—that of your name." His voice was as warm as his eyes, his hands, like Hopkins, moved as he spoke.

"Graie," Jonathan said, not sure why he was here, and he felt dirty and clumsy.

"So formal," Michael said, sobering. "Well, Master Graie, the Assizes will go on for several hours yet, you will not miss much. We have found many evil women to be tried today. I have been up since before daybreak, and if I know my master he will keep me working until well after the sun has gone down tonight. I broke my fast more hours ago than I remember, and I do not like to eat alone. Would you refuse God's bounty? Will you not join me?"

Jonathan sat, clumsily, feeling rough and unpolished, knowing that he was nothing better than a smith and a common soldier. "And wilt thou tell me thy name?" he asked at last. "For I canst not call thee by thy Christian name."

"Giddings," said the man, breaking the bread in half and giving it to Jonathan. "My name is Michael Giddings."

"Thou must forgive me," Jonathan said, frowning, "but I am completely a stranger to this town. In truth I hardly know how I found myself here. I knowest not what goes on here, or why everyone has come to see—who is this Hopkins? For I have been told he is a witchfinder, and I have heard of them only in legend."

"Not heard of Matthew Hopkins?" Giddings exclaimed. "Have you, *hast thou*…been living in a cave for the last year?"

"Not a cave," Jonathan said, shortly. "No."

"In the Americas then, for you must have been far afield not to have heard of the great work we do here. 'Witchfinder.' Nothing so mundane, he is a *general*. He is at the head of a burgeoning army, which will sweep across the nation routing out evil in its path. A Witchfinder General." He poured them both a drink, and looked Jonathan over. "Army. You were in the army."

"And thou wast not?" The bitterness seeped out in Jonathan's voice; the Midlands had been so embroiled in the conflict, it seemed like it had been his life for so long. He couldn't really understand that somewhere there had been places it had not touched, that people still went about their everyday business without worrying about the desperate struggle for the survival of a country.

"I had other work to do, work just as vital as yours, soldier Graie. You were ridding the world of one evil; I help rid it of another. The Devil knows," he said, leaning across the table to Jonathan, his clear face full of earnest zeal, "when the barriers to this world are at their weakest. Times like now, when all men's eyes are turned away, when the Church is split, when the divine right of a ruler is questioned, when brother slaughters brother on fields of blood. The Devil knows, and he sees his opportunities. In the years since the war began, my friend, hundreds of witches have been found, biding their time, waiting for the opportunity to strike and *then*," he said, bringing his hand down hard on the table and rattling the plates, "it will not matter who is in charge of the country, for we will *all* have lost our souls."

Jonathan found himself listening, glad of the food and, if truth be told, very glad of the company too. Giddings was impassioned, committed, and he spoke from the heart. He told Jonathan about their methods, confirming what Jonathan had heard from Hopkins' words, that they did not just take people's accusations as proof, they questioned the accused, they searched their houses, they used the trials to give the accused every chance to prove their innocence.

"For we do not want to hurt the innocent. They have nothing to fear from us. Hopkins insists that in the trial by water, ropes are tied around the accused's waist, and if they sink, why then we thank the Lord and pull them back to life and redemption." He went on to praise Hopkins and Stearne, saying how it was a crusade now, and that the more good they did, the more good they had to do, for every day another village or town contacted them, begging them to come and make it clean. "The Devil is *everywhere*," he insisted. "At the moment it is just a few of us, but Hopkins dreams of an army. I was recruited in Swaffham, and I have been doing the Lord's work ever since."

Much, much later, Giddings wound down, and began to gently question Jonathan about his own life. Jonathan was unwilling to speak at first. He had no idea where to begin, and he didn't really know if he wanted even to do so. He was unused to speaking to strangers at all, and he was reluctant to speak of life before the army. In his regiment he had no friends to speak of, save his brother for a while—and that had been strained; nothing had really cleared between them since they had left their parents' home. He had been nicknamed "the Stoic" by some wag for his tight-lipped behavior. He held the memory of pre-Naseby David against his heart like a talisman. No matter what had occurred between them, David had loved him once. David was a subject he did not wish to speak of. He hardly knew if he wanted to tell this man anything, but after the man's hospitality it was hard to be unmannerly, so he spoke a little, and answered the best he could.

Michael Giddings sat and listened with the same degree of patient concentration that he had given to Hopkins. His chin in one hand, his light blue eyes steady and welcoming, he drew Jonathan out skillfully, almost imperceptibly. Asking a subtle question here, interrupting at a vital point, and artfully changing the subject then returning to it later so that the two streams did not seem to connect.

And while Jonathan spoke, at first haltingly and then with more confidence, Michael listened, and as he listened, he learned.

It was a gift he had developed young. Inquisitive and bright, he'd been called; the son of a clergyman, he had learned to read early. He had been fascinated with the glorious, golden glow of illuminated Latin long before he had managed to make any sense of English. He had learned the trick of observing people; perched up high in the gallery during his father's sermons, he absorbed the edicts of the church like a sponge, believing every word of fire and brimstone, pain and redemption, hell and damnation that spewed from his father's mouth. Fascinated, the boy had watched the congregation. He watched the pious and the bored. Learned when people were not paying attention and when they were dissembling. Discerned who did not believe, who pretended to do so and who truly did. While he was still young, before his father even considered him able to be a part of the church, he would mingle with the crowds after services, hearing, listening, learning what people said, gradually knowing that sometimes it was not what people said, but what they did *not* say that was important. Not their words, but how they acted, the looks they gave each other, the way their bodies spoke when their mouths did not.

In Michael's world, his father's church was everything—a place of worship, a meeting place, the center of the village. The pastor was the hub of it all, the driving force, God's own guardian against the Popish threat. Michael's father was a holy terror; anyone who did not come to church was shunned, and their place in village life destroyed piecemeal, until the offender fled or crawled back, repenting on his or her knees. Absenteeism was rare. No one missed church unless they were unable to walk. Samuel Gidding's ways of forgiving the defaulters were so stringent that grown men did not repeat the offence, and their fear of such violence being administered to their wives and children was enough to make them ensure that the entire family attended, regular as clockwork.

This then, was the world that Michael grew up in, flourished in. He learned to count by counting the congregationand reporting back any missing names, he learned his arithmetic from counting the offerings from the faithful, and he learned that it was not what you knew, but rather what you could convince others what you believed that was important.

And all this he learned in his father's church.

Jonathan was an open book to Michael. The young man did not want to say anything about his home life. He was deliberately coy about his time at a forge at Kineton, and yet he had already let slip the duration of his indenture and the date of his anticipated qualification. Michael now knew that Jonathan had not qualified, had been at Nottingham, bought by another master, and was then pressed by the army before he could earn his papers as a qualified smith. He learned that Jonathan had had a friend once, one he missed, that he'd lost a brother, and that he felt sorrow at letting people down. All he had to do was fill in the blanks. It was not difficult.

He watched and he saw through all the evasions and holes in Jonathan's story that the man had a darkness, a misery that he could not express.

Under Michael's studious gaze, Jonathan did not stand a chance of truly concealing his past. He was so guarded about it that all Michael had to do was to ask simple guileless questions, and that was for Jonathan, Michael could tell, just what he needed—a listener and a new friend—and gradually he raised his eyes and met Michael's warm stare.

What are you hiding? Michael wondered. Secrets fascinated him; all men had them, and all men were capable of spilling them, given the right incentive. It was simply a matter of finding the best way to bring them into the light. So, slowly, with friendship and companionship, he let Jonathan speak. At first there were just words, as Jonathan attempted to tell his tale, although it was obvious to Michael that he skipped important sections. But gradually, Michael drew him out, like a fisherman teases a trout from the reeds before gutting it and throwing it into the frying pan. Jonathan relaxed, and told Michael more than he ever realized he did, even down to the name of a friend he was clearly missing deeply.

And Michael smiled.

ᕤ CHAPTER 19 ᕥ

July, 1645

Two days had passed since his first meeting with Michael, and Jonathan found himself still in Chelmsford and strangely unable to leave. Dazed, numb, physically and mentally exhausted, he had simply run out of energy. There wasn't much further he could go, no further to the east at any rate, and he had no ambitions to go to London. The meager pay that he'd got from the army had almost been eaten up, so after Michael Giddings had offered him the place of somewhere to sleep, he'd accepted.

"It's nothing much; a blanket on a floor in my room at the Queen's Head, but you are welcome to it," Giddings had said as they had walked back to the Assizes after their meal. "Unless you need to be somewhere else?"

Jonathan had shaken his head and said he would think about it, but even then he knew he would take Giddings up on his offer. Now that he had let go, had let the world back into his life again, he found he was so tired that the thought of a bed indoors, even a floor, seemed like home. *And after all, where else do I have to go?*

For the remainder of the afternoon's proceedings Jonathan stood at the back of the courtroom, his arms folded, watching case after case come up. The evidence presented was meticulous and detailed, statements from neighbors, catalogues of herbs grown in gardens, lists of familiars, together with their behaviors. Not all the suspects were pricked, for some had already undergone the trial by ducking and it was not needed—the guilty had floated. That there was so many would have surprised Jonathan, if he'd thought about it at all; but after having listened to Giddings, the reasons for the influx of witchcraft throughout the country seemed logical and rational. Of course the Devil would find this time a perfect breeding ground for his evil—the whole world seemed corrupt to Jonathan's eyes; it needed an army for God to beat back the darkness.

Giddings didn't take any part in the trials themselves, but sat with Hopkins' other companions. He occasionally caught Jonathan's eye, as if to reassure himself that his new acquaintance was still there. Noticing this small attention, Jonathan felt the ice in his soul begin to thaw almost imperceptibly, for to have one person care whether he was present or not made him feel wanted, and that was a feeling he had all but lost.

Eventually, after a day of listening to further catalogues of evil and desecration, the cases came to an end. Hopkins had proved the guilt of more than ten women in one day, and they would be hanged at the next session.

The women accused had reacted in various ways. Some, like the first case he'd seen when entering the Assizes, had been limp, hopeless, seemingly uncaring of what was said either to them or about them. Others had screamed their innocence, even as the knife drew no blood, or a damning birthmark was shown for all to see. Some cursed the court and all the onlookers—proving, if proof were needed—that if they lay importance to curses, they must be guilty indeed.

As the final verdict was issued the crowd began to applaud Hopkins, cheering and calling out his name. He stood and took a short bow, before gathering up his papers and companions. He seemed eminently professional, and Jonathan was impressed with both his bearing and his good work.

Giddings waved as the party stood up, and gestured for Jonathan to join him. Weaving his way through the throng, he reached Giddings, who caught his arm and said, "Matthew, John!

This is the man I was telling you of." Hopkins and Stearne looked Jonathan up and down appraisingly, and Jonathan wondered what exactly Giddings had said to them, what they were expecting to see; surely not a footsore ex-soldier with dust on his boots and moth holes in his jacket.

He shook both of their hands. The woman had disappeared. "Did you watch the Assizes?" Hopkins asked. His voice was startlingly different in conversation than it had been in court, enticingly soft, and with a countryside burr to it that it did not have in his public address.

Jonathan nodded, a little tongue-tied.

Hopkins led the way out of the court and Jonathan fell into step beside him at the invitation to join them. "And what is your opinion?"

"I don't know if I have one, as yet," Jonathan said carefully. "'Twas clear to me that the women were guilty, but I should like to know more of thy methods, to see how this is proven."

Hopkins gave a short laugh. "A veritable Doubting Thomas, Michael, this soldier of yours! We will have to see what we can do to convince him. Let us hope that he does not wish to put his hand into the spear's wound." Jonathan frowned at the near blasphemy, but Hopkins' next words caught him by surprise. "You will dine with us?"

Jonathan attempted to refuse, but his eyes and disheveled appearance must have belied his words. Hopkins would not brook any refusal. "We will feed you and then we will convince you, Thomas. Evil is spreading through this country like a plague, and we need rational solutions, not baying hysteria. Your questioning is what this army needs, for I think we need to have you, Thomas. We need a converted doubter who can convince others. Come." He pushed open the door of the inn, and in no time Jonathan found himself clean, fed, and sitting by a large fire with the three men as they talked on and on about their crusade.

Hopkins and Stearne disappeared for an hour or two, and while they were away Giddings went to his room to fetch a huge pile of papers and notebooks that he placed before Jonathan, and sitting close to him, his blond hair almost touching Jonathan's dark locks, he read out previous successes, trial transcripts, and confessions; most of which Jonathan found dreadful to hear in their wickedness. By the time Hopkins returned, alone, Jonathan was as convinced as he would be that if they asked him, he would join.

Hopkins quizzed him with none of the twisting subtlety of Gidding's earlier talk, but this time Jonathan was receptive and more open. He knew that if he had been interrogated so frankly by Michael he would have shut up like an oyster, and probably left the town that night, but now he was intrigued; he had met people who were doing good, doing something to improve life for everyone. That had been the talk in the army, that they fought to improve the lot of the English, but now Jonathan could see all they had done was wallow in bloodbaths and that Cromwell's war would improve life for few.

This cause seemed real to him. Here was evil he could see, right in front of him. Not hidden away in a palace swathed in golden robes, here was evil he could touch, a canker spreading through the land, a sickness that had to be cut out. The need to belong loomed large in his mind. He wanted to work, to be useful, and most of all he wanted to stop running.

"You have come along at an opportune moment," Hopkins remarked, lighting a clay pipe. "Michael has already explained to you that we are nothing more than the advancing scouts in this battle of ours? We have laid the foundations of our work, and now we feel that it is time to emulate our Lord—to gather in disciples to our cause, and to spread the word of the evil that threatens us all."

"Master Giddings was most eloquent," Jonathan said quietly, "and thy cause can be nothing but just, for witchcraft must be rooted out."

Giddings gave him a slow, warm smile at this, which melted the remaining ice in Jonathan's soul. "And shall he join us then?" said Giddings, turning to Hopkins with a strange look. Jonathan was briefly reminded of the way a puppy eagerly looks to his sire, Gidding's deep voice holding a tense edge of frustration. "I am ready to teach *now*, Matthew, you have said so yourself. Now is the time for me to branch out, with a neophyte of my own, to expand our operation, at last Please, Matthew?"

Hopkins looked at Giddings for a long while, without changing his expression. The smoke in his pipe poured upwards towards the rafters and the group was silent. Jonathan found he was digging his nails into his palms, for he wanted nothing more than to stay with these people, good, pious, God-fearing people, and learn their ways. He wanted to look at Hopkins with the same pleading expression as Giddings, but he dared not, so he kept his eyes on Giddings himself, pleased and surprised that his new friend seemed to want him to stay as much as he did himself.

Finally, Hopkins turned to Jonathan, "Well, young man—what do you say? Would you wish to join us, seek the truth, have Michael guide you? Do not say yes lightly, for the path is a hard one." The full force of Hopkins' attention was unnerving, making Jonathan feel unsure and vulnerable

"I would, sir. I am only a blacksmith—and a soldier..."

"And now you are a soldier in the army of the Lord," Hopkins said, holding out a slim, pale hand.

Jonathan's returning handshake was firm, his eyes bright and eager. He belonged somewhere again.

Now, two days later, Jonathan sat waiting for Giddings. They were to break their fast together, and then go to the village of Writtle to investigate reports of a woman who had been seen wringing the neck of chickens at midnight under a full moon. As Giddings joined him, calling for the wench to serve them with a breakfast "fit for hungry soldiers," he gave a wink at Jonathan, and Jonathan could see that Giddings' face was lit with the anticipation of a case of his very own.

Jonathan felt the lightness of his purse and attempted to convince Giddings that he was not hungry.

"Firstly," Giddings said, "from now on, you are to call me Michael. At least for now," he added mysteriously. "And secondly, I'm hungry, and I had a large dinner last night whereas you, if I remember, had a chicken leg and a piece of bread. I don't want you to hide things from me. If we are to be friends, and I hope we are, friends and colleagues, I need to be able to trust you." He put a hand over Jonathan's as it lay on the table, "I think trust is one of the most important things between friends." He took his hand back and looked Jonathan deep in the eyes. "Without trust you have nothing."

Jonathan flushed. Michael had a way of seeming to look inside his head. He seemed to be able to pull out the thoughts and worries, to read all his doubts and concerns. Jonathan was unused to talking about money, but two nights in an inn was something he'd not done before, and he was unsure if he had enough money to cover his expenses. On the march he had stayed at inns before, but that was as many men into one room as could be squeezed in, and the army didn't bother to recompense the landlord—he'd be lucky if the place wasn't burned down, especially if the battle or skirmish was lost. Even sleeping on a rug on the floor of a rented room seemed luxurious, particularly if you could not pay your way.

He looked at his empty plate and tried to make his stomach stop growling. "Thou hast been very good to me, and I appreciate Hopkins' offer, but I must now go and get work, for I have been a burden. It is not something I have been before."

He looked up to see Michael's eyes full of surprise. "But you *have* work, Thomas," he said, using the nickname the group had been employing since their first evening. "Did you not realize that Matthew is now your employer? It will never make you rich, but it would seem that you are not used to excess. You may get a little spending money from time to time, but you need not ever worry about food and shelter. We are your new family, Thomas, and if we did not make your mind easy on that matter, and if you ate lightly last night for our lack of explanation, then we are all at fault, and ask your forgiveness."

Jonathan felt as if a weight had lifted from him. "Hopkins, is he a gentleman or a lord?" He'd seen lords, riding incredible horses, their uniforms pristine, their harnesses dripping with ornamentation. They all looked the same, though, when they were dead in the mud.

"I do not know," Michael replied, "but I would imagine so; he knows so much and speaks many languages."

Jonathan nodded; that spoke of proper schooling, something else he had never known, something reserved for the rich.

Michael went on. "He has a commission from the government to pursue this work. We are authorized by the country, and of course by God, to ask for up to twenty shillings per witch. People pay, of course; they are only too glad to be rid of the evil influences in their towns and villages. We have more work than we can do."

Jonathan was startled at the sum, but he did not comment. He needed no pocket money; he did not gamble or drink for pleasure. If his accommodation and food were paid for, he had nothing else to worry about. Whatever the salary, meager or nonexistent, he didn't worry if his living expenses were paid. After all, isn't that how an apprentice lived? He was simply another apprentice, learning a new trade, one for which some day he would be paid as no doubt Michael was, maybe not in money, but, like him, being allowed to take on a student, a neophyte under his wing, and pass on the knowledge that Jonathan was about to learn.

For a young man with no education, his future now seemed assured and full of purpose. He thought for a long moment, thinking how to sell himself, how to seem someone worthy of Michael's time. Then he realized that Michael had already decided to teach him, had already championed his entry to the Witchfinder Army, and that he was already accepted.

"I...was embarrassed," he saidi honestly, "for having no money."

"You have—nay..." Michael's voice dropped to a dark purr which made Jonathan warm as he changed his mode of speech to suit Jonathan's, "*thou* hast nothing to be embarrassed about. Thou wert honest, and I do not feel that thou hast any deception in your soul. I feel here," he touched his own chest with the flat of his hand, "that thou art searching for answers thou canst not find."

"Art thou mocking me?" said Jonathan, his brows constricted with a little anger.

"Nay, sweet Thomas," said Michael, touching his hand once more. "I was simply attempting to make you feel more at home. Matthew Hopkins is a committed Puritan—as are we all, but we have all broken away from much of our lives, simply because of the need to travel further afield, to be accepted wherever we go, to make our work easier." He called for a second time for a breakfast for Jonathan, and this time Jonathan did not object but ate it, under Michael's happy smile.

The day David was offered the job at the livery stables, he had returned to the house and waited for a Tobias who didn't come home. All day and through the night David fretted, unable to sleep soundly, waking every time he heard a sound in the street. As dawn lit the sky with pink and orange, he rose, worried and tired, and walked down to the stables, knowing it was pointless to search for Tobias in the maze of streets and seemingly endless taverns.

He was sick at heart, terrified that something had happened to his friend, and despaired at knowing no one in this seemingly vast and unfriendly city. Ashwell was not about when he arrived for work, but there were a couple of young lads grooming horses and cleaning harness. When David's questioned one of the boys, it seemed clear that Ashwell was expected. The boy led him up a ladder to the loft space above to show David where he'd be sleeping. David's heart sank; it was just that, a loft. A huge space, ranging across the whole of the stables, used for storing hay and straw, old smithing tools, and dry, crusted harnesses. At one end of the loft was a straw-filled mattress, a grubby bolster, and one rickety table, at the other was an obviously well-lived in area for the two other boys.

The bareness depressed him. He'd never been used to luxury, but he'd been used to better than this, even at the Oxford barracks. Slowly he put his meager belongings on the floor by the bed, then went downstairs to light the forge.

By noon he was tired, by six he was physically drained. There had been no live-in farrier for several weeks, and the horses had been seen to on a needs basis. That meant there was a lot for David to do, and more nags out of commission than not. As soon the stableboys realized there was to be a farrier on the premises full-time, they brought their charges to him. Shoes were missing, hooves were overgrown, some horses needed bleeding, some drenching, others rasping. David worked hard, and when he'd finished tidying the forge and banking the fire, he was ready to climb the ladder and sleep the sleep of the dead. But he'd been worrying about Tobias all day, meant to find out if he'd been back to the house on Addle Street.

As he pulled the main door open to leave, Ashwell entered, a stink of stale beer and urine hanging about him. "Where do you think you are going?" he demanded, blearily.

"Out," said David. "I'm hungry and would have thought for the pittance you are paying me there would have been some food available, but seemingly not." Any trouble from this man now and David knew he would swallow his pride and sweep the floor of a tavern rather than come back.

"It's curfew at sunset," was all Ashwell said. "Make sure you are back by then. There are troops on the street at night, and I'll not be getting you out of trouble with Cromwell's Apprentices."

"Of course," said David, fuming, though he hadn't known about the curfew. He had seen gangs of the Apprentices, though. Shaven-headed thugs in uniforms. He'd not like to run foul of them during the day, let alone at night. He fairly flew back to Addle Street, in the door and up the stairs. "Tobias?"

His lover was not back. David paced the small house as the day darkened, made a hasty meal, but when the sun started to disappear he had no choice but to leave and run back to the stables.

Thankfully Ashwell was not about. David could hear the man singing drunkenly in his shed, so he climbed the ladder as silently as he could, his shoes in his hand, and, filled with a sense of loss, he fell onto the bed in a heap trying not to imagine where Tobias might be.

The next day he was still worried, but resigned. He would look for Tobias tonight, curfew or not. London might be enormous, but Tobias had set out from here—someone must have seen him. Parliament controlled London, and David's biggest fear was that Tobias had been arrested for being in the King's Army, but he refused to acknowledge that might be a fact, not yet.

The second day of work was as hard as the first, but by noon David had shod all of the shoeless horses to his own satisfaction, even though his spine ached, and he felt he might never be able to straighten up again. It had been a long time since he had shod horses, and he'd never done so many, one after another like this.

When lunchtime came so did meat and beer and bread, but as pleased as David was that his words had gone home to Ashwell's conscience, he was almost too worried about Tobias to do it justice. To try to distract his mind from the vision of Tobias dead in an alley somewhere, he got talking to one of the boys, learned both names and a little about them. They were both orphans, as far as the boy knew, and he was a little reticent about what they had both done before getting jobs with Ashwell. At first David was concerned that the boys were little more than slaves, but they seemed happy; they got a shilling a week each, and they were fed and had somewhere warm to sleep. The boy in turn questioned David, and he easily told him the same lies he'd told Ashwell.

The afternoon he spent working on one of the carriages for hire, reforging pins and checking the strength of the axle. Lying flat under the carriage, banging out one of the bent connections, he felt his boot being kicked.

"I would recognize those legs anywhere, even with too many clothes on."

Tobias... With a grin a mile wide David pulled himself out from under the carriage and scrambled to his feet, just managing to resist the temptation to gather the taller man into his arms and kiss him until their lips bled. "So this is where you've been all day," Tobias said with that slow sensual smile that had David's blood pounding in his veins.

"Where *I've* been!" David's temper nearly snapped at the injustice and the sleepless nights. "Where have *you* been?"

"Getting work, Davey-boy!" Tobias beamed, and David realized the man was more than a little drunk. Ashwell was lurking around in the back, so David shoved Tobias down onto a bench and got on with some work, unable to resist checking on Tobias from time to time. At first the man watched him work, a stupid smile on his face, but after half an hour, David looked over only to see he was fast asleep. David was glad of it, for it gave him an excuse to leave with Tobias at the end of the day. "My cousin," he explained to Ashwell, when the man finally noticed the stranger. "And I am ashamed to say he was celebrating new employment. I'll take him home—to make sure he gets home safely." David woke Tobias, none too gently, and together they wove their way the short distance back to Addle Street. Once home he closed the shutters, then pushed Tobias into a chair and started to take his boots off, but he had only just managed that when Tobias made a spectacular recovery from his drunkenness and pulled David onto the chair with him.

"You were pretending?" David asked, getting more annoyed by the moment,

"Absolutely," Tobias said with a grin, unlacing David's shirt, "or mainly so, at least. If I hadn't been so drunk, your scowling and most attractive employer would likely have thrown me out, and I wanted to feast my eyes on this pretty face," he kissed David, "and this delectable fundament." His hands slipped beneath David's buttocks and cupped each muscled cheek.

David attempted to stay angry as he jumped up. "You could at least tell me what employment you have," he scowled as fiercely as he could, but it was not an expression he was used to, and it simply made Tobias laugh.

"I've missed you," Tobias whispered, kneeling on the floor as he undid and pulled the breeches from David's legs. "I've missed this." He kissed David's flat stomach, teasing the sparse hair with his tongue. "And this." He suckled the swollen head of David's cock. With rough, eager hands he pulled David down onto the floor with him. "But most of all I've missed this," and he claimed David's mouth again in the kiss he'd been waiting for all afternoon.

Everything melted away after that: anger, time, place. There was nothing except Tobias. Perhaps it was because of the time he'd spent fretting, perhaps it was because he had been so very tired, but David's limbs felt like lead; his mind slowed to a crawl, and it was as much as he could manage to lie on the floor and to be worshipped, for that's how it felt. Tobias, always a gentle and considerate lover—never the desperate vortex of passion that Jonathan had been—was that evening so tender and languidly demonstrative that it brought tears to David's eyes. Every time David attempted to repay the compliments of kisses and touches, Tobias pushed him back down, it was if he was apologizing for his absence in the sweetest way, with his mouth and hands, when he was uncertain that mere words could manage the task.

On and on Tobias went, his fingers teasing David's tenderest places, cupping his scrotum, sucking his member for what seemed like hours, until David's body, tantalized beyond reason, rebelled. In desperation he began to push his cock through the imprisoning hands, and in seconds he climaxed with an almost inaudible sigh of contentment. Tobias lay still, holding him close, and David suspected they were both thinking of the same moment, of their first encounter long ago in Kineton, when Tobias had given pleasure to a receptive, wanton boy. It seemed a lifetime ago.

They ate there, on a blanket on the floor of the kitchen, in front of a fire that Tobias had lit, with Tobias sitting, propping up David's weary body. They talked of David's work while Tobias fed

David as if he were a baby bird, popping a morsel in his mouth whenever he turned for some. As the meal progressed, kisses would sometimes be substituted for food, hands that should be slicing the next piece of meat were roving to a newly erect cock, and before the end of the meal they had slid back down onto the floor, food forgotten.

Afterwards, Tobias watched David sleep, having promised he would wake him before sunset. He knew, had known almost from the first moment they had been reunited, that he would fall in love with David, but he had not expected that it would be as deep as the well of feeling he now had. Just to look at David hurt, made him feel fiercely protective. But he knew life was too uncertain to fall in love, particularly for men with men. They could be betrayed, arrested, murdered, jailed, executed. London was a good place to disappear, but it was still fraught with dangers, each one as terrifying as the Roundheads.

Tobias knew that he must guard his heart, and not let David know just how much he was loved. David must be free to go if he wished, and that very thought was almost too much to bear.

Tobias wondered if David would leave him if he found out the truth about him, and hoped to God that he never would find out.

✬ Chapter 20 ✬

Tobias folded his arms. "It's my choice, David. It's what I can do. And you were the one who thought working in an inn was beneath me."

"I think I would rather you had got work in an inn, after all." David pulled on his shirt. He knew he was frowning, knew he was being unreasonable, but couldn't stop himself. He was tired, and the nap had hardly been enough.

"We can't live on the money you are earning, and a potman's job would pay no better," Tobias said, evenly.

"Yes. You said." The argument was going round in circles. "But we could manage on it."

Tobias sighed and stood up, pulling on his breeches. "This is good money, and after a trial I'll get an increase, with bonuses if I actually do something positive, like protect my Patron—"

"Get yourself killed, you mean."

"No... If Roundheads couldn't do it, then footpads are not going to manage it, are they? Give me a few months, then you can give up this slavery you are doing, and we can be together here."

"It's too dangerous, and I don't like it," grumbled David, realizing that Tobias was not going to back down. He rammed his hat on his head and left, without letting Tobias answer. He was fuming at Tobias' stupidity. Did he not think that three years of war was enough? Was that not dangerous enough for him? Surely there was something else he could have done rather than join the personal bodyguard of some nobleman David had never heard of. As he stalked through the darkening street, Tobias' words came back to him. *"There's nothing more useless than a soldier in peacetime..."* Technically they weren't at peace yet, but he knew Tobias spoke truth. Tobias had actually suggested more than once that if they went to the continent, they could both join the armies of the Dutch, who were, according to Tobias, on the King's side. But David had had enough of war, of losing friends. Had enough of lice and starvation and mud. He didn't think it would be any better in Europe. More than once he had even considered going home; he hated the way he had left his father, and now he knew that Jonathan had also deserted the forge, he worried how his father was managing. The shame he had brought on his father remained an ever-present stigma, and the thought of his father's disappointed face had stopped him from contacting him. It was more than likely that Elizabeth had had her child, and some other man had taken her on, but he couldn't rely on it, and there was no way of finding out, not safely. So he had convinced himself that it was probably better for everyone if Jacob believed his son was dead, although the weight of his guilt and sadness never faded. *And what would I say to Tobias if I went?* He couldn't exactly expect the man to be satisfied in Warwickshire.

Tobias had been so pleased about his new employment, at least until the argument started. His delay in returning to his uncle's house had been caused by meeting men in various inns who had pointed him on to another place where he might find work, and then to another, until he was too far away to try and break curfew to get back to Addle Street. And he was too much in his cups to attempt it.

On the second day he had trawled further afield and eventually got lucky; he had been given the address of a nobleman who had recently lost a guard and was looking for a militarily-trained man to replace him. Tobias had to prove his worth, showing his skill in both sword and musket before the man accepted him on a month's trial. It was a Godsend, Tobias told David. After all, the city was flooded with military-trained men.

"And it is not as dangerous as you think," Tobias had said, going on to explain that his new drinking companions had told him that there was better law enforcement in the city now than at any time before.

David was still unconvinced. Tobias had not told him what had happened to the previous man-at-arms, and the deft way Tobias had changed the subject worried David even more; he had learned that Tobias' skillful manipulation of a subject meant he was hiding something.

As David threw himself onto his mattress in the stables' hayloft, he wondered about all the other gentle evasions Tobias had given him. Now that he came to think about it, there seemed to be a lot of them. David realized he knew almost as little about Tobias now, as he did back in Kineton.

Work at the stable settled down once all the neglected animals had been attended to. Ashwell had copied Thomas Hobson's method of hiring out: the freshest animal was the one placed nearest the door, and this rotation meant that no one horse was overused, and usually, the shoes received equal wear. The bulk of David's day was spent repairing tools and implements brought in by others, or with the horses of travelling men, put up for the night. These were the most irksome because often a horse would be brought in late at night, the owner bashing on the barn door until he was heard, and he would need the horse again early in the morning to continue his journey. If the animal needed a shoe, it was up to David to start the forge, however late it was, and to attend to the beast. The horses Ashwell owned and the horses at livery were a known factor. The boys who attended them knew their quirks and vices, and between them and David's experience, they managed to avoid accidents, but the temporary boarders were always a risk. Having to deal with a biter or a rearer, single-handed and late at night, was always an unpleasant experience.

As for Tobias, David saw little enough of him. His job being of higher importance than David's, Tobias was granted a full day off each week, but it was changed from week to week, and it rarely coincided with David's Sunday afternoon. In his precious few hours of liberty, David would walk down to the Thames or up to Spitalfields and pretend that he was back in the country, back by the banks of his river. He had plenty of time for introspection, and he found that more often than not, Jonathan's accusing, suspicious face was in his thoughts. He prayed that Tobias was right, that Jon's injury could have been treated, that he had survived the war. He hoped beyond hope that one day Jonathan might forgive him, if he lived, and would find a life with some happiness in it. *God knows that you deserve it, Jon.*

There were a very few hours in a week that David and Tobias did manage to be together; evenings when Tobias would creep into the stables, they could do nothing but sit and talk, mindful of the two young boys, curled up together like puppies in a basket on the other side of the loft. The best times of all were the Sundays when they could be together. They usually spent them in bed, relearning each other's body. Each time was an exciting reunion, made sweeter by the time they spent apart.

Writtle, Essex

The village was quiet as Michael and Jonathan entered, men were out in the fields, women busy in their houses. It seemed unnaturally quiet to Jonathan however; there was a lack of movement so noticeable that even the very birds seemed stilled.

"It's so quiet," Jonathan said.

His friend's face was a picture of concentration. His head was lifted, he seemed to be listening and scenting the air all at once, his face beautiful as the late summer sun lit it. "It's typical of the atmosphere of a cursed village," explained Michael. "Supernatural forces are keeping even the children and animals in check. See how the cows are lying down, and there are no dogs on the street, no children? There is fear here."

"Perhaps we should have brought one of the others," Jonathan suggested, looking around him as they moved forward.

"No, this is my test," Michael replied, his face fixed with a firm expression. "And my reward will come after." When pressed for what reward he meant, Michael did not answer but kept walking until they came to the small, cobbled, village square. Michael sent a man to ask for the Elder of the village and they waited by the well, Michael's concentrated silence curbing any conversation. Suddenly feeling chill with fear of what they might find, Jonathan dropped to his knees and prayed. He wondered if God was listening to him, after his denial of Him, *but surely*, he thought, *he must know that I plan to atone for straying from his path? I do His work now.*

After a lengthy wait, a red-faced man approached them. Introducing himself, he led them down the hill to a grassy lane. "The hag's name is Margaret Wenham—"

Michael stopped him with a wave of his hand and a smile. "We will not begin our investigation by judging her in advance," he said. "We will speak to her, and if necessary question her in front of witnesses. We will need to speak to those witnesses too. We are not barbarians," he said, and he gave Jonathan the golden smile that he was beginning to know so well, the smile that drew him in, made him feel part of the family, important.

The Elder refused to come any further down the lane, but pointed out the tumble-down cottage with the decaying thatched roof that they could see in the distance.

Jonathan was struck by the normalcy of the situation. It was a beautiful day, two friends walking down a grassy track, what could be more ordinary? Michael whistled as he strode beside him. Jonathan could hardly believe that they were going to see someone whose very life was in their hands—who, by the end of the day might be confined, awaiting trial. The responsibility made him clench his fists and his mouth compressed into a tight line. His new friend noticed his expression and the fact that his pace was slowing, so he stopped and turned to face him.

"Thomas," Michael said, "sweet, doubting Thomas." He leaned forward and tucked a rebellious strand of hair behind

Jonathan's ear.

"I am…frightened that we may judge wrongly." Jonathan said, haltingly. "Hast thou ever sent an innocent to death? What would be our punishment in the next world if we killed, *murdered…*" Jonathan's mouth was dry, his thoughts tumbling over themselves.

"Sit down for a moment," Michael said gently. He sat down on the verge and pulled Jonathan down with him. "It is best that we discuss this now, for if you show any fear or uncertainty when we start, the Devil will take advantage of you. I had the same fears when I began, believe me. My mortal soul is the most precious thing I have, and I guard it as zealously as I do my chastity." He took Jonathan's hand in both of his. "How could I ever consider taking an innocent life, when I would be damned for eternity? Would God allow it? Of course not. God will not let this happen, and we must trust in Him. I am not as adept as Mistress Phillips, nor do I have the insight of Matthew or know the right questions as infallibly as John Stearne, but I trust in the Lord. He has never let me down yet."

"What will we do?" asked Jonathan, flushing as he realized that Michael still held his hand. He pulled it away, feeling awkward, but Michael took it again, firmly, and with a gaze so serious, so honest, that Jonathan could not help but be persuaded by his words.

"We will talk to the woman, and we will use our eyes. If we have any suspicions we will say nothing, and leave it to the others. We cannot search her person for signs of witches' marks or strange additional malformities such as witches often have; not without Goody Phillips. But if we suspect her of harboring familiars such as the Clarke witch did, or of performing the rites her neighbors say they have witnessed, then we have the right to have her arrested and charged. We can perform the trials, if we are in any doubt—ducking, pricking, either will suffice, but I would rather question her first. I don't like ever to duck an innocent." Michael slid his fingers to intertwine with Jonathan's. "Please don't worry. If she has nothing to hide, then she has nothing to fear."

Thus reassured, Jonathan stood, pulling Michael up with him, their hands still linked. Michael was too close to him as he stood, his slender body brushing against Jonathan's as he gained his balance, giving him that smile that Jonathan hadn't seen him give to anyone else. Was Michael trying to tell him that he knew? That he understood Jonathan's perversions? Shared them? Jonathan shook these thoughts away; Michael was a friend. He was handsome, it was true enough, but not all handsome men were attracted to men. Jonathan had learned that this was anything but common.

In the army, Jonathan had learned much about men's sexual needs. Away from women, many men turned to men as being the next best thing, not for companionship or love, but for sheer physical gratification. There were a few there who took what they wanted, but most were safe from unwarranted advances; it was the slighter, more boyish soldiers who were favored, and Jonathan, being tall, broad, flat-cheeked, dark-haired, was not considered attractive enough to bother with. He had received an occasional hint here and there, but experience soon showed him that the best way to deal with it was to pretend complete ignorance. He found that his disgust was no protector from sin however, and he was often aroused when he heard the unmistakable sounds of creaking beds in the night, slapping flesh and groans of completion. He had been ashamed to be so aroused, but he had been unable to control the lusts of his body from responding.

Nor had he been attracted to any other man, in all the time since David had deserted him, *betrayed* him. How could he even look at the unwashed beasts who shared his billet when he'd known someone like David? He knew, for certain, that he would never love a woman, but his eyes had not been drawn to anyone since David. Even the younger, prettier boys did not tempt him, for they were too popular, and his skin crawled to think how many beds they had shared.

The signals that Jonathan picked up from Michael were subtle, but to Jonathan they seemed bright and clear, and for the first time in over a year Jonathan was uncertain whether to squeeze that hand in his, to pull Michael a little closer, to let his breath gust over Michael's neck in an acceptance of the soft invitation. But this was not the time. He knew that much, at least, so he let their hands separate.

"I trust you," he said simply, merely as something to say, to break the lingering silence. "And I will be guided by you." It seemed that this was precisely the right thing to say, for Michael's smile was as wide as he'd ever seen it.

"And I will be your guide," Michael said. "And I will be your path." He took the lead, as if to strengthen his words, marching briskly up to the cottage and knocking hard on the door.

That first day passed in a blur of questions. Margaret Wenham was an old and decidedly unattractive woman. Her cottage was horrendous—broken down, filthy with a stench that made the eyes water. Jonathan had to put his handkerchief to his nose and mouth to enter, as the smell was overpowering.

"You smell it?" asked Michael. "They make their hovels like this on purpose, so that we do not smell the stench of evil."

Although the old woman had been warned of their coming, Mistress Wenham was suspicious and guarded, and this put Jonathan on edge from the beginning, wondering why she was so cautious, so unhelpful, for she did not act as if she had nothing to hide. He had no part to play, so he was able to sit and listen to Michael as he questioned the woman about her life, her past. Hours slid by and still Michael kept up his barrage of questions: did she believe in God? Yes, of course. Did she attend church? Yes, although not as often as she should. Why not? She was old and it was a long walk to the village. Did she keep animals? Yes, she had cats and a rabbit. Where were they? Somewhere about. Throughout it all, Michael stayed calm and smiling, patient, chiding almost, like a father who has been disappointed at the behavior of a loved child and simply wants them to tell the truth. Jonathan was forcibly reminded of his own father, for he had spoken in these same tones when one or other of his sons had let him down.

Finally Michael straightened up and turned to him. "I am uncertain," he said. "There is a stench of evil here that I cannot abide. The animals, or possibly her familiars, are missing, and that bodes ill, for they are perhaps with their master this moment. I do not think there is any other choice. She will need to endure the trial."

The old woman blanched and clutched at Michael's clothes in desperation. "Nay, master!" she cried, her wizened face creased in horror and fear. "Not the water, please, never the water! I am innocent of any wrong-doing."

"Why then," said Michael, returning his gaze to the woman with a swiftness that surprised Jonathan, for in their short acquaintance Michael was usually deliberate and steady, not whip-like. "Why then have your neighbors testified against you that you are a witch?"

"I don't know, master," the woman wailed, her gnarled hands tangling in her apron. "I have done them no harm, only good!"

"Tell me then, if you have done them no harm, what *good* you have done them," Michael said softly, and Jonathan had to muffle a gasp, for he saw what Michael was doing, and it was obvious the crone did not.

"I have looked after them," she said, desperately. "They come to me when they need something, something to…" she stumbled over her words.

"Something to help them!" prompted Michael. "Something you made for them?"

"Y…yes." The woman was crying now, pitiful thin streaks of water running down her dirty face and splashing onto her twisting hands. "I meant no harm by it, but people begged me and it had worked before…"

"I understand," Michael said, casting a triumphant glance across at Jonathan. "Potions, brewed up and given to others." The woman nodded, gulping.

"It's all right." Michael put a hand on the woman's shoulder.

"You need not fear the water, you will not have to endure the trial."

The woman looked up, her face blank in shock. "You mean that, master? I won't be ducked? Oh *bless you*, master! You look like an angel and you surely are!" She dropped to her knees and clutched once more at his clothes. Michael disentangled her with some little difficulty, and they left without another word to the sobbing, grateful woman.

Outside, Michael examined the woman's garden, and although he didn't say anything out loud, Jonathan could see his face was shining with some hidden exultation.

Back at the village the Elder invited them into his house, where they were fed and offered a place to sleep. The next day the witnesses were called—Michael asked for each person who would give statements against Mistress Wenham to come and speak to him. The witnesses were mainly women, who were all as scared and as pale in the face as the accused herself had been. Little by little, a picture built up of a woman who the villagers believed was consorting with demons and had been poisoning the villagers with her vile potions.

"My husband met her on the road two months ago and he got to talking, like," one large-bosomed goody with a red face declaimed, "and she said that she could give him something for the sleeplessness he had been experiencing. He went to her house, and she gave him some brew or other. On his way out he trod on one of her cats, broke its leg. He had to kill the beast. She was furious, gave him a right telling off, so he said, but he took the potion anyway. I told him not to take it. I told him that it was the Devil's work and that she had probably gathered the ingredients by the light of the new moon or something, but he didn't listen, oh no, not him, never listened to a word I said. And what happened?"

"What *did* happen, Mistress Carter?" Michael asked with the patience of a saint.

"Well, it was poisoned wasn't it? Or if it wasn't poisoned it must have been bewitched, and only against him, for hurting her cat.

He took some, and he gave Old Jim Barnaby some too, it didn't do him no harm, but my husband came up all in boils and lumps, all over his body. Not natural, the priest said, he couldn't work for a week."

That was the most important evidence; although there was plenty more testimony, it was more of the type that had no evidence to back it up. Strange sounds coming from the cottage at night, a "funny look" given by the crone one day which led to a pain in a leg the next, and so on.

In the afternoon they took their leave and made their way back to Chelmsford. For the walk back Michael seemed unwilling to speak of the Wenham matter, so they spoke of past cases Michael had experienced while being in Hopkins' company, stories of many women proved by the Witchfinder to be in league with the Devil. Once back in Chelmsford, Michael reported his findings to Hopkins.

"You did well," Hopkins said. "It seems clear that she has been using witchcraft on the village for some time."

"May I file the warrant?" Michael asked.

This time, Jonathan watched Hopkins' face carefully. The Witchfinder's face was blank, but his eyes seemed to glitter as he stared into Michael's eager face.

"Not this time," he said. "You know that you will have your own establishment soon enough, and so for that I may need to send you off at a moment's notice. If your name is on a warrant, that's something I cannot do. Patience, Michael. Your time... is yet to come."

Michael's face seemed to contort as if he was struggling with himself, and then he looked up and smiled at Hopkins. "I trust you, sir."

"So you should," Hopkins said, even though his face was still serious. "Now take our new friend away and lead him into the fold. Worry about *him* now, Michael, and let me worry about your future. Stearne and I go to Yarmouth this day, and will be back in a month for the next Assizes. I'll think again on your future—

both of yours, when I return."

As Jonathan watched, baffled at the conversation, Michael's eyes filled with tears as if Hopkins had given him a gift, but for the life of him, Jonathan couldn't work out what it was. They said their goodbyes and left Hopkins sitting in the bar.

Michael led him through the muddy streets and was unusually quiet. Jonathan's curiosity got the better of him and finally he asked, "You said to the old woman that she did not need to fear the trials."

"Nor does she. Not for her the barbarism of the village pond and the jeering of the local people. She will get a fair trial and if acquitted, no one can further accuse her."

Michael said no more but strode ahead, and Jonathan mulled this over as he hurried after him. *It seems fair enough*, he mused. A court trial was evidently a lot better than the dreadful torments of ducking, and the evidence had to be real. It was better this way.

They came to a stop outside a small back-street tavern Jonathan hadn't been to before. They drank together for a long while and talked over the day's work. Michael seemed to get distracted, anxious, and Jonathan, even more convinced of their cause, thought he had done something to displease his new friend, and had tried to apologize for his earlier doubts.

"No need, Thomas, or rather, *Jonathan*," said Michael, smiling. "You needed to realize the importance of our work, to see it in action, to understand. *'For none of the wicked shall understand; but the wise shall understand.'*"

"I understand, really, I do." said Jonathan.

"Do you?"

"I do...At least, I think so."

"Do you trust God to bring you to understanding? Do you trust His judgment, and His choice of judge?"

"I do," said Jonathan, wholeheartedly, wanting to convince Michael of his zeal for the work. "I do."

"Then come with me." Michael put out his hand and Jonathan took it, gratefully.

◖◕ Chapter 21 ◕◗

With his hand fast in Michael's, Jonathan followed his friend down a steep set of steps behind a wooden door, then through another thick oak door. A corridor turned back on itself and opened out into a circular room with no windows. Jonathan stopped, in shock; it was not what he expected, for the room seemed to be nothing more than a cell.

As if reading his mind, Michael shook his head, a strange expression in his blue eyes. "You cannot yet possibly comprehend what we do here. You cannot be trained to do this work; you are called, tried, *judged*. Everyone who works on the side of right, on the side of God and the angels, must be tested himself. In order to be wise, you must submit, be tried."

Jonathan frowned at his friend, confused and suddenly worried. "Surely thou dost not think that I am a witch?" Michael continued to smile his ethereal smile, but in this place it took on a different context; instead of being enigmatic and beguiling, in the bloodstained cellar it seemed to Jonathan to be the smile of a fanatic, unstoppable and terrifying. Jonathan watched Michael, hardly daring to break the eye contact, frightened of what a sudden retreat would bring to him. At a noise behind him, he started and turned his head to see two men at the door, large men.

"Do not be frightened, Jonathan. You have nothing to fear. Not from me." Michael's   smile still played on his face as the two men entered the cell. "Only from God." The men took hold of Jonathan's arms and slammed him against the wall, half stunning him as his head collided with the stone. Manacles were placed around his wrists and ankles as he attempted to struggle, chaining him to the wall. Strangely, apart from the initial force of the assault, the two men were attentive, almost careful. Jonathan looked across at Michael again. He had moved closer now Jonathan was restrained.

"Why art thou doing this?" he asked hoarsely, his breath taken from him in shock.

Michael moved in close and kissed him lightly on the lips, giving him his breath back. "We all endured the trial," he replied softly, caressing Jonathan's hair. "You cannot search for the Devil in others if he resides within you. You must realize that." His voice was almost sad. "I believe you are pure, truly I do. I feel in my heart there is no evil in thee. But you know as well as I do that the Devil is the great deceiver; we must be sure you are doing God's work," and with that they left him alone, shocked to his core and scared.

Throughout the night he called out many times, still half believing that Michael meant this as some sort of joke. He thought he *knew* Michael, he thought they were friends. If he had been told that a trial was the price of joining in with their grand plan, he didn't know whether he would have been so sure of his volunteering. His wrists and ankles chafed and his shoulder, still sore from the bullet, was agonizing.

The top restraints were too high for him to sit down on the floor; they kept his arms out in a crucifixion stance, and after an hour or so his muscles were cramping badly. He tried hanging from the chains, finding he was able to squat down on the floor if he did this, but the pressure this put on his upper arms caused such excruciating pain that after only a few minutes, he knew he would never be able to sleep in that position. In the end he just stood and waited through the longest night of his life, his mouth drying out slowly, as he used every ounce of strength in his muscles to get through the pain.

He was badly frightened. This room, this treatment could not be a secret held only by Michael and the two unnamed men. *Hopkins must know, must have authorized this, and Hopkins works for the government.* Fear kept him awake, wondering if he'd live to see daylight again.

As morning broke, he found himself getting angry as sounds were heard faintly somewhere in the building.

He started to shout again. "Hey!" His voice was hoarse through exertion, and pointless calling. "Michael? *Michael!*" When he'd almost given up, the door finally swung open, revealing Michael looking refreshed and as beatific as ever. Michael came close and watched Jonathan carefully as he struggled to control his breath and his temper. Jonathan glared at him, furious, "Get me down from here, Michael! This is *not* funny. Thou hast made thy point. I am no witch and thou knowest that."

"You told me," Michael said, ignoring him, "that you wished to join us. Do you still wish it? *'And he called unto him the twelve, and began to send them forth by two and two; and gave them power over unclean spirits.'* Two by two, Jonathan. Master and acolyte. Teacher and neophyte."

"And if I were to change my mind?"

"Do you?"

"Wouldst thou then release me?" he half-whispered the question, knowing the answer before it came.

"Of course not, Jonathan. We would then have to discover *why* you changed your mind. Did you volunteer simply to infiltrate us, learn our methods, the better still to avoid detection? Or did the Devil change your mind?"

He's mad, thought Jonathan, *and I am going to die.* He tried to swallow, but his mouth was so dry he could hardly manage it.

"So I am to die then, whatever my answer?"

Michael's face became full of concern. "If you are human, Jonathan, there is no question of that. Only if the Devil has you in his thrall should you fear what we do here. But in order to pass that test you must learn obedience. For is it not said in

Isaiah, '*If ye be willing and obedient, ye shall eat the good of the land: But if ye refuse and rebel, ye shall be devoured with the sword*'?" All Jonathan could do was stare as, to his horror, Michael took a knife out of a sheath around his waist. "I asked you a question."

Jonathan's mind went blank. *Question? What question?* Michael was so close now he could feel the man's breath on his face. With the knife, Michael cut away all of the clothing Jonathan was wearing above the waist: coat, waistcoat, and shirt.

"It's a simple answer to a simple question," he whispered, running one hand up Jonathan's muscled torso. He pressed his body against Jonathan's, and Jonathan was shocked to feel Michael's arousal against his hip.

"This is madness," Jonathan said angrily, twisting away as best he could. "I don't remember a question. Does Hopkins know I am here, does Stearne?" He attempted to tear the hand restraints from the wall, but all he managed to do was further hurt his wrists.

"So much anger," Michael said quietly. Jonathan felt a searing pain in his side and he cried out, falling forward; if he had not been chained he would have landed on his knees. Michael stepped back. There was blood on the blade, and a warm trickle of liquid poured down Jonathan's right side. The pain was like reddened glass behind his eyes.

Michael's voice was so soft that Jonathan nearly did not hear it as he rode out the pain with huge gasps.

"*Obedience*, Jonathan. The teacher asks, and the pupil responds. Your first lesson." He threw the dripping knife onto the floor and left the room.

Jonathan hung on his chains, almost blind from the pain. He couldn't understand what he had done to deserve such treatment. Surely he had given no indication to Stearne or Hopkins that he was a threat? Could they really have authorized this? As the agony passed to a dull throb he twisted in position to see the damage. Michael had been skillful—slicing the layers of skin to cause as much bleeding as possible without damaging the muscle beneath. His breeches were soaked with blood, but the material was thick and no blood had reached the floor.

The pain dissipated a little as he thought frantically, attempting to remember what they had been talking about, to remember what he had been asked. Michael had been quoting the Bible as usual...his mind cleared. Michael had asked, *"Is it not said in Isaiah?"*

There was no way of telling how much time had passed, but it felt like several hours before he heard footsteps and a key in the door. He called out as Michael pushed open the door. "Yes, Michael, yes! It *is* said in Isaiah. You are right."

The fear returned as Michael picked up the knife from the floor and examined the blade.

"It seems you did not quite learn the point of the lesson, Jonathan, and that makes me truly sorrowful." He stepped up to Jonathan's other side and ran his hands down the unblemished skin. "Can you tell me what it was?"

Jonathan could not think of anything except the cold steel against his skin, anticipating the slice he knew must come. He dared not say anything. *Surely that will be safer?* This time Michael kissed his cheek as he cut him, his lips on Jonathan's tears. He spoke so softly in his ear that Jonathan had to stop his screaming to ensure he did not miss a word.

"'Behold, I send an Angel before thee, to keep thee in the way, and to bring thee into the place which I have prepared. Beware of him, and obey his voice, provoke him not; for he will not pardon your transgressions: for my name is in him.'" His hands stroked Jonathan's cuts, causing fresh waves of pain, then he rubbed his bloody palms on Jonathan's chest with a drugged look in his eyes. "Hast thou learned the lesson?"

Jonathan was sobbing in pain, his tears splashing onto the bloody palms on his chest. Somehow his mind dragged back the last thing Michael had said before. Teacher. Pupil. "Yes. *Yes.* Thou asketh. I answer."

Michael put his hand under Jonathan's sagging chin and raised

it so they were looking at each other. "You please me." He motioned to the guards who had entered unnoticed, and Jonathan's
arm restraints were released. "It proves that you can learn. I am
encouraged." He turned to go and spoke two simple words to the
guards. "Walk him."

When he'd forgotten how to it might feel to be still, they'd finally
stopped walking him. *Such an innocent expression,* Jonathan
thought, dazedly. *"Walk him."* What harm could that do? At first
Jonathan thought it was a reward for his doing what Michael had
asked of him; exercise to stretch his cramped limbs, to bring life
back into the numb muscles. He was grateful to the guards for the
support, pleased to be out of the cell and being walked up and
down the dank corridor. But the walk stretched on interminably,
and Jonathan's hungry and desperately thirsty body cried out for
rest; to lie down, or even just to sit down, at the very worst be
chained back to the wall, but the guards didn't stop, and he had no
strength to resist them. When they did halt, after more hours than
Jonathan could know, it was only to swap shifts. The new men said
nothing, just took hold of his arms in that same gentle, firm manner and continued to walk him. Up and down. Up and down. His
lips had become so dry they were cracked and flaked, his mouth so
scorched he could hardly swallow. He was only allowed to relieve
himself when they permitted it. Talking to them was pointless, for
they never replied, never looked at him, and he saved his strength
in the end. Kept walking and tried talking to them no more.

When his legs gave way they would stop, in a semblance of
care, wait in total silence for him to recover his strength, and
when he had managed to force his knees to straighten again, they
walked him on. More than once he knew he must have passed out
because the guards revived him with cold water or with none too
gentle slaps across the face.

When he woke for what he thought was the second time in an
unknowable number of days, he was chained to the wall again,
and someone was giving him water, tiny sips of water, cold and

fresh. Michael was with him, the first time he'd been back in the cell since he'd ordered the guards to walk him. He stroked Jonathan's cheek as he helped him to drink, his face such a picture of love and concern that Jonathan was utterly confused.

"Why are you here, Jonathan?" Michael asked.

Jonathan tried to speak and choked on a build up of fluid in his tortured lungs. "To be tested?"

He knew the answer was wrong, knew it as soon as it was out of his mouth. He didn't know the real answer. A silver-white-hot trail tore down his chest as Michael slid his hand from his throat to his navel, rending the flesh with a razor-sharp blade concealed in his palm. Jonathan cried out, meaning to scream, but the higher notes wouldn't sound, only a hoarse emptiness resounding around the cell.

"Stupid," Michael said calmly. "Lazy and stupid."

"Redeem me then, for the love of God," croaked Jonathan. *"'Teach me, and I will hold my tongue: and cause me to understand wherein I have erred'."*

"My poor Job," breathed Michael in a sigh of rapture. "You begin to see. But you do not yet understand. Why are you here?"

Jonathan began to panic, and Michael soothed him with kisses and gentle stinging caresses over his bloodstained torso. "Let me help you remember." He took his knife and slid it without breaking the flesh down from Jonathan's navel to the waistband of his breeches. He cut the buttons off one by one without taking his eyes from Jonathan's face, then sliced open the stiff, fetid material of the garment and the lining and pulled them off his legs. "So beautiful," he breathed. "So very beautiful." He stepped back and stared at Jonathan's naked body as if allowing himself pleasure. To Jonathan's shock Michael dropped to his knees, his eyes glued to the bloody body before him, as if in worship. Then he closed his eyes and began to pray.

Jonathan watched his torturer without emotion. He was too tired to think, too weary to hold his head up. He heard Michael's voice, but the man did not seem to be speaking to him, he was quoting his beloved Job again, talking to himself. Or God.

"*What is this man that thou shouldest magnify him? And that thou shouldest set thine heart upon him? And that thou shouldest visit him every morning, and try him every moment?*" Jonathan watched him shake his head and step up again close to him. He felt one hand on his balls, warm fingers and cold, cold steel and he began to shake.

"Now," Michael whispered, "Tell me about all about David."

⟪⟫ CHAPTER 22 ⟪⟫

Jonathan was stupid enough to try and be clever. He had been relieved to have the opportunity to talk. While Michael was there,
sitting on a small stool in front of him, listening, he was allowing
Jonathan to eat a little, and drink. His strength was returning to
him, but at only a fraction of what it had been. So he pulled out his
memories of David, giving to Michael what he thought the man
wanted. He talked for hours, telling Michael about Kineton, the
forge, the battle, David's injury. Holding nothing back of their
friendship, but going no further than that. He thought that was
what Michael wanted, but his heart chilled when Michael stood
and took the cane from the corner of the room.

He woke and immediately regretted it, did not even open his
eyes and tried to lull himself back into sleep or unconsciousness,
but the soles of his feet hurt so much they wouldn't give him the
peace he sought. There was an orange glow in his head, but he ignored it; he'd seen every color flash behind his eyes at some point
or other since his incarceration. That very thought gave him
pause. He realized groggily that he could not remember exactly
how long he had been here. *What day is this?* He had no idea
what day of the week it was, nor how many days he had been
chained. He shook his head. *It was definitely Wednesday, wasn't
it—when we went to Writtle? Wednesday?* He wasn't sure. He
was suddenly more frightened of his own incapacity to be sure of
such a simple fact than he was of Michael's reappearance. Taking

long deep breaths, he risked opening his eyes, and found to his surprise that the cell was brightly lit. Four silver candlesticks stood on the table, their candles giving an unaccustomed brightness. He squinted, letting his eyes become used to the light, which seared through even the slightest slits of his eyelids to ravage the back of his brain with a pain equal to any of the cuts he had received. Slowly, painfully he became aware of what the illumination revealed.

With an animal cry of despair his head rocked back, hitting the stone wall and sending a sharp pain down his spine. The cell was a bloodbath. His bloodbath. Around his feet a channel was cut through the floor to the cell door. The depression was dark and shiny. The walls on either side of him were splattered with blood; some splashes brown and rusty, some red like the channel beneath him, where the blood was not yet congealed.

Michael had given him this light. His last words as he had thrown the cane on the floor and kissed him were, "*Soon you will come to your illumination... Reflect.*" The man said nothing without meaning. Nothing.

Nothing Michael did was arbitrary, Jonathan realized at last. If that were true, his shattered mind reasoned, then perhaps everything he did was for a purpose after all? *Was it my destiny then, to be here? Is Michael truly God's instrument?* He whimpered in the empty cell. Fearfully he looked down at his body in the light for the first time; bile and bitter vomit surging to his mouth as he saw the lacerations covering his torso. His skin looked like old parchment, yellow and waxy, *like David's had been the night of his accident....*

Oh God, Jonathan thought. *Illumination...* He suddenly remembered that night. David as still as death, and how desperate he had been that David would not die... He almost laughed at the recollection. *Illumination.* He'd had no idea of the meaning of the word back then. Closing his eyes, he now understood the reason why he was here, why he had been delivered into Michael's lethal hands. Hands so talented that he could, and did, use the bastinado so skillfully that he never broke the skin until he wanted to.

"*Michael...*" His voice was almost unusable, his throat hurt clear down to his stomach. "Illumination..." He heard the door open and froze, not daring to say more, waiting for permission to speak.

"And what have you learned?" Michael's eyes were still the blue ice of the bastinado.

"That it is my own fault...my...cardinal sin that brings me here." He struggled for the strength to speak. "I asked God to spare David. I...promised Him I would follow whatever path He set me upon." He coughed blood and sputum onto his chest. "He heard me. He granted me that wish."

"And why did you want David spared? You knew he was an abomination."

"He was... hurt."

Jonathan was begging for mercy even before the cane reached his skin. When he looked up at Michael, it shocked him to see that Michael was crying.

"Why must you lie to me! Why must you hurt me so? Did you want him saved for *yourself?*"

"*No!* His father feared for his life!" Jonathan screamed then as he didn't think he was able to scream any more, as Michael began to flay him with none of the subtlety shown in their earlier sessions. Skin came away on the split cane, and Michael wept with every stroke he dealt.

"Why...did...*you*...want...him...spared!"

"I *loved* him!" Jonathan cried. The whipping stopped as suddenly as it had begun, and the next thing that Jonathan was aware of was Michael cradling him in his arms, holding him up in his chains, wiping the blood and saliva from his face, unmindful of the fact that he was soiling his own clothes.

"'*Behold, happy is the man whom God correcteth: therefore despise not thou the chastening of the Almighty.*'" He was almost purring into Jonathan's ear. "At last, we come to it. You loved him, this abomination. And did you lie with him?"

"Not then...*No!* This is the truth, Michael! Not then... Later...yes." He was releasing it all, could feel it all falling from him with the tears which burned his mutilated body as they slid down his face before dropping onto the floor.

Michael kissed his forehead and his eyelids. All Jonathan could do was lie there, feel Michael hold him. "My good Jonathan. Confess it now. God will not cast away a perfect man. Wilt thou confess it to me, or shall I bring a priest to hear thee?"

"You." Jonathan's voice was hardly audible but he could see Michael's joy. He felt Michael's lips against his own, the warmth of Michael's tongue in his mouth, and felt a communion forge between them, bonded by blood and faith. It was like no kiss he'd shared before, nothing base. It was confession. As Michael held him, wiping the blood from his skin, Jonathan spoke only of David, their friendship, their unholy union in blood brotherhood. Jonathan could see the stain that David had left on his soul, and it all drifted from him as the words fell from his lips. When he finally spoke of the first time they had mated, Michael knelt before Jonathan and took his prick, heavy and soft, into his mouth.

Jonathan's eyes were closed, and he spoke slowly and painfully as he remembered each touch, each kiss of David's upon the body of a man whom Jonathan could hardly remember. When he paused, Michael bade him continue, and Jonathan was slowly aware of Michael's mouth on his member, so gentle and with the same attention that he gave to everything he did. As the words tumbled from him, a catharsis of loss and despair, revelation and surrender, he felt heat in his loins as Michael did what Jonathan would have considered impossible: aroused him. It was not the remembrance of the golden body of David that was filling his loins with a slow starting inferno; it was this man who had shown him that only through the fire could he escape his own hell.

Unable to do anything else, he hung there as Michael swallowed him as a man dying of thirst, his hands between Jonathan's ravaged legs kneading his balls with firm subtle strokes. Powerless, Jonathan felt his very soul leave him and fly to Michael's hand like a trained hawk, his for the bidding. Just when he felt a surge, a deep thrumming in his ears which begun somewhere in the recesscs of Michacl's mouth, his torturer stood up and left his member cold, hard, and aching for release. Michael kissed him, sharing again the taste of sweat and blood, then put his lips to Jonathan's ear.

"Repeat the story of your first congress with the Devil and this time, miss no detail." Jonathan obeyed, dumbly, only praying his compliance would be what Michael really wanted, closing his eyes as Michael's hand slipped to his weeping cock and closed around it, fisting it slowly. He thought back to the first time he had entered David's body, and his erection faltered as he spoke of their sin.

"Confess it, Jonathan, and free yourself of it for ever. *'Because thou shalt forget thy misery, and remember it as waters that pass away.'*" Michael's voice was eager and persuasive, his hands working Jonathan, encouraging him back to hardness. Jonathan told the story again and again as Michael whispered suppport into his ear. On the third time of telling it, Jonathan felt a searing pain in his side as Michael slid his blade along his flesh, urging him to continue, to give every detail of plunging his cock into David. The pressure in Jonathan's loins was fighting with the pain in his side, liquid dropping from his side and from his tortured member. His breath was shallow, his pulse pounding in his head as he searched for the words to obey Michael, to please him, to say anything to make him stop the pain.

Jonathan's reason was near to fracturing. He felt he was walking a sword-edged path between ecstasy and agony; the pleasure and pain so enmeshed that there could be no taking one without the other. The paths were divided before him, and the only recourse remaining was to take both and tear himself apart. He surrendered utterly, relaxed into the pain, learned to ride it. In his mind it became a frozen slope and he slid down it into the darkness beyond. As he felt it overcoming him, he was plunged forward into the same vision he had when first he had fucked the

Devil; he again he saw the Angel at the end of the path, a flaming sword in his hands, and the sword was his own cock, splendid and on fire with a righteous light.

He knew now who it was, and in his vision Michael raised his head, opened his arms and said, "You are mine." Then all was conflagration. He felt his climax hit him, and he remembered nothing else.

Jonathan lay on the cold stone floor, his body not even able to shiver for the cold, his muscles weak and completely useless. He was released from his chains, but couldn't even remember when that had happened. Last night Michael had at last given him water, an entire skin full. What should have been a life-saving blessing had turned into another terrifying nightmare as he forced Jonathan to drink and drink; his stomach, empty of food, swelling abnormally as the liquid stretched it. He tried to drink fast to get it over with, but every drop spilled was rewarded by a vicious yank of his hair, which made him gag, pulling liquid into his lungs, choking him. At one time he thought he would drown, thinking that by drawing the water into his lungs he could breathe death and make an end. He needed an end. But Michael was too careful for that—he forced just enough past Jonathan's lips to swallow, not to choke. Suddenly Jonathan understood: he only had to agree to the help he was being given... It was all so clear. He took a deep breath, fixed his eyes on Michael's, and, ignoring his distended stomach, *drank*, slowly and deliberately.

Michael raised his eyes to the roof and shouted, "Praise God!" He reduced the rate of the water's input drop by drop, but never stopping until it was all impossibly gone.

Michael sat with him for a long while afterwards, stroking his filthy hair and his broken face, softly praising him for submitting without fight. "You are so close to glory now," he whispered, his eyes glazed and unfocussed. "Your reward will come tomorrow." Then he stood and was gone, leaving Jonathan unbound overnight for the first time, coughing blood onto the floor.

Jonathan truly felt that he was close to glory—he doubted that he would last the night. Despite his newfound freedom, he did not sleep. The pain of the night was excruciating, his stomach screamed at him for hours, overburdened by its load, and when his bladder started to complain, he dared not stand without permission, knowing that he was being watched as closely as ever. He hardly noticed it as he pissed whilst laying in his own filth.

The candles were nearly burned down when the door opened. Michael and the two guards lifted him from the ground, although he barely felt it. All he could see were Michael's eyes fixed upon his, smiling and loving. He did not know whether he slept or whether he had passed out again, but he was revived by water over his head, not freezing this time, but warm, scented, and gently poured. His eyelids forced their way open and Michael was there, as he was always there, smiling. In his face there was now no disappointment or sadness, but joy and love. As Jonathan's nerve endings registered with his sluggish brain, he realized he was sitting in a large tub of water in a room he did not know.

He was soaped tenderly, his cuts washed, the grime and corruption rinsed from his body. Everywhere hurt; the lavender-scented water stung bitterly. Through his half-closed lids he could see the cuts and welts on his thighs, his torso and arms, but when his head strayed too far Michael brought his face back to his gaze with a firm hand. Jonathan didn't resist. Michael's eyes held him captive still, and he dared not move one muscle without his master's word. When it came, it was like a benediction, a sudden rush of release.

Michael leant forward and kissed him gently on the lips, bringing fresh pain as the cuts there split open even at such a butterfly touch. "My Jonathan." Michael's voice was a white light to which Jonathan clung in a happy daze. "You are indeed pure, although rarely has it taken so long to prove. The battle for your soul is won."

Tears fell from Jonathan's eyes, and within seconds he had started to sob convulsively. He drowned in Michael's eyes. He knew now without fear that Michael loved him and would look after him, as it was meant to be. Strong arms surrounded him, his master's voice told him not to cry, and his sobs shut off immediately in sudden obedience. He was praised again, helped from the tub, dried with such attention that his heart nearly broke for shame that his master should be tending *him* in this way, and was lowered onto soft linen sheets. Sleep crept upon him as he felt hands rubbing ointment into his wounds, heard muffled voices speaking softly, and warm covers pulled over him. The last thing he felt before darkness claimed him was gentle lips on his, and he knew that it was his Michael, his Archangel, blessing him, keeping him safe.

It was days before Jonathan was lucid, and Michael sat with him nearly every moment, finding sleep by simply dropping his head onto his arms on the bed. His heart was light, his soul rejoicing; Jonathan's soul was clean, the man had submitted to the Trial and was one of them, and his submission was complete.

More than furious, Hopkins had taken one look at Jonathan and denounced Michael for bringing the new recruit so close to death.

"You had no authorization to cut the man!" He'd roared at him. "These things are outlawed, you know this—they are not part of the Trial! Did I cut you? You could have put us all under suspicion, Michael."

Michael reassured Hopkins that Jonathan was not in any state to complain to any authorities—and that Jonathan's spirit was his, now, to do with as he wished, but it hardly assuaged Hopkins' anger. "We don't need *sheep*, boy," he'd thundered, before ordering him out of the room.

In truth, Michael cared little for Hopkins' opinion regarding Jonathan. The emotions he felt for this young man were vindicated. He knew without a shadow of a doubt that God had given his permission for him to love Jonathan; they were disciples both, joined together by their shared suffering. As he watched

Jonathan sleep he remembered his own Trial, at Hopkins' own hands, six days and nights of torment and accusation. In reality, he'd had nothing to confess, although he told Hopkins anything he wanted to know, just to stop the questions and the walking. Anything at all for the questions to stop, to be allowed to sleep.

At odd times Jonathan would wake suddenly, his breath like a death rattle in this chest, and his eyes would fly open, unseeing. Michael would soothe him, sustaining him with the word of the Lord. *"'And they overcame the Devil by the blood of the Lamb, and by the word of their testimony.' He is gone Jonathan, he will never trouble you again. Sleep."*

Jonathan knew no other course; he obeyed.

Finally, Jonathan's gray eyes opened sluggishly and there was intelligence within. Michael whispered a swift prayer and held his hand tightly. "Welcome back to this path we make for their redemption, my love." Jonathan gave a deep sigh, tears falling from his eyes as Michael kissed him. *"'Unto you it is given to know the mystery of the kingdom of God: but unto them that are without, all these things are done in parables.'"*

Jonathan smiled, his very face muscles causing him pain as Michael stood up and started to undress. He tried to lift his hand to touch Michael's arm, but his muscles wouldn't work properly.

"'Thou shalt lie down, and none shall make thee afraid; yea, many shall make suit unto thee'," Michael said gently, dropping his clothes to the floor.

He lay there happy to watch the man disrobe; his body now revealed at last to Jonathan was slender and pale. Michael's chest was tautly muscled and covered with golden hair, his waist slim, his prick dark and very erect. Michael slid in next to him and gently put one arm around him, the other hand slipping between Jonathan's thighs, stroking his flaccid prick. To Jonathan it was as painful as any of the lessons his master had given him—it was *wrong*. He should not be the one to be pleasured, even though his prick was unable to respond, he knew that *he* should be plea-

suring Michael. He tried to tell his master this, but Michael
hushed him, saying he understood his concern,

"But you must not object to what I do to you, Jonathan. Surely
you realize that by now?" Sharp nails dug into his balls and
Jonathan arched up in pain, hissing his acquiescence. For this he
was kissed and stroked and praised again. Compliance meant
praise, he remembered that lesson. Compliance meant he made
Michael happy, and lying there, his very soul aching, making his
master happy was what he wanted. Michael turned him on his
side and ordered him to raise his right leg. He tried hard to obey,
but the muscles were so badly bruised he had difficulty lifting it.
A sob broke from him at his failure to comply, but Michael reassured him, his own hands helping the leg, bending it painfully
into the position he wanted.

"You tried, which pleases me." Soft lips kissed the back of
Jonathan's neck, strong fingers held his hip in position, and a
hand slipped down between his buttocks. "Now, my beautiful
Jonathan, now." The voice sounded frenzied as fingers pushed
their way between his sweating arse-cheeks and found his opening. Jonathan tried not to panic; to show nothing but welcome
for his new lover, who was not aware that he had never been
breached. He breathed out, forcing his muscles to relax as the
fingers pushed their way past the tight, virgin ring. *I must not
cry out, I must not cry out*, he thought in a litany of preserva-
tion, but he could feel the muscles there tightening against his
will. He knew Michael would punish him, so he shut his eyes in
anticipation of the retaliation he knew would come. Teeth bit
into his shoulder right on top of an unhealed wound, and he
gasped in pain, but he knew that this was what he had been
trained for—pain he could control. He rode out the waves of
agony by breathing deeply as the teeth worried the wound, his
head falling back. As the torment receded, he realized that the
fingers had gone; Michael was pressed up tight behind him, and
was sliding in and out of his body. The burning in his fundament replaced the pain in his shoulder tenfold, but now that

his lover had entered him, it was a matter of control, and one thing he had learned was control.

"'Blessed are they that do his commandments, that they may have right to the tree of life, and may enter in through the gates into the city.'"

With those words, Jonathan felt his sin drop away from him. The ice of his degradation and corruption melted away as he renounced David and all of his works. He saw himself as in the vision he'd had many times, on the path with Michael before him. It was if he had stepped eagerly into the fire of Michael's redemption, and as Michael's seed flowed into him, it seemed to purge the taint of David completely.

Jonathan's eyesight dimmed, as sleep blanketed him again while Michael held him gently, mindful of his injuries once more, purring his name. Jonathan was safe and warm and happy. *How could I have mistaken the feelings I had before for love?* His master had made his past clear to him—his love for David had been wrong, sinful. It was the reason that he had been suffering. Now that was past. The only love that mattered was God's love, channeled through Michael. The ethereal vision of David's face melted from his mind like smoke in a breeze. He had finally forgotten it all; forgotten everything except that he belonged to Michael.

Forever.

◖◉ CHAPTER 23 ◉◗

After a slightly shaky start, David and Ashwell, whose first name was Robert, managed to work together fairly well. The smithy work, although tedious and repetitive, was of a level to suit David; he would soon have shown his failings if he had been working under a swordsmith. His experience with horses, and his speed and professional work on their feet and teeth, soon proved his worth to the seemingly surly owner.

The two boys who worked there were named Christopher and Stephan. David never knew their surnames, and discovered later that they didn't know them either. Christopher had untidy straw-colored hair, and Stephan—the smaller of the two, although both seemed small to David—had black curls and a look of mixed blood about him. David, when he had the opportunity to speak directly to Stephan, found the boy was mute.

"He ain't deaf though," said the cheerful Christopher, "he just don't talk." As Stephan brought David a bucket of water and put it on the floor with a shy smile, David could see a shadow of something in his black eyes, and wondered what it was the boy was keeping to himself. Twice when David attempted to question Christopher on who they were, what their history was, Ashwell called out to the boys in a gruff voice to get on with work.

"I don't pay you to stand around gossiping," he said to the three of them, as the younger boys scuttled off. The boys' tasks were primarily concerned with the welfare of the horses, both the hacks that Ashwell rented out, and the mounts of people who rented stable space there, permanently or just for the night. They seemed to be constantly on the go, mucking out from early light, then grooming, feeding, watering, cleaning harness and tack, and a thousand other little jobs.

Both boys, according to Christopher, were grateful beyond words that David had cured the biter. "That's all we called him," quipped Christopher one lunchtime, as they ate together at the table in Ashwell's shack, "the Biter." He rolled up a sleeve, revealing several sets of teeth marks of various ages, the bruising ranging from black to yellow. "But you've sorted him out now, good and proper. We'll have to think of a new name for him. Probably, the Kicker. He ain't no angel yet." He rolled his sleeve back down, and David wondered what the thin, gray lines were he had spotted at the top of the boy's arm. Both of the lads seemed too fragile to deal with tons of horseflesh, and he asked Christopher if he'd ever been hurt.

"Other than kicks and bites yer mean?" he asked. "Nah, not really. Stephan broke some toes once when a carthorse stood on his foot, but I think the horse was more sorry about it than Stephan. Some of the big ones are right soppies," he said with a laugh. "It took long enough to get the horse to notice that Stephan's foot was there, they aren't the brightest of animals neither." He turned to Stephan. "You should've shouted at him," he told his friend. "I know you can do it." He looked back at David. "He used to talk, you know, a while back, but he just got quieter and quieter, and one day he just stopped." He smiled sadly. "'He's got a loverly voice too, it's like singing." Stephan rewarded this with a slow smile.

"Stead of which the silly bugger just stands there and is hitting the horse on the shoulder, and the great lump takes as much notice of him as a fly. Eventually he gets the bright idea of hitting the trough with a brush, and I comes running. We made a code after that. Like this," he tapped his hand on the table quickly, "means help. But we've been all right."

Fate however, as David now knew well, did not like to be challenged. Three days later a customer brought a gray gelding into the stables. It was temperamental and fractious, and David, as he walked down to the storeroom to get more nails, heard Christopher speaking to Robert about the horse.

"He's just nasty. Not surprising really, seeing as how many sores the poor bugger has all over him."

"It's not the horse's fault," came Robert's voice, in that gentle tone he only used with the boys when he thought no one was listening. "A little kindness now will do no harm at all, and the man is a regular. I daren't turn him away, he might ruin me."

"I know that," said Christopher. "You've told me enough times that money don't make kindness. Can I have the horse on my side? If Stephan gets into trouble he might not be able to let anyone know quick enough."

"Of course," said Robert. "I'll help you with him."

"No need," said Christopher. "It wont take but a minute." Christopher came out of Robert's living area whistling, cocked a jaunty salute at David who was returning up the aisle with the nails, and then ducked into the gray's stall. For a second there seemed to be a hiss of something, as if the gods were holding their breath, and swift footsteps sounded behind David. Stephen pushed past and barged his way into the stall. David stopped and watched, worried at the furious expression on the darker boy's face He walked up to Christopher where he was untying the rope of the horse's halter, and grabbed it, ripping it from Christopher's hands with such force that the young man cried out in pain and brought his palms to his mouth.

"God's *blood*, Stephan, that hurt!" He opened his palms showing the rope burn, but Stephan's eyes were still full of anger. He hit Christopher in the chest, pointed to the horse, and then to himself, then put both hands into his pockets and turned them out.

"Yes," Christopher said, catching Stephan's meaning immediately. "Yes—I know, he's a good tipper, but the horse is a bloody menace. Remember last time? When he had me up against the stable wall? You can't—"

Christopher's words were cut off as Stephan shoved him backwards, his face utterly furious, as if Christopher were cheapening him for simply not being able to express himself. The horse was stamping and snorting, its eyes red-rimmed and fractious.

"Stephan!" cried Christopher. "We can still share the tip—like we always do!" Stephan spat on the floor, turned his back on his friend, and moved away, leaving Christopher in the stall. As David watched, time seemed to slow, and although he started toward the boys almost as soon as the horse did, it was all too late. Stephan barged out of the stall, with Christopher staring after him. The horse, realizing the rope was untied, attempted to swing towards the boy, but David's movement made it turn around. Quick as a striking viper its quarters swung around, and with his face to David, he kicked out at the vulnerable boy behind him. There was a scream and a meaty sickening thud. David ran into the stall. He grabbed the dangling rope, slapping the horse's muzzle as it bared its teeth, and yanked the horse forward out of the stall, letting it loose in the stables before dashing back to where Christopher was crumpled on the ground, like a puppet with its strings cut.

Dropping to his knees, he gathered the boy in his arms and ran out, meeting Stephan and Robert, both already pale and worried. He ran past them into Robert's living quarters and laid Christopher on the bed. "You'd better get the horse," he said to Robert, who nodded.

Christopher was deathly still, but a touch to his nose told David he was still breathing. Stephan's face was a tragic mask, and he pulled at David's arm, to attempt to let him get closer.

"No," David said. "I need to see if he's all right." Stephan crumpled onto a chair, weeping unnaturally silent tears. As David examined the boy's limbs, Robert came back in and moved to his side, saying nothing, but looking concerned. "His leg is broken, I think," David said. "Or maybe something worse, I can't tell. The horse kicked him with both feet."

"I'll go to the monastery," said Robert. "They'll send someone." He moved away and put his arm on Stephan's shoulder. "He only wanted the horse moved because he was worried about you, lad. You shouldn't have distrusted him." Stephan's face was so full of guilt and fear that Robert softened. "It's only a bone break, lad. I doubt his head is hurt. Hopefully he'll be all right."

Stephan threw himself on the floor, pulled a rosary out of his pocket, and began, wordlessly, to pray.

Hopkins took a piece of bread, and dunked it into his watered-down ale. He was still angry, but he had calmed since Jonathan's recovery. "I've told you before that you went too far with the boy," he said to Michael. "I thought you were ready, but you are not. If I'd had any idea of how hard you would have pushed him, I would not have allowed him to join us." He looked over to where Jonathan was sitting quietly by the fire, reading the Bible. "As it is, I was wrong; he's more than a member of the team, he's become irreplaceable."

"I knew he would be," Michael replied quietly, so not as to let Jonathan overhear. "I saw something fine in him, something bright and shining that had been badly corrupted by a past friendship, but he has given that up. He is a single-minded man, and he will do one thing to the best of his ability."

"He certainly does that," said Stearne, knocking his pipe on the fireside. "I had thought that you, Michael, were like a bright light who illuminated our dark path when you had joined—but Jonathan is a fiery brand held in the hand of an angel of vengeance. Such devotion to rooting out evil. He makes us look positively lazy in our aspect."

"Then give us more scope," Michael said, gazing at Hopkins in supplication. "Let us go out and do it for ourselves. We can begin in Cambridgeshire or Lincolnshire. There is work here aplenty, but you can manage that without us." His eyes were bright and pleading. "He will blaze a trail through the ungodly."

"I don't think the boy is ready," said Hopkins with a frown. "He has only been with us for such a short time."

"But *Michael* is more than ready," Stearne said sharply, glancing at Jonathan. "I think the way he's broken that colt proved that." Stearne had made it clear to Michael that didn't trust Jonathan at all, despite his outward praise. He'd said that the lad was too quiet, too damned compliant.

Since his recovery, Jonathan had been allowed to manage some of the questioning of the women under suspicion and his manner was truly daunting. When questioning the accused, he was a man possessed, thundering and terrifying where Michael was soft and deadly; but when not working, Jonathan was almost completely silent, needing nothing more, seemingly, than his Bible, food, and drink. Stearne didn't like the way that Michael ordered the taller man about, fearing that one day the simmering violence that he knew he had once seen in Jonathan's eyes when they had first met him, would erupt upon them all like a dam bursting. But he joined Michael in his praise of their newest recruit, encouraging Hopkins to send the pair of them away from Essex. "Michael can control him—it's clear he'll do as he's told, and no more."

In the few weeks Jonathan had been in their company, he had changed from a questioning, uncertain, almost awkward young man, into a silent, somber, and forbidding figure. He stood behind Michael like a menacing shadow, the dark eclipse of Michael's aureate fire. With a Bible always in his hand, he dressed in deepest black, wore a wide-brimmed hat, and his uncommon gray eyes with that black rim around the irises gave him a look of unearthly knowledge. Stearne had noticed that when they entered a town or a village to do their work, it was increasingly Jonathan's name that he heard whispered by the onlookers, Jonathan's mere appearance that could still a crowd.

Stearne was frankly jealous. Once people had been awed by him and by Hopkins, but neither of them, for all their eloquence and meticulous methods of keeping notes of confessions, had Jonathan's presence. Jonathan fitted the mould; when people thought of Witchfinders, they now imagined Jonathan, dark, pious, and silent except when exhorting the victims to confess.

"Michael was your acolyte, Matthew. You trained him, tested him. You know he's capable," Stearne went on. He looked slyly at Hopkins, envious of Hopkins' fondness for the blond-haired young man. "Matthew is right, there is not enough work for us all in East Anglia. This is your home ground, you are needed here. Let them go and prove themselves."

Hopkins was silent, puffing at his pipe, his face shrouded in the flickering shadows of the candles and the firelight. "So be it," he said finally. "It shall be as you ask." He smiled at Michael's grinning face. "You have served your time, and now it is time for the disciple to go unto the world and preach the word. You will have letters of introduction and enough money to keep you for a goodly while." He clasped Michael's arm. "Just be careful, for I would not lose you, either of you."

Michael shook Hopkins' hand, then flew to Jonathan's side and whispered a word to him. Immediately, Jonathan closed his book, stood, and followed Michael out of the room.

Hopkins caught Stearne's expression and tapped him affectionately on the arm. "You need not worry about Michael, John, he was born to do this work."

"I do not worry about the work," Stearne said, a muscle twitching in his cheek as he watched the young men exit the bar. "But I worry about Michael. I do not like that relationship. It does not seem natural to me. What did he tell you about the testing? It was over by the time we got back from Yarmouth, and I was concerned enough when I found that the boy had been treated no better than a witch."

"Each man's testing is his own secret," said Hopkins quietly. "You, John, know that as well as anyone. Have I ever divulged what went on between us? Have you?" Stearne shook his head, but he continued to look at the door where the men had left. "What is it that makes you concerned?" Hopkins asked.

Stearne frowned, remembering his own Trial. No, he'd never spoken of it to a soul, and never would. It had been a time of darkness, and prayer—Hopkins had shown him the light and had proved that his soul was worth saving. "I wish I could put it into words," he said. "It sounds a blasphemous thing to say, but sometimes I feel that Michael has a little too much belief. If he ever loses control of his pupil, it might be the worse for him."

The nights were drawing in, and that meant that David and Tobias could spend less and less time together as Parliament continued to enforce the curfew at sunset. David dreaded the winter, when it would be dark by four, and they would only have three short hours together on any Sunday when their lives coincided. They still met in Tobias' uncle's house. There was no sign that the man would ever return.

Neighbors had not been helpful, saying only that the old man had moved away at the start of the war, perhaps to stay with relatives. After David told Tobias this, the man was never mentioned again by him. David noticed more and more that there was so very many things he did not know about Tobias. He didn't know where his parent's farm had been, or why he never spoke of them. He didn't know if Tobias had any siblings, or any relations other than this uncle, the name of whom David had never heard the man speak. With little else to occupy his mind but work and thoughts, it had become an obsession with David. He took every opportunity to attempt to draw Tobias out on the subjects, but it was like trying to capture smoke in basket. Tobias smiled, changed the subject, or ably avoided the questions with many practiced methods.

Once, David had simply lost his temper. "You know everything about me!" he had shouted. "Why won't you tell me even the smallest fact about you?"

Tobias had simply shrugged at this and said, "Because I'm not a terribly interesting person." And that had been all David could get out of him that day, other than one remark, said with guilt inducing softness. "After all, do you ever talk about your father?" That had stopped David's questions for a while.

He did think of his father, a great deal; the bad memories of

Kineton, the battle, and leaving Jonathan were often wiped away by the memory of warm days, dozing on the riverbank, or remembering when he was small and his father carried him on his shoulders. Just thinking of Kineton hurt him, for the good memories and the bad.

A month had passed since Christopher's accident. The monks who had come had confirmed that it was a broken bone. They'd strapped the lower leg and ankle tightly with bandages lined with comfrey. For days Christopher had been insensible, and those days had been hard. Stephan was inconsolable, and spent as much time by his friend's bedside as he could spare, which wasn't much as Christopher's absence was hard felt. After four anxious days Christopher had come to himself and slowly began to make a recovery. For a week he had stayed in his bed in the loft, carried there by David, and had had a long and lonely time of it, for work kept the rest of them busy.

Robert had been reluctant to employ a new boy, even temporarily. "I trust who I have," he had said, shortly, when David asked him about it. The gray horse had been removed, its owner informed that because of its violent nature it was no longer welcome. The man, to his credit, had given the monastery a contribution, but it did not take Christopher's pain away, nor Stephan's guilt. *Nor,* David thought grimly, *does it absolve the owner from making his horse into a killing machine.*

Time healed, as do young bones, and after a while Christopher was able to get out of bed, and with the aid of a crutch, to move about. He was unable to work, however, and the sadness in his eyes showed his boredom, frustration, and worry whenever he didn't think anyone was watching him.

Silent and affectionate, Stephan attended him as if he were a sultan. Christopher's every need was anticipated and granted. Like a dervish Stephan swept through the stables, doing both boys' work, and then looking after his friend in a frenzy of guilt and care. It was soon obvious to David, if it was not to Robert, that the boys were more than just friends. The way that Stephan fawned for affection, the way the Christopher would touch Stephan's hand to let him know how pleased he was that he had been brought this thing or that thing, soon made it clear to David that their relationship was sweet and strong.

Although Christopher was able to get about with the aid of the crutch Ashwell had fashioned for him, he was unable to do much more than sit on a bench and polish harness. David had taken him to work with him in the forge, for he could sit and use the bellows and pour water as directed, but the boy's heart wasn't in it. David would watch him as he turned his pale face towards the horses, and the expression on his face was once that David knew all too well—a sense of longing for something that he thought was gone forever. It made David think, and during the times when he was not working, or the Sundays when he did not see Tobias, he hatched a plan. He went to Ashwell with a few rough drawings. Fortunately, Ashwell took one look at them, and understood immediately what David was trying to do.

The next few days were the most fun David had experienced since he had started at the stables, as the items he had to make had to be done secretly, not letting Christopher see what he was doing. He was a sharp-eyed youngster, though—he had to be with so many equine charges—and Ashwell kept him occupied by telling him stories of his life before he had moved to London, of days on a farm in Kent, with acres of apple fields and huge plough horses. In the evenings, after Robert had carried Christopher up to the loft, David would let Elijah Cook, a carpenter from a neighboring street, into the forge, and they would work together, fitting iron to wood, until they both looked at their creation with pleasure.

"It's not attractive," laughed David.

"No, it ain't," said Elijah, "but it's useful. In here, at any rate. Wouldn't be no use on the street with them cobbles."

The next evening, after everything was tidied away, and they gathered together in Robert's one-room dwelling for the evening meal, Robert revealed the surprise: a small wooden chair with large wooden, metal-bound wheels. The boys just stood and stared at it, while Ashwell roared with laughter at the expressions on their faces.

David glared at Robert in mock fury, then turned and explained it to Christopher. "We knew you were missing working with the horses, and you can't stand for long yet, not long enough or strong enough to groom and harness them, so we thought—"

"*David* thought of the idea," said Robert, giving David his due, "and we roped in Elijah here."

"Who thought they were mad," Elijah added, smiling.

Stephan leapt forward, beaming, and stood beside the chair, but Christopher turned and clumsily launched himself into Robert's arms, giving him a heartfelt hug, which made Robert go as red as a cherry. After a moment or two, Robert disentangled himself from Christopher, who was grinning from ear to ear, helped the boy to sit in the chair, then pushed him out into the main stable area for him to have some space to navigate.

"And of course, the bad news is that you have to stop lazing around pretending to help me, and you get to carry on slaving for Robert!" said David, laughing, taking pleasure from Christopher's evident joy in the little chair. "You can hang a bucket on these hooks," David pointed out. "And anyway, it's not forever." The bones would mend, although it was probable that the boy would always walk with a limp, the monks said.

The men left the boys to it—Christopher in place and learning to navigate the chair up and down the aisle, and Stephan pushing him when required.

"You did a good thing, Robert," said Elijah. "Those boys are very fond of you."

"And me them," Robert said, pouring the three of them a drink. "I have no family, and I'm planning to leave the place to them when I die. If the boy is crippled, then at least he'll have an income, such as it is. Or they can sell the entire concern, and go and do what they bloody like."

Elijah blinked. "Generous! And rather premature I would

imagine."

"What do you mean?" Robert asked with a frown, not a man to have his decisions questioned.

"I mean nothing by it," said Elijah. David could see the carpenter knew his friend and didn't want to make a scene. He just stood and shook both their hands. "I must go. I have commissions to finish, and they won't carve themselves."

After Elijah had gone, Robert was still scowling, and to lighten his mood, David asked him more about the two boys. The ploy worked and soon Robert was talking happily about them.

"Don't rightly know how old they are," he said. "I found them begging from my customers outside the door here, one freezing day in February, cold enough to freeze your balls off. My first instinct was to cuff them and send them on their way, but Stephan was almost blue, hardly knew where he was, poor bugger, so I took them in. 'Just for one night, mind,' I said to them." Robert smiled at the memory. "And five years later they are still here."

"They look about fourteen," David remarked.

"Aye, they are small," Robert agreed, "but I think they are older than that, both of them, not that they even know how old they are themselves. Christopher says he remembers being taken to see Old Tom Parr, and that was ten years ago. He could be around seventeen, I reckon. They'd be about the same age as each other, I'd wager."

"Tom Parr?" asked David, curious.

"Claimed he was the oldest man alive, said he was over 150. I don't believe it meself, but he came to London and was introduced to the King, paraded about like a sideshow for a while. He shouldn't have come, London ain't good for everyone. It killed him. If he hadn't've come he'd probably still be around." Robert roared with laughter.

"What happened to the boys before they came here?"

"I've pieced together a bit of it, but Christopher doesn't like to talk about their past much. Seems Christopher woke up one day and his parents were dead; he were too young to know how, could have been plague I suppose. No one wanted to take him in, so it must have been some disease or some neighbor would have adopted him. He started begging after that, met Stephan on the streets, then they huddled together like orphan lambs often do. Must have been hell. Too little food, always cold, they didn't grow much, stayed stunted-like, and were eventually taken in by a man called Lewis, a sweep who treated them badly, from the little Chris does comes out with. And I've never heard the other one say a word, leastways not to me, but I've seen the soot-stained whipmarks on their backs, like black stripes. I'd better not meet that sweep, that's all I can say. Poor little devils."

"They've fallen on their feet here, and no mistake," said David. He was surprised by the speech, the longest he'd heard from Ashwell, and touched by his employer's generous nature.

"They work hard, and they make up for their previous lack of vittles," laughed Robert. "You'd think I had six boys working here, the amount they eat. I don't begrudge them." The two men continued to drink for an hour or so, and by the time he was ready for bed, David's impression of his employer had changed quite radically. He might act like a loud-mouthed bully in public, but his heart was most certainly in the right place.

David took off his boots as he mounted the ladder to the loft, glad that the ladder was closer to his side of the space rather than where the two boys slept, as he didn't want to wake them. As he reached the top, he heard what sounded like crying, a small slight sobbing, and David worried that Christopher was in fresh pain. He moved across the floor as silently as he could, not wanting to interfere if he was not needed. What he saw made his breath catch in his throat— the two boys were as naked as the day they were born, lying as close together as two spoons. It was clear that David's suspicions were correct, the boys were certainly closer than friends, and he tiptoed away hoping he hadn't been heard. He looked forward to telling Tobias of his discovery.

⟪ CHAPTER 24 ⟫

That is the problem, thought David, the day after, as he molded shoes for a gentleman's carriage horse, *not being able to tell Tobias what I want, when I want to tell him.* He never knew when he would see Tobias from one meeting to the next, and he was lonely. Not just for the warm body at night, or the gentle passion the trooper had always shown, but for companionship. He missed Tobias in many ways, and just to be able to turn to someone who cared and tell them about your day was a pleasure sadly missed. He had been used to calling into the house at Addle Street after his work finished, just on the off-chance that Tobias would be there, and when he was not, David would pace the increasingly chilly streets until the curfew forced his return to the stables. As a young man used to companionship, this routine soon began to pall. Finding few opportunities to talk to at his place of work, and with Tobias was becoming increasingly hard to find, David began to frequent the local taverns to seek out company, much as he had in Kineton.

This act had a surprising and positive effect on their relationship. One night Tobias came to the stables unexpectedly, only to find David missing. He went to the house, and then back to the stables, sought out Robert and questioned the man. Eventually and reluctantly, Robert admitted that David had started to go to the Dog and Duck, a few doors down, on a fairly regular basis. When Tobias finally found the grubby, dark alehouse, he stopped at the doorway where David could not see him, letting his eyes adjust to the light. His young lover was sitting at a large table with a group of four or five men of a similar age, although from their demeanor, obvious to military eyes, it was clear that they had not been to war; they did not have that age-old weariness about their eyes that Tobias suddenly realized that David had.

Nevertheless, Tobias was taken aback by how at home David looked with them; he was an obvious favorite. Apart from the pockets of quieter, staid drinkers around the bar, David's table with song and laughter, was the center of attention, and David unmistakably the flame that drew the others to him, shining in the dim and smoky atmosphere like an alchemist's flame. With a pang of jealousy, Tobias had a sinking feeling. He didn't want this relationship to go the same way as his with Hal had gone. Hal was something never discussed between David and himself, both of them seemingly ashamed of the liaison. Tobias himself *was* ashamed, but ashamed of his own behavior. He had neglected Hal, and he had lost his former lover to other men's beds. He felt something akin to physical pain when he realized that he had been doing the same to David.

In his desire to get settled and secure with his patron, Lord Albury, he had been working harder and longer than he needed, always accompanying his employer, even when there were others to do so. This zeal had not gone unrewarded; Lord Albury had been more than generous, increasing his pay, as well as giving him accounts at a swordsmiths and a clothier, for the lord loved his men-at-arms to be smartly dressed, kitted out and armed in a fashion that was foreign in its influence.

However, looking at David now, laughing and joking with a new set of friends, Tobias realized it was time he stopped working quite so hard, and spent a little more time on what was most important to him, before he lost it forever. This place—dark, dingy, and filled with young, half-drunk wastrels and silent, unfriendly men—was not the background for a man like David. With his looks he deserved to be at court, or at least in Tobias' opinion. It was ironic that there was no court anymore.

He walked past the laughing men and up to the bar, bought two mugs of ale, and returned to the trestle, rudely elbowing one young lad out of the way. Foolishly the lad seemed about to complain, until he realized how much taller and broader Tobias was, and seemed to recognize the soldier in Tobias' bearing. Then Tobias gave one of the mugs to David and smiled at him, hoping it would say all he could not.

David's tongue was a little slurred with drink. "So, you found me." He didn't look pleased to be interrupted, and his voice was harsh.

"Eventually," Tobias said, guardedly; he didn't want an argument, not here in public. "How is Christopher?"

"Lording it over Stephan, when I left them" David smiled slightly. "Christopher was having the toes of his broken leg scratched. He is a master at getting what he wants."

Tobias smiled at this, thinking that it took one to know one.

"Will he walk again?" he asked, feeling pathetic that they had to maintain this pretence at small talk, but aware of the other young men around the table, who were listening and watching the exchange. No doubt, one or more of them were willing for Tobias to break with David, so that they could step in. *That*, he thought fiercely, *is never going to happen, not while I have breath in my body*. He had found and lost David once, only to be blessed enough to find him again in the most unlikely of places.

"The monks are confident that he will," David was saying. "But he will not find it easy—they say the leg is shorter than the other." There was an awkward silence between them, and one of the young men started to sing; this was taken up by the others around the table until all were singing. All except David and Tobias, locked in an island of uncomfortable awkwardness.

"I can't stand this," said Tobias suddenly. He touched David lightly on the knee. "Let's get out of here."

"The curfew," murmured David, though his eyes lit up at the touch, making him look happier than he had for a while.

"The Devil take the curfew," Tobias growled, loud enough for a man next to him to hear. "I want to talk to you, and I can't do that here." He drained his drink and waited for David to do so. He did, but then took an annoyingly long time saying good-night to everyone. It was, as Tobias had seen when he came into the tavern, obvious that his lover was a favorite and a regular. *How could he not be a favorite,* he thought, *with his beautiful face and friendly manner.* He charmed all he came across, women, children, and most especially men. One of the youths looked at Tobias curiously as he stood to lead David out of the tavern, and Tobias had a sinking feeling in his stomach.

As they left the smoky atmosphere for the street, the cold air hurting their lungs, he voiced the concern he'd been feeling. "What do they know about us, about you?"

"Do I appear to be stupid?" David snapped, the smile sliding from his face. "They didn't even know of your existence until tonight. I can't imagine what they are thinking now." He glanced sideways, taking in the finery of Tobias' black and silver uniform, his new sword and dagger, and buckled shoes. "A fancy gentle-man such as yourself coming into a place like that, and leaving with the pretty boy after buying him a drink." The last words were almost spat from his mouth.

"I didn't think of it like that," Tobias said quietly.

"You didn't *think*," corrected David, getting angrier. "You never do though, Tobias, do you?" He increased his pace, head-ing towards the river, his long legs carrying him forward. Tobias hurried after him and grabbed his arm, spinning him around, shocked at the fury on David's face.

"What do you mean by that?" He felt wrong-footed, confused; he hardly knew what he had done to deserve this fierce wall of sullen anger. David pulled away again and attempted to keep walking, but Tobias' composure cracked and he grabbed hold of David by the upper arms, threw him against a brick wall, and yelled at him. "Damn you! Keep still and stop trying to walk away from me! Just talk, will you? Do you have to run away from everything in your life?"

David gave a sharp gasp, and as soon as the words were out of his mouth Tobias knew he had made a terrible mistake; the hurt on David's face tore a hole in his heart, but Tobias' anger still raged, a jealous, paranoid anger. David tore himself away and ran ahead of him back to Addle Street. He was through the door mere seconds before Tobias. Inside, he lit the candles and turned around, his eyes blazing, ready to continue the argument.

"And whose bloody fault is it that I've had to run away, that I have no home—no father?" The force of David's voice almost knocked Tobias backwards with the shock of hearing such rage coming from the boy who had never raised his voice to him before. "*Yours!* You and Hal! Yes, he told me all about you two—how you'd go from farm to farm, and find the prettiest boy you could find, and 'teach him about love', which basically meant you would fuck him—fuck him and *leave him!* Like it was a competition!"

"It wasn't—"

"Wasn't like that with me? Wasn't it? You didn't come back, did you? Had your fun and left. Hal told me how it was your turn!"

Tobias reeled as the words spat from his lover's mouth, words that David had clearly been keeping back for weeks, every bitter thought he'd been harboring.

"Hal told me everything one night—when he came in, drunk and rambling about you. How he loved you—and how you set up your little game. How he had to watch you fuck your way across the country! You arranged it all, didn't you? And you were so good at it by the time you got to me—forgetting your ale, distracting Jonathan, you wandering off—yes, he told me *everything!* How do you think that made me feel? You took me, introduced me to something so wonderful, and then you left! Left me to deal with it. If you had left me alone, gone to the next farm—do you think I would have done what I did to Jonathan? Would have even *considered* it?"

Tobias was staggered. He couldn't believe that David had all this fury hidden away inside him, that he blamed Tobias for everything that had happened to his family.

"You can't blame me for that!"

"Why the hell not?" David raged on. "You destroyed us both! Jonathan was a good man, he believed in hell and damnation and all that. Thanks to you, I made him do things that he thinks he's going to hell for!"

Tobias temper snapped. "*Jonathan!* I'm sick to death of hearing about the saintly Jonathan! I didn't do anything to you that you didn't want done, David. You'd have turned to Jonathan eventually—I just hurried it along for you. And what happened to that 'true love'? He drove you away, didn't he? He wouldn't believe you when it really mattered. He was going to *shoot* you in that wood, and yet still you moon over him like some lovesick maid!"

David's face paled. He seemed to struggle for control. "*No.* He was never unfaithful. I was the cause of everything that went wrong for him. I'm beginning to think that I should have stayed after all." He turned to face the fireplace.

Tobias spun him around. "I've never been unfaithful to you, David, I swear it."

David refused to look at him. "Hal told me just how faithful you were to him."

Tobias shook his head. "You don't understand. Hal and I—we had a different kind of friendship. But you are right, it was like a competition."

"What I can't bear the thought of," said David sharply, "was that it might have been *Hal's* turn that day. I wonder what difference that might have made, to all of our lives. You hurt people, deliberately. Jonathan only hurt me because he was hurt himself."

Jonathan. Damned Jonathan. He tainted every thought of David's. Tobias thought back to the nasty little scene in the woods at Naseby, overhearing that conversation and feeling sick to death every moment the Roundhead had his musket aimed at David.

He hoped Jonathan was dead, and he hoped he could find *out* he was dead, and tell David of it, so David could stop thinking backwards thoughts and simply move on, with him, make a new life, instead of yearning for something that he could never have.

"He was a *boy*, David," Tobias whispered. "Forget him. The world has moved on through fire and war. Those Kineton boys don't exist any more. You can't recreate what has been destroyed. *God*, David, I should know that more than anyone. Move forward. I can't compete with a phantom, I can't compete with a saint, and you know as well as I do, Jonathan wasn't a saint."

"*No!*" David shouted. "No, he wasn't. He was jealous and possessive and suspicious and brutal, but that's how I liked him! He was passionate—he *cared!* He cared if I looked at anyone else! He cared where I was—he worried and looked after me. He cared enough to be around…" His voice dropped suddenly. "He may not have been perfect, but he was there, and he wasn't afraid to say that he loved me!"

Something inside Tobias broke open at this; David thought that he didn't love him? He pulled the young man towards him, not an easy task as David was nearly as strong as he was, shorter but full of muscles born from hours at the anvil.

Twisting David's hands behind his back, Tobias held him fast. "He *loved* you? If he loved you, how could he have let you go? How could he have doubted you? He should have begged you, forced you to stay if he'd loved you one fraction as much as I do." He closed his mouth over David's, kissed him in spite of the fact that David was making it clear he didn't want to be kissed. Then he broke away and looked down at the man in his arms. David was looking up at him with a mixture of distrust and fear, but also a faint haze of hope in his hazel eyes. He tried to shake free, but Tobias was not letting him loose. Tobias almost laughed at the disbelief in David's eyes. "Yes, I love you, you stupid, selfish little idiot—didn't you know that?"

He moved towards the stairs, dragging David with him. David was still unyielding, but he allowed himself to be manhandled, knowing that Tobias was strong enough to win in any serious wrestling contest. Once in the bedroom, Tobias began to tear the clothes from David, feeling that the only way he could truly show David what he meant was to let loose the passion that he felt, he had been holding back, for so many reasons. Buttons tore, fabric ripped, laces unthreaded as David was laid bare. Pushing his prize back onto the bed with one shove, he undressed in seconds and fell on top of David, pinning him down by his legs and wrists. He began to graze upon David's body with teeth and lips, murmuring the reassurances of love that he had been holding back for so long.

He wanted to write his name on David's flesh, to brand him with permanent marks so that he could lay claim to this ethereal boy, who, Tobias was certain, would forever be pursued by every like-minded man he met. He wanted to split open the beautiful head and tear out every thought, every last memory of Jonathan, and to replace the surly Puritan's face with his own. He'd never felt so proprietorial with anyone in his life before. Where Tobias' mouth moved, small red and black bruises sprang up. Throughout the sweet torture David lay writhing in a torment of being marked, possessed, Jonathan's claims being overwritten, erased.

"You are mine, David Caverly," Tobias said, rubbing his cock against David's hip as he kissed his neck and cheek. "Mine, and don't you ever forget it." He feathered kisses over David's upturned face, his eyebrows, his closed eyelids, his temples. He slid his hands around his lover's waist, dug his nails into his back, and pulled him hard against him, buried his mouth in his neck and bit down harder than before as his erection slid between David's thighs and rubbed against the sensitive skin of his balls. David gasped, his fingers tangling in the sheets.

"Tobias," David said, panting slightly, but all Tobias did was slide down, silent at last.

David felt him move down his chest, leaving damp trails of saliva and tears, lips kissing him in a silent benediction. He knew now that Tobias loved him, but right this moment, he felt that Tobias was worshipping someone that wasn't David Caverly, but some unknown idol; it seemed almost blasphemous. He tried to pull Tobias back up to his face, to kiss him, to calm him, but Tobias was heading southwards with tender deliberation, his fingers grazing his balls and pushing David towards sensual madness. Tobias' hot and so familiar breath was on his cock, and with a desperate groan David slipped into his lover's mouth, just as Tobias slid a slender finger into his entrance.

Tobias was humming, his finger working him deeply, causing David to feel like there was molten liquid pooling around his groin, that possessory mouth swirling around his cock the way he liked it best. David was crying out, his body Tobias' instrument, all of his control lost to the man who played him tenderly and as expertly as any musician. He'd mislaid all the boundaries of where he ended and Tobias began.

His orgasm was like a dam breaking, beginning with a rumbling of walls and building up till it could sweep away cathedrals, softer, sweeter and more intense than anything he'd experienced since Tobias' return to him. As the waters receded, he lay almost catatonic listening to Tobias' voice, now shorn of all anger and violence, still telling him how much he loved him.

Tobias moved back to his face, and touched it lightly, tears rolling down his face. He looked almost as if this moment was their last on earth, and he wanted to capture David's face in his eyes forever. As David understood what the words meant, how Tobias had made them his very own, his own tears mingled with those his lover dropped onto his face.

Taking both of his hands in his, Tobias moved between David's legs, smiled sweetly at the limp and depleted youth, and with eyes burning with a love David now knew was real, he entered him with a soft hiss of pleasure. There were no words to describe Tobias' face, and David was almost frightened by the intensity in his eyes. He didn't know if he could live up to

Tobias' perception of him, but as Tobias began to move slowly within him he forgot about the darkness, and remembered that their tunnel had a bright light at the end of it that was not canon fire, nor the blaze of war. That was over, and the future was here and now.

For Jonathan, it felt like being reborn. In the days and weeks since his Trial he had been tended to by Michael, prayed over and cared for in a manner unlike any he had ever experienced. Even his mother, fond as she was of him, had been unable to spend such singularly devoted hours with him as Michael did now, hampered as she had been with so many other charges dependent on her time.

He felt light; that was the only way he could have described it. He felt as light as a feather, as an angel's wing. All the weight of his guilt and shame had been torn from him and he was released from his torment. He floated above Michael's golden head, held only to the earth by an invisible chain that linked them.

In Chelmsford, after his recovery, Matthew Hopkins had had one interview with him, alone. That had been a terrifying experience. The man asked him to his room, and Jonathan had looked to Michael for instruction, but had found none in his face. Unable to refuse the Witchfinder, he had followed Matthew into his chambers and sat in response to his bidding.

Matthew had spoken gently to him. "I know what you have been through, Jonathan," he had said, quietly. "I have spoken to Michael, and he told me what you were harboring in that quiet soul of yours. Be advised that we rejoice that you have put it aside, but know this—no man will ever ask you to discuss your Trial, and we do not judge a man on who he was before he was saved. We hoped you were one of us before this, and are rejoiced to find you purged." Then he had joined Jonathan in prayer for many hours as the Witchfinder begged God to keep the Devil away from Jonathan. In Jonathan's mind there was no doubt who the Devil really was, and he had no fear; he knew that he would never see that silver-haired, silver-tongued devil again.

When he had returned to Michael, Jonathan had thrown himself onto his knees and wept, kissing his master's hands, begging never to cut him loose without instruction again.

At this request Michael gave Jonathan a soft, secretive smile and had gathered him into his arms. "If you are the pupil you promise to be, then I will never need to." This reassured and chilled Jonathan in equal measure.

Michael asked for little at first except utter obedience, as swiftly and as easily as Jonathan could give it. If he was asked a question, however innocent or casual Michael appeared to frame it, Jonathan was expected to answer in as full and as frank a way as he could. At first Jonathan stumbled in these lessons, being unused to such openness of speech, preferring the more introspective nature of his Puritan upbringing. Michael never became angry over stuttering honesty, but if he suspected an evasion or a half-truth his retribution was swift.

Jonathan soon learned that most question and answer sessions took place in bed; he learned to wake swiftly, to listen attentively to everything Michael said, even when his hands were sweeping over him, or his mouth was hot against his neck, or his cock was breaching him. Jonathan kept alert, and he learned to answer openly and quickly, for if he did not, pain followed gentleness with the certainty of night following day.

But pain was not the worst that Michael could inflict. Far more terrible than any pain, or fear of pain, was the threat of being cut loose, to have their slender connection severed. This was a punishment that Michael used only when he had exhausted every other method of teaching Jonathan a particular lesson, and it took a very few times before Jonathan would do anything, *anything* to avoid this disassociation, this…horror. Michael simply withdrew himself from Jonathan, for as little as an hour but sometimes as much as several days at a time, and it was as if Jonathan was blinded, made deaf and dumb. Without guidance, without permission, he was not a human. He was incapable of leaving their rooms, unable to walk down to the dining room, unable to use the piss pot, and eventually he would end up shuddering and rocking, crouched in a corner like a tame fox who had been freed but has slunk back to the only home it had known, starving and covered with filth.

When he had reached this black pit of despair, Michael would return to him, and it was only the thought that this was just a punishment, and that Michael *would* return to him, that kept Jonathan from teetering over the edge of madness. For if he didn't truly believe that Michael would return to ensure that the lesson had been learned, then that thread between them would truly be severed, and Jonathan knew he would lose himself. Only Michael had his soul safe, he knew that with a fervent certainty he hadn't felt since first he read the Bible.

Jonathan's lusts had been razed and torn from him, his prick unable to respond to anything that Michael did to him. At first Jonathan was surprised that Michael was not angry about this, until he learned that it was not his body that made Michael the happiest, it was Jonathan's obedience that aroused him, made Michael turn to him with eager hands and loving words, tangled with Biblical texts. Jonathan knew that after a lesson well learned, after however many punishments it took, it was all forgotten, all wrongs forgiven, and Michael would bathe the cuts he had inflicted upon him, or wash the filth from his body and praise him.

It was the praise that healed Jonathan better than any balm or bandage. Knowing that he had pleased Michael, that he had done something so right to deserve praise, was like drops of ambrosia on a parched tongue. Jonathan could live on one word of Michael's praise for many days, or at least, until the next time he displeased him.

◖◗ CHAPTER 25 ◖◗

Parliament's troops swept across the country. Chester,
Bridgewater and Bath all fell to the Roundheads and
Cromwell's New Model Army marched across the West
Country, putting down any insurrections he encountered.
By the time the inclement weather drove the King back to
Oxford for the winter, most of the country was in Parlia-
ment's hands.

After the plans to expand their operation was given its blessing by
Hopkins, and the second wave of the Assizes were over, Hopkins
arranged for them to leave their lodgings at the Queen's Head, in
preparation to move everyone back to his base at Mistley, to the
hostelry known as The Thorn. The entourage, consisting of Hopkins, Stearne, Goody Phillips, Michael, and Jonathan traveled back
by coach. Jonathan marveled that when once he would walk everywhere—or at most travel by cart—now he seemed to have gone so
far up in the world as to be taken everywhere by coach, even though
the two young men were riding in the basket on the back of the
roof, rather than in a little more comfort inside. Jonathan didn't
care; it seemed inconceivable that in such a short time, his life had
changed so much. The journey of forty miles took an easy two days,
instead of the same time in a painful route march, or a four-day
hike by foot. Jonathan found the county of Essex beautiful, but
much flatter from the country near Kineton, or his home village.

From Chelmsford to Colchester the road was good, straight and wide, running past well-tended farmland and manorial parks, even if some of the place names were disturbing, places like the ominous sounding Gore Pit. But after a night's stop in Colchester, the landscape changed. The roads closed in, became narrower, the villages were quieter, and as they passed through, children would run from the street into the cottages. It gave Jonathan a frisson of fear, and he turned to Michael to seek some explanation.

Michael touched his arm in that particular way he had when he was pleased with his pupil, and Jonathan's heart raced at the contact.

"This is where Matthew came from," Michael explained. "Here, south of the Stour. This was the nest, he says, where it all sprang from, but he of course was born sixteen hundred years too late. By the time he was here, the threat was dispersed around the world."

"I don't understand," Jonathan said, worried that his incomprehension would be misconstrued as disobedience.

"I know you don't," said Michael. He took Jonathan's hand and tangled their fingers together, his eyes alight with passion for his subject. "But it is simplicity really, when you think about it. When the Christ was given his chance on the world, had his opportunity to find disciples, so too did the Anti-Christ. When Joseph of Arimathaea was bringing the Grail to England and planting his staff over in the west, the Devil was landing his disciples here, in the east."

Jonathan watched Michael as he spoke. He found his friend beautiful to watch whenever he talked of the cause. To Jonathan's eyes he became almost golden, the glow that he carried with him shining around him like a halo, obvious to those who had eyes trained to see it, those like him, who believed. How different it was to the quicksilver of David. Beauty but no truth. And like quicksilver, nothing you could hold or touch without poisoning yourself.

They sat in silence for a long while after that, Jonathan happy for the simple touch of hand on hand. As the light began to fade, a smell Jonathan had only encountered once before became apparent. "It's near the sea?" he asked with growing excitement. He had only seen the sea once, when his regiment had camped high on some windswept northern cliffs. The sight had startled him, made him feel so small. It had seemed to him that God could have put his hand down and plucked him up and thrown him into the waves, and he would have been grateful. It had been unsettling and magnificent all at once. He longed to see it again.

"Not really, but the Stour is at the beginning of the estuary, leading out to the sea by Harwich. The Thorn is by the quay, but the sea is no distance at all, really."

Jonathan peered out, eager to catch a glimpse of the water.

"What do you see, Jonathan?" Michael asked.

Jonathan recognized the tone as masterful and answered swiftly. "I see... fog," he ventured, knowing how this was a stupid answer, as the low-lying mist was obvious to all, but it was what he felt. "The landscape is a disguise for something else," he added lamely. "I ... know how impossible that sounds..."

"You answered," Michael said, squeezing his hand with the casual familiarity that meant so much to Jonathan, "and it might be nonsense or you might think so, but it was from the heart. You, my stalwart, see clearer than you think." Buildings loomed ahead in the mist as Michael spoke, and the village came in sight. "This is a strange county and it has more legends and evil associated with it than any other I know. It is also the home to these mists which are strange, changeable, and too thick to be natural. But this," he said, as the coach slowed, stopping outside an inn, "is where we gather our forces against it. The Thorn."

The chilling mist from the river was creeping across the quayside in a ground-blanketing sheet, its ragged edges like rotting, questing fingers. Jonathan shuddered, and Michael followed his gaze to where the mist crawled along the ground. "Horrible, isn't it?" he said. "Let's go in."

Jonathan had never been so glad to be out of the dark in his life. The sight of that unearthly fog, the like of which he'd never

seen before, had unnerved him. He was more than happy to occupy himself helping carry the luggage to the rooms and then
join the others in the bar.

While Hopkins and Stearne spoke to the locals and dealt with
what appeared to a large amount of correspondence, handed over
to them by the barman, Michael introduced Jonathan to Edward
Parsley and Frances Mills, the final two members of the team.
Jonathan felt shy and provincial again; these men seemed as self-
assured as Michael, but older, sterner, and dressed like him in
unremitting black. He noted that they greeted his friend with
loud and effusive welcomes, but their eyes were wary, and they
exchanged glances with each other, as if they thought less well of
him than their greetings showed.

Jonathan sat and let the talk wash around him. It was mainly
of the war, the current rebellions flickering here and there
throughout the country, and the treachery that the King had compounded by inviting Irish Catholic mercenaries over to fight
against his own subjects of the true faith.

"You are a quiet man, Master Graie," said Parsley, after half an
hour of talk had passed and Jonathan had said very little.

Michael cut in so quickly that Jonathan did not even have a
chance to do more than open his mouth. "He does not say much,
but he listens well to what he hears."

Jonathan knew that for a veiled instruction, and he said nothing
for the entire evening; even when addressed directly he looked
down or away to the fireplace. He hated to do that, for he was not
used to being uncivil to others, but he dared not disobey. He had a
distinct feeling that this did not win him any friends amongst his
newest acquaintances, but he was sure that it was worth it.

His reward came quickly. Michael touched his arm and led him
upstairs to their new quarters in the Thorn, turned to him with the
most beautiful smile and told him how good, how very good he was
getting to be, how perfect a pupil he was. *Yes,* thought Jonathan, as
Michael undressed him, kissing every scar as it was uncovered, *it
was all worth it, and other men's opinions mean nothing com-*

pared to Michael's praise.

The Thorn, he soon learned, was not simply a base of operations for Hopkins' campaign to rid the country of evil. Although Jonathan had little idea what was really going on, he knew it was not all to do with witchfinding. There was a constant stream of visitors to the tiny town, and Hopkins was rarely seen downstairs in the bar after that first night. He had rooms of his own, although Jonathan had not seen them, rooms at the far end of the inn, and there were footsteps up and down stairs at all hours of the day and the night.

Occasionally Jonathan would hear voices as they passed his door, or he'd catch a few words in the bar, but words that baffled him, nothing seemingly of their shared cause. One night, as he sat reading at Michael's feet, his friend's fingers carding through his hair, he plucked up the courage to speak.

"Matthew has many visitors," he ventured. "I was wondering—" He realized it was a mistake almost instantly. Michael's fingers tightened in his hair, and his head was yanked back sharply. He felt on his neck the silver chill of the small knife Michael had been using to peel an apple.

"Jon," Michael's voice was a low growl, "you will learn to be honest with me. Have I taught you nothing?"

"I meant nothing by it."

"*Liar,*" hissed Michael. "Liar! How could you still lie to me? Is the Devil still within you? I should cut him out. Is that what you want?" The knife's point nicked Jonathan's skin but he held perfectly still, knowing it would make it worse should he move. "You wish to wheedle out of me what Matthew plans? Are you a spy, Jonathan Graie?"

"No. No! How could you doubt me?" Jonathan said quietly, breathing shallowly as if his very breath might tip Michael into further ire. He felt hairs tear from his scalp. "I merely wondered…who all these strange men are…I meant nothing wrong, Michael. I was incautious perhaps, that's all."

The sun returned to Michael's face as quickly as the storm

clouds had gathered. The knife clattered to the floor and Michael slid down, pinning Jonathan to the ground, kissing him brutally. "My Jon," he breathed, "we must all be cautious—for it is not only God's work we do here."

Jonathan let the fear fall away from him, relieved that Michael's furies were sometimes easily deflected. But as Michael slid his hands over Jonathan's skin he couldn't help being reminded of another young man who would use sex as a diversion.

Michael forgave him as swiftly as he punished him, as long as Jon was penitent, and he always was. After that evening he dared not ask more questions, but he kept his eyes open and listened to all he overheard, whilst seeming to be busy or ignorant. The more he heard and saw, the more he became convinced that witchfinding was not the only work that Matthew Hopkins did. *However,* he thought to himself, even if he didn't entirely convince himself, *it is none of my business unless Michael makes it so.*

As the autumn mists gave way to the first frosts of winter, he found he was too busy to leave the inn and had been unable to visit the sea as he had long wanted to do. Michael kept him employed in learning his new "trade." First he had him read *Daemonologie* by King James, and in fact he was so insistent that Jonathan get the full flavor of the book, he had him learn great chunks of Philomathes' speeches. He seemed to know most of Epistemon's lines by heart and would require Jonathan to act out the speeches. Amazingly, to Jonathan, mistakes in the recitation were never punished, and Michael was never so patient as when tutoring his friend on the harder concepts or words that Jonathan might not have encountered in the little reading he had done prior to joining Hopkins' cause.

When he was satisfied that Jonathan understood the *Daemonologie* in a manner that he could apply it to the work they did, they moved on to *The Wonderful Discoverie of Witches in the Countie of Lancaster.* Michael was most particular, pointing out the similarities between the cases there and here, particularly that of the evil Demdike of Lancaster with the infamous

Elizabeth Clarke, one of Hopkins' most famous cases. His master kept him so busy with studies that Jonathan, still eager to explore, found that he had no time to see the village, let alone go to the sea, for all that it was so tantalizingly near. The scents and sounds beguiled him, pulled at him.

Next came papers, more paper than Jonathan had ever seen in his young life. Once, when he begged the local pastor in Kineton for used parchment upon which to draw, he couldn't have imagined there was so much paper in all the world as there was now scattered around their room.

The two young men spent further days closeted away, poring over maps, newspaper reports, and correspondence from preachers and laypersons that had been received by Hopkins since the campaign had begun. They needed to find out where they would be of the most use, and working together, they marked on the maps available where reports had been made, accusations given, and tales of supernatural events were witnessed.

Michael worked his way through the paperwork tirelessly, like a man possessed, finding more and more information to work from, up early and not going to bed until late. But Jonathan was happy, because while Michael worked like this, he was less demanding, asking only that Jonathan be ready with a quill to make notes at a moment's notice. When Michael was occupied like this, he was affectionate in an absent-minded way; while they were alone in their room working, he strode about reading from letters and kissing Jonathan sporadically as he passed him. Each tour of the room seemed endless, and each kiss seemed a lifetime apart.

After too short an idyll of busy intimacy they had their new target area: Cambridge. Nathaniel Bacon, a member of the Long Parliament and a good acquaintance of Hopkins, had received numerous complaints about witches from people in that area and sought Hopkins' assistance.

"The timing could not be more perfect," proclaimed Michael jubilantly, when Hopkins called them both to meet Bacon in his rooms. He unrolled the map of Cambridgeshire they had marked out, and showed the prevalence of supernatural activity dotted around the villages on the outskirts of that city. "We will sweep in and cleanse the county, as Matthew has done here. Believe me, we will be famous men this time next year."

"Young Giddings here I know well, of course," said Bacon in an approving tone. The stranger was, to Jonathan, of a stern and quite forbidding aspect, gray-haired, and an obvious Puritan. "But I know not this young man he brings with him. Is this the Graie boy of whom you speak so highly?"

Jonathan waited to be addressed, but he did not miss Stearne, lounging against wooden paneling at the back of the room, shoot him a look of sheer hatred at these words. Over the last few weeks it had become obvious to Jonathan that Stearne resented him for some reason, and he couldn't think what he had done to deserve it.

Hopkins stepped in and summoned Jonathan forward. "Aye, we had the very good fortune to meet up with Jon in Chelmsford and he learned fast, but then," he said, with a hard look at Michael, "he had a firm taskmaster."

"And so he should," Bacon said, walking around Jonathan as if he were a horse, or at a hiring fair. Jonathan kept his gaze firmly on Michael, whose eyes were blazing with command and strength. "Not everyone can do the Lord's work, and do it well." He stopped in front of Jonathan and looked him up and down, but addressed his question to Michael. "Well, Giddings, can he do it well? I trust you in my parishes, I have seen you work, but I fret about letting a stranger loose, even if he does look like the storm-crow of doom. Do you vouch for him? Hopkins gives his assurance, and if you do also, then I will give you leave."

"Unreservedly, sir."

Jonathan's heart swelled with a pride that he thought he had lost. "He is ready," Michael went on, "more than ready. He learns so fast it is almost too hard to teach him." Jonathan just about managed to avoid smiling at this inaccuracy, as he knew what a burden he had been to his master over the past few weeks. The gratitude and affection he felt for Michael broke any banks of will he had left. He loved Michael—he knew that more assuredly now than he knew his own name.

"Well, that's good enough for me," said Bacon, pulling Jonathan's attention back to the subject at hand. Bacon offered Michael a sheaf of letters, "There's more than enough work for the two of you, God knows." Included in the bundles were sealed letters, Jonathan noticed, the seals heavy and decorative, but he thought little of it. They were ready, and soon they would be off to Cambridge together.

Michael was ecstatic. "Once we are there, you will see, more witches will be found than we can manage. We will soon be re-cruiting more helpers, just you wait."

At this Jonathan felt a tiny twinge of jealousy, and vowed to himself that he would work himself to death to avoid needing new recruits; he would not share Michael's attention with anyone.

Michael seemed pre-occupied the next morning, and Jonathan was on edge, worried that it was something he had done in the night to displease his master. Once or twice previously Michael had punished him for talking in his sleep—Michael said he had speaking the name of the Devil he had been enslaved to at Kineton. As he poured ale for Michael now, Jonathan became so anxious that the cup he was filling spilled over. He dropped to his knees in accustomed penitence and begged forgiveness, his soul lightening in relief as Michael's hand tipped his chin up so he met his eyes.

"What do you think you have done?" Michael asked softly, his eyes raking Jonathan's face in query.

"Nothing in consciousness," Jonathan said, tears pricking his eyes, "but if I have displeased thee, if I have reverted to evil in the night—"

"You have not," Michael said abruptly as he stood, leaving Jonathan kneeling. He took his cloak from the stand. "I am to go with Matthew to a meeting."

Jonathan remained where he was, unable to ask anything for

fear of sudden violence, but he wanted to ask, to beg not to be left by himself. He looked up and found Michael watching him with a strange expression.

"Your eyes are clear windows to your thoughts, my Jonathan," he said, smiling and gesturing for him to stand. "You have been wanting to explore, have you not? Take the morning to look around the village. We will meet at lunch, and I will listen carefully to all you have seen."

Jonathan was left alone then, pleased that he had permission to do something that he wanted to do, but feeling suddenly bereft, and also a little unnerved that his master had misinterpreted his inner thoughts so completely, when he thought that Michael had understood him more than anyone else on this earth.

After David and Tobias' reconciliation, certain changes were made in their relationship. Both of them realized that they could not go on seeing each other on such a sporadic basis, for it was rotting away the small foundation they both had worked hard to build and keep secret. David talked to Robert one evening, and spun him a long and complicated tale about Tobias' uncle, who (he lied) had returned from war, injured and invalided.

"We were staying in his house, uninvited," David told him, trying to keep as close to the truth as he could. "And he wasn't at all pleased to find us there, as least at first, but after a while he came to rely on us. Then we both found employment, and since then the poor man has had to fend for himself. When we visited him last night, he was quite ill with neglect. Tobias was wracked with guilt, and although I hardly know the man, I was a little ashamed that we both so casually forgot him."

"You are not thinking of leaving?" Robert asked, stirring his broth and looking over his shoulder from where he crouched by the fireside.

"No, not that, *no!*" David said, relieved that it was going well. "But if you would allow me to spend nights there at the house—

not all of them, for Tobias and I can share the load—we can be
sure he's got someone with him, at least at night."

"That seems fair," Robert said, putting a bowl of stew out for
them both, "but three nights only. It's not *your* bloody uncle, and
your fancy friend should do the lion's share of it." David gave
Robert a pleased grin. It was enough.

Meanwhile, the rolling chair was a great success. Christopher
had learned to maneuver it as best as he could. It ran well up the
straight lines of the stables, and needed help around corners, but
the boy was thrilled; it meant that he could be left to groom, feed,
and water along the aisles, and if he took a little longer than
Stephan did, or if Stephan ran around and helped a lot more than
he used to, no one remarked on it. The monk who had set the
bone came back on a regular basis to check on the boy's leg.
David never knew what he was looking for, but he always seemed
to be satisfied. David promised himself that once the splint was
off the boy's leg, he would go to church and give thanks.

As he hammered horseshoes that afternoon, Christopher
wheeled up to him, hot and smiling. "You look like your thoughts
was off with the fairies."

"I was trying to remember the last time I was in a church."
David shoved the shoe into the furnace, and leant against the
brickwork as he waited for it to get red hot.

"What made yer think of that?"

"No reason, really," David said, evading the issue. Images of
churches he'd known rose in his head. Kineton church: with the
inevitable vision of his father—pious, good, *unchangeable*—
kneeling beside him. Memories of kissing a reluctant Jonathan
by the side of it in the biting winter wind. Joining his troop in one
before a battle to ask—pointlessly—for victory. Running for
cover into a church at Leicester. Setting light to another, where
Roundheads sheltered; a sacrilege full of screaming horses and
the shouted prayers of dying men. However he tried, he could-
n't clearly picture himself in earnest, heart-felt prayer. He knew
there must have been a time when he believed with the same

strength as his father, but it seemed two lifetimes ago. Some time long before the war, before Jonathan. Those days were fading, he realized. The farm, seemed caught always in an endless summer, almost impossibly beautiful, in a country idyll, lightly scented with primroses, far from London, and therefore quite unreal.

⫷ CHAPTER 26 ⫸

There was nobody in the bar room except the innkeeper as Jonathan walked down the stairs. His boots seemed to echo with suppressed guilt, and with every step to the doors he expected to be called back. He was sure that this was a test; and by the time he reached the door and stretched his hand forward to turn the handle, he noticed that his fingers were shaking. The cold air hit him hard, and a flurry of snow blew in, bringing an angry yell from the innkeeper. Even after he had closed the door behind himself, and stood blinking in the daylight, his heart was still pounding.

Outside, the bright white sky seemed to burn his eyes after the long days of seclusion surrounded by the dark oak paneling of the inn. It was breathtaking; the air burned his lungs, but it felt so good to be outside. He wrapped his cloak around him, thrust his hands deep into his pockets, and walked across the track to the river, losing himself as he watched the boats unloading and the ungainly swans as they waddled between the busy sailors. He wondered for a mad moment what it would be like to step aboard one of these ships, and be swept away somewhere unimagineable—London, France, Spain, Holland—or maybe somewhere even further. He frowned to himself at the very thought, his blood turning cold at what Michael would think if he knew what Jonathan was contemplating. It was not as if he had any money of his own—Michael looked after his pay, such as it was, and Jonathan had not dared to ask for any.

To take his mind from such treachery, he turned and walked along the quayside towards the east, following the line of small ships moored up and those still anchored in the narrow twisting channel, waiting for their chance to unload. Warehouses lined the quayside, and the scents of the ships mingled with the smell of the river and the elusive scent of the open sea, giving this little town an exotic and exciting flavor. In the cold winter's sun, the quay presented a much different appearance from how he'd seen it the night he arrived. It no longer seemed menacing, but bustling and lively.

The cobbled way finished long before the line of ships; a muddy frozen track lay beyond it, and Jonathan walked as far as he could before running out of land The track was merely for animals, running alongside reed beds and treacherous looking mudbanks. Reluctantly, he turned back towards the town, unwilling to incarcerate himself in the inn before he had to. He had no idea of when he would be granted time to stretch his legs again. He walked into the town, taking note of the shops on the main street, but with no coins burning holes in his pockets, the only thing that caught and held his interest was a blacksmith's forge in the square at the back of the inn.

Drawn to the art he knew, he leant against the edge of a horse trough and watched the blacksmith work for a good hour, casting a critical eye over the man's technique and style. After a while, the cold began to trouble him. His feet began to tingle and complain, and his fingers were so numb he had difficulty moving them without pain. Instinctively he moved into the forge and warmed his hands at the furnace, wanting to say something of the craft to the large sweating man, who didn't seem to notice the chill. Jonathan remembered how that felt.

As he turned to thank the smith for letting him warm himself, he heard a clatter of hooves, and saw a pair of magnificent chestnut horses being led across the square to the forge. They were of a type he hadn't seen before, and, always appreciative of horseflesh, he marveled at their compact strength, short, strong necks, and powerful legs.

The young man leading them was as unlike his charges as could be, apart from his hair which was the almost the same ruddy shade. He was as reedy as a pike, his face thin and pale, his lips seeming almost blue in the cold air. As he led the horses past where Jonathan stood, his face, half obscured by a strangely shaped hat, came into clear view. His skin had seemed pockmarked from a distance, but now Jonathan could see that it was nothing more disfiguring than freckles, livid on his pale skin. Jonathan watched the blacksmith give the newcomer a broad smile, teeth white in his grimy face, then set to removing the shoes from the great beasts.

It was surprising to Jonathan that there were so few people about, even in this cold. It seemed such a different scene from the old days when he'd worked at a forge. Back then, more particularly the forge in Nottingham than Kineton, the forge had been a place to meet and exchange news. In these more paranoid times, when Cromwell's spies were thought to be everywhere, Jonathan noticed that people didn't loiter or gather to gossip; they left their houses, did their errands, and returned home. The atmosphere seemed unnatural to him, and after a while he noticed that, instead of nodding politely at him, people were dropping their eyes and hurrying past. With a sinking heart, he wondered if it was because they knew with whom he was associated. He had never felt so lonely, not even in the army—and as he continued to watch the blacksmith, he was reminded of happier times.

An image of a bronzed, smiling David surged unbidden into his mind. He could see him as clear as day, as clearly as he could see the Mistley's smith. In Jonathan's mind David was bent over a horse's hoof, then he straightened, pushed his infernal hair from his eyes, and looked straight at Jonathan. With a guttural cry, Jonathan turned on his heel, leaving the forge behind him, and marched straight back to the inn without looking to the left or the right.

Back at the Thorn he flew up the stairs, and, gaining his room, he dropped to his knees and prayed with all his might. He was still on his knees, stiff and hoarse with repeated prayers, some two hours later, when the door opened.

"Jonathan?" Michael's voice cut through the fog of Jonathan's desperate pleas to *take the evil away, take the evil away...*

Michael was beside him in a heartbeat, forcing his hands down and ordering him to open his eyes. "*Now.*" It was the voice that brooked no resistance, the voice that drew him in, because that way was fear, but that way was also safety and redemption. He looked up and told his master what had happened.

"I thought he was gone. I thought thou had seared him from my mind," he said, quietly. His hands, cradled in Michael's, were shaking.

Michael kissed his forehead, then held him close, his lips reassuring and warm against his ear. "I had hoped it for you, but he won't let you go. You are not out of danger yet." Jonathan relaxed into the inevitable. "It happens betimes, and I had suspected it for some time. You know I hear you speak of him at night—sometimes I see him in your eyes. But we can defeat him, Jonathan. *I* can defeat him. If you trust me."

They prayed until Michael was satisfied of his penitence. As they ate in the bar that night, Michael made it clear that company was not invited, but read the Bible to Jonathan whilst they dined, and then read to him again later in their room. Jonathan felt safe under Michael's protection, knowing that his sins would be purged eventually, but troubled that he was even having these thoughts, these images of David. *It is a sign,* he thought, *of Michael's trust in me, that he is using the power of prayer, rather than his more extreme methods.*

Although Mistley was so small, its importance as a trading port meant that news was received in good time. Cromwell, now commander in chief of the army, and Parliament were tightening their grip on the country, to Michael's delight. Laws, new laws, Puritanical, stern laws, were filtering through from London. Singing and dancing had been banned. Jonathan had heard tales of street minstrels arrested, theatres closed. Holy Days other than the Sabbath were dwindling away, and here, in this Cromwellian stronghold of Essex, they were done away with completely. The innkeeper said that it would lead to the Thorn losing business, but whilst he grumbled in front of Stearne and Hopkins, he did not, Jonathan noticed, say anything when Michael was around.

Their routine changed; Cambridge was still part of their plans, but the date of departure had been postponed. Whatever Michael was doing with Hopkins—and Jonathan dared not ask what it was—it kept him busy for most mornings, and Jonathan found himself at liberty to do what he liked. He sought permission from Michael to be able to go out when he wished, and it was granted, with a proviso.

When Jonathan had asked this boon, Michael had been playing with him, with his blade. It was a regular occurrence, and one that seemed to arouse his master. Although Jonathan didn't understand it, he always wanted to please Michael, even though he was often terrified in his presence. Michael would run the knife all over Jonathan's body, most of the time never breaking the skin, just seemingly fascinated by the contrast of steel against the yielding flesh and muscle.

"I want you to visit that forge every day," Michael had said, that lost, dreamy look in his eyes, which Jonathan knew meant that he was actually at his most aroused, his most alert. "I want you to immerse yourself in that place—and when you return to me here, we will talk about what you've learned, and we will pray. Do you understand?"

Jonathan had nodded.

"When you return, we'll talk more about those thoughts of David...."

The next day Jonathan woke to find the usual warmth of Michael's guarding arms missing, his pillow empty. He dressed quickly, in case he was needed, and sat on the bed awaiting Michael's return. But the morning crept forward, the sun melting the swirls of frost on the windows, and Michael still did not come. As time went by, Jonathan began to get hungry, and his bladder hurt, but he knew better than to move. It wasn't until the sun rose above the ships in the harbor that a rap came at the door, causing his heart to leap. The innkeeper entered, a tray in his hands.

"Ah. Master Michael said you'd be up here," he said, putting the tray on the dresser. There was something like pity in the man's face, as he looked at Jonathan. "He's a-gone, with Masters Hopkins and Stearne."

"He left me a message?" Jonathan was almost disgusted at his own voice, at the fear in it, the fear of abandonment.

"Can't say he did," the man said, spitting in the bucket by the door. "All Master Hopkins said was that they'd be gone a week at least, and that you'd be staying here." He nodded at the tray and was gone, leaving Jonathan with his fear. *Is this another test?* Cold sweat beaded his forehead. *Should I stay here? Wait until released? Or do I dare to leave, without permission—without orders?* His fingers clenched in the fabric of the bedspread, tearing the thin blankets, and his breathing came shallow and fast. He called on Michael for guidance, and slid to his knees in prayer for fear of doing the wrong thing. For all he knew, Michael might be outside waiting to see what he did. Slowly, as his breathing calmed, his mind cleared and he remembered last night, and the knife. Michael *had* given him instructions, it was if his prayer was answered—Michael had told him to go to the forge. Relief flooded through him and he pulled himself upright, retrieved his tray and ate a little, the bile of his panic attack preventing him from doing much justice to his breakfast.

Out in the town again he felt strange. Before, he always felt he was on a long slender thread, and that wherever he was, Michael only had to tug and he would feel it. It gave him security, a sense of belonging. But, that morning, as he made the short walk down to the harbor, it seemed to him as if the sky were too big, the light too bright, and that he was alone, with no connection to anyone or anything. With every step he wanted to flee back to the inn, but he dared not. He would do as he was told.

He watched the boats for a while, but the business of loading and unloading was repetitive, and in the cold wind he soon became chilled. He turned, pulling his cloak around him, and walked slowly back toward the center of town. As he loitered outside the forge, the blacksmith looked up from his hammering and nodded in greeting. He straightened with a grimace and said, "Come in and get warm, young man. You'll go blue out there in the frost."

Jonathan had fallen out of the habit of striking up casual conversations, and his shyness had kept him from making friends easily. He hesitated until the blacksmith seemed to recognize his shyness and laughed, his weathered face creased and welcoming, but with a subtle wariness in his eyes. "Come in, lad. I'm not going to bite you, and if the fire frights you, well, you'd be better to be careful not to touch anything." He turned and put the metal he was working on into the coals again, "I saw you yesterday—the cat had your tongue then too, I believe. What's your name?"

"Graie."

"Master Graie, is it?" the blacksmith went on. "Staying up at the Thorn, b'ain't you?"

Jonathan guessed this was common knowledge, so he nodded, not knowing what else to say.

The blacksmith pulled the metal out of the coals, hammered it without further comment, and plunged it into the bucket beside him, then repeated the process while Jonathan sat awkwardly, directionless, on a wooden bench. After a while, the smith set the hinge pin he'd been working on beside Jonathan on the bench, and lifted a stone jug to his lips. After drinking deeply, he handed the jug to Jonathan, who took it, not wanting a drink particularly, but not wanting to be rude.

"I've heard tell you're one of the Witchfinders," said the smith. There was no malice or suspicion in his tone, and Jonathan realized that Michael's teaching had paid off, that he was already looking for signs like that, without realizing it.

"Not really one of them," Jonathan said, bending the truth

somewhat. "Been travelling with them a while."

"Army?"

"Yes."

"Cromwell?"

"Yes. And thee?" He could have bitten his tongue off for his curiosity; it wasn't a safe question to be asking in these times, but then the smith had asked him, so he was pretty sure of the man's reply.

"Yes," he said, confirming Jonathan's thoughts. "Don't think many people would admit to different, this side of the country."

"Not so clear cut, where I came from," Jonathan went on without thinking.

"Oh? Where's that then?"

"Further west a bit." He was regretting speaking now, was fairly sure that Michael wanted him to gather information, not give it out.

"Don't worry, boy," the smith said. "You chose the winning side, and then landed on your feet, *some* would say."

Jonathan didn't miss the slur about Hopkins, but twisted the smith's words to see if he could trick him. "I was injured," he said. "I didn't desert."

"Hey! I wasn't meaning that, young master!" the smith said quickly, putting the jug down as he stood. "Just meant that Hopkins is a well-thought-of man in these parts, mostly. Me—well, I think that he does good work, the Lord's work. Thing is..." The man's hands twisted in his apron and Jonathan suddenly realized that the man was attempting to curry favor. It stunned him, and he swelled with confidence. This then was what Michael had meant him to do, and he was succeeding!

The smith moved closer, his voice suddenly low and confidential. "There are a few, well...some who think less well of him, perhaps you could pass that along. He might be grateful for that information."

Jonathan looked up. The big man was clearly anxious, as if worried that he'd said too much. "I'm sure that he would be more than grateful for any information thou couldst give him," Jonathan said quietly and carefully. "And The Lord, too, in whose name he works."

"Aye, of course," the smith said, holding out a hand. "I should have introduced myself of course. Hopkins knows me by name, I'm sure. Webb, William Webb—and you won't find a better smith between the Wash and the Thames." He grinned.

Jonathan took the massive hand, and shook it, unsure as to how to proceed; he'd had no training in this, he couldn't interrogate the smith the same way they did the witches. "Hopkins is a man from these parts," he said. "I would have thought that he'd be more appreciated, but then," he said, changing his voice to emulate Michael's when he was inviting confidences, "a prophet is always denied in his own country."

"Most do," agreed Webb, with a shrug, "but some people think he's a fraud. *Not* that I do, mind!" he added, hurriedly, as Jonathan frowned angrily. "I can't help but hear things, working here."

Jonathan nodded, as he turned the information over in his mind and spoke to fill the gap. "I know what that's like. I was a smith, before the army. Still am, I suppose. Men gossip just as much as women, I find."

Webb laughed. "They do at that." He left Jonathan deep in thought and continued his work at the fire. Jonathan knew he should ask for names, addresses of these people, but something stopped him. He looked across the square, watching the residents about their business. Just a word from him could do terrible things, all on the word of a man he'd just met. He felt he couldn't, in all conscience, do that. He decided that he would simply pass this information on, and let Michael do with it what he wanted. He was still staring out at the square, not really seeing, when a shadow passed in front of his eyes, and he looked up.

The red-headed man he'd seen the day before was shaking hands with Webb, talking slowly in a heavily accented voice. Jonathan watched with interest, wondering where the man was from, as it was certainly not from England. He'd never met a foreigner, and had no reference to place his accent. The smith saw Jonathan's gaze and turned towards him,

"Master Graie? Allow me to introduce Master Domine Johannes. For all his outlandish fancy name, his family are good folk. Hollanders—weavers from the road toward Harwich. Domine, this is Master Graie. He's at the Thorn." The smith said nothing more of Jonathan's circumstances, but from the man's startled glance between the smith and Jonathan, it seemed obvious Johannes knew well who his companions were.

Jonathan couldn't help but scowl as he shook the young man's hand, annoyed that his questioning of the smith had been interrupted.

"Thou art a weaver too, Master Johannes?" Jonathan had trouble with the pronunciation of the strange name.

"No," Johannes said, "and please, Domine call me. I work in the brewery on the quay, but today I bring wagon wheels for repair."

"Talking of that, you two clear out now, if you want these done by noon," Webb said, as he went over to the farm wagon. Jonathan and Johannes walked into the square and watched the smith pull the massive wheels out of the back of the cart as easily as if they were feathers. Jonathan felt awkward; he'd wanted to at least get something more useful from the smith, but he supposed he had a couple of days to go back before Michael's return.

He was glowering at the water trough, lost in thought when his companion spoke. "I have seed to buy, but the wheels will be an hour or two. I invite you to take with me a glass of something?" Jonathan didn't want to, but found no reason to refuse and let Johannes lead him back to an inn near the hustle and bustle of the quay. It was busy, far busier than Jonathan had ever seen the Thorn, thronged with traders and sailors. They found two seats at a crowded table, then Jonathan watched with a sinking heart as the four men who had been sitting there stood and left the inn, their looks dark and suspicious. No others joined them, and Jonathan wanted to escape. He would have, had it not been rude to his new acquaintance who had bought him a drink.

Johannes put a tray down on the table. Two small glasses of a clear liquid stood side by side with the mugs of local ale. Jonathan looked over at Johannes as the man sat down with an honest smile on his freckled face.

"You are a handy man in a crowded inn," he said, laughing, distributing the drinks between them. "To get a table cleared that quickly is impressive." Jonathan merely shrugged his shoulders and the young man went on in his strange accented voice. "I think it is not you they object to perhaps—"

"What's this?" he asked, ignoring Johannes last comment. He pointed to the little glasses. "I'm not a man for strong spirits…"

"It's a drink from my country," Johannes grinned conspiratorially. "I keep a bottle here, as my master… he's a little like your fr…you, perhaps. Not one for strong spirits. I thought you would like to try it. I always start a friendship with a drink, and here we have the English ale and the Jenever from my country." He smiled as Jonathan lifted the little glass in his large fingers. "You must drink it all in one, like this." He swallowed the drink in a swift, upending movement, then slammed the glass on the bar. Assuming by Johannes' easy action that it couldn't be that strong, he tipped it down his throat…and immediately straightened up, coughing and spluttering as the fumes hit his lungs.

Johannes laughed. "Such a large man, to be defeated by such a little thing."

Jonathan gulped his ale to take the burning away from his mouth, and glared across at Johannes. "I'm just not—"

"Used to strong spirits, yes, you said. I should not tease you. I apologize, but we are friends now, yes?"

Jonathan glowered at Johannes for a moment, but the spirit hit his stomach, and a slow, creeping warmth started in his groin and moved outwards like an warm cloud. He couldn't help but smile.

"It seems so," he said simply.

◄◙ Chapter 27 ◙►

Over the next day or so, Jonathan did what Michael expected of him: he studied a little, prayed a lot, and spent several hours of each day in the forge in the town square. He already had the measure of Master Webb, a man who was willing to sell out everyone he knew for nothing more than the good graces of the power in the area, and he had given Jonathan more information than he really knew what to do with. He had pages of notes, scribbled down hastily when he returned from the town, for he dared not sit writing in public. They ranged from the clear-cut accusations against women who were known to have put spells on others and on livestock, to other, murkier news. What the local people really thought of Hopkins, and what they thought of Cromwell. Who among them was suspected of being a Royalist sympathizer, who was saying Mass in private, and many other betrayals. Jonathan doubted any of the leads to suspected witches would be viable; Hopkins had been in this area for too long, it was unlikely any would have slipped through his net, not this close to his base of operations.

Webb had let Jonathan show his skill at the forge, and Jonathan had loved to be reunited with fire, metal, and water after so long, slipping back into the routine of smithing effortlessly, gaining approval from Webb as he saw the mastery the young man had over the craft. The townsfolk were wary at first, but seeing Webb accept Jonathan into the forge, and watching his obvious skill they warmed, stopping to gossip while their horses were shod, or whilst their metalwork was mended. Nothing much was gleaned by this gossip, nothing much he didn't already know, but he knew it was useful; to be accepted by the town would prove a valuable token in his career with Hopkins and would please Michael.

Then there was Domine Johannes. Jonathan met up with his new friend each day and found himself increasingly eager to be in his company; sometimes the Dutchman would bring one of the brewery horses in to be shod, or he'd pass the forge with a sack over his shoulder, giving a friendly wave as he came into the town for provisions. But mostly they met after Johannes' work was through. Jonathan was alone without Michael, and the lively chat of a man who had seen countries across the sea interested him greatly.

Johannes seemed strangely incurious as to his new friend's past and asked no questions, and for that Jonathan was grateful, happy to sit and listen to his more garrulous friend, although after the shock of the Jenever, he stuck to the malty local ale made in the brewery where Johannes—or rather Domine, as the Hollander wished to be called—worked.

When darkness fell each evening, Jonathan returned to the Thorn, but he didn't linger in the bar after the evening meal was over. Stearne didn't seek out Jonathan's company, and Jonathan was pleased to maintain the distance between them. After eating he would retreat to his room, to read and try to sleep. He found it difficult, for the familiarity of being at the forge raised demons in his mind, memories he didn't want to remember. Memories of David, laughing—always laughing—his face alight with the simple pleasure of being with Jonathan. Memories of the stolen moments they'd shared when Jacob left the forge, when David would slide his arms around Jonathan and kiss the back of his neck—or slyly touch his cock through his breeches, or cup a buttock cheek. Jonathan spent hours on his knees praying for the memories to leave him, but to no avail—somehow, without Michael's assistance, he was too weak to push the temptation away.

On the fourth day after Jonathan had been abandoned by Michael, Domine had an afternoon off and, by previous arrangement, Jonathan met him outside the brewery, a small sack of provisions over his shoulder. The day was bitter, the wind coming in from the east, cutting through any amount of clothes pitiful humans could wrap around their frames, cold enough to freeze the marrow. Domine came striding out of the yard, his wide-brimmed hat jammed down hard on his head to save it from blowing away, and the two of them turned right along the road towards Harwich. Domine had promised to show Jonathan the sea, but first the two of them had to battle the freezing wind in their faces for nine miles. It was a hard journey, even though they tucked their hands into their clothes, the wind slicing their faces with invisible ice-shards straight from Russia. They hardly spoke a word to each other, except once when Domine touched Jonathan's arm and passed a flask of Jenever over with a word that the wind snatched away unheard. In spite of his loathing for the taste of the stuff, Jonathan took the little flask gratefully, letting the spirit spread all the way to his numb fingers and toes, warming him for a good half a mile or so, before the cold encroached once again. Jonathan thought of the warmth of the Thorn, the fire in his room, and yet somehow he felt happier out here in the freezing wind.

Their luck improved a few miles along the road, when a trader taking cloth down to the market at Harwich took pity on the two of them, and let them ride in the back of his covered wagon. They huddled together, back to back, for warmth, blowing on their fingers and grinning like a couple of children who'd run away on a grand adventure.

As they bumped along the rutted road, Domine at last showed some curiosity in his friend, casually asking Jonathan where he was from.

With his usual inability to dissemble, Jonathan was pleased that they were not facing each other, and that Domine couldn't see the pain Jonathan was sure was in his eyes. "My parents live near Coventry. But I served my apprenticeship in several places."

"You finished it? Why, then surely you should be in business for yourself?"

"No, I didn't. The war…"

"Ah, yes," Domine said, and Jonathan felt Domine's head nodding from behind him. "I understand. We have no choice when we are ordered to fight."

"I would have preferred not," Jonathan said, shortly.

"You are a man of God. I have not fought, but my father has, at home. He also does not like to talk of it." He was silent a moment. "Now you fight for another cause, I think."

Sitting there, watching the frozen landscape receding behind them, Jonathan heard the words and mulled them over, before nodding. "I do what is needed." There was a long silence before Domine questioned him again.

"And, after the war? They must have been pleased you were alive?"

"I…" Jonathan stopped. How could he explain that his family must think he was dead? No one who had a family of their own could understand. "I have not yet been home," he managed at last. That at least was true. "I left the surgeon and went in the other direction." Adam's face rose accusingly in his eyes, then a vision of his mother crying—but he could express none of it, none of the guilt.

Domine swung around in the cart and faced him. "You are a difficult man to know, Jonathan Graie. You make it sound like you have no one but your friends here in Mistley, and now I discover you have a family somewhere. Is there more? Is there a sweetheart waiting for you to come home—"

"*No!*" The word was out of his mouth almost before Domine had finished the sentence, and Jonathan swung out of the wagon. He shoved his hands into his pockets, and, his eyes on the road, started to walk back towards Mistley. His stomached roiled with emotion; he felt sick. The sky was too big, too open. He needed Michael to help him; he was miles from the Thorn with nothing to sustain him, nothing to stop his thoughts from drifting where they did not belong.

Domine scrambled out of the wagon and dropped into step beside him, keeping silent, his freckles the only color on his pale, pinched face.

Ashamed of his outburst, Jonathan stopped. He struggled for words as he looked back up the road towards Harwich. "I'm sorry," he said. "I should not have..." He was relieved to see Domine give him a small smile, the worry evaporating from his face.

"Many have things they do not want to share."

Domine's words were soft and inviting. Jonathan wanted to talk, but dared not. He felt he had so much bottled up inside him that if he were to start talking, he'd never be able to stop. He wanted to speak of Michael, and the work they did. He wanted to explain his own sins, and the way they beset him. He wanted to talk of the war, and try and make some sense of why it had destroyed his life, but he couldn't. He'd only known Domine for such a short time. It was nice to have someone who didn't want anything from him but his time, and Jonathan wanted to cling to that for as long as he could. He didn't want to see incomprehension or, worse, disgust cloud his friend's face. Instead he shrugged, returned Domine's smile, and, allowing himself to be turned around, they raced after the cart together.

Tobias had been away for ten days, and David missed him more than he would have guessed. He had got used to the man's gentle manner and his patience, and selfishly he had admitted to himself that he missed being loved, being treated with kindness and tenderness. Lord Albury had business out of town and had taken Tobias with him as part of his retinue.

Lonely and irritated that Tobias had been gone twice as long as he'd anticipated, David threw himself into his work, but the days dragged without the promise of companionship back at the house. Neither Robert's nor the boys' conversation were fulfilling substitutes for Tobias. For entertainment and release he started to frequent the taverns again, much to the delight of his friends, who had thought they had been abandoned.

This time, though, he found the companionship there hollow and brash. He was constantly having to lie about his interest in women, and found that he was having to get drunk simply to enjoy himself. He soon found that the headaches and empty pockets that followed suited him less and less. Eventually he spent more time at the Addle Street house, staring out at the street below, and trying to not worry that something had happened to Tobias.

"He would send word," Robert said, when David expressed his frustration.

"He might not be able to; his job is not the safest."

"Nor are the roads at this time. Many desperate men out there. But lad, no word is better than evil tidings." He untied the horse that David had finished working on. "Worry when there's something to worry about." David knew Robert was right, but still the concern lingered.

Later that day at Addle Street, he shut the door against the dark and cold of the night, and was splitting the logs into kindling for the fire when a knock sounded, making him turn in surprise. Tobias wouldn't knock. It was past curfew, and for a second David panicked, afraid that someone had finally caught up with them.

"What do you want?" he asked, gruffly, in an attempt to disguise his voice

The voice that answered stunned him, for it was a woman's. "Forgive me for disturbing you unannounced." The woman, whoever she was sounded tired and weak. "I am looking for the whereabouts of Tobias Aston, and believe that his uncle once lived here. If you do not know of him, sir, I apologize."

David wrenched open the door—now easier to do since Tobias had planed the base down—and held the candle out. "Who are you, that want to know this?" he asked, suspicious. The woman was pale and fair haired, a woolen shawl around her shoulders, with ragged gloves and dirty shoes peeking out from a muddy hemline, which told its own tale of a long journey.

"I'm his wife, sir," the woman replied.

The shock of her words hit him like a cold wave. He stepped backwards, feeling nauseous. "You…had better come in…Mistress," he said, clenching his fingers around the candlestick. "I am making a fire, and by the look of you, you are in some need of one." He felt numb at her declaration; not for one moment had he ever guessed that Tobias was married. The man never spoke of his family, other than the uncle whose house he had blithely commandeered. In all truth, David didn't even understand how Tobias *could* be married, if he slept with men.

While these thoughts swirled around his head, he continued to make the fire and put a chair out for the woman. When the fire was struggling into life, he opened a press and produced a jug of wine and a mug, pouring a measure and handing it to her. At first she declined, but David insisted. "It will take me a while to get us some food ready," he said. "I was not expecting company, as you can see." He waved a grimy hand around at the room, which was littered with clothes, bits of metal, boots, and tools.

The woman merely smiled, meeting his eyes once and then dropping them, her face coloring, and as she concentrated on the wine, her hands clutched the man-sized mug so hard that her knuckles showed white. David washed his hands in a bucket, then set out some of the food he had in store, cheese and black bread. He cut slices of pork from a spit-roast he'd had a day or so ago and put them on her platter. They ate in awkward silence, David's eyes ranging over her face and form, watching the way she ate with dainty little bites. Apart from Elizabeth, he had rarely been in the sole company of a woman, and from this one's manner and voice, if it had not been for the dirt and wretched clothes, she might have been mistaken for a lady. David wondered at the many mysteries her appearance had brought to light and how he would manage to summon the courage to ask her, without betraying his true relationship with her husband.

Husband! His mind turned the word over and over. *Was this really Tobias' wife? Could he have kept this a secret from me all this time?* David wondered—if it was true—what it was that could have made them separat. Or was it, he suddenly thought, that Tobias, like himself, had simply not gone home?

The woman said nothing. David would have expected her to have asked further about Tobias, or to have queried who David was, whether he knew him, or even what he was doing in her husband's uncle's house. David surmised that she would have taken shelter with Old Nick himself, judging the state of exhaustion she appeared to be in. After clearing their platters away he poured himself another drink, though she refused one

"Master Aston is away from home," he began carefully. Her eyes moved to his with an expression he couldn't quite fathom, a little like hope and a little like fear. "My name is Caverly—we were in the army together," he continued. She nodded. "I have been expecting him back for a few days now." He watched as her expression faded to one of blank resignation. He wondered if he should lie, should tell her something to lighten her load, to tell her that Tobias had spoken often of her, when in fact he had done nothing of the sort. Instead, he said what he had been thinking. "You should have written, perhaps."

She looked down, twisting the edge of her shawl in her fingers. "I did. Several times, to this address as well as to his…the village where his parents lived. After we received word of Naseby I didn't know whether he was alive or dead. He should have let us know. He should have…" She trailed off, leaving David with pangs of guilt for having been as thoughtless with his own father, who didn't even know he had been in the fighting. His mind digested what she'd said. *Us? What more am I to learn this night?*

The woman was silent a moment, then seemed to force herself to composure, and stood. "I am sorry to have intruded like this. Perhaps you can recommend somewhere I might stay for this night?" Even though her face had more color, David could see that she was clearly exhausted.

"You'll stay here, of course, Mistress Aston," he said, his voice as confident and authoritative as he could make it. For all that he was confused and full of worry, he owed something to Tobias' wife, if that was who she really was. "At least for tonight, perhaps he will return tomorrow. He is long overdue."

She didn't reply, but sunk back into her chair. Her cheeks were flushed, but she didn't raise her eyes again. She looked broken, somehow, like the life had gone out of her. A thousand questions bubbled into David's mind. *Are there children? Where is their home? When did they…?* But he forced them down. There was no point in interrogating the woman. After all, she was not the transgressor. If anyone belonged in this house, she did, and not himself.

"I will prepare a room for you," he said, and went up the stairs. There was only one bedroom, and it was not much tidier than the downstairs room had been, but he did his best, picking up bottles and trenchers and stuffing them into a sack. He was prepared to yank the sheets from the bed, but the smell of Tobias rose from the bed. So male, sweat and sex in a delicious mixture. Just for a second he was tempted, as jealousy finally hit him like a hammer, to leave them on the bed, but his conscience won. Tobias had hurt her badly enough, by the looks of her. He found clean bedclothes, made the bed, then went downstairs.

The woman was asleep, her head resting on her arms on the table. In repose, David found her quite pretty, and younger than he'd first thought. He touched her on the shoulder but she didn't stir, so he gently lifted her into his arms and carried her up the stairs. He left her on the bed covered with a blanket, then went downstairs to sleep in front of the fire.

He woke in the dark, after what seemed like mere minutes. The night was well advanced by the moon's position, but it was not yet dawn, and for a second he wondered what had woken him. Hearing a creak, he realized the back door was being opened. He stood up, reaching for his sword in one fluid movement. His fear

turned to relief when a tinderbox flared, a candle was lit, and Tobias' face emerged from the darkness, his own sword naked and
raised, its edge glittering gold in the candlelight.

"By'r Lady!" Tobias exclaimed. "My heart near stopped! What
the Devil are you doing sleeping down here?" He moved toward
David to embrace him, but David sidestepped him and sat down
at the table, roughly taking the candle from Tobias and lighting
the others in their wooden holders.

"The bedroom is occupied," he said, shortly.

"The Devil it is! Who have you got here?" Tobias' face darkened in jealousy. "Is this what you do when I'm not around? One
of your young bucks from the inn?"

David's anger flared at the false accusation, when Tobias was
the one... He spoke bitterly, keeping his voice down. "Yes, as soon
as you left, the very second you left, I went and found a bed
warmer—in fact, I have too many of them that I am unable to fit
in the bed myself—as you can see." The temper got the better of
him. "In fact, why don't you just go and see? I'm sure my bed
warmer will appreciate a visit."

They glared at each other for several seconds, David not dropping his gaze, refusing to back down. Tobias spun on his heel,
grabbed a candle, and clattered up the stairs. David listened as
the door was flung open, and footsteps sounded overhead. He
heard them speak to each other, but he couldn't hear the words.
David's anger drifted away slowly, seeming to dissipate like a
dying flame, leaving him numb. The voices continued overhead,
they were arguing, but the words were indistinct. "Why?" he
heard from the woman more than once. "I cannot," from Tobias,
but the sentences eluded David's straining ears. On and on they
talked, while David sat and watched the candle burn down, carefully not thinking of anything. Eventually the woman began to
cry, and then there was silence, nothing but creaking of wood and
the occasional sob.

After that, he put on his boots and left the house. *Curfew be
damned*, he thought. *I can mope just as easily at the stables, and*

if there's one thing I don't want to see, it's Tobias' face when he comes back down those stairs.

When Jonathan returned to the Thorn, it was dusk, the freezing fog already creeping out from the mudflats towards the town. He was tired but exhilarated, his face feeling warm in the bar after the cold of the outside. The day, after a rocky start, had been a success, and he'd enjoyed Domine's company. They'd been to the docks, where Jonathan had watched the activity with some awe—so many ships going to places he couldn't even imagine—and then Domine had taken Jonathan to meet his family, or rather his mother and his sisters of various sizes, all as talkative and as red-headed as Domine himself. Mistress Johannes did not speak much English but Domine translated, only how he did it so easily was a mystery to Jonathan. As Jonathan dandled a baby, ate cakes, and had everyone talking to him at once in different languages, he realized with a smile that he'd been missing this simple family happiness from his life.

Domine had been delighted to share his family, but at one point had left the house for a quarter of an hour, reappearing with a young woman with blond hair and a face that blushed as red as Domine's hair.

"Jonathan Graie," Domine had said, gravely, "I have the honor to introduce Mistress Marie Vigne." He didn't have to explain what the girl meant to him, for the looks they exchanged, and the way they were holding hands, gave it away, to Jonathan's amusement.

After that it had all been more chaotic than ever, and when it was time to leave, Jonathan was almost dizzy from the welcome they'd given him. All the way back Domine had talked of his Marie, entreating Jonathan again and again to tell him how fine he thought she was, which Jonathan was only too pleased to do. Back at Mistley, they parted in the square, shaking hands, and promising to see each other again the next day, and Jonathan ran the last hundred yards back to the Thorn.

Just opening the door to the inn was like entering a different life. Jonathan could almost taste the tension in the air. He skirted the bar, which was already frequented by black-clad figures, the air blue with curling smoke, and made his way upstairs, only to find, as he opened the door, Michael waiting in the room, a look of annoyance and sheer bloody rage on his handsome face.

CHAPTER 28

The room seemed as oppressive as the rest of the inn, with the curtains drawn against the night. Jonathan felt guilty, horribly guilty, for he had hardly thought of Michael since his disagreement with Domine earlier that day, and had certainly not been doing Michael's bidding by travelling to Harwich. He waited to be spoken to, twisting his hat in his hands, but Michael said nothing, stretching the silence until Jonathan could stand it no longer. He had displeased his master, unwittingly, carelessly, selfishly. He must pay the price. He fell to his knees.

"Forgive me," he said, dropping his gaze to the floor.

"What have you done?" Michael asked. Jonathan heard the deliberately even tone, which denoted his master's anger. He knew, all too well, that Michael, whilst deceptively calm, was a coiled spring, a living crossbow of violence, and he *would* strike—it was simply a matter of when, and how hard.

The joy of the day had been ripped from him, although he could still feel the pleasant, warm numbness of the cold on his face. He clung to the sensation, for it held memories of a day that was almost normal.

"I neglected my work today." Jonathan pointed to the sheaf of papers on the window table. "I thought the information I had was enough and—"

With one step, Michael was in front of him, a hand twisting in Jonathan's hair, pulling his face up to read his eyes. "You have not the wit to know what is *enough*, blacksmith." He spat the last word, and Jonathan's heart contracted in fear and pain, Michael had never belittled him in his punishments before. "After all I've taught you, all I've given you, you disobey me the first time I leave you to some responsibility. You do not *deserve* the honor Matthew gives you!"

Jonathan had no answer. He knew it was pointless to argue; it would just fuel Michael further.

Michael's next words turned Jonathan's guts to jelly. "Who is this weaver's brat you were with? Tell me that you were observing him—observing his family—tell me they are under suspicion! Are they Catholic? Dutch Catholic?" Michael's voice was little more than a growl. "*Tell me*, Jonathan, that you did my work this day, or is the Devil still so deeply rooted within you that you turn away from your God—and me?"

Michael had given him an escape, and Jonathan struggled with himself for one long terrible minute that seemed like black hours. On one side there was duty to Michael, duty to everything the witchfinder done for him—held against the new-found friendship with an ordinary young man and his family. He could invent something—say that he'd spotted a rosary in the Johannes' house, and the punishment would be avoided, but he knew, as surely as he knew that Michael was going to hurt him, that he could not tell falsehoods just to save himself. That would be untrue to everything he was, and he could not betray Domine and his family just to save himself some pain. He *had* been negligent, he knew. He had, without permission, taken time to himself instead of doing God's work, *Michael's* work, but if he believed anything at all, he had to believe, deep down, that Michael would not do more than punish him for his laziness and sin of sloth and disobedience. In truth, Michael had not given him firm instructions, but he didn't dare say that while his master was so angry.

Jonathan pitched his voice as quietly and evenly as he could when he spoke at last. "He hast done nothing. He nor any of his kin."

"Ah. You know him well, it seems."

"Not too well, in truth, but—"

"Then how can you know they have done nothing wrong? His name?"

"*Michael*, please..." Fear rose like a well of bile in the back of his throat. He couldn't. He just couldn't.

"His *name*, Jonathan? Do you think I could not find it out? This town is *mine*. Of course, there is the chance that I know it already, and am simply testing you."

"If that be so, then what good—"

The strike when it came was more brutal than anything he'd felt, it was like a kick in the face, and when he raised his head again, he felt blood in his mouth. On Michael's right hand was a chain-mail glove. Jonathan had never seen it before.

"Let me be the wise man in the room, Jonathan," Michael said quietly. "I will decide whether it has merit, or not. Now, you *will* tell me his name."

"Johannes. Domine Johannes." Blood trickled down his throat as he swallowed, and fear claimed him totally. He was terrified. Not for himself, but for Domine, his happy family, his fiancée. In all the time they'd been together, not since the very first day when he had found himself bound in that cellar, had he begged Michael for mercy, but now he did, he had to. "Please, Michael, he is just a friend...just a man I met at the forge. He has no affiliation with anyone. I do have names." With disgust in his heart, he heard himself denounce the names on his list, even the names that he had been planning to edit, erase, burn. He named everyone he could think of, people he knew, people he didn't. Anything in an attempt to deflect Michael's interest in Domine. Michael listened, all the while running the fingers of his bare hand through Jonathan's hair. Jonathan could hear his breathing calm, and when he looked up, the fire had gone out of his master's face, and Jonathan dared to hope that the crisis was past.

"So, you *have* been working."

"I have," Jonathan said quickly, as Michael reached for the papers. *God forgive me*, Jonathan thought, knowing that the town's gossip and tittle-tattle was not deserving of Michael's particular attention. He watched Michael scan the papers, and when he looked again at Jonathan, his eyes were soft, and his mouth was curling into a smile.

"Confess it, then," he said simply.

Jonathan didn't hesitate. "I was disobedient, I went to Harwich with him to meet his family, and I did not do thy bidding. But every day other than today, I have—"

"Today is what I want to hear about," interrupted Michael. "Why did you disobey me? "

"I don't know."

The second slap was as hard as the first, but as his face was still numb, it seemed to hurt less.

"*Liar!* Why did you disobey me?"

"Because I am still filled with corruption," Jonathan said, the words tumbling over themselves to be said. If it was what Michael wanted to hear, and if it *was* a lie—Jonathan didn't care. He didn't even know if it was a lie. He had disobeyed. "Because..."

"Because the Devil still has you captive?"

Jonathan nodded, too numb, too afraid. Pulling the glove from his hand, Michael helped Jonathan to his feet and kissed him, licking the blood from his mouth.

"My poor Jon," he said, his voice silky. "The Devil must love you greatly to withstand me the way he does. You must tell me that you want him gone." Michael unbuttoned Jonathan's clothes slowly and deliberately. He had a fervent look in his eyes, a gleam of anticipation that chilled Jonathan to the very bone. "Or is there some glimmer inside you that rejects your salvation? That still clings to the dark, to David? Do you dream of him still? Does your flesh rise at the thought of him when it should lie quiet?"

"No, you—"

Michael dug his nails into Jonathan's side, silencing him. "Or is it this Domine that your body wants now? Do you hope to touch his prick like you do mine? Do you want to corrupt him—like David did you, like you did *me?*"

Jonathan dropped his eyes, unable to meet the blue fire that seared into his inner thoughts. *It is me?* he wondered in his confusion. *It's I who is the corrupter, is that what he means? How can that be?* He was led towards the bed and pushed down onto it, lay still under Michael's hands as the man undressed him with a familiar, swift violence. "No. No, Michael," he kept murmuring. "No. I feel nothing for him," but Michael said nothing further, and after a while Jonathan heard his footsteps sound across the floorboards. The door opened and closed, leaving Jonathan alone and shivering. He struggled for control, used to such abandonment, but unable to decide whether he was more afraid of Michael's return, or that he might never do so. It seemed forever before he heard Michael come back, and he found his fingers tangling in the bed covers almost of their own accord, tearing at the thin blankets. Michael moved to his side, placed a gentle hand on his hair, then withdrew. Jonathan could hear the unmistakable sounds of clothes being removed.

"Open your eyes, Jonathan," Michael ordered. Jonathan didn't hesitate. What he saw made him want to close them again, but he did not dare.

Michael stood by the side of the bed, and next to him was a boy, surely not more than sixteen, thin and blond, his hair in dirty ringlets to his shoulders, and as naked as Michael. "It's just another test," Michael said quietly. "A final test, and then once I have spoken the Lord's Prayer over you, I will know you are fully healed."

Jonathan knew his eyes betrayed him as he looked up, frowning in confusion. Michael pushed the boy forward, and Jonathan had a baffled second to wonder where Michael had found a whore in this tiny town. He knew, seeing the anger in Michael's face, that he would pay for the question, the rebellion, even if he had never voiced it.

"This is David," Michael said, running his hands down the boy's skin. The gorge rose in Jonathan's stomach, imagining watching Michael doing to the boy what the witchfinder had done to him in that basement in Chelmsford. "It doesn't matter what his true name is, for our purposes he is David. *Your* David." Jonathan went to speak but was silenced by a sharp glance. Michael put his arms all the way around the boy and cupped his privities. "Same blond hair, same brown eyes."

Jonathan knew that to contradict Michael in his description of David would be madness, so he kept silent and kept his face as blank as he was able.

"I'm sure you can close your eyes, and imagine him—the way he used to be."

Jonathan closed his eyes again and lay still, feeling the bed creak as the boy clambered on. Even with the fire roaring in the grate, the boy's skin felt cold, almost clammy.

Michael's voice sounded quietly, right by his ear, whispering directions to the boy, telling him to not be put off by Jonathan's lack of response. "Take him into your mouth, *David*. Make him hard. Jonathan? You have my permission to be hard. If it is David you want, then grow for him. I'll even let you fuck him, the way you used to."

In response, all Jonathan could do was to shake his head, feeling his flaccid organ sucked in by an all-too-experienced mouth, cool hands on his skin. Michael's knife was inches from the whore's throat, he knew that without seeing, knew it without being told, for the boy was shaking too hard to be merely cold, and Michael's breathing was that icy intensity that he had when he was aroused by another's fear.

Jonathan had not experienced a hardness since his Trial. There was no way that Jonathan could become hard under the circumstances. Michael's knifeplay had never aroused him, but that fact had never concerned Jonathan, for Michael had never insisted upon it. Jonathan often feared what he'd do if Michael had done so. Now, as the whore's mouth worked him thoroughly to no effect, he realized he couldn't remember the last time he'd had an erection.

Robert had said nothing at David's early arrival at the stables that day, although David had caught a questioning look in his eye. David's thoughts were muddled, so much so that for the first hour, as he helped the boys with the mucking out, he shoved them down, attempting to force himself think of other matters, such as Bryn Talbot's dog-fight that weekend, or whether the worrying rumors of the King's arrest could possibly be true. But the anger kept surfacing. It was not until the palfrey he was rasping nipped him hard on the arm, that Christopher, grooming the sides of a gray carthorse beside him, laughed and said, "She knows you were not paying her the attention she needed. Women need to be fussed over, David. I'm younger than you, and even I know that!" He laughed again as the palfrey tore a rent in David's breeches, making him swear. "Seems like she would disrobe you, but more than one woman would fancy that, I'll wager." The smile died on Christopher's face as David glared at him, threw his rasp to the ground, and stalked off, clambering up the ladder to where he still slept on the nights he wasn't at the house.

He had hardly been up there a quarter of an hour when the ladder creaked, and Tobias' head appeared above the platform floor. "The lad said you were up here. Annoyed a mare had bitten you, he said. I did not disabuse him of the notion." He didn't approach, but stayed by the ladder.

Tobias could see by the young man's stance as he stood at the attic window, the way his face was set in that particularly stubborn way, the way his eyes were dark and hard, that David was hurt—and that he was angry. *He has every reason to be, too*, Tobias thought.

"He was right then, wasn't he," David said, his voice harsh.

"About the mare?"

"About me being up here. Now you've seen me, you can go. It is not likely I'll throw myself from this window from grief." David's tone was bitter, and he turned his back on Tobias, pretending once more to look out of the window.

Tobias could hear the chatter of the boys down in the stable, the sounds of the London street as the city churned into life, and the sound of the owner whistling somewhere in the back. It was fairly obvious that whatever was said up here would be heard, especially if it was said in anger. "I have duties to see to," he said at last. "Catherine has gone to The Crown and—"

"You'll join her, and good riddance," David snapped.

"What I'll *do* is see you later, when my work is done. There is much we must discuss."

"I am sure your lord awaits you," sneered David, "so don't let the idiot farmboy with the callused hands keep you from your *duties*." He strode past Tobias, shaking off his hand when he tried to stop David. "Don't *touch* me," he muttered furiously. "You still reek of her." He was gratified to see Tobias' cheeks pale a little, but Tobias restrained him.

"Don't run away from this again, David. Not without the whole story."

"And are you going to tell me the whole story?" Their voices were hushed, but David's anger still simmered under the surface.

"Not now. I cannot take the time now, but as God is my witness, I will tell you it all tonight. Just—"

"You've had a long time to tell me your secrets, and there is not one of mine you do not know." That it was a lie didn't matter, David thought. *I can fight lies with lies*.

"You should have asked me." Tobias' face was full of a silent entreaty as he answered simply.

"Asked you what? Are you *married?* I somehow thought that actions spoke louder than words." He couldn't continue without shouting, so he turned away and slid down the ladder to the stables. The day had truly begun, customers trickling in, street vendors clogging up the stable doors, horses whinnying for food and water. There was no time to spend arguing with Tobias, or thinking about his secrets or his wife. David threw himself into the day, and before Tobias had descended the ladder, David had decided he would not go to the house that night. *A little absence*, he thought, angrily, *will make the man realize what he is missing*.

Tobias came over to the forge and stopped, looking swiftly around, obviously noticing the attention that the boys and Robert were trying to disguise. "I will be back, later," he said, but David didn't look up or acknowledge that he'd heard him. Tobias stood there for a second or two, then turned away and strode off.

David had to bite the inside of his cheek to stop himself from calling him back. To David it seemed like history was repeating itself, that once more a woman was stepping between him and the life he wanted. *If I had one place I could go*, he thought bitterly, *I'd go today*. At that he couldn't help but remember his father, and wondered if he could ever go home; or did Jacob, like Tobias' wife, imagine that David was long dead, buried in some field with hundreds of nameless others?

Tobias was angry too. He was angry at Catherine—for seeking him out, for coming to London when she had not been answered. She could not have been certain that he was alive, let alone living in his uncle's house. *She should have waited!* He was angry with David for being childish and stubborn. He wanted to shake the young idiot, for evidently nothing but violent, jealous passion, the kind that Jonathan Graie used to give him, was the only proof of love that David understood. But most of all he was angry with himself, knowing he could have told David of Catherine, and they would already be past the arguments that were yet, inevitably, to come. So many times had he told himself that he must tell David of her, but he'd never found the right moment. At first they had been running, trying to stay alive, and then when they were finally settled, their time together seemed to be too precious to risk their happiness with a long-dead past, and the threat of the David's jealousy.

He'd married almost without helping himself. He'd had always known that he was different, that it was the flat, firm bodies and the hard-planed muscles of men that attracted his desire. With young friends of his acquaintance, he had various encounters, but they consisted mainly of comparisons of growth and a youthful curiosity. None of his friends showed any signs of sharing his inclinations, no one wanted to handle the other's privities, no one wanted to press flesh to flesh as Tobias had, and Tobias had been too frightened of discovery of his unnaturalness to try it. In London it was easier to hide with a male lover, but in a small town it was impossible. Daily he had lived with the fear of being found out—it was considered such a detestable vice that other men would rarely bother with a prosecution. Tobias remembered, as clearly as he could recall David's face, the time when a boy from a nearby village had been caught with a local farm hand. Both men disappeared. The gossip was that they'd been driven away from the village, but Tobias was sure they hadn't, for why did no one mention their names again? After that, he forced himself to play a part—to do as other young men did and talk of nothing but maids.

As he strode through the London streets towards his master's house, he couldn't help but remember the years past. Tobias' mother and Catherine's mother had been best friends since their own childhood, and both women's dearest wish had been that their families would be joined in wedlock. But to Tobias, Catherine was nothing more than a younger sister. He had always loved her, it was impossible not to do anything else. She was everything Tobias could imagine in a girl, sweet and kind, modest and innocent. Like her mother, she had been raised knowing in her heart that she and Tobias would someday marry. So did Tobias, but as much as he tried to push forward his feelings for her, to think of her as a wife, he could not. He thought of her as a sister and nothing more.

He'd said nothing about it to anyone, although he wanted to—wanted to tell his father that he was sure he wasn't the right man to make Catherine happy. When the banns were read, the happiness in his mother's face was enough to keep him silent, as was the soft, warm grip of Catherine's hand when their names were announced. Eventually he half-managed to convince himself that it was the best he could have. *After all*, he'd reasoned, *my true longings are impossible, illegal, and immoral. Never to be realized.* He may as well marry someone that he loved, a sweet girl who loved him back, even if he had no carnal desire for her. *And anyway, isn't carnal lust a sin?* he'd asked himself. *Wasn't marital coupling meant for the procreation of children?* The Bible said so. The marriage service said so. Tobias knew he could manage that, at least.

Having no frame of reference, he felt that the marriage was more successful than he deserved. The wedding was a celebration, and if the groom was slightly more drunk than he should be, nobody complained. The wedding night was managed, more or less. They were both as embarrassed as each other, but matters reached a conclusion, even if it wasn't a mutually satisfactory one. Tobias had rolled off his wife, feeling sick and brutal, and Catherine had cried herself to sleep in his arms.

Out of the bedroom, their friendship made the day-by-day relationship easier than that of many a more unsuitable couple, and to everyone's eyes, including the doting mothers, the marriage seemed a success. However, as time went on, and despite both mothers' prayers and cajoling and hints, there had been no children. Gradually they drew apart physically, and Tobias sensed that his wife had no less relief in that than he did, although after they finally stopped trying, Tobias couldn't help but notice that Catherine was quieter and even more retiring than before, as if she blamed herself for a barren womb. She spent hours at the church, praying for God's intervention, and she would throw sharp glances at Tobias when he tried to give excuses why he wouldn't pray with her.

Tobias had blamed himself. He was sure that it was his sinful coupling that brought no issue, for when he fucked her he closed his eyes and thought of men. No particular man, but any naked flesh he had been privileged to see, whilst swimming, or when pissing beside his friends. *How could God*, he thought, *allow the issue of children, when I am being unnaturally unfaithful to my wife, and imagining her to be a man?* Before they gave up, he had been wont to turn her over in bed and take her like dogs did with bitches, running his hands over her back and imagining that it was the back of some young man.

The lack of children was his punishment for that, he was sure of it. The guilt he carried that he knew, in his sin, he was withholding a baby from his wife, ate at him like a canker-worm, gnawing and twisting his guts and mind until he could hardly bear to look at her in his shame. It was made no better by his wife's growing piety and her patient entreaties to ask God for intervention.

He gave in, eventually, knelt beside his wife and prayed with her. But his prayers did not bring a child—it brought an escape for him in the form of war, and he'd ridden away from his home with a sense of relief—leaving his mother and wife supporting each other, both in tears.

As he pushed open the side door to his master's house, he shook his head, trying to clear his thoughts. His work here could often be dangerous, and it behooved nothing to dwell on matters already soured with sin. Anyway, it all seemed like a lifetime ago and another Tobias, a Tobias who wanted to please everyone, and ended up pleasing no one but himself under the guise of a hero by going to war.

◖ CHAPTER 29 ◗

Something woke Jonathan, and he sat up with a start, inhaling as if surfacing from a cold, dark river. Night's terrors clung to him; he'd been drowning in the dark, *breathing water whilst the torches of the righteous shone above him....*

It took him a moment to calm down. The morning was gray and the windows filled with snow, the light hardly making it through the obscured panes. Michael's side of the bed was empty, the pillow cold. The fire was not lit, which was unusual as Michael, a colder body than Jonathan, usually lit it the moment he woke. Jonathan shrugged the quilt around his shoulders and padded across the icy floor to light it, then he grabbed a wash cloth and a ewer of water before clambering back into the still-warm bed. He felt his jaw, gingerly. It didn't seem to be broken, but the skin was almost too painful to touch. The links of the chain-mail had pierced the flesh in several places, and although Michael had been tender later, as he always was after his rages, and had cleaned the cuts, some of them had opened again in the night, leaving a crust of blood on his cheek and a tell-tale stain on the pillow.

After the whore had left, Michael had been triumphant. "He has gone, Jonathan!" he said. "I have beaten the Devil. You will be troubled by David by no more!" Then he'd kissed him before falling into a sound sleep. Jonathan realized that he must have fallen asleep eventually, too, but first he'd lain awake for a long while knowing that Michael was wrong, terribly wrong, The memories of his love for David had not gone.

The water in the jug was so chilled as to be almost frozen, but he damped the cloth and cleaned his face as best he could. Then he dressed and sat by the burgeoning fire, waiting for the cuts to clot, for he could not face the others with blood trickling down his face. He couldn't shave either, unless he left half his face untended. The only option was to stay in the room until Michael came back. *And that would be quite the best option too,* he thought, mindful of his obedience. He hadn't been given permission to leave. He doubted after the day before that he would be let loose on the town alone again, not until he could prove to Michael that he was trustworthy.

He prayed alone, simple words and prayers. Not the Bible quotations and lofty communication that Michael had taught him, but words learned from his mother, prayers from the heart. He asked for strength and the gift of obedience, but deep in the core of his soul there seemed to be a faint, rebellious voice of doubt calling to him from a place that Michael had locked. *It is the Devil,* he thought, *it is the last remnants of evil clinging to me. Memories of David.* Whatever Michael had promised, he hadn't succeeded in driving David from his mind. Jonathan found that he could remember him even more clearly since Michael had dubbed the boy of the night before with David's name. His face, his body, the way his skin felt in the sun…and in the pitch dark… All these things were clearer to him than they had been for weeks. *And if Michael failed,* he thought miserably, *then he must never know of it. I'll carry the memories, and hide their evil away.*

Finally, aching and confused at Michael's mistake, he rose and sat at the table to read the verses Michael had marked for him. He noticed that the notes he had given to Michael had disappeared. He hoped that whatever was delaying the move to Cambridge would be resolved quickly, for if Michael acted, and began to question those mentioned in those notes, he did not wish to face the town again.

The maid arrived to change the water and make the bed. He could see her looking at his face, which was beginning to puff up, but she said nothing. She had rarely spoken to either himself or Michael, and once or twice Jonathan had caught her looking at Michael with naked hate in her eyes. *She is lucky*, he thought, as she finished her work, *that Michael has not seen her look at him that way*.

She bobbed a curtsey at him as she stood at the door. "Master Michael said you would come down for breakfast, sir."

"Have it sent..." he began, but then he thought again, and stood. "Tell him I'll be down directly." If he disobeyed Michael now he couldn't imagine what would happen.

He hardened his heart, and set his expression in granite as he made his way down to the bar. Out of the corner of his eye he could see heads turning to watch him pass, as he cleared the last newel post and stepped down into the main room. There was no sign of Michael, and for that he was grateful—even though the instant he had that thought, guilt racked him through like a wave of sickness. He was prepared for some snide remarks from Stearne about the injury to his face. The man had not thawed in his attitude in the least.

It surprised him that no one made any remark as he passed by, even though they all seemed to notice. There were very few in the bar, far less than normal and as Jonathan took his small beer he wondered what had made the place so empty. *Perhaps everyone is planning to move on, like us—before the weather gets any worse*.

Hopkins' dominant presence was also missing, and Jonathan resolved to wait until one or the other returned, for Michael would tell him what he thought Jonathan needed to know.

Stearne was at the bar with a pipe, the smoke leaving the bowl in blue wisps which hung around the beamed ceiling. Jonathan sat at a table, asked for porridge, and managed half of it, the pain taking the edge off his hunger. As he drained his mug, he saw Stearne signal to him, then walk towards the door to the yard and stables. Jonathan frowned for a second; Stearne bore him no good will, and he couldn't imagine any reason for a clandestine meeting with the man, but the atmosphere in the room was wrong: dark, like someone had let the marsh fog in during the night. *Perhaps Stearne knows something.* Jonathan kicked his chair back and followed the man outside. The air was chilly, the snow falling thick and heavy, muffling the ever-present sounds of the town and harbor. He was grateful when Stearne opened an empty stall and stepped inside. The sudden change from brilliant white to the musty darkness of the stable made it hard to see clearly for a moment, but he could make out Stearne, propped against the long wooden manger.

"I can't imagine what thou wants with me," Jonathan said, aggressively. He hadn't meant to be so direct, but the pain in his face was heightened by movement and stung from the cold, and any conversation he'd ever had with Stearne had been combative and unpleasant.

"Nothing you can give me," Stearne replied with a sour glance, "and if anyone asks me, we didn't have this conversation. But if I were you," his eyes moved over Jonathan's face, "and I'm damned glad I'm *not*, I'd get out of this place. Fast as you can and shake the filth from your shoes. Go now and as far as you are able."

"I am going, and soon," Jonathan said, with a shake of his head. "Thou knowest that."

"Not to Cambridge you ain't. And *not* with him," Stearne said quietly with an edge of impatience. "Go home. And if your home isn't standing, go elsewhere, for you'll go nowhere but the Devil with him." Jonathan made as to leave, but Stearne held him fast by one arm. "I know I've been harsh with you, but believe me boy, I wouldn't want to see a *dog* treated the way you are. I know Michael's methods, for I know who taught him them." Startled, Jonathan stopped resisting. *Was it possible that Stearne meant that Matthew had....* He listened as Stearne continued, nodding gravely. "Aye, I was purged too. Yet the difference between Matthew and Michael is that Matthew does what he does for a cause—and he knows when to stop."

"So does Michael—"

"Wake *up*, boy," Stearne snapped. "Michael does what he does because he *likes* it. God has nothing to do with it. If he hadn't met Matthew, he'd have found some other way to torture...and murder."

Jonathan felt himself go red with anger. "Thou dost the *same* work, thou knowest it is not murder, it—"

Stearne's face flashed with a strange expression. He didn't reply at first, but let go Jonathan's arm. When Jonathan showed no sign of leaving, Stearne knocked his pipe out against the brick wall and spat into the gutter. "I don't deny that your absence would be advantageous for me, so maybe I'm not as kind as I sound. Think on what I've said, and if you ever need something to drive you away, look for the knife."

"I...I don't understand."

"Look, you aren't a bad lad," Stearne said with exasperation in his voice. "I've watched you, and you trust that what you look at is the truth. Perhaps it's time you stopped looking and started seeing."

Jonathan started to get angry again. "No riddles! Just *tell* me what thou insinuates. I hadst thought that thou wast loyal."

"More than you know," Stearne said. "I'm loyal to Matthew, and what he believes in, and he's harbored trouble with that one. But God will see that Matthew can weather it. He's well-known, respected, has some powerful friends. I don't think you'll do so well. There now, I've said enough," he finished. "More than enough for your pretty monster to make my life very uncomfortable if he so chose."

Confused and a little frightened, Jonathan couldn't help but look over his shoulder. *Monster? He's lying. Michael believes— I know... I'm sure...*"Just answer me one thing," Jonathan said. "Why now?"

"I was in the bar late last night," Stearne replied, his voice dropping to a near whisper. "I saw Michael bringing that boy in.

And now the boy's missing... or so the town is saying."

Jonathan went cold. *Monster...* He tried to speak, but his tongue seemed too dry to wrench from the top of his mouth.

"Heard of it when I went to speak to the priest, I did," Stearne continued. "Seems the boy shared a pit with other poor wretches who can't get regular work, and he didn't come back last night. The word is that he's found himself a patron and taken himself off, but—well, I wonder if he could have had the time. Did he? Do *you* think he met a rich patron on the way home from here? Or did he meet God?"

Jonathan swallowed. *If the village ever found out where the boy had been...* "No! You can't think that of Michael?" He felt unable to accept Stearne's words. He searched his mind for some explanation. This smelled like extortion, and he accused Stearne of the same.

Stearne just looked at him, his face grave. "If I needed any reason to accuse you, boy, I'd have more proof than a tumble with a half-wit." Jonathan paled again, realizing how completely he was in this man's power. "Think on. Do you think that Michael considers a whore to be any better than a witch? Nay, lad, I don't know what happened to that boy one way or the other. I've no proof. But I've seen Michael's liking for his work increase, and so have you. That ain't natural. No one can like what we do here. Do *you* enjoy it?"

"No...No, I don't. I am gratified when we find evil, but I don't like the fear. Some of the women..."

"Are innocent? Who knows. No one but God. But Michael— he lives for the fear. Not God's will. You know that better than I. It's as important to him as the Gospel. It's more important to him than truth. Have you never seen his face during a trial?"

That little voice he'd been hearing in his soul was crying out to be heard. *Yes, you have!* it was saying. *You took it for saintliness, but it's the same expression he has when he sees your fear, when he cuts you. It's love. You just thought it was love of God, love of you.*

He forced the thoughts away from him. It was disloyal, betrayal, *disobedience*. He wanted to defend Michael, to tell Stearne of the good he did, the glorious vision Michael shared with him, the passion he had for a world without witchcraft, but he couldn't speak. Michael was saving him, Jonathan knew that—whatever his perversions were, he was fighting for Jonathan's soul —and winning. Stearne wouldn't, couldn't understand just how hard Michael was fighting for Jonathan's soul. Michael was hot tempered, Jonathan knew, but Michael quoted the commandments at him daily, he could never do what Stearne suspected. He'd never *kill*.

But, Jonathan had to acknowledge as his shoulder gave him a jolt of memory, recalling the men he'd killed and the bullet that David had fired at him, he'd thought that about himself, once— long ago.

A rattle and a creak announced the opening of the back door to the inn, and Stearne froze. He pointed up at the hayloft. "Get up there," he whispered.

"He'll want to know where I went!"

"I'll say you went to the town.Better that than found in conference with me, in here."

Jonathan doubted that, very much. Better to be found here and punished here than to have to lie to Michael, but he obeyed. He climbed the ladder as swiftly as he could and lay down in the hay, hardly daring to breathe. He heard Stearne open the stall door. "Any news?"

"None." The answering voice was Hopkins', and Jonathan could have cried out in relief, but kept quiet. "There's no family to speak of," Hopkins went on, "so no one really cares enough to search. He's disappeared before, they say. Most people are saying that he's gone off with someone."

"You don't sound convinced, Matthew," Stearne said.

"I'm not."

"Could be he got tired of the place and jumped on a ship…"

"You don't think that, anymore than I do." Jonathan heard the crunching of their footsteps in the snow, and their voices becoming indistinct, as the two men walked away. "Ever since that girl in Ipswich I have…" and then Jonathan could hear no more.

They had gone, leaving Jonathan to the darkest of thoughts and a terror of the unknown.

He scrambled down from the loft, and spent a frantic few minutes removing every scrap of hay from his hair and clothing before re-entering the inn. Stearne and Hopkins were on the far side of the room, deep in conversation, and to Jonathan's huge relief, Michael had still not appeared.

Looking up as Jonathan walked towards the stairs, Hopkins called out, "Jonathan, stay a while." He pulled a chair from the nearby table and placed it between himself and Stearne. Jonathan sat down, keeping his eyes on Matthew, though he could feel Stearne's eyes on him.

"How are you, lad?" Matthew said, solicitously. His glance slid to Jonathan's cheek and back again.

"Well, Master Hopkins, I am well." Jonathan's voice was defiant, but he felt that he was standing on sand. "Ready to do thy will."

"You have heard of the news in the town?"

Jonathan felt himself coloring. He could not help it. The implied guilt, the sins of the night before washed over him. Even if Michael had nothing to do with the boy's disappearance, using a boy for money was a terrible transgression. "I have, sir."

Hopkins glanced at Stearne, his expression unreadable. "I think, then, that your dispatch to Cambridge is timely. You've done good work while you were left alone, remember that." He opened the calf-skin folder in front of him on the table and pulled out the same papers that Jonathan had given to Michael the day before. "There are names here that need investigation."

Jonathan's fingers itched to grab the documents and throw them on the fire. "When do we leave?"

Matthew's face was grim. "I've decided to send you alone. You are more than capable of the work involved, John here agrees with me. You can find an assistant perhaps on the road, or when you come to the city." A shadow seemed to pass over Jonathan, but when it passed he felt a glimmer of something that he'd long forgotten.

Alone? He swallowed. "I am grateful to thee, that thou thinkst I merit, but—"

"Stay your thanks, lad," Hopkins said. "You'll work hard for your money."

"And Michael?"

"I'll speak to Michael," Hopkins said grimly, "and he'll do as I say."

"But Master Bacon—"

"Will understand." Hopkins took a sealed letter from his folder and passed it to Jonathan. "Give that to him when you arrive, and he'll know why you travel alone. Where is Michael?"

"I have not seen him all this morning, although the maid passed me a message from him not an hour since."

Hopkins and Stearne exchanged a further glance, then Hopkins put a bag of coin on the table.

Jonathan felt sick with panic. "I should wait. I should—"

"Jonathan, you have your orders." Hopkins fixed him with a firm eye.

Jonathan nodded. "You'll tell him? Tell him that they were your orders?"

"I will. John offers his horse. You'll travel faster alone anyway, for the roads are often impassable by coach this time of year. In the spring, we'll join you and gauge your progress. And you'll write as often as you can. Get yourself packed up, take what you need. You go today."

The last words were a definite dismissal. Jonathan shook both their hands, catching the subtlest of nods from Stearne when he took his. As he packed what little he owned, the seeds of doubt that had been planted in his mind last night—about Michael truly being his salvation—began to flower as he relived his conversation with Stearne.

In the cellar of Lord Albury's mansion, Tobias shucked off his jacket and donned the livery of his lord. He was, he realized, as he armed himself with the exquisite daggers and the sword his master supplied, more torn than he'd ever been in his life. With all his previous dalliances with farmboys and ensigns, he'd never had his heart taken like David had taken it. On one side he knew that his relationship with David was wrong; there was no doubt of that. Illegal, dangerous, sinful. On the other side he knew he'd been hiding from Catherine. She'd shocked him with her accusations, for it seemed, as she had made very clear the night before, she had long known of his preferences. She had noticed his easy manner with Haldane when the two men had come home on furlough, and in subsequent conversation with his erstwhile companion had been convinced that they were unnatural friends.

It was her tearful acceptance that tore him to ribbons. Somehow she had convinced herself that it was her fault, that she had been wrong to marry him knowing that he did not love her as a husband should, hoping she could change that somehow. The implication that Tobias caught from this was that she thought he should have told her, and he had been surprised at the steel beneath the sweetness, a hardness he had not noticed before. Now he had them both to deal with. Both of them hurt, both Catherine and David angry with him, and both of them in London, which was much too close together, as far as Tobias was concerned.

Belting his sword around his waist, he grabbed a cloak from a peg and followed his compatriots up the stairs. Their master had business with a rival, and a meeting had been arranged, at a neutral location for both—the Black Bull in Cheapside. This rival, Bulstone, had requested the meeting, and although Tobias had attempted to dissuade his master against it, the man was adamant. "He hints of an alliance," the lord told him. "I have a son, and he has a daughter."

"He's your greatest enemy," Tobias had reminded him. "Do you trust him?"

"Not at all," Lord Albury had said easily, "but his ships reach the Continent with less loss than mine, and that sort of protection is worth shedding a little family weight for in the short term. He has no son."

Tobias understood this; a son would inherit both businesses when the rival was dead. He could not say that he did not understand his master's reasons, but still he was uneasy. It seemed too simple after years of bloody rivalry, for the man to throw his daughter away like this. His shoulder blades itched—he had been a scout for too long not to smell an ambush, but his lord was set in his mind. He listened to advice, but he rarely took it, relying on strength of his guard, rather than the sense of any counsel. Tobias couldn't help but be reminded of the arrogance of the King. *He had thought the same way, and where was that King now?*

His gloomy thoughts were interrupted when the sedan was announced, the men waiting in the hallway. Tobias searched the hired bearers thoroughly before allowing his master inside, and then as they moved out of the courtyard into the snowy street, he swung himself up onto the horse his master provided and guarded the chair on the left. Will Palmer, on his wall-eyed mare with the red ribbon in her tail, rode on the far side.

It was less than a mile from the mansion to The Black Bull, but Tobias didn't let his mind wander. Even in daylight the streets could be dangerous, and there was always the fear that he might be recognized as a deserter, although the chance lessened with each day that passed. He was fairly certain that Palmer was a deserter, too, for he'd recognized the way the man fought. And once, on a day when Palmer had suffered a cut in a brawl, Tobias had seen a blurred ink mark on the man's arm—quickly covered up—something that looked very much like a regimental crest. Tobias liked him; he was monosyllabic, illiterate, and while he seemed to have the same acquaintance with soap as David had with women, Tobias had never seen a man faster with a knife, nor quieter in the dark. He worked for money, same as Tobias now, and Tobias was happy to have the man on his side.

He wheeled his horse to a standstill outside the Bull. Two of Bulstone's men lounged outside. They levered themselves off the wall as Tobias threw a leg over the pommel of his saddle, and slid down to face them.

Palmer took the reins of Tobias' horse and gave them, with a coin and a curse, to a waiting stableboy, then stood between the chair and the inn as Tobias opened the door for his lord.

"Sire," he said quietly, "I can get them to carry you all the way in. I like not the look of the men here."

"He'd take it as weakness."

"At least let me come in with you." Albury always insisted on Tobias being left outside; his presence would show a lack of faith in business negotiations, he always said. *What trust could you have that a man would sign a contract of his own free will, if an armed man stood behind him?"the lord had said.* As expected, Albury he shook his head, stepped out of the chair, and put on his hat. Tobias accompanied him to the door but stopped, respectful to his master's wishes but regretfully, at the threshold.

CHAPTER 30

Christopher wheeled himself up to where David was attempting to straighten his back and grimacing in discomfort. David had been working on four massive dray horses he'd encountered once before. It was a job he dreaded, for the horses didn't co-operate.

"'Ere," Christopher said, reaching to the back of the chair. "You look done in." The boy reached to the back of his chair, pulled out a grimy bag of small wrinkled apples, and threw one at David, who had to dodge to avoid it hitting him in the face. He looked up indignantly to find Christopher in fits of giggles. "Thought you might fancy a break, them drays are a nightmare. The last bloke we 'ad, he made Robert do 'em."

David nodded, still stretching his arms and trying to realign his spine. "The bloody ostler never taught them any manners," he grumbled. "With a horse this size, you've got to teach them from the start to pick their feet up and not to nibble the farrier's hair."

"Robert says they lean on you." Christopher patted the massive horse's chest, the highest point he could reach. The horse snuffled around Christopher's chair, seeking the apples.

"They do, and it's too late to teach them any different." David sat on the edge of the horse trough and bit into his apple, which was still sweet with the last flavors of the autumn. "Very handy man, they think, takes away one of your legs, then bends down in exactly the right place to rest your weight on. I swear that ostler laughs all the way home. The joke is that Robert charges him double because of the extra time it takes to shoe them. If they were better trained, his master would be paying less. Serves the bastard right."

There was a silence between them for a while as they both chomped their apples. The horse in the stall nearest to David nickered at him, so he stood up and he fed his core to it. Christopher wheeled next to him and said quietly, "Yer man went in a bit of an 'urry this morning."

David shot the boy a look, startled. "It's all right," Christopher continued. "You know about me and 'im. You must do, you was up there and I ain't exactly quiet, even if Stephan is."

David nodded, but he didn't look at the boy again; instead he stroked the neck of the horse. His cheeks were flaming with color, he was sure; this wasn't something he'd ever talked about. It was frightening just to hear the words spoken out loud.

"Stephan and me, well, we got each other and it's right? You see? Girls is all right, but different. Stephan listens. Not that he does much talking, though he can a little—when he wants, you know." Christopher sounded defiant, defending Stephan against nothing. "But what we've got is, like it's nat'ral. Like we've always been together. Like brothers. But more'n that. I jus' wanted to let you know that we understand. Robert don't, so we don't tell 'im. But I knew you did, first time I saw the way yer man looked at you."

My man... David gave a swift glance up the gangway to where Robert was hauling feedsacks to the loft, "He doesn't suspect?"

"P'raps," said the boy. "But he ain't never said nothing. He ain't exactly one of them Puritans, is 'e?"

Not like my Puritan, no... David shook his head. "Not something I'd like spread about."

"No. Same as us. None of us fancy getting 'anged or worse— does we? He looks like a gentleman, though. Yer man," Christopher added, "is he?"

David shrugged. He wasn't sure what Tobias was. *I don't think I have ever known..*

"He cares though, you can see that. He didn't look too happy this morning. And you ain't smiled once, since, till now. It's difficult enough to find someone like us, you know. Not without going up Lad Lane…" Christopher went pink then. "Well, you know…."

David wanted to yell at the boy, to tell him to mind his own business, but he knew what Christopher was trying to say. Sulking never achieved anything. If he stayed away from Tobias, he'd only hurt the man, and that would feel good for a while, but David wanted the tension between them over, once and for all. Even if it meant that Tobias went back to his wife. He clenched his jaw at the very thought of that, then patted Christopher on the shoulder.

"You win. I'll talk to him."

Christopher grinned and wheeled off without another word. David wondered briefly how the ragamuffin had got to be so perceptive, then gave up wondering. The boys had led a feral life before Robert, one that he could hardly visualize. He didn't know how they'd managed to survive out on the streets like they'd been. He took the dray horse to tie up next to the other three, and returned to have some food. Despite the miserable weather, he felt more determined. Now that he had decided not to run away from Tobias, he was also determined to fight for him.

It was dark long before he finished his work. This early in the year they had to light the lanterns that perched on the pillars of the large barn at around 3 o'clock, sometimes even earlier than that if the weather made skies dim. Stephan would run out with a torch and borrow flame from the link boy who lit the few public torches in the streets. David's area, being the nearest to the door, was lit first. Even though he could have shod a horse in pitch darkness, he would prefer not to.

He sluiced himself down, wiping the worst of the smuts and the sweat from his body, then changed his shirt and breeches from the small supply he kept in the loft. He caught Christopher's eye as he walked out—the boy was grinning from ear to ear, so

David gave him a wink, in an attempt to look more confident than he felt.

When he got back to the house, he was surprised to see that there was already a candle burning in the window. David's stomach gave a jolt; he hadn't expected Tobias to be back—his master often kept him late into the night when he was entertaining. Pushing open the door, he could see Tobias at the table, looking worn and tired. The remains of a hardly touched meal lay in front of him, and the table was set for two. Guilt coursed through him at having added to his lover's troubles. He had enough of them God knew, what with his wife resurfacing, and the constant danger of being discovered as a deserter or a sodomite. David threw off his cloak and hat and closed the curtain before sliding into Tobias' arms with murmurs of love and apology.

David felt the man kissing the top of his head as he buried his face in Tobias' neck, ashamed of his childish outburst earlier. "David," Tobias said, his fingers soft in David's hair, "don't, please..."

David sat up, and clutched Tobias' hand, bringing it to his lips. "I was foul to you—God's blood your hands are *cold!* Why have you not made a fire? I'll make—"

"No...stay," Tobias said gently. "You are far warmer." He coughed. "I've had a hard time of it today, ridden hard...and I think that the cold has claimed me."

David held Tobias' hands in his own, rubbing them, trying to put the life back into them. Tobias looked paler than he'd ever seen, and, with a further pang of guilt, David realized the strain his friend had been under at work as well. "Let me make that fire," he insisted, breaking free of the embrace and ignoring Tobias' protests. "We aren't so rich that we can afford you getting sick." He layered kindling with larger blocks of wood. "Catherine? Have you seen her?" he asked, trying to sound as casual as he could, although the shade of Tobias' wife hung like smoke between them.

He heard Tobias sigh, a deep, rasping noise, and from the

sound of his breath it seemed like the man already caught a cold. "I have," he said, heavily. "I called at The Crown before dusk and told her..." He paused with a small grimace, as if the very memory was too painful, then continued. "I told her...well, if not everything, then everything she needed to know. She...shouldn't bother you again." He held his hand out for David to return to him, but after leaning over for a quick buss, David got some wine.

"Why did she come in the first place?" He poured Tobias some of the strong red wine and cut meat from the joint of lamb. His heart was pounding, and he felt happier than he had for many weeks. *She is gone. He chose me!* "Surely, if she didn't think you dead, she should have realized you were not coming back?"

"She wanted to make sure, as sure as she could." Tobias spoke slowly, every word denoting his weariness. "The army told her I had fought at Naseby, so there were several options: either I had died, or I was still in the army, which obviously I was not. She worked out that I was either captured or I was a deserter. I think this house was her last hope on a long journey. She didn't expect to find me here. If we had been away from home, she would have been none the wiser."

Cursing himself for opening the door to the woman, David sat back down, helping himself to the food. Tobias was *his*; the man had done the impossible—turned his wife away like a beggar and chosen a life of sin with him. He knew should have been feeling sorry for the wench, but he couldn't help himself. He felt it was a fitting retribution for the injustice that Elizabeth Woodbine had done to him, for the pain she had caused him. Chewing on some black bread, he wondered about Elizabeth, how her belly would have proved him right when the child was born as dark as any of the lads she had tumbled for. He lost himself in thought for a moment, wondering if she'd managed to get herself a husband, and whether his father had ever realized the truth.

Tobias interrupted his reverie, for which David was grateful. For the memories of Kineton—other than those of Jon's passionate dominance—were dark and bitter. The thought that

Jacob might still think him false rankled deep.

"Do you want to know about her?" Tobias asked. "I promised you that you would know it all. Just remember this, my heart, that I never knew what love was till I met you. I was dead to everything, except the thought of war and Hal's false friendship. You bewitched me that day, and I have never since been free of you…nor would I wish it otherwise."

David grinned, but was embarrassed, not used to such endearments out of the bedroom. "No. Well…yes, I do, but not tonight. You are too tired, and I'm just happy to have you here, when I was certain that I'd driven you away."

"I have things I need to say, things you do not yet know," Tobias began. He yawned, but it turned into a cough, and David was immediately concerned.

"You will be ill, if you don't get some rest. Whatever we have to say can wait." He slid an arm around Tobias's waist; he could feel a chill on the man's skin, even through he was still wearing his outside clothes—no doubt to keep him warm. "You are frozen still!" He went to unfasten Tobias' jacket, but the older man stopped him.

"I'm tired, that's all. As I said…it was a hard day, and tomorrow will be harder still… I may have to travel again for a while." David didn't care now he knew that Tobias was his. His jealousy had been snuffed out as if it had never been. Tobias stood, and ruffled David's hair, smiling, for he knew David hated that. "I'll go and rest for a while, for I feel I could sleep for a week… Wake me later, and I will remind you of how hard and strong my love is for thee…"

David watched him as he made his way up the stairs, and then finished the food, suddenly hungrier for being happy. Then he tidied up a little, determined now to do better in every part of his life—now they had been given a new start, a new chance. For an hour or so he sat by the fire, warming his feet and drowsing, seeing pictures of their future in the flames. He didn't fool himself, he knew that life wasn't going to be easy for them—they would always have to lie to people, always have to hide their natures. But after the fear that Tobias would leave with Catherine, and learning how much he had *cared* about that, David knew that Tobias could take Jonathan's place in his heart. *Maybe one day*, he thought sleepily, *the thought of Jon won't hurt so much.* Jon's face still haunted him at night. Not the earnest, kind Puritan who had nursed him back to health and had been his blood brother when he was needed, but the bitter, angry soldier he'd seemed back in the wood at Naseby. *Where are you, Jon? Are you happy?*

He blew out the candle, and made his way by touch alone up the narrow stairs and into their bedroom. The draught from the window rattled the glass, and David pulled the thick, stiff curtain across to try and minimize the chill. It was cold and the morning would probably bring more snow. *We should have slept downstairs by the fire*, he thought. *It's almost too cold to be upstairs.* He took off only his boots, and slid onto the feather mattress.

Tobias gave a sigh as David wrapped his arms around Tobias' back and pulled the covers over them both, right over their heads to keep their warmth in. He kissed Tobias' neck and fell to sleep, smiling.

◖◗ Chapter 31 ◖◗

Cockerels sounded from across the street, and David stirred, waking slowly. The street sounds were louder than usual, and he realized, without a shred of guilt, that it was probably long past the time he should be at work, or at least making his way there. He peered out at the dim room from the edge of the tent the blankets made. From the looks of the muffled light that leaked from the curtain, it had snowed afresh and he didn't want to get up, to have to put his feet on the cold floor. It was warmer, if not terribly much so, under the covers, where the blankets still swathed them both, trapping what heat there was in the darkness beneath. *Tonight*, he thought, *we are definitely sleeping on a mattress in front of the fire.*

He had been restless in the night, having dreams he hadn't had before, strange dreams of drowning, ghastly wet seaweed slapping his skin as he had twisted and turned in a cold wet nightmare, and he woke to find himself turned around, facing the window. He rolled back and considered whether he should disturb Tobias. David was loathe to wake him, tempted to let him sleep on, to send word to Lord Albury, and make his excuses. Perhaps he would do the same to Robert, and they could stay here in the warm all day.

Gradually he became aware that his left arm was cooler than it was before, and he put his other hand down to feel. The bed was not just damp, it was wet, and David swore in surprise. *Is To-*

bias so ill that he'd pissed in the night? His mind knew the answer, almost before he threw back the covers to see, and he blanched in abject horror—the bed was soaked with blood, the sheets so saturated that at the edges, beyond where David had been lying, it had dried to a dull brown, but beneath Tobias it was still dark.

"Tobias!" He pulled the man by the shoulder, causing him to land on his back in the center of the bed, and David's heart contracted in fear. Tobias was icy cold and stiff, his eyes closed as if still sleeping, but his face was the color of milk and his lips were blue. *"Tobias!"* David screamed and shook him, kneeling up in the bed, taking the man by the shoulder and pulling him back and forth—although he knew, deep in his heart it was hopeless, that he was gone. Tobias had left him in the night without managing to call for help.

Words of denial tumbled from David's lips, nonsense words and streams of reassurance. "No! *No*...you can't be..." He ripped aside the blankets to find that Tobias' shirt was almost completely drenched in gore. With shaking hands, David lifted the shirt to find the cause, turning his friend's body now with gentle but trembling hands until he found the culprit, hidden by a bandage and crusted over with congealing blood. He wiped it with his own shirt, revealing the smallest and most innocent of cuts. Not a musket wound, the skin was not torn and the wound was flatter. Any musket fired in London was likely to be fired at close range, and even at fifty yards they were deadly, David knew, to his cost. It was a small slit, no more than David's little fingernail in width—probably a rapier, or a stiletto. David closed his eyes in grief; he'd heard tales of blades so sharp and so thin that they would kill you from the inside out. It seemed from the bandage, and from the way he'd been acting the night before, grimacing with pain, that Tobias had known he was wounded, but had no idea of the seriousness. David stared in misery at the cut that had taken Tobias from him, and remembered his own first sword wound, the terrible laceration across his buttock and thigh. It had seemed twice as serious as this tiny puncture. And yet...some devilry had caused this cut not to knit, but to leak Tobias' life-blood so slowly in the night that neither of them had noticed it until it was far too late.

He touched the cold lips, his fingers shaking so much that they pulled the dead flesh back a little, and he leant forward and pressed his mouth to Tobias'. *So cold...* His breath coming in ragged gasps, he slid down into the blood-stained sheets and wrapped an arm around Tobias, rested his head on the cold chest, and pulled the blanket up and over them both.

The morning crawled by. David stared at Tobias' face for hours upon hours. Outside the windows, tradesmen shouted, milkmaids sang, carriages rattled, and from time to time a troop of soldiers would march by, unmistakable synchronized boots, all whistling of some bawdy song or other. The world moved on, unaware that David had lost yet another love.

He must have slept again, for he woke, disorientated and cold. He looked up. In death Tobias had lost the beauty that he'd had in life, his skin now blotchy and sickly. With a groan, David crawled out of the bed, and leaning down one final time, he kissed Tobias lingeringly, as if he could transfer some of his own life to the dead man, and he would have done, if he'd had the power. Dimly he was aware that someone was thumping on the front door, and he turned towards the stairs without thinking, pulling a blanket around him with cold, numbed hands. Somehow he made it down the narrow stairs, holding on to the walls for support as his damp stockings slipped on the polished wood. Without a thought that it might be troopers, he pulled open the door. Snow swirled in, buffeting him in the face and making him take a step back.

"David!" A muffled figure pushed past him, dragging him back into the house. "What the *Devil?* What's this blood?" As if emerging from a trance, David focused to see Robert standing in a pool of melting snow, putting a lantern on the table. The man pulled off his cloak and unwrapped a scarf from around his face.

"Are you hurt? When you didn't come to work... *Damn* this house is cold! Why haven't you got a fire?"

In a daze, David looked at the state of his clothing. His shirt and breeches were stiff and brown with dried blood. He touched the blood with shaking hands, then looked up at Robert. "Not mine," he whispered, hardly seeing his employer. The light of the lantern seemed dizzying, and he sat down heavily at the table.

"You're covered in it, lad," Robert said more gently, coming closer. "Your hair, your face..." He rubbed his palm against David's cheek and showed him the sheen of dried blood that came away. He went to lift David's shirt, looking for an injury, but the gesture was so like the one David had himself had so recently given Tobias, it was too much to bear. He wrenched himself away, backing into the dresser, causing tankards and trenchers to clatter onto the stone floor.

"*Not mine!* I'm not hurt," he said, and returned to the table, poured a mug of last night's stale beer, drained it, and poured another. He wanted to get out, to get as far away from Robert and the questions he could already see forming in the man's eyes. "He's up there." He didn't need to indicate where up there was. He could see Robert's concern, his face half worry, half fear, not knowing what he'd find. "It's all right," David said calmly. "He's dead."

When Robert slowly began to climb the stairs, as if expecting a wounded adversary to fall upon him any minute, David wondered why he'd used that expression. Why was it all right that Tobias was dead?

He listened, while the beer warmed him, making him even more unsteady—he had eaten nothing since the night before. He heard Robert's footsteps cross into the bedroom, move around on the creaking floorboards, then silence. Finally the man reappeared at the foot of the stairs, his face almost as pale as David's own. David guessed that he knew what the man was thinking—murder might not be unknown, and the Night Watch less than useless, but it was no easy matter explaining a man dying in bed with a dagger wound.

Robert cautiously approached the table and sat. David closed his eyes and tried to imagine that Tobias sat there instead of the big red-headed blacksmith. Not the pale and shivering man of last night, but the summer trooper of long ago, with a slow, secret smile and a world of new experiences in his hands and lips. He felt Robert shake him.

"Don't you get drunk on me now, David! I need answers from you, before that man's a moment colder! Did you kill him?"

David held the mug to his lips, mouthing the rim. *Tobias put his mouth here...* At Robert's question he opened his eyes slowly, and stared at him. *Why*, he thought, *am I always being accused of things I have not done?* "No," he replied. "*No*. Of course I didn't kill him!"

Robert's eyes were harder than David had ever seen them. "But you are covered with his blood? What did you do then? Sleep next to him all night?"

Sick of lying, sick of it all, David snapped. "Yes! That's right. *All* night. Every night!" He almost laughed to see Robert's incomprehension. "There's no invalid uncle. I made it up so we could be here—together!" He was on his feet, shouting and not even realizing it. "But even us keeping it secret wasn't good enough, though, was it? God took him away like he takes everything away! My father, Jon... And if you hadn't come..." He wiped a sleeve over his face at the inconvenience of tears that were finally coming. "I slept with him in my arms. One more time... Just once more." He glared at Robert. "I loved him. I *loved* him and God took him. Punished me, punished me!"

"God didn't hold that blade," Robert said quietly. He acted as if he hadn't heard David's confession. "Hush down, lad. The streets don't need to know our business." He pulled David's cloak off the wooden settle and placed it around David's shoulders, as he was shaking with shock and grief. "Now, tell me what happened."

Somehow, David got the words out, how he'd thought Tobias had caught a chill, how he'd gone to rest early, and how he'd himself had too much to drink before falling into bed beside Tobias.

"His master needs to be told," was all that Robert said when David finished. "Likely as not this injury was taken in his service. He'd want to know. Will help us deal with the Watch, at least. What's his name?"

"Albury."

"I know him. Or of him. My place isn't good enough for his flashy Spanish beasts, takes them elsewhere. But I'll send word." Robert paused for a moment. "Now wash and change. You come back to the stables, lad. You can do no more here. I'll send for a brother or a goodwife to lay him out."

"I'm not leaving him."

"David. Be sensible—"

"I'm not leaving him! We didn't have enough time. You don't know!" David's could hear his voice breaking with grief, like waves over rocks.

With a sigh, Robert nodded. "All right." He ordered David to get busy, set him to boil water in the biggest pot he could find, and told him again to get washed and dressed. The message sunk in finally, and almost seeming to need the orders, David got up and set to work.

"I'll be back soon," Robert said, muffling himself up again for the cold journey back to the stables. "Bolt the door. Don't open the curtain or answer the door."

When the half-frozen water was on to heat, David stripped, unmindful of the cold, pulling the clothes from his body in silence. He folded them on the table, blinking with emotion as he realized just how bloodstained they were. He stared at them for long minutes, and then came to himself, working swiftly and efficiently, wanting to finish before Robert returned. He washed, fast but carefully, even dipping his head into a bowl of the lukewarm water to rinse his hair before tying it back with one of Tobias' black ribbons. Then he dressed and brought all of their clothing down from upstairs, sorting it into two piles, one smaller than the other. The larger pile he tied up with sackcloth and two of his own belts. Taking his dagger from its hook on the fireplace, he cut a small, stained edge from Tobias' bloodstained shirt and kissed it before tucking it into the dagger's sheath. Then he took the remaining clothes and fed them all into the flames.

He didn't turn away from the fire until the last piece of fabric had been consumed. When he did, it was to scribble a short note to Robert.

"Robert. You've been more than good to me, and you deserve more than being left to deal with this in my place, but I cannot stay. What good byes I have to say, I've said. His wife can be found at The Crown, if she's still there. Let her mourn by his grave, for I will not. My wages should cover the cost of it. In grateful thanks. David."

The night was full dark and snowfilled once more when he pulled open the front door for the last time. He didn't look back. He had fought all the wars he wanted to on his home soil, fought and in fighting, had lost everything that he'd cared out. *There are always other wars to fight,* he thought bitterly. *Tobias had said that, more than once. Perhaps if we'd gone abroad after Naseby, like Tobias had suggested, gone to fight for the Dutch then—he'd still be alive....*

All he took with him, as he headed for the docks and a ship to Holland, were clothes, weapons, a blood-stained piece of fabric, and one long, brown curl of hair.

Jon had little enough to pack. He was tempted to leave the clothes that he'd been bought since joining the Witchfinders, but they were finer than any he'd owned in his life before. He'd more than likely need respectable clothes where he was going—he couldn't imagine that Master Bacon would welcome him in the same rags he'd left the war in. His head was spinning, though, with the speed of it, and his nerves felt shredded. He winced and his stomach jumped at every sound from the corridor—imagining Michael reappearing and... Just the thought of what Michael might say or do made him feel nauseous—not even the protection that Hopkins and Steane gave calmed him. But, in spite of his fears,

Michael made no appearance, and soon Jonathan had as much in his bag as he could carry. The bulk of the books and manuscripts would have to be sent on after him, when he had somewhere for them to be sent.

At the door he stopped and looked around. On the table lay one of Michael's blades, the knife he used for pricking the suspected witches to see if they bled or not. Michael said had it never failed him. Jonathan found himself picking up the knife and slipping it into his pocket. He'd need it, and Hopkins had said *"Take what you need."*

Even with his suspicions of what Michael might have done, he found it hard to leave. Michael meant so much to him, had tried so hard to exorcise him of the demons Jonathan knew he would carry all his life. It was easier that the bar was empty, and that Stearne's horse was saddled and ready, no more goodbyes to be said. But once he was on the road he felt a little better, even if he was cold, outside and in what he laughingly called his soul. The sense of loss and sorrow only increased the further he rode, and he was not even a mile down the road before he pulled the horse to a standstill, sitting uneasily on its back as it swung round in circles, the animal snorting in its eagerness and impatience to be off. Jonathan's hands were sweating, in spite of the cold, and he couldn't understand how he could have been so utterly stupid. Why was Michael missing? He never was.

Then he saw, with clarity, as if he was looking directly into Michael's mind: *Domine*. It wasn't just that he was going without telling his new friend—for Jonathan couldn't imagine that Domine would care all that much—but he had a horrible feeling that he knew exactly where Michael would have gone.

He pulled the reins taut, wheeled the horse around to face the village, and spurred it into a clumsy canter. He had never been the best of riders; that fact alone had saved him from being pressed on that one occasion, but he'd learned a little in the army, and now determination drove him on. In no time at all he was clattering past The Thorn and along the coast road towards Harwich. The horse was sweating and blown before they were halfway there, and Jonathan was forced to slow, to walk the animal the rest of the way, but Jonathan's heart thudded in fear with every hoofbeat.

Reaching the outskirts of Harwich, he pushed the horse into a trot and navigated the narrow streets until he found the house, and slid down from the saddle. There were hopeful urchins hanging around him so he threw the reins to one of them, then pounded on the Johannes' door, feeling foolish and yet terrified. The door swung open and a girl's face peered out, one of Domine's sisters.

"Mistress Johannes," Jonathan said, with a sigh of relief. "I...I was leaving Mistley, and wished to give my leave to thee, thy family... and to Master Domine."

"Please," the girl said with a smile. "Come in, sir." Stepping aside, she let Jonathan inside the cottage.

The tableau before him was the very worst he could imagine, and to Jonathan's eyes it was a terrifying nightmare.

The kitchen was lit with the golden glow of candles and the hearth fire, everyone was laughing and singing. The family sat around the table, and holding one of the smallest children on his lap, sitting next to Domine, was Michael.

For all that the room was warm and heated by the kitchen fire, the heat leeched from Jonathan's face, and he felt as chilled as he had been on the horse. He could hardly see anyone else in the room, couldn't concentrate on anyone other than Michael. The man seemed to pull Jonathan's will and mind from him, making it his own.

Domine was the only one who wasn't laughing, and Jonathan could only imagine why he was as pale as milk. Michael must have waylaid him on the road and brought him back here, knowing that Jonathan would eventually arrive. Something cracked in Jonathan's head. *I must be going mad....* All he could think of was what he had seen Michael do—*what I let Michael do*—to the boy prostitute the night before. It was as if he was reliving that moment and Domine was in the whore's place, suddenly falling back with a knife at his throat.

Jonathan fingered the blade in his pocket, tempted to draw it from its sheath and force Michael from this happy—normal—house. He would have, too, if Michael didn't have his fingers tangled through the auburn curls of the smallest Johannes. The moment seemed frozen; Jonathan felt he'd been standing gaping at Michael for hours. Michael's eyes were at their most dangerous, entrancing and seductive, flickering from Jonathan to Domine to Domine's mother, who didn't see anything wrong with Jonathan's friend, or the way he was holding the baby.

With a growing fear, Jonathan saw Michael's hand move down to the child's neck, seemingly casual, almost affectionate.

"Michael." Jonathan spoke, just to stop Michael touching the child further.

"Jonathan," Michael replied, his voice cutting across the shrieking laughter of the children. "We thought you might come. I was just telling these good people here that there was one person missing—and here you are."

"You...should have sent word."

"Oh—I didn't need to, did I?" Michael said, his lips curling up at the edges. "I knew you'd work out where I was. You were always clever. Saw things that others didn't." He looked appraisingly at Jonathan's travelling cloak and thick gloves. "Going somewhere?"

Jonathan's heart was thumping so loud that he was sure everyone in the room could hear it. If only he could see Michael's other hand....

"Welcome, Master Graie," Domine's mother said. "Will you take some oysters? Some cheese or some ale?"

Jonathan shook his head, trying to stay normal. "I cannot stay, Mistress. Master Hopkins has..." He had a sudden idea, and prayed that for once, he could lie convincingly. "...decreed we should go to Cambridge this day. There has been a death at Mistley," he explained and turned to the family, trying to keep his tone as natural as possible. "A boy, found in the mud. There has been some bad feeling in the town, people are blaming evil spirits, and Master Hopkins thinks we should expand our operations westwards while he finishes his work here." It was as near to the truth as he could make it.

"Master Giddings has told us a little of your work," said Domine, his earnest face still pallid under his freckles. Jonathan wanted to look at him, to explain—to try and explain why he hadn't told Domine more about his companions. "I'm sure that there is much for you to do in Cambridge."

Jonathan nodded, numbly. "Hopkins sent me to fetch thee, Michael."

"There's so much to do, everywhere," Michael said, still smiling up at Jonathan. "But it seems that I am needed." Jonathan's knees felt weak with relief as Michael delivered the child into Domine's care and stood, taking his cloak from one of Domine's sisters. "My visit here has yielded fruit, and I will keep you no longer." He bowed politely to Mistress Johannes, then turned suddenly and smiled directly at Domine. "I am sure that we will meet again, Master Johannes. I look forward to that."

Jonathan's anger surged. *How can a man of God threaten children?* What had this family ever done that he would arrive like a wolf in sheep's clothing—eat their food, take their hospitality, and then leave with a threat to Domine who was suspected of nothing.

Nothing except make me his friend. His blood ran cold at the risk he'd put his new friend under, him and the innocent family. The children. As his temper rose in him, his fingers curled around the haft of the knife in his pocket.

Somehow, Jonathan managed to say his goodbyes as naturally as he could manage, which took far, far longer than he would have wanted. He expected that Michael would do something dreadful—for if he *had* killed that boy last night, what did he have to lose? But the farewells passed without incident, and eventually they left the warmth and fear of the cottage to emerge into the cold street. The street boy handed back Jonathan's horse, and by silent accord the two men walked through the Harwich streets toward the Mistley road, the horse between them.

"Thou shouldst ride ahead," Jonathan said dully. He could almost feel the bands of Michael's control wrapping around him once more. "I can walk. By the time I get there, we can leave together."

"Oh, I don't think so," Michael said, quietly. "There was something about your tale that didn't ring true."

"I spoke the truth," he tried.

"Some of it. The horse is packed for a journey, but why would you burden the beast unduly to ride all the way to Harwich on the chance that you might find me? Why not wait until I returned?"

"Hopkins was anxious that we—"

"Liar." Michael stopped and stepped around the horse. "Hopkins told me that he was sending you alone. Days ago."

Jonathan felt himself flushing, as he always did when Michael found him out. Why did Hopkins not tell him the whole story? "I wanted to get thee out of Essex—"

"*Liar!*" Michael tackled Jonathan, startling the horse who plunged backwards, over the ditch that ran next to the road, before finding the verge where it stopped to graze. Michael tripped Jonathan and they landed heavily on the muddy track. "Why would you want to?" he hissed, his eyes mad, his fingers at Jonathan's throat, hard on his windpipe. "You are a born sinner, Jonathan. You don't deserve what I could have given you. I wasted my time trying to cure you."

"The boy..." Jonathan said desperately, his fingers fumbling in his pocket as he tried to breathe.

"*Ah*, now we come to it: the boy—delicious, wasn't he? He was so pleased to see me again, you know, the little fool. The Devil had him as tightly as he had you. The stupid whore thought to make more money. He dropped to his knees and didn't even see the danger until it was too late."

"No..." *Monster—monster...*

"Yes. You *know* the truth. You knew it when you came into their house—you knew when you heard the news. He was evil. Like you, like that pathetic Johannes. The whore struggled more than you ever did, but then, I hadn't spent the time with him that I'd spent with you. Perhaps Johannes—"

"*No!*" With black spots before his eyes, Jonathan panicked. The chill of the frozen water seeping through his clothes kept him focused, and he summoned all the strength he'd once had fromworking with steel and fire. He pulled the knife free from the sheath in his jacket, plunging it upwards into Michael's side. The knife fell from his hand onto the ground. Michael's eyes fluttered in surprise, and he coughed as the knife and fist hit him hard. Scrabbling for advantage, Jonathan bulled upwards. He had hardly noticed it before, but he was bigger than Michael, and he *knew* now that he was stronger.

Stronger and a better man.

He punched Michael again, watching with satisfaction as Michael's head snapped backwards before he fell into a frozen puddle, his face muddied and his lips bloody and split. With a glance down at Michael's side he could see something was wrong: Michael wasn't even bleeding.

Jonathan picked up the knife and stared at it, uncomprehendingly. It wasn't blooded at all. There was a bubbling laugh from Michael, and Jonathan looked at his face then down again at where he'd stabbed him, where blood should have been pouring from his wound. There was nothing.

"You ignorant…oafish…*clod*," Michael spat through the blood around his mouth. "You poor stupid fool."

"What is this? What Devil's trick?" Eager to stop Michael's vile laughter he reached down and clamped one huge hand around the man's throat, threatening him again with the blade.

"Even now you do not see, you do not *learn*." Michael's voice was strained as Jonathan throttled him. "You never did see, for you are the most stupid fool I've had the displeasure of purging.…"

"Thou—*you* dare call me a liar and yet…" Jonathan looked in disbelief at the blade.

"And yet you cannot see what's under your nose."

With his free hand, Jonathan punched him again for good

measure, and while he was half stunned, divested Michael of the blade he knew was tucked under the other man's jacket. Then he touched the blade of the knife that had failed to injure Michael. As he put pressure on the point—although it was sharp and left a mark on his palm—the blade slid almost effortlessly into the handle, disappearing completely.

His mouth was dry as he realized the import. "The witches…no blood…"

Michael was laughing again, high and unnatural, mocking and sneering. "Finally, the clodhopper has the truth of it."

"But the women—"

"Were worth twenty shillings each. *Now* do you understand?"

"No. You...you *believed.*" He put his hand back around Michael's throat. "Tell me you believed!"

"I believe in the Devil, Jonathan." Michael's smile was pure evil.

Hoofbeats sounded somewhere at the edge of Jonathan's consciousness and a cart pulled up beside them.

"What be the trouble, good masters?" A man jumped down from the cart and pulled Jonathan away from where Michael lay in the mud. He didn't resist. He was cold. Cold from the bitter wind, cold from his soaking clothes, and cold from the soul outwards.

He stood over his former master, feeling sick at the look of him. Michael's face was no longer the face of an archangel—his jaw was bruised, his nose broken, blood pouring from his mouth. Mud covered his face and hair, but still he was laughing.

With ice in his heart Jonathan stepped forward, shaking off the newcomer's restraining hand.

"I am of the Witchfinders' party," he said, evenly. "A witch killed a boy in Mistley yesterday."

"Aye, we heard of it," the man said.

"This is he. Take him." He put every effort into the command, using the voice he'd perfected under Michael's tuition.

Michael's laughter trailed off as he looked up at Jonathan in confusion. He attempted to stand up.

"This one, a witch, master?" The carter's two companions grabbed Michael and held him fast.

"No…" Michael's face contorted in anger. "Jonathan. No!" He struggled, futilely. "I meant none of it—*Jonathan*—sweet Jonathan—"

"A witch will say anything to save its skin," Jonathan said in a flat voice, the words learned by rote from the many interrogations he'd witnessed and performed. "A witch fears to bare its skin for fear of witch spots." Jonathan ripped open Michael's shirt, and using the fake blade, drove it against Michael's skin, over the mole on his chest, then stepped back and turned to the carter. "And a witch does not bleed. Behold!"

"Jonathan… *don't.*"

"Thou hast rope?"

"Aye, that we do, master." They all ignored Michael's wretched screams shouting it was a trick, that he was innocent, cries Jonathan had heard a dozen times or more. From others. "What should we do with him? Hang him?"

Jonathan stared straight at Michael, feeling nothing, at long last. "No. Do not sully thy hands. Take him back to Hopkins and swear before God what thou saw here. Hopkins will do what is necessary."

"You will not come with us?"

"No." Jonathan watched as Michael was manhandled onto the wagon and secured to the rail. "I go to Cambridge—to carry on God's work." He stood in the filthy road and watched until the cart turned the corner and was out of sight.

When the cart was gone Jonathan turned at last. It felt as if a dark shadow had fallen over him. He caught the horse, mounted, and for a long while he stared at the road, looking east to west. Finally he swung the horse around and took the road west, for Cambridge.

⟪ CHAPTER 32 ⟫

30th January 1649 –Whitehall, London

In the years since Naseby, the King's fortunes slid further and further towards disaster. Oxford was put under siege after Naseby, but the King managed to slip out of that city, surrendering himself to the Scottish Army. It was, perhaps, a sign of his overweening arrogance that he thought he'd be safer with the Scots than fleeing abroad. This confidence was to prove ill-founded when, disliking his negotiations with them regarding the establishment of Presbyterianism in England, the Scots sold him to Parliament for £100,000. But even after Parliament had the King in their hands, no one, it seemed, wanted to make a decision as to what should be done with him, and he was moved from prison to prison, until finally, after two years, Parliament decided to try him for high treason and found him guilty.

David was a different man than he'd been when he'd scrambled aboard a ship for the continent three years previously. He knew that, outwardly, he retained a certain remembrance of the other-worldly beauty he'd had as a boy, although it had been tempered by a sword cut on a cheek. There was cold, steely cast to his eyes, and his mouth, once so mobile, was now set in a line that rarely smiled.

Inside his chest was a heart protected by fortifications that would do credit to any siege town. He'd vowed to himself that he'd never let himself love again—and in the armies of the Dutch, and in the post-war scrabble for a quiet life, it hadn't been hard to keep that resolve.

The crowd was thickest around the raised platform, but the street was so busy with people it was difficult to push through without annoying anyone. Using his height to spot a space on a roof on the far side of the street, David persevered, his face grim as he shouldered aside soldiers and common-folk alike. He was regretting the decision to come to London—he'd been away for so long he hadn't imagined himself ever coming back to England. But when he'd heard they were going to try the King, he'd packed up and taken a ship without a second thought, leaving behind the little forge in Bruges he'd been working in since the fighting in Holland ground to a halt.

In Bruges, he had managed, with the smattering of Dutch he'd picked up in the ranks of the Orange army, to get work and to keep it, but he was not much liked, for he let no one near him. No one gave their trust to the stern young man who did nothing but his work, and spoke few words to any save the horses.

Scaling the steps at the side of the building, he pulled himself up onto the roof. From the vantage point, above the seething—but strangely quiet—crowd, he could easily see the scaffold outside the Banqueting House of the Palace of Whitehall. Troops surrounded it, footsoldiers and cavalry. David gave a wry smile. *What do they expect? That a rescue attempt will be made?* Although the executioner's block itself was partially obscured by black drapery on either side, it was impossible to miss the executioner. His very presence seemed to contribute to the stillness of the crowd as he waited, motionless, on the scaffold.

Men, soldiers and clerics emerged onto the scaffold accompanied by a man in a white shirt and dark cloak, his hair loose upon his shoulders. What little noise there had been faded away as the soldiers and crowd looked upon their King for the last time. As David watched, it became clear that the King was giving his final speech, although David could not hear a word that was spoken. He spoke for a long while—and as he did, David found himself becoming angry. Not that a man was about to be beheaded, or that his King was about to lose his life, or even about the rights of Parliament to order such an event, but that this man, this elegant little man in his white shirt, could have caused so many to die. *And for what?* he thought savagely. *Will his death bring my friends back?*

The King took off his cloak and handed to one of the men beside him, then stepped out of David's view. The killing blow was screened from David's sight, but the crowd was as silent after it as they were before. When David saw the headsman lift the King's head from the platform and hold it up for the crowd, and spotted relic hunters crawling under the scaffold for drops of the King's blood, David had had enough.

Feeling chilled and sick at heart, he dropped down off the roof and pushed his way through the dispersing throng. He had little thought of where he would go, what he would do. The thought of his future had surfaced from time to time on his journey from Bruges, but he'd pushed it aside. Now he felt worse— his future seemed as hopeless and dark as England's own.

There were two places he could go in England, but as he wasn't sure of his welcome in either of them, for now he'd find somewhere to stay and take stock. He asked one of the street sellers for an inn and was directed to one on a nearby side street. For a second he hesitated; the inn was thronged with Cromwell's troops, then he chided himself. *It's been years since Naseby. No one will remember one lowly musketeer who deserted.*

Calming himself, he pushed into the busy bar-room and ordered some ale, found a corner where he propped himself against a wall and considered whether he should risk returning to Kineton or not. He'd heard no news about his village in the years he'd been away, which wasn't surprising. It was a small place, its significance to the world's theatre lost after the war had moved on. The only thing that put him off was not knowing what might have happened to the forge and farm in his absence. *Would Father have managed the place alone? Would he have sold it? Is he even alive?* The thought of that caused something to constrict in David's chest—he'd served his father badly, and the thought of never being able to make amends, rather than the pathetic excuses and apologies he'd given the man for years, had gnawed at him for years. He knew, deep down, that he had to go and see, that he'd never sleep soundly until he did. *I have to know if Father is alive—if he can forgive me. I have to know.*

A group of troopers were singing "Love Lies Bleeding" at the table next to where David was standing, and they were singing it extremely badly. The captain, a large, straw-headed man, waved his arms on the final crescendo and spilled his drink, splashing David, who moved backwards rather than say anything and cause trouble. He missed his sword against his hip; it had been part of his life for so long, but he'd had enough sense to realize that going armed in London was a bad idea with Parliament's men on every corner. The captain turned and gave a half-drunken grin.

"Oh, now, I'm sorry for that," he said. "I love that song, and get carried away."

"It is of no matter," David said quietly. Ale dripped off his hat, which he pulled off to wipe dry with his sleeve. His hair swung around his cheeks in the blunt bob that he'd been wearing for a year or two.

The captain gave him an appraising look, the sort of look that David was not unused to. "Let me buy you a new drink," he shouted, as the singing had started up again without him.

David shrugged, and then nodded his head. He wanted to leave, but he'd learned that drunken men could become offended if their offers of hospitality were rejected. The captain made space at the table for him, and David reluctantly joined the party.

"You've got a look of a Dutchman," said the captain, bellowing with fetid breath into David's ear.

"Been fighting overseas, yes," he said.

The captain frowned, then nodded knowledgeably. "Sold off abroad were ye? After Naseby?"

David kept his face completely blank. He didn't like being questioned and regretted coming into the bar. *I should have left the city. Found lodgings away from here.* Being associated with Naseby, either as a captured Royalist who'd been sold to the Dutch, or as a deserter, wasn't healthy.

"No," he said easily. "I had friends in Bruges and was living there at the time, joined up over there." It sounded weak, he knew that, but perhaps the soldiers knew no better. It seemed so, for the captain didn't ask him anything further about it but encouraged him to join in the singing, which he did, as best he could, looking for an opportunity to make an excuse to leave. Eventually, several of the troopers seemed more the worse for drink, and the captain stood and ordered them into line. He leaned down to David. "I'm Captain Gerold," he said. "It was good to make your acquaintance, sir, your name?"

"Gray," said David. He took the captain's outstretched hand and found himself held fast in an iron grip.

"Unusual-looking man, ain't he, boys? Master...? What did you say was it again?"

"Gray," said David firmly, attempting to pull his hand away.

At some signal that David hadn't seen, two of the guards grabbed his arms. He struggled against them and shouted for help, but the crowd moved away all of a sudden they were interested in something else. Within seconds the area was cleared apart from the four of them. The soldiers dragged him into the street.

"What do you think you are doing?" David yelled, struggling.

"Shut yer mouth!" the tallest Roundhead sneered. "Do you know what, lads? I think this is the ruddy King's man we've been looking out for, and here he is, pretty as his description and watching the show all the time."

"Unhand me!" shouted David, attempting to put as much

authority into his words as he could. The tall man backhanded him so hard that David felt his lip split. Blood dripped into his mouth, coppery and warm.

"I don't think we'll be doing that, Master *Gray*," drawled the captain. "We've got orders see? Some of the local lads been on the look out for you for a long time now, and I found it a bit too much of a coincidence that you look like your description on your warrant, but have a name like yours. Such a coincidence, isn't it lads?" He pulled a piece of paper from his belt and held it up. David had no idea what he was talking about and tried to free his arms.

"I'm surprised you can read," David muttered thickly through bruised lips, words he was soon to regret as the same hard fist pounded into his stomach, making him gasp for breath.

The captain spat at David and read aloud. *"Reward offered for the arrest and apprehension of David Caverly of Kineton, Warwickshire. Description: White blond hair, green-brown eyes, red birthmark from left hip to knee."* The captain narrowed his eyes and removed a small knife from his buff coat. "Only way to make sure we got the right man." David began to struggle again, but the other two men held him fast. The knife sliced into the material of David's breeches and the captain straightened up.

"Yeh, this is our man. Although after him being so unwilling to come quietly, I would have arrested him anyway. Take him. The General will be very pleased that we've finally caught up with this one." The man leant close into David, leering. "I don't s'pose we'll be seeing you again, but then, I don't s'pose no one will be seeing you again."

David had stopped struggling and glared straight back at the vile bully. "What is my crime?" he demanded.

"Well, I don't actually think I needs to be telling you that, but as you asks so nicely—I would have thought it was obvious with your unnatural looks, and that mark of the Devil on you." He glanced down at David's thigh. "The General interrogates witches. He'll ask you what you've done. And soon, you'll be telling him everything, whether you did it or not." He laughed, seeing the incomprehension on David's face. "Never heard of him? You soon will. If the General wants to see you, then he'll see you, and he'll be the last man you'll be wanting to see, but the last one you'll be seeing, I'll warrant." He laughed out loud at his own clumsy wit as he turned away, leaving David to be dragged along behind.

They took him to a tall building in a main street not far from the palace of Whitehall, through a side alley, down some stairs, and along a long corridor dark with blackened walls. The few candles were unable to make much employment of the flames, the very light seemingly sucked back into the walls. David realized that he was now one of the Forgotten, from tales he'd heard, even back when working with Robert—about men taken off to be questioned by Cromwell's gangs. If he were never seen again, who would know his fate?

A door was opened. David had expected a cell, but he was pulled into another corridor, this one with lighter paneling and portraits hung on either side. The troopers moved on. Wherever they were, David realized, the building was large and maze-like. Finally they came out into a large hall with a great wooden staircase, and they ascended, turning left into a gallery bright with candlelight and filled with beautiful pieces of plate and art. At the end of the walkway was a large, carved door where they stopped. The captain removed his helmet and, to David's astonishment, swallowed, clearly petrified of what was beyond that door. He knocked at the door, and they all waited, subdued, as if they were waiting to hear a whisper.

David heard nothing, but the captain obviously did, for he entered, and, to David's further surprise, left him outside with the other men. From within there was what sounded like a one-way exchange. The captain was either conversing with himself, or he was speaking to someone who was talking in such a low voice he could not be heard through the thick oak. The troopers holding his arms were clearly as nervous as their captain had been, and for the life of him David could not imagine why they felt as scared as he did.

Finally the door opened and the captain stepped out. David was shocked to see that the trooper had a cut under his eye, as if someone had hit him. With a strange look of relief on his face, he gestured to the soldiers to release David, took him by the arm almost gently, and pushed him into the room, closing the door behind him and leaving David alone.

The room seemed dim after the brightly illuminated hall, no lit candles in here. The curtains were drawn nearly fully across the tall windows, the velvet hangings allowing only a little of the winter's light to encroach upon the darkness. There was a huge stone fireplace containing a glorious fire; David could feel the benefit of it from all the way over by the doorway, which was also draped with velvet to stave off the draught. A tall man in leather stood by the fireplace, facing David but his face in shadow. He stayed there, menacingly silent for a long while, until David felt that he had to speak.

"Sir," he tried to keep his voice even, belying his pounding heart, "I would that you would let me know my crime, so that I may answer for it. Your men waylaid me with drink, and when I gave my name they arrested me." There was no response from the man at the fire. "For pity's sake sir, tell me my offence, for I am sure I have caused none to you." *Surely*, he thought, *his desertion at Naseby was still not a concern to Parliament after all this time?*

The man inclined his head very slightly and gave something that sounded like a sigh. Then he turned sharply and exited the room through another door on the far side. David strode after him, but found the door locked. He flew back to the door through which he had entered, but that was fastened also. He briefly considered shouting, though there didn't seem to be any point. He went to the windows and was not surprised to find that they were also securely locked and bolted. He pulled back the curtains; the vista looked out onto Whitehall and from here, on a lower level, the execution platform was clearly visible. Anyone watching from this window would have had an unimpeded view of the King's death. A shudder went through him as he thought of the man who had been here, watching silent and brooding as the King's head was cut from his body.

The windows were breakable, that was certain, but the drop was rather high. David knew he'd have to be desperate to take that route, hoped it wouldn't come to that.

He hazarded a guess that things did not look well for his future—*but I'm not dead yet.* He examined his surroundings. There were worse places to be imprisoned; he could certainly vouch for that, having been a captive more than once in his campaigns. The room was large, dominated by a luxurious, four-poster bed opposite the fireplace. Ewers of water, one cold, one warm, a bowl and cloths had been set on a table, together with meat, fruit, cakes, and wine with two glasses. Someone was interested in his comfort then, at least for now. He lit the candles from the fire, and the room gradually grew bright and cheerful, the vibrant reds and yellows of the wall hangings and the bed linen coming to life. He tried to relax, and not to think of what he had been arrested for, or what that might mean.

He was not particularly hungry, but he was still a trained soldier—he ate when he had the opportunity to do so. He took some food and the wine and went to sit on the bed, noticing for the first time that there were papers strewn over it. The counterpane and bolster were disordered as if someone had been resting there not long since. Pulling off his boots, he slid up onto the bed, feeling a little guilty; never had he been on such a decadent piece of furniture, and he was far from clean after his journey. He propped himself up on the enormous pillows and sipped his wine. *Well,* he thought, *if I am to die tomorrow, my last night will be pleasant enough.* He felt oddly calm, as if it had been inevitable that his life had led to this very room, as if this was a place he had once known, or had dreamed about. For all of his thoughts of that morning—deciding to finally go to seek out his father—he could no longer see beyond this moment.

Idly, he picked up one of the papers. Written in a small and even hand, it seemed to be a record of someone's observations on various people, none of whom David had heard of. *Some kind of journal?* He picked up another which was of a similar ilk. He reached out for a third piece of parchment, expecting more of the same, and was surprised to find it was a poem. There was no title and no author, but David read the lines over and over, entranced.

Since first I saw your face I resolved to honour and
　　renown ye;
If now I be disdainèd I wish my heart had never known ye.
What? I that loved and you that liked, shall we begin to
　　wrangle?
No, no, no, my heart is fast, and cannot disentangle.

If I admire or praise you too much, that fault you may
　　forgive me;
Or if my hands had stray'd but a touch, then justly might
　　you leave me.
I ask'd you leave, you bade me love; is 't now a time to
　　chide me?
No, no, no, I'll love you still what fortune e'er betide me.

The Sun, whose beams most glorious are, rejecteth no
　　beholder,
And your sweet beauty past compare made my poor eyes
　　the bolder:
Where beauty moves and wit delights and signs of kindness
　　bind me,
There, O there! where'er I go I'll leave my heart behind me!

David's cheeks were wet with tears when he finished reading; the poem had torn into his heart and released so many of the

demons he had shut away, tearing into his shuttered memories of
Tobias and his gentle loving hands. What the Devil was his cap-
tor doing with this poem? Surely a man with such sensibilities
could not be someone whom Roundhead captains feared? It
seemed irreconcilable. Frowning, he pulled a sheaf of pages towards him, hoping to find more clues to his poetic jailer. He
found a large folder of loose-leaf pages and opened it.

They were drawings—some no more than a few simple lines,
depicting a leaf, a horse, an old man on a bench, swallows in
flight; others more detailed—a sleeping cat, a man with tight
curled hair, a woman crying, a rose, its petals scattered. To
David's eye they seemed skillfully done.

He turned to a smaller set of pictures and frowned. They appeared to all be scenes of some sort of courtroom, many of them
obviously the same place, but in each one there was a different
face in the dock. They were mainly women. *What is this man?
Some sort of scribe for the courts?* There were several dozen of
these little pictures, and the strangest thing was that each one
was named. *Presumably the person facing justice*, he thought to
himself, curious as to what their crimes might have been and why
on earth this man would have kept records of them. Some of the
names seemed familiar, but he could not call to mind where he
had heard them before. He took a drink of the wine and continued flipping through the pages.

The last batch were close studies. Detailed, attentive work,
but the subject matter was disassociated. A hand, some fingers,
legs, perfectly proportioned and again, skillfully executed.
They seemed to be of male anatomy, but it was hard to tell
whether or not they all belonged to the same person. He came
to a bundle tied with ribbon and, uncaring whether he would
be allowed to do so, he undid the ribbon and shook the last
pictures loose.

His heart seemed to stop in his chest. There, repeated over
and over, was his own face, his own body. His face and form from
years ago, smiling, always smiling; his hair loose and tangled over

naked shoulders, then a study of him working in the forge. Small and simple sketches of him lying on his bed, a few wildly erotic poses of him kneeling, being fucked by a blurred figure. Page after page of detailed portraits of his hands, his body, his cock, his neck, his chin, his eyes. Tears fell onto the last drawing. David remembered it so vividly it hurt to remember it. It had been two days before their final parting. They had made love in the barn, then Jonathan had raced away to get his paper and charcoal, ordering David not to move one muscle till he got back. He had obeyed him, laid there in the scratchy hay, his hair tumbled and filled with dust, his body still aching with the pleasing violence of his lover's hands. Jon had returned and drawn so speedily that David could not imagine how he had captured him that fast, but when he handed over the finished sketch, it had taken David's breath away.

It still did. The portrait of love created was one David had never forgotten all these years, had never expected to see again.

A perfect face with no trace of the guile it contained. This he could admit now, distanced as he was from that moment in time. Eyes that looked at the artist with such love, trust, and tenderness. This portrait was the David that Jonathan had loved, he knew now. *It is a picture of a boy that never really existed*, he thought, *except in Jonathan's loving imagination.*

He stood, strode to the far door, and banged on it with both fists.

"Jonathan!" he called. "Jonathan! I *know* it is you. Show yourself!" He knew that the man would not have gone far. He had left all that there for David to see, to prepare him for whatever Jonathan had planned for him. He went back and sat on the edge of the bed, unable to look at any of the drawings again. Within seconds, the door creaked open and Jonathan stepped into the room. David's eyes blurred, and his breath caught so hard in his chest he thought he would die. His love had hardly changed at all in height and breadth, but so very much in other ways. At Kineton he had always been tall, as strong as an ox. Now in the full flush of his maturity, he was as imposing as ever was. *But how forbidding—what dominance, darkness, and power.*

Power Jonathan always had; he had unveiled that on their last night, but now David could see that Jonathan had learned how to harness it, how to command men with it. He said nothing, but gazed at David with those otherworldly eyes, showing no emotion, and in that alone David recognized the change in him. His Jonathan always wore his heart on his face, had been unable to hide his thoughts. This man with the granite face, the shorn hair—could this truly be the passionate blacksmith he'd once known?

David stood, unable to think of anything to say. His first thought was that nothing he could say would bridge the gap between them. He wasn't even sure if he wanted to. Jonathan moved to the table, poured wine for them both, and handed David a fresh glass. He gestured to David to sit down, and they faced each other like wild dogs uncertain of the other's status. He felt suddenly as vulnerable as he had the night Jonathan had thrown him across the forge, but he had to speak, if only to try and save his own life from whatever this "General" had in store for him.

"Why am I here, Jon?"

The first words from those lips were cold. "Because I ordered it."

"You ordered my arrest?" Jonathan nodded and sipped his wine, his eyes never leaving David's face. "Do you still hate me so much? Is there no forgiveness in you at all?"

"I have forgiven you for too much." His words were factual, but without accusation, and David was startled at the change in his voice, the formality, and wondered when he'd stopped using his Puritan speech. "There are some slights that can never be condoned. Have you forgotten Naseby? You tried to kill me."

David's eyelids fluttered in shock, at first unable to understand what he meant.

Jonathan went on, his voice still leaden and icy. "At Naseby. It was only that I fell in the mud that saved me, they told me afterwards."

"You thought that?" David gasped. He leant forward, trying to read something, anything in the gray ice of Jonathan's eyes, seeking his Puritan inside this frozen commandeering exterior.

"I was told what happened, yes," Jonathan said coldly. At that David smiled, in disbelief, and for the first time Jonathan's face showed a glimmer of something, something other than stone.

David's gut warmed when Jonathan's reserve broke a little. He wondered how long it had been since anyone had smiled at Jon, had tried to melt this man. He pushed on with the advantage. "And these *informants*? Did they tell you of the King's man with the discharged musket and his head blown off, found ten paces behind you? Did they tell you of the Royalist musketeer who was dragged away before your comrades could kill him? Or did they miss those small details out?" He found he was almost whispering. "I tried to pick you up, Jon. To get you help, you were bleeding...." His voice faltered. "But T—someone... Why am I here, Jon?" he repeated. "I thought you were dead."

Jonathan tilted his head to one side and blinked rapidly for a second or two, as if confused. "I have had warrants out for your arrest for a good while." He stood up and walked to the fireplace. "I wanted to meet with you again, like this...to hear your excuses if you had them. You always had excuses."

"I do not excuse myself to you, Jonathan," David said quietly. "We fought on different sides from the day we first met."

Jonathan walked away from the fire, blowing out some of the candles that David had lit. David watched him banishing the golden light from the room, and wondered then what had happened to this man, the man whose very soul had been alight with joy once upon a time, the man who had drawn pictures of life and love. When had he turned into this impenetrable wall of darkness?

"I had given up on ever finding you," Jonathan said.

"I was abroad."

"I had assumed so. Or were dead."

"I hardly went for my health," David said bitterly. "But there came a time when I sought war. Rather than life."

"I did not imagine you would return. Not even for the death of the traitor."

David rose to the taunt, fighting ice with fire, letting his anger out at last. "And *your* man? Cromwell? Parliament's great hope? The great cavalry butcher? Will he bring peace and prosperity, restore the balance, and re-home the homeless? I assume from all *this*," he waved a hand blithely around the room, "that you have been favored amongst the mighty. How else can a simple blacksmith rise up to such heights, Jon?" The word "favored" was etched with bile, and it clearly hit home.

Jonathan spun around, his eyes full of something David had not seen before, a terrifying emptiness.

David stood—shaking, unsure, suddenly frightened of the menace, the sheer physical presence of the man. "Jonathan? Forgive me."

But Jonathan had moved to David and had one hand around his throat, the other twisting his arm around his back, his eyes mad flickering between inferno and glacier. "*Favored?*" he ground out. "Favored...thou thinkest this...this is *reward* for my work? This is a hell of my own making, begun the day thou kissed me, and paid for every day since. Thou canst not know what favours I have done...the things I have done... Then there is thou, my David, alive, after all this time...." His voice slipped into a whisper and his gaze raked David's face, anguished life returning to his slate-gray eyes.

"Why now? Why today of all days when I couldst not find thee before? I lost thee, and myself. They told me that thou wert evil...." His hand moved gently from David's throat over his face, tracing the scar on David's cheek with shaking fingers. "I caused this, all of this. Everything I thought was true was lies, and I killed them, David.... I was there, and they lied to me, and it was all a trick, and I killed them...and it was thou, all the time—telling me the truth. In the end it was the Angel who lied." His face was desperate as he fell to his knees, leaving David horrified at the sudden collapse of the man's terrifying veneer. "But the others...? If the Angel lied—were the witches telling the truth? I could not bear it."

David was hardly breathing, his mind filled with shock at Jonathan's private hell. He had no idea what the man was talking about, but he understood the emotion. They had all been through death and beyond, out there in the mud.

They had all been lied to.

He knelt down and softly touched Jonathan's face. Desperate and hunted, the gray eyes met his and David found his Jonathan at last, hidden deep inside the black and cadaverous figure.

"There you are, my beloved Puritan," he whispered. With gentle fingers he touched the familiar cheek, drifting down to touch Jonathan's lips, watching them part as they always did. He dipped a finger into that mouth and then brought it to his own. "Still as sweet as ever," he said, and leaned forward, pulling Jonathan to him and kissing him as softly as he could, tasting wine and tears, wondering at how passive Jonathan was. Jonathan was shaking, and he looked strangely unfocussed, as if his mind had slipped away. David felt a chill of fear. Perhaps seeing David again, coupled with whatever nightmare he had been through, had been too much for him.

He pulled Jonathan to his feet. "Sit," he whispered. Leading him to the edge of the bed, David placed him upon it, knelt between his knees, and made him drink some wine while stroking his hands, wondering at how soft they now were now. Then he stood and began to light the candles once more. Jonathan made no move to stop him this time, but sat immobile and pale with his eyes fixed on David as he moved around the room. David walked back to the bed and felt the love he had for Jonathan wash over him. He slipped out of his jacket and breeches, saying a fond prayer to Tobias' memory. Then wearing just his shirt, he sat on the bed, to be accepted or killed, whatever Jonathan decided.

He slid his mouth up to Jonathan's ear; the man had not even reacted. "*Since first I saw your face,*" he whispered, "*I resolved to honour and renown ye.*"

To David's joy, the dour and frightening man seemed to melt away, and it was his beloved Puritan who turned to him and replied. "*If now I be disdainèd I wish my heart had never known ye.*"

"Never disentangle," David murmured. His hands controlled the moment; he remembered the raging torrent that Jonathan had been, and after all this time he wanted to prolong, delay, *enjoy*. His lips claimed dominion over those of his long-lost Puritan, tasting the sweetness of the wine from them, his tongue softly re-encountering its mate, pulling it into his mouth. His passion swept through him, making David as hard as he'd ever been. His teeth nibbled their way along the line of Jonathan's jaw, worrying his ear as eager fingers strayed over leather and metal and wool, unburdening, unbuckling, unembellishing.

As David pulled the shirt from Jonathan's back, he stopped in shock when he saw the scarring on the once perfect skin. He sat up, startled, his eyes wide with pity. But the sorrow he felt was nothing to the look of gentle tragedy mirrored in Jonathan's.

"There is much to tell thee," Jonathan said simply, "and there are darker tales than this."

"How?" was all David could say.

"It was a lesson designed to teach me what I felt for thee was wrong, what I am feeling *now* is wrong. I have been in the dark since thou left me, but thou hast relit the lights, and I see now that the lessons were false." He glanced sideways at the dresser and smiled. David followed his eyes, seeing nothing there but a small black dagger. For one dark moment it seemed to David as if all the candles had gutted in their holders, and the man the soldiers called the General had returned, dark and brooding beneath him. When Jonathan spoke it broke the spell, for his voice was the same as it was on a frozen day in Kineton. "Can'st thou standst it...David?"

For answer David threw one leg over Jonathan's hips and
kissed him full on the ravaged chest, his arms tight around him
as if he would never let him go again. He clung to him; tears
pricking his eyelids as he kissed Jonathan's skin over and over,
murmuring words of reassurance, and love.

"We are both marked men, my Jon."

There was a sudden warmth in Jonathan's arms, a heat he had forgotten, and Jonathan fell into an almost forgotten memory as he
reached tentatively for David's body. He tore the coarse linen away
so swiftly that it was discarded like bad dreams on a sunny morning. Something jarred him—the friction of his hand on the pale
skin was just as he recalled it, but it was upon skin that should be
brown, brown as berries, brown as an autumn leaf. New sensations,
for the aggressive contours of a more mature man; angles where
there used to be curves, and an achingly familiar remembrance for
the form he could once have mapped with his eyes closed. This
well-known frame which he used to be able to draw with just a few
charcoal lines, but could never do justice to its symmetry. This he
remembered, the flat stomach, the bony hips; but the scars on the
birth-marked flank and on the broad chest—still hairless for all its
breadth—these were new. He kissed them both softly as an admonition that they spoiled a perfection, then again lingeringly as a tender welcome that they were now part of David and as such,
belonged to him.

This mouth he remembered, as his own lips trailed over it;
the taste a beautiful regression. These teeth that caught at his lip,
the way they always did, this was unchanged. But these lines beside the mouth were new, hinting of past sadnesses. This brow
was the same, as his fingers traced the flaxen hairline, but this
frown had never been in the laughing summer boy of '42. *This is
a stranger, this muscled man, who is he?* What body was this,
where was the boy who had left him behind? *When did he grow
so solid, so hard, so tall?* Where did this battle-hardened veteran

come from? What happened to the beautiful hair he used to hold so tightly in his fists?

What tragedies made those eyes so sad?

But the prick, Jonathan remembered that. "This is David, this is my love." In the dark, or with his eyes torn from his head, as long as he had fingers and hands and a tongue to trace it, he could say this. It curved back proudly into his welcoming hands, and the groan David gave was the keening of a homecoming.

David turned beneath him and his hands moved over Jonathan's skin as if he too was recalling all that they had shared and lost. Jonathan closed his eyes and he was instantly transported, to memories of the Caverly cottage, warm in their shared bed, the older visions clearer than the thoughts of yesterday; back when all there was to worry over was not breaking his indentures and the secrecy of their shared sin. Before the cold and the blood and the fire and the lies of the Archangel. Before his work for Bacon, before he began to hate himself. Began to hate the man he had become. When David touched him he felt younger, cleaner. It was a promise of purification—with David's warm palms on his skin, he could almost believe that those hands could erase the horror. Perhaps they could put him together again.

The skin beneath his hands was absolution, and Jonathan's mouth traced the words of his confession upon it. He could feel the muscles ripple beneath his lips as he mouthed the sins that he could never dare to speak aloud. Somehow he knew that David had forgiven all without even knowing them, as he always did, as he always would.

David unfolded beneath him, and the tawny eyes were half-closed as he gave the old invitation, unforgotten by them both, but now it was urgent and needful, a mature and long overdue desire. Tears fell from Jonathan's eyes as he knelt between the pale thighs; water fell onto the precious skin and his hands brushed it away, savoring the feel of the flanks under his fingers. He pushed his hips tight between David's legs, reveling in the heat of buttocks on his cock, his eyes closing, praying for a miracle of arousal. But his own cock was not healed, his sins were *not* forgiven, and his soul was not absolved. He knew then he had nothing to give, and the shame made him turn from the writhing figure on the bed. He slid to the floor and cried in silent grief, hunched and broken. The Archangel stood over him, laughing, a fiery sword in his hand.

There was a rustle and then David was on the floor with him, cradling him into those new-familiar arms, muttering into his hair with that forgotten-remembered voice with the silk behind it. Words of love, words of loss and rebirth, rebuilding by inches the mightiest of bridges over the long and bloody years. Gently, David helped him back onto the bed and as rough hands stroked his cheek, Jonathan opened his eyes, trembling for fear of finding Michael there and not this new dream. David was propped up on one elbow and staring intently at him, his brow furrowed. The boy had gone, but Jonathan knew he could love this man just as he loved that boy. David kissed him then, a kiss the like of which he had never felt, not then and not since. Not until now; and he realized that he had been waiting all of his life for this one kiss. It was soft, dry and gentle, a tender brush from side to side, then it was a wet and salty communion, David's tears falling into the mixture of lips and tongues, wine and memories of too much blood.

David's hand slid down Jonathan's torso and trailed confident fingers down his hipbone, moved inwards, and with eager hands encompassed Jonathan's flaccid cock. Jonathan groaned in shame and disgust, and attempted to roll away again, but David pinned him down with surprising strength, opened his mouth wider, and subdued any thought of escape or rejection as he held Jonathan's body still with the power of his tongue. Jonathan surrendered to David's unspoken command and lay shaking with unreleased sorrow, helpless; hopeless.

"Jon...."

There was the voice that had haunted his dreams and his nightmares for many long years. The voice that the Archangel had tried to wipe from his soul. The voice speaking that one word that Jonathan had heard every night since their tragedy at Naseby, the voice he had been convinced that he'd never wanted to hear again.

"*Jon.*"

If Jonathan kept his eyes closed, he could almost pretend that the past years had not happened. That he wasn't a trusted inquisitor for Parliament, with spies and informers in every tavern, on every corner. That his men weren't downstairs, waiting to deal with this man they had arrested for their leader. If he kept his eyes shut, he could fool himself that the luxurious linen beneath him was woolen blankets and coarse linen sheets, that the ornate bed was a simple cot. That the night outside held no city, no soldiers, no dead king, or a terrifying future, nothing more than water meadows, grazing cows, and sleeping chickens. If he held on to that thought, the sun might rise and Jacob would call the boys to breakfast. If he could only hold on a little longer. The memory was so sharp, so razor thin that he saw his summer David imprinted on his eyelids, silver hair loose and tumbled to his waist, his mouth in a twist of pure ecstasy, as he once rode the wildness that was Jonathan's cock.

That he remembered. *That* he remembered. His eyes slowly opened and finally he understood the vision of the blond angel in the dark. There, like a miracle, was the beloved face, and the smile was all his. As he blossomed in David's eager hand, he knew he had won his battle against the demons and pulled David into his arms where he belonged.

ACKNOWLEDGMENTS

Many thanks to Ingrid, RW Day, and Tracey who read each new chapter and never failed in their encouragement. Much thanks to the Sealed Knot, The English Civil War Society, and all the other people, too many to mention, who helped with research and facts. Thanks especially to Lisa, my editor, who kept asking questions that needed to be asked.

ABOUT THE AUTHOR

Erastes is the pen name of a female author who lives near the Norfolk Broads in England with 2½ demanding cats and an even more demanding computer. She decided to specialize in gay historical romance because it was the sort of book she wanted to read—and so few people were writing it. She's the Director of the Erotic Authors' Association, and *Transgressions* is her second novel.

Please visit her at www.erastes.com